UNDER A NORTHERN SKY

LL MEYER

Cover by: Murphy Rae at Indie Solutions

www.murphyrae.net

Formatting by: Farah Faqir @craftedbyaf

www.craftedbyaf.com

Email: lisalynn_meyer@outlook.com

Instagram: @author_ll_meyer

Facebook: Lisa Lynn Meyer

Goodreads: LL Meyer

TikTok: author_ll_meyer

Amazon Author Central: LL Meyer

UNDER A NORTHERN SKY

BOOKS BY LL MEYER

The Barbarian Realms
Under a Northern Sky, #1
Beyond a Savage Heart, #2 (coming in 2023)

The Worlds Collide duets:
Not So Far Away (Scott and Ellie, #1)
The Here and Now (Scott and Ellie, #2)
Fall from Grace (Alejandro and Sophie, #3)
The Devil's Own (Alejandro and Sophie, #4)

The Penny Books
His Lucky Penny, #1
Pennies for Wishes, #2
Find a Penny, #3
Pennies from Heaven, #4

LiSA LYNN MEYER

A Touch of Silence

DEDICATION

This one is for that girl sitting in the movie theatre, watching *Gladiator* for the first time, asking herself, *I wonder what that guy's story is?* when the 'barbarian' held up that soldier's severed head.

TRIGGER WARNING

While I wouldn't classify *Under a Northern Sky* as a dark romance, it does contain dark themes that may be triggering to some readers, including attempted sexual assault. Please have care.

CHAPTER 1

RINA

D awn has finally leached the inkiness from the sky. As their backdrop fades, the stars have disappeared one by one until only the brightest remains; the North Star. I watch its valiant attempts to stave off the inevitable.

I wonder if that will be me soon, swallowed whole by circumstances beyond my control. Probably. But I take strength in knowing it endures. Whether it can be seen or not, it'll be back tonight, as permanent as ever.

North marks the direction we've been traveling in for the past five days. I have the silly notion that when we finally arrive at our destination, the North Star will be directly overhead. I say *silly* because, so far, all my questions about our journey have gone unanswered and I've been forced to dream up my own answers.

From my spot sitting on the creek bank, I lean over to dip my fingers into the icy water. I'm already chilled to the bone so its temperature doesn't so much as elicit a shiver. I won't complain though. No matter how miserable I am now – cold, hungry, and unable to sleep – I know it could be worse. Last week I was living my three hundred and seventy-fourth day locked in a chamber by order of my cousin, Gaden, the King of D'heilar. At least here in the wilderness, I can see the sky. At least here in the wilderness, I can muster some optimism for my future.

A future which includes marrying a man I've never met. A barbarian no less.

My empty stomach turns over. I'm not sure if it's dread or hope that causes it, but I wish I had something *certain* to cling to. All I know of my betrothed is his name, and I only learned that much because I overheard him mentioned in conversation among my five-man escort.

His name is Luka, and he's one of their kings – *or deves* – as they're known in the barbarian realms of the north.

"Rina!" hisses through the air, startling me. "What in *the Mother's* name are you doing down here? Noé is about to send the twins out to hunt you down."

I turn to find Bron, the youngest of my escort, halfway down the short embankment, looking slightly panicked.

My shoulders sag at the thought of another grueling day of travel. "I'm just washing up."

"Well, hurry!" He traipses back up the hill, and then in the distance, I hear him reassure the others that I haven't run off.

I want to roll my eyes. *Run off to where?* There's nothing for miles and miles around. It's been days since we've passed a single homestead . . . which probably means we're nearing the River Colundra, the natural border between D'heilar and the Realms.

No one in their right mind would live this close to barbarian territory. Though the incursions have eased off considerably in recent years, barbarian raids into the northern regions of my homeland are infamous for their callousness.

Figuring I won't like it if Noé uses *callousness* to come and get me, I push to my feet on aching legs. Not only is my cloak too thin for the very late autumn weather this far north, but my cold muscles are unaccustomed to riding after my year-long incarceration. Wincing with every step, I slowly make my way up the hill.

I'm sure my cousin, the King, would be thrilled if he could see me now. His lifelong campaign against my family culminating in my being brought low before these barbarians would be a dream come true for him, what with them being our sworn enemies and all.

The relationship between our two nations has always been contentious, but the origins of the tension remain a somewhat murky subject. Even if the monarchs of D'heilar have done everything to convince their subjects it's a cut and dried, good versus evil situation, I've read conflicting accounts of the Northern Rebellions against the Crown. Some claim that it was actually the Crown's cruel taxation and conscription system in the face of floods and famine that forced our northern people to rebel and ultimately move across the River Colundra. Maybe they left of their own accord, or maybe they were expelled. Either way, they weren't supposed to flourish or become a permanent thorn in the monarchy's side, but that's what happened.

Nowadays, however, D'heilar and the Realms have a more pressing problem: the rise of the savages along our common border on the eastern flank. Over the last five to ten years the situation has become dire enough that the two sides have been forced into a tentative truce. And apparently my marriage to a barbarian is meant to stick the two halves more firmly together, the two halves that have been at odds for more than two centuries. The phrase *sacrificial lamb* comes to mind.

At the top of the small rise, I spy the barbarians through the trees, packing up the camp. I still haven't gotten used to them. They're nothing like the groomed and mild mannered men of the south who prefer pretense and doublespeak to get their points across. These men don't bother with anything of the kind. They say what they mean, and mean what they say, unafraid to insult one another or even me.

Noé, the leader, has been cranky from the start, obviously unhappy with being assigned the task of chaperoning me north. "You've missed breakfast," he gripes as I approach, the ivory beads in his long black hair clinking together. "You'll just have to go hungry."

I give him a terse nod instead of the crude gesture I want to shove in his face. His attitude toward me has really begun to chafe, but so far I've kept my temper. There's no sense in making an enemy of him before I have a complete picture of what my new life will have in store for me. I can already see that I'll have an uphill battle though. These men have completely rebuffed my attempts to make conversation with them. It seems they're not willing to let bygones be bygones with our peoples' long history of hatred and ill-will hovering over us like an ugly spectre.

"I don't know if starving her is such a good idea," is drawled from behind me, sending a jolt through my chest. "She's already so scrawny."

Jerking around, I come face to face with Cayson and Carson, their eerily identical sneers sending an unpleasant chill down my spine.

"And combined with that dung-colored dress? Ugh," one of them continues; I still haven't figured out how to tell the twins apart. "A fine bargain Luka has struck."

"Shut up," snaps Noé. "If you cannot control your tongue, Carson, I'll cut it out."

The casual violence of the words curdles in my hollow stomach, probably because I can imagine such a scenario playing out. There's a physicality to these men that often makes me uneasy.

"Oh, I'd love to see that," Cayson says with a snicker to bait his twin, using the back of his hand to whack the other man's chest. In retaliation, Carson shoves him.

"Mount up," Noé orders like he's sick of both of them. At least we can agree on that. I don't really trust any of them, but it's been obvious from the start that the twins are the worst of this group. Their insults don't bother me as much as the way their unnerving, light-colored eyes constantly follow me around. I try to keep constant tabs their whereabouts just to be safe.

I make my way around my horse to where Bron is finishing up with my saddle. "Thank you," I whisper, hoping he understands I'm referring to the help with my horse and the warning down at the creek. He nods as he slips me a piece of dried meat before walking away. I quickly squirrel it away into the pocket of my cloak, feeling a spark of gratitude toward him.

Mounting my horse is painful. Every muscle in my body protests and it takes a mountain of will to keep the whimper that rises up inside of me stoppered. These men already believe me a weakling, but I refuse to give the idea any credence.

As we start off down the road, rather than focus on my aches and pains, I ponder Bron's connection to the terror twins. Yesterday, I learned he's their youngest brother and I still haven't gotten over the shock. While the twins have been devoid of even a scrap of human decency from the beginning, Bron attempted to befriend me when we first set off on this journey. Noé put a stop to it, but that wasn't Bron's idea. I wonder if Bron's uncharacteristic, easy-going manner compared to the others has something to do with his different style of clothing. He's the only one who wears a tunic. The others all wear a thick leather vest with an insignia of a large cat burned into the leather at their left breasts. I assume it's a uniform of sorts, marking them as soldiers.

Is my betrothed a soldier? With my luck, chances are high and he'll be equally unpleasant as Noé or the twins. I won't be deterred though. I don't have the luxury. There's no going back for me and I have every intention of making this marriage work.

This marriage to *Luka*. I wish I knew *something* about him. His age, or his disposition, or –

My horse sidesteps, causing my ankle to bang against the stirrup, and for the millionth time since we started this trip, a bolt of pain shoots up my leg. What I wouldn't give for a proper pair of riding boots. To steady myself, I take some deep breaths and try to concentrate on my surroundings. The sun's attempt to break through the bows of the endless evergreens today gives me a bit of a boost, but it's just not enough to distract myself from the pain or the cold.

I tune into the rattle of the cart in front of me, over which I can make out Dix – the last man of my escort – complaining to Noé, once again, how it was such a waste of time to have brought 'the infernal contraption'.

Dix has been annoyed about it from the beginning. The first time I met these five, enormous men, all of them except Bron had been wearing scowls worthy of an angry and suspicious crone on their pale faces.

"Where are your things?" Noé had demanded from atop his horse in a strangely accented voice that rang with scorn.

I'd lifted my chin and projected what I hoped was confidence. "My cousin, the King, has seen fit to send me to my new life unburdened by the past."

His fierce expression had remained unchanged and it occurred to me that polite speech was lost on him. "It's just me," I'd clarified. I was wearing everything I owned.

That was the first time the terror twins had mumbled something about Luka getting the short end of the stick.

"Skeevy bastards," I mutter under my breath. As if I'm not already nervous enough that my tan skin, black hair, and small stature won't put Luka off. Then there's . . . reflexively, I press the inside of my left arm against my side. Through the fabric of my clothing, I can feel the ugly, mottled skin that mars my ribs.

Memories of that horrible day begin to surface; the coal-hot blade, the taunting slurs, the unspeakable, penetrating agony of my singeing flesh. The contemptuous face of my tormentor forms in my mind and I do everything I can to banish it. Dearest *Mother*, how I despise him, Mattice Dulat, High Advisor to my cousin and all-around worm. Even if it's been over a year since I've seen him, his cruelty still haunts me.

Desperate for *any* distraction now, I strain to listen in on the terror twins' conversation from further behind me. I catch snippets of their usual degrading talk of women and boasts of exaggerated sexual exploits. To say the least, it does nothing to fight my falling spirits.

I sigh, pulling the strip of meat from my pocket to nibble on it.

A few hours later the trees start to thin out and we come to what must be the banks of the River Colundra. I gasp with wonder. I've heard of the natural boundary between D'heilar and the Realms, but I've never laid eyes upon it. Dismounting, I join Noé at the water's edge and watch the dark, cloudy water move past me like some kind of a creeping monolith. The far side is barely visible and I'm sure the placid surface hides a wicked undertow.

"We're to cross that?" I marvel aloud.

A derisive noise comes from the back of his throat. "Don't fall overboard. I won't save you."

"I'll do my best," I say wryly, earning me a look of mild surprise. It's as if he didn't believe I had a personality. I wonder if these barbarian men react to all women this way or if it's only me. "Is this the end of our journey, then?" I ask.

"No," he scoffs like he's offended by my ignorance. "This is but the mid-way point."

I want to point out that he's responsible for my *ignorance*, but men in the black uniforms of the Royal Army emerge from the trees on horseback and he goes to meet them.

Turns out the horses we've been riding are the property of the King, loaned to the barbarians for their use on the southern side of the river. The presence of the soldiers has me on edge after a year of being kept under lock and key and my 'meeting' with Mattice Dulat fresh in my mind. Being a prisoner is not an experience I want to repeat, so I remain as unobtrusive as possible. I don't trust my cousin not to revoke the marriage deal and take me back into custody.

The provisions from the half-empty cart are loaded into a large, wide-bottomed boat. When it's time to go, I eagerly climb in. Though I know how to swim, I doubt I'd make it to shore if we capsized, something that sends a zing through my veins and voids out the fear inspired by the King's men. It's wonderful to be out in the world and *living*.

I sit in the bow, soaking up the sun, while the men pull the oars in long strokes. They don't fight the current that carries us swiftly downstream, but work with it in order to hit a designated landing point on the opposite side. It's all perfectly timed and gauged. They may be uncouth, but these men are clearly competent.

The heartfelt welcome of their barbarian comrades on the far side of the river takes me by surprise. Even though it's not meant for me, the good-natured teasing makes the very air easier to breathe. A man wearing one of the leather vests and a wide smile wades into the knee-deep water and holds up his arms, offering to help me from the boat.

"My name is Dion, my lady. Let me get you back on dry land."

There's nothing untoward in his demeanor and I can't help but respond to him with a smile of my own. "Thank you," I say with what is undoubtedly too much feeling, but it's been a very long while since anyone has offered me a civil word.

After setting me down on the bank, he leads me past fortified buildings that must be part of an outpost, complete with manned look-out towers that line the shore at intervals for as far as the eye can see. The place appears ready for war. Maybe the truce between D'heilar and the Realms is weaker than I realized. Maybe this marriage really will make a difference.

I'm shown to a large corral where the provisions are being re-loaded into a new wagon and horses are being brought out from the stables for our party. It seems with hours of daylight left, we won't be lingering.

"She's a beauty, isn't she?" Dion asks as he saddles a mare for me, probably noticing my astonishment.

"I've rarely seen a finer mount," I admit. It takes everything in me not to confirm that I have permission to ride such a beautiful animal. "Does she have a name?"

"I don't rightly know. But she's yours now, so it's –"

"Mine?"

"Yes, a gift from the deve."

"From the deve?" I echo stupidly.

Dion hesitates. "Yes. *Deve* is the word for . . ."

"Ruler," I finish, not sure if I should curb the hope that blooms, fierce and deep, in my chest. *Luka.* "The mare is from him? Truly?" I say, fully expecting him to confess to jesting.

"Yes, of course. Come closer. Let her know you."

Throwing a nervous glance over my shoulder for Noé or the twins, I pat the horse's neck. Her midnight black coat is warm under my palm as she nuzzles me sweetly, and a certainty I haven't experienced in *years* takes hold of me. I'll do everything I can to make the best of my new life. I'll learn how to love my new husband no matter the cost. Just for giving me this moment, one that feels like joy being poured directly into my soul, he deserves my all.

Dion helps me into the saddle and adjusts the stirrups. "May I –" I stop myself from asking for permission. I doubt an *a'deve* – a ruler's wife – would do such a thing. Eyeing Noé where he's preparing his own mount across the paddock,

I amend to ask, "Is it safe to ride ahead? To get a feel for her?"

Dion gives me a jovial laugh. "Just stay on the road heading north. They'll catch up."

Before anyone can stop me, I urge the dark beauty into a trot, then a canter, and on into a gallop. My spirit soars right along with her hooves. Her gait is so smooth she seems to barely touch the ground. With the wind in my hair and my sore muscles protesting, I name her Glory, for that's what she is, pure and simple. And the knowledge that my betrothed isn't above acts of kindness? It leaves me breathless. Because who needs air in their lungs when their chest is bursting with optimism.

When I allow them to catch up, Noé isn't thrilled with my initiative, but he doesn't chastise me, and Bron offers me an encouraging smile. In fact, on this side of the river, they're all more relaxed. Over the next few days, as we journey steadily north, I begin to let down my guard, turning most of my attention to caring for my new mount. I can't remember the last time I had something other than myself to worry about. It's heady and sweet.

Until it isn't.

Three days after leaving the river, with the dawn barely breaking over the horizon, on my way back from relieving myself in the trees, one of the twins catches me unawares.

"Finally," he jeers. "Alone at last."

Despite his intentions being as plain as day, I can't quite comprehend. "What are you doing?" My voice turns shrill on the last word as he takes a threatening step toward me.

"I think that's obvious."

I back away, my heart beginning to pound in my chest. "But I'm to be your a'deve."

13

He laughs coldly. "Doubtful."

"I'll scream."

"Excellent. I love a good struggle."

Terror swamps me as he lunges. I barely get a half-cry for help out before his hand clamps over my mouth. I fight and claw and thrash with everything in me. But the horrible realization that this is going to happen no matter what I do hits me when we topple over and his weight squashes me into the dirt. Despair fills me. This can't happen. It *can't* ha–

An opening comes.

He lets go of my wrists to start scrabbling at my skirts, and I frantically shove at his shoulders. Except it barely registers with him and now his hand is fumbling under my dress.

No. No. No.

I begin groping at the ground around me for something, anything to use as a weapon. There! I swing instinctively, without any conscious thought at all, and the dull thud of the rock against his skull reverberates up my arm.

He slumps down on me.

Reeling with shock, I barely hear the bellowing that ensues. It's all a steady, pitchy buzz until the body on top of me abruptly disappears. "What have you done?!"

I can only lie there, trembling.

"You thrice damned whore!"

It's the other twin and he's enraged. I need to move, but my quaking limbs are far from cooperative. My leather slippers and the heels of my palms slip in the fallen pine needles as I desperately try to retreat from him.

With a roar, he kicks out at me. In his frenzy, he misses, but I'm not so lucky on the second attempt. Or the third. Then he falls on me and the punches come.

Curling into a ball, I try to protect myself, but the blows are like hammers, driving the breath from my lungs and the sense from my mind. My vision goes dark for a second. When it flickers back, I realize everything has stopped and that Noé is yelling . . . at me. "What were you thinking?! You stupid woman. *Father's* tit, what do you have to say for yourself?"

My short, panted breaths aren't enough to allow for words and I'm not sure I could come up with anything coherent even if they did.

"She led him out here," a twin accuses at the top of his lungs. "Said they could have some fun. And look what she did! She killed him."

"Wha –" *Fun? Killed?*

"You will speak!" Noé roars.

"I did no such thing," I wheeze.

"She calls *me* a liar after slaying my brother?!" the twin rages to Noé and then at me, he spits, "I am a warrior of the Mountain Lion Range."

Mountain lion. That makes sense. The cat insignia on their shoulders has a long body. It must be a mountain lion.

Vaguely it occurs to me how useless these thoughts are. I should be listening to Noé. He's saying more, things I'm not processing. Abruptly he leans down and grabs my wrist, dragging me along the ground back to camp. If I could scream, I would. The pain radiating along my already-bruised ribs almost pales in comparison to the feeling of my shoulder about to wrench free of its socket.

"Noé, what are you doing?" comes the urgent voice of another. Bron. He meets us at the wagon where Noé dumps me in a heap.

"You don't move," Noé growls at me. "Do you hear me?"

He leaves me there with Bron. "What happened?" he whispers urgently, helping me to sit up with my back against a wheel.

I bring a very unsteady hand to my head and it comes away bloody. "Hhhe . . . he attacked me." My survival instincts really kick in and I start searching for my horse. *Would they pursue me? Hunt me down?* My brain lurches and sways in its attempts to form a plan, any plan, to get away from here.

"Noé? Noé attacked you?"

"No . . ." I can barely concentrate on Bron's words. "Will hhhhe let me go?"

"What?"

"Will Noé let me go?"

"No, he won't let you go," Bron says like I'm daft. "He must deliver you to the deve without fail."

We hear cursing, and Bron looks over his shoulder. The sight of Noé and a twin carrying a body between them has Bron's very wide, brown eyes swinging back in my direction. "Is he dead?"

"I think so," I whisper, tears now blurring my vision. I must get away from here. *But where will I go?* "Will Noé kill me?"

"What? No! I told you, he has to deliver you."

Dix appears. "What in all the horrors of *the Abyss* happened?" he demands, watching them slide the body onto the cart bed.

"The D'heilarian whore," a twin scorns, "lured Carson into the trees, and when she didn't like the results, she killed him."

"That's not true," I cry, struggling to my feet with Bron's help. "He attacked me."

"You're disgusting!" It must be Cayson if Carson is dead. "You've been making eyes at us since we left D'heilar."

I don't know if the dizziness is sparked by his despicable statement or the pain in my ribs, which is quickly growing intolerable. "That . . . is . . . not . . ." I weave, and though Bron catches me, everything goes dark.

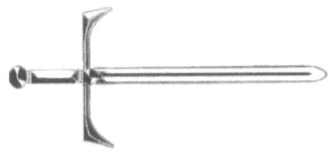

I wake up chained in the cart, an ankle restrained at one end and a wrist at the other, laid out next to the body of my attacker. Noé will not hear my pleas. All he says is that the deve will settle things once we arrive. Beyond that, he won't acknowledge me except to threaten to stuff a rag in my mouth if I don't shut up.

That was yesterday. Already bruised and battered from the assault, I'm a wreck now. After spending the entire day on the move, with my wounded mind, body, and soul being rattled into oblivion on the planks of this forsaken cart, they left me where I was overnight. Without a campfire, the bitter cold worked its way deep into my bones and has not left since.

Now, today, what little warmth *the Mother* has granted me will soon be lost as the sun begins its descent toward the horizon. I don't know if I can face another night of shivering in this cart, shackled like an animal. The only thing holding me together is the fury that underpins my physical suffering. *Because how dare they do this to me? How fucking dare they?*

The cart jolts heavily and my anger falters with the cry that leaks from between my compressed lips. My ribs ache and the roughly hewn manacles have scraped my skin raw. I'm almost grateful that I'm half-numbed to the pain by the cold.

Bron comes into view. From horseback, he offers me a skin of water.

"Bron!"

Noé's angry voice snaps through the frigid air like a whip.

"If she dies," the younger man says evenly, "the deve will not be pleased." There's no response, but the offer of water is rescinded and he disappears from sight.

Despondency presses deeper. My thoughts are sluggish as I try to remember the last time I was given water. *Was it this morning?* I don't think the lack of water will kill me, though, before the cold. My free hand clumsily feels along the waist of my dress to where my mother's ring is sewn into the gathered material, the last piece of my family left to me.

"I'm sorry, Mama," I whisper to the darkening sky. "This isn't how it was supposed to be, is it?" In the days before her trial and execution, Mama had been adamant that if I was ever given the chance, I should seek out happiness and live. But she's been gone for eight years now, and my father and my brothers for fifteen. At this point, I'm just so tired.

Later, something tugs at my consciousness, and I realize the sway of the cart has stopped. Loud, angry voices begin to funnel into my brain. The specifics are lost to the numbing effects of cold, thirst, and hunger, but a whooshing sound brings with it the light of a torch. I clamp my eyes shut against the sudden brightness, then hear the high-pitched wailing of a woman crying for her dead son. Carson was luckier than he deserved if he has . . . had a mother to grieve for him.

18

The clanking of my irons rouses me further and I find a man with the fiercest of scowls looking down at me over the edge of the wagon. With hatred burning in his eyes, he declares, "Lock her up."

CHAPTER 2
LUKA

They should have been back yesterday. And their continued failure to turn up at the gates of the stronghold has me pacing my chamber like a caged animal. This marriage contract has proven itself to be an irritation many times over, and the damnable woman hasn't even arrived yet.

A gust of air through the window draws my attention to the darkening sky. I doubt they'll travel at night, not with the pampered princess in tow, which means another sleepless night of wondering what's gone wrong. I make to pull the shutter closed when, from across the courtyard, I hear a duty guard's cry of, "Riders approaching!"

"Finally," I mutter darkly.

By the time I make it downstairs to the Great Hall, it's obvious that word has spread. Warriors and villagers alike are abandoning their evening meals to file out into the courtyard to greet the returning party and, most probably, to catch a glimpse of their new a'deve.

It's absurd to think that I know nothing but the name of the woman I'm supposed to marry. When I first heard that there would be a marriage treaty between the Realms and D'heilar, it didn't occur to me that the First Deve would saddle *me* with her. Though as the youngest and newest ruler in the realms, I shouldn't have been surprised. Now, after having the summer and most of the fall to adjust to the idea, I can't say I'm any less revolted by it than I was in the spring during the Realm Council meeting when it was announced. But according to my lord and commander, I'll be tying myself to this woman whether I like it or not.

An odd mixture of dread and anticipation claws away at my insides as I cross the cobbled courtyard. Over the heads in the crowd, I scan the scene in the light of the torches. *Where is the woman?* A pulse of disquiet shoots through me when I count only three men on horseback. One of the twins is missing. *Where in the name of the Mother is he?*

Worst case scenarios rush at me. *They were attacked by eastern savages. Or wild animals. The princess has been taken. Killed. Drowned. Mauled. Thrown from her horse. Maybe she ran off with the twin. Or maybe she refused to come at all.* Yes, that must be it. But my relief is snuffed out by the expression on Noé's face.

"My deve," he says gravely. "There's been . . ." He looks down and away before he hauls in a deep breath and re-meets my eyes. "There's been an incident. Carson is dead."

"What?!" is shrieked by a woman from the back of the crowd. Carson's mother, Zola, pushes her way forward. "What do you mean he's dead?"

21

My question exactly, right along with, "Where is the woman?"

"They're both in the cart," Noé says. "She, uh, killed him."

My thoughts tangle and trip over one another. *She what?*

"No!" Zola yells as a torch is brought closer and we peer over the sides of the wagon, joined by half the village.

"The wanton slut tempted him into the trees," Cayson announces bitterly for all to hear. "And then she caved his skull in with a rock."

It takes a moment, but once his declaration sinks in, a full-body rush of hatred consumes me. Deep down, I always *knew* the woman would be unfit for marriage.

Over Zola's shrill wails, the villagers start shouting for the woman's blood, calling her a witch, a harlot, a murderess. I can't say is disagree with them as I watch Noé unhook her shackles from the cart bed.

"Lock her up," I order, watching Cayson yank her prone body from the cart.

The worthless realization that I should have gone south to collect her myself assaults me. Or I should have at least sent Eldon. I lift my gaze to Noé for an explanation. To the man's credit, he doesn't flinch, but he does look ill at ease. "Things didn't go to plan," he admits from the other side of the wagon.

"To plan?" I grit out. "A Range Warrior is dead at the hands of my intended bride under the watch of my Warrior Commander. Things are *far* beyond the plan, Noé."

He grimaces, those stupid molars he takes from his kills and threads into his hair glinting in the torch light. "I admit I underestimated her," he says, coming around the cart.

I glare at him, rage beginning to bubble just below the surface. I have to check the urge to beat him to a pulp, right here and now. But that's something my father would have done. And I am not him. To distract myself, I watch the woman being dragged off to the holding cells between two warriors, her head flopping about, the still-attached chains clinking against the stone.

"My deve!" Zola's sharp voice pierces my skull. "My son is dead and I will have retribution. Do you hear me? Swift and sure. I want that traitorous bi–"

"First," I say loudly, cutting her off. Zola Cyrun has been a thorn in my side since day one of my rule. "We will have Carson lifted to *the Eternal* as is befitting a Range Warrior." I look pointedly to her son's body which is being removed from the wagon.

"But –"

"Enough!"

Mouth twisting with grief, she turns her back on me and follows her son's corpse as it's transported to the clearing outside the stronghold's walls where the pyre will be lit with the morning's first rays of light. There is nothing more sacred in the Realms than a warrior who has been lost.

"That woman is a menace," Noé grumbles, watching them retreat.

"No, that woman has lost a son. And we have lost a warrior."

A noise approximating a growl comes from his throat, but I hold up my hand to stop him. "Hold your tongue for now. Over food, you can explain this to me in a way that makes sense." Because, so far, I see no sense whatsoever in this situation. After Eldon, there's no one I trust more than Noé. He may be a bit of an uptight prig, but missteps of this magnitude are unheard of. In fact, buried somewhere under my fury lies an entire slab of disbelief.

We enter the Great Hall, which is much busier than usual. Though everyone from the village is welcome at the Great Hall, most of my people are farmers who live and work on the surrounding land. Usually they have little time for a trip to the stronghold if it's not market day.

A hush falls over the room, the high stone walls magnifying the silence and our booted footsteps. Obviously, the story has spread like wildfire. I'm sure everyone feels vindicated. I know I do. Taking a wife from among the snakes of D'heilar was an absurd notion from the start.

I head for our usual table in the far corner of the room, steering clear of the dais, which I sit upon only when I must. I notice with satisfaction that someone has already removed *her* chair from the head table.

As soon as we sit down, Lorna is there with two tankards of ale.

"My deve," she coos. "So sorry to hear that your intended has lived up to her ancestors' reputation." My eyes catch on her full red lips and I almost let thoughts of what she can do with them fill my head. "If you need comfort at all," she continues, "you know where I'll be."

Without waiting for a response, she leaves and Noé stifles a laugh. "When is she going to give up on you? She should be married by now."

I can't stop a smirk. "If Lorna married, there would be a revolt among the men."

Noé gives a knowing nod. "Her cunt is where I'm hoping to land tonight."

"You and half this room."

"I'm not against sharing," he retorts as Eldon slaps him on the shoulder.

"Noé, my friend," Eldon says, sitting next to him. "Wouldn't you rather have one, permanent woman to warm your bed? One you don't have to hunt down and cajole onto your cock every night?"

Both Noé and I grimace. My second in command and cousin is famously besotted with his wife of the last seven years, Daysa . . . and their three children.

"Fuck no," Noé chokes out.

Eldon only laughs like it's not him but Noé who's the fool before he turns to me. "So, is what I hear true, Luka? That Carson Cyrun has finally met his end?" He says it with a bit of relish, but I suppose it's no secret that Eldon never liked Carson . . . or Cayson for that matter.

"Though," he goes on, "I guess we've got bigger problems, considering who brought that end about." A huge grin splits his face, showing us his teeth from behind his shaggy blond beard. "Looks like your bride has some unexpected claws, dear cousin. You've always been a lucky son of a bitch."

"Lucky?" I counter. *He can't be serious.*

Lorna returns carrying three trenchers of stew. "Don't upset my deve, Eldon. He has enough going on without you –"

"Leave," I order her. I've always appreciated Lorna's ability to read my mood, and right now, I'm not mucking about. She makes herself scarce without another word.

I jab an accusing finger in Eldon's direction. "Explain."

"Well," he starts, still with the obnoxious cheer. "Your intended can't be a fragile little flower, can she? And that kind of spirit usually spills over into other . . . areas."

"What the fuck are you talking about?"

"Bed sport, Luka," he says dryly. "You've got yourself a hell-cat."

Am I hearing this correctly? I have to unclench my jaw to speak as he shovels a bite of food into his mouth. "Are you out of your mind? You still expect me to wed her?"

He surveys me as he chews, considering. "You expect not to? With the First Deve breathing down your neck?"

Something cold turns over in my gut. It's true that this marriage is a done deal in the eyes of the Realms and D'heilar. But surely they can't expect me to tie myself to a snake-tongued killer. Things have changed.

I shove my plate away.

Eldon leans in, lowering his voice. "You know you'll have to go through with it. You took the title for better or worse, *my deve.*"

The title. *Deve.* I loathe it. And I hardly *took* it. My father's actions forced it on me. What he did to Gray – the twins' oldest brother – pushed me over the edge, and at twenty-two, from behind a haze of rage, I'd challenged my sire for leadership.

The next day, in realm tradition, we met on the training ground and I did what needed to be done; I sank my sword into his heart. No regrets. Only lingering bewilderment as to why it had to be me to do it. *Why had Dunthor Djothar's cruelty been allowed to run amok for so long?* He was in power for longer than I've been alive. I mean, I understand the power of tradition. My grandfather was deve before my father, but surely someone could have found the courage to stand up to him. Of course, it *is* a lifetime commitment. The only way to rid oneself of the title is to lose it to a challenger . . . in a fight to the death.

I shoot Eldon a hard look. "You think I don't know that I'm bound to this title until the end?"

"You make it sound like a fate worse than death, Luka. It's not. Not even close. Now quit your moaning and tell me what this princess of D'heilar looks like."

Noé's face pinches. "She's actually very puny."

What an ass. The both of them. I push to my feet, almost knocking the bench over behind me.

"Deve," Noé says quickly. "I have much to tell you and a letter that must be dealt with."

"It can wait. I have pyre rights to prepare for."

Stalking from the room, I ignore the weight of everyone's stares. Leadership has always chafed. It fits ill against my skin and I'm eternally expecting to be seen for the imposter I am. I never wanted any of this; not the pressure, not the responsibility, and certainly never a Mother-forsaken, murderous bride. I consider storming down to the holding cells and confronting her, letting her feel my wrath. But unfortunately, I spoke the truth when I said I have pyre rights to prepare for. As a Range warrior, Carson is entitled to be lifted to the Eternal with words from my mouth, as well as the priest's. And those words must honor him.

Because Eldon is right. I need to stop moaning and get on with doing.

I make sure the men in the barracks know their attendance is mandatory, I send out runners to the furthest village farms, and, along with our cantankerous old priest, I inspect the burial pyre being built in the sacred clearing. And in between, I rehearse what I'll say about a man I spent much of my childhood with. Though we drifted apart during adolescence, he was a solid warrior. His loss will be *felt* in our community and on the battlefield.

During the ceremony, my tribute is . . . adequate. At least no one raises any objections, and when I lead the chants heralding Carson's arrival in the Eternal, the whole village joins me. It isn't until after the pyre is lit and Zola's sobs rip through the dawn that my simmering rage finally boils over. What an absolute waste of life. That foreign bitch's title isn't going to save her. She's going to pay for what she's done.

With purposeful strides, I head for the holding cells.

"Deve." I don't slow my pace for Bron. There are five brothers in the Cyrun family, four of whom became Range warriors, but Bron is the odd one out. He does enjoy some status as my personal aide though. "May I speak with you?"

"I'm busy."

"This shouldn't wait," he says, his breath pluming in the cold morning air. "It's about Rina."

"Who?"

"Your, err, intended?"

My steps stall out and he recoils at my glower. "Unless you want my dagger embedded in your heart, Bron, I suggest you keep your thoughts to yourself. I'm in no mood to discuss *my intended.*"

Worry flickers across his features as I start walking again. *I thought her name was Amarinata.*

"Please?" he calls after me.

Ignoring him, I make my way back through the stronghold's open gates to the north eastern corner of the courtyard and take the stairs down to the holding cells. Somehow it's colder down here than it is in the open air. A single torch in the wall bracket illuminates the recruit on guard duty. My lip curls when his gaze skitters away from mine. He may still be young, but the show of weakness is still aggravating. By his age, I'd already been a fully-fledged warrior for a year.

"The key," I order, my voice echoing off the stone walls.

He swallows. "It's not locked, my deve."

I stare at him until he stutters, "Mother Cyrun didn't return it."

"Mother Cyrun?" I drawl in a way that says he better explain immediately. *What was Zola doing down here?*

"Yes," the boy gets out. "I asked for the key's return but she chose not to hear me when she left."

My mind sifts through what he's telling me. "She came alone?"

"No, sir. She came with her youngest . . . at least I think he's her youngest. She has so many sons."

Bron? No, Bron avoids her meddling. He must mean Crion, who's a year older.

"Is the prisoner still among the living?"

His eyes bulge. "I . . . I don't know. Should I check?"

I slam my fist into his ribs, sending the air whooshing from his lungs. He goes down onto the dirt floor like a stone. "Report to Noé. You'll be cleaning chamber pots for a month. Now get gone."

He does his best to scramble to his feet, choking out a, "Yes, Deve."

In the corridor there are four doors, but only the second is closed. For a moment, I hesitate. If this woman is dead, there will be consequences. I should have known Zola would try something and made sure that an actual warrior was put on

29

guard duty. Stupid. But there's nothing to be done for it now.

Pushing the door open, I'm greeted by a wall of complete darkness. Backtracking to grab the torch, I return and hold it up to illuminate the small, dank room. She's there, sprawled on the floor, her body arranged at an odd angle, seemingly bent in half.

"Oy," I call. No response. Since her actual name is a mouthful, I use the shortened version Bron gave me. "Rina!" Still nothing. Moving closer, I watch for any sign of life, but with the way she's positioned on her side with her hair over her face, I can't discern anything. "Hey, Rina," I try again, this time using the toe of my boot to nudge her. Not even a twitch. "Shit."

Sliding the torch into the bracket by the door, I bend down and jog her shoulder. I get nothing, but she's breathing, and I see now why she's bent into such an awkward position. The shackle on her wrist and its counterpart on her ankle have been affixed to the same iron ring that's embedded in the floor. I feel a twinge in my chest. She's not a battle-hardened soldier, just a woman, a small one by the look of her.

Carefully, I move her hair back. Her chapped lips are an unnatural shade of blue and her left eye is partially swollen shut by a bruise that runs from her jaw up to her temple. I squint at the black hair plastered there. *Is that blood?* I lay my hand on her forehead and instantly pull it back. She's ice cold. Turning her more fully onto her side, I catch sight of a fresh, bright red stain on the skirt of her dress at about thigh level.

"Rina." Still nothing.

Father damn me. I tilt my chin up and stare at the ceiling. *She deserves to die,* I tell myself. If I leave her here, she won't last a day and she'll no longer be a problem . . . until the First Deve comes sniffing around for an explanation. And I suppose at a minimum I should listen to her side of the story before I do anything. Though what is the word of a snake worth? Not a lot.

Unsure, I grunt with frustration and fall back on my tried and true system.

What would my father have done?

A short and bitter laugh comes out of me. He definitely would've left her to die. No question. And therein lies my answer.

Fuck.

I inspect the shackles. The damage they've wrought has me frowning. Her wrist is bruised and bloody, and her ankle is worse, barely recognizable with all the swelling. *Why was she shackled at all? Couldn't they handle one small girl?*

I guess there was the whole issue of the murder to consider.

I could ask Noé for the key, but I have a feeling he'd lobby to leave her here, and I'm not interested in defending my decision. Pulling my dagger from my belt, I work at slipping the iron pin free. It takes some doing but I get the shackle off her wrist.

Holding my dagger up to the light to inspect it, I mutter, "If it chips or cracks, I'm going to have to kill her anyway."

I'm more careful with her ankle, which is in rough shape. When the pin finally gives and I open the cuff, I get my first sign of life in the form of a small whimper. Sheathing my knife, I get her up and over my shoulder. She weighs less than nothing, and again, I wonder why she was shackled.

I head up to the courtyard where Bron is still hanging around.

"Is she okay?" he asks urgently.

"For now. Bring some fresh water and a blanket to the baths."

"Yes, Deve. Right away. And thank you."

That stops me cold. "Thank you?" But he's already gone in search of what I've asked for. *What kind of a man thanks me for helping his brother's killer?*

It's then that the smell hits me. Ugh. She's pissed herself at some point. Wonderful.

The hot springs baths are less than a quarter mile away, bubbling up into a small system of rocky outcroppings and half-formed caves. The pools are empty of people right now but that doesn't mean I won't encounter any eventual prying eyes, so I haul her back to the furthest pool. Pulling her off my shoulder, I place her on the ground on her back.

In the growing light that filters down through the fissures in the ceiling, the twinge of disquiet I felt earlier, becomes a full-on pang. She looks like she's been beaten to a pulp. And the circumference of the blood stain on the front of her dress is larger.

A slight shiver rolls through her and her head lolls to the side. "Rina," I say loudly. I'd slap her to bring her around, but it would probably kill her.

Since she's in no condition to consent, I go ahead and dip the fingers of both hands into the neckline of her filthy dress and yank. The flimsy material gives easily and once I've ripped the entire garment right down the center, it reveals . . . another dress. Not an underdress, but literally another dress, though this one is even more threadbare than the one on top.

"What in the . . ?" *This is a princess of D'heilar?* Suspicion doesn't just whisper to me, it blares. Once I've got her arms out of the sleeves of the first dress, I tear the second and almost stumble back at the sight of her. Her torso is a painted canvas of purple, black, and yellow bruises. She's not wearing any undergarments and I find the source of all the blood: a stab wound to her thigh.

Mother all mighty.

I hear boots on the path and whirl.

"What have they done to her?" Bron hisses.

Ignoring him, I turn back to work on freeing her arms from the second dress.

"Just leave the –" My words die in my throat. Under her left arm, along her ribs is a row of four marks. Burn marks. Made by the flat side of a heated blade if I'm not mistaken. They're not fresh, but they're ugly. And systematic. Meant only to inflict pain. A rush of compassion drowns my good sense for a moment, but I promptly pull myself together. Who knows what she did to deserve such treatment.

"What is it?" Bron asks, coming closer.

I block her from his view as best I can. It's irrational since there's nothing sexual about the situation. Plus, I know Bron has no interest in women. But somehow I don't want him staring at her brutalized, naked body. "Nothing," I snap. "Leave the things and make sure no one enters the pools." When he hesitates, I raise my voice. "Go!"

Listening to his retreating footsteps, I take a better look at this girl who I may have to take to wife. With the swelling, it's hard to discern her features, but her long hair is loose and creates a black-as-night frame around her face. There's a sickly waxiness to her skin despite it being a rich tan color. And the dry, chapped state of her full lips reminds me that she needs water if she's going to survive.

Uncorking the skin Bron brought, I support her neck and

pour a small amount into her mouth. Most of it leaks back out, but when I try again, I see her throat work, weakly at first, then with more purpose. So she's not fully unconscious, only weak and dazed. That's a good sign I suppose.

While she drinks, I finally get a look at the rest of her. She's mostly sharp angles and ruined or abused flesh. Her small breasts are tipped with dark nipples and the apex of her thighs is covered with jet-black curls. The stab wound to her thigh is deep but not gaping; however, it's still oozing blood. I've seen thigh wounds kill a man within minutes on the battlefield. She's lucky Zola didn't want her dead.

When the water starts to become too much for her, I pull it away and turn my attention to the pool. I groan, realizing I'm going to have to get in with her. I strip myself and then lift her from what's left of her clothing.

Holding her slight, much-too-cold body to my chest, I step into the shallow end of the pool. Knowing the temperature change will come as a shock, I mutter a warning of, "This is going to hurt," as I move deeper to slowly lower us into the warm water.

It doesn't take long for the heat to bring on a reaction. Soft whimpers start up, quickly becoming more and more distressed. Soon uncoordinated limbs join the protests and I'm forced to use some strength to hold on to her.

"Easy," I admonish, lifting my shoulder to keep her head from flopping back. "After all this effort, I'm not keen on you drowning."

She stills, but as soon as my voice fades, she's back to struggling. "Hush now. No one's going to harm you." Again she calms, so I keep it up, feeling like a fool for conversing with a semi-conscious woman while gently rocking her in the water.

A croaked word interrupts me and I look down. Her eyes are open and they cause an unexpected, visceral tug in my gut. Though unfocused, they're the most stunning amber color, made all the more striking against her tan skin and black hair.

"Water," she rasps.

Tearing away from her mesmerizing eyes, I give her a terse, "In a minute."

Her response is an irksome little mewl.

"Relax. I'm trying to help you."

Moments later, her body starts to tremble. "H-hh-hurts," she stutters.

"Well of course it does," I gripe as I study the matted hair at her temple. Actually her hair is beautiful as well. It's a deep black, like onyx or a raven's wing. Dipping her back, I attempt to rinse the blood away, but panic at the motion has her jerking in my arms and then going limp. Great. She's fainted. "Bron!"

"Yes, Deve?" he calls.

"Come and help."

When he appears, I wade toward the edge of the pool. "She's passed out. Get my shirt ready. You'll put it over her head and get her arms into the sleeves." Transferring her legs to straddle my waist, I cradle her with one arm under her ass and the other across her back as I get out.

"Be quick about it," I scold, when he just gawps at her bruised back. "She'll lose all the heat she's gained." He snaps to it and gets the job done despite the material sticking to her wet skin.

"Can you handle her weight?" I ask as he brings the blanket and folds it around her.

He rolls his eyes so I pass her over. "She doesn't weigh

much, does she?" he comments while I tie the drawstring on my pants and pull on my leather vest. "She hasn't eaten in a few days," he informs me, then notices the hem of my shirt is slowly turning red. "Uh, is she bleeding?"

I sigh as I get my boots on. "Your mother didn't appreciate her son's murder."

"Murder," he scoffs, followed up by, "My mother?"

Not bothering to respond to something so self-explanatory, I hold out my arms for the girl. "Will you leave her in the cells?" he asks, handing her over.

I shake my head. "Run ahead and have a bed placed in the east tower, then go and find Elsy." The old healer won't appreciate the early morning wake-up call, but that's not my problem.

Bron's relief leaves me weary. It's been a long night. Arriving back at the stronghold, more people are milling about, but no one dares approach me. They'll have to content themselves with guessing at who I have in my arms.

CHAPTER 3

RINA

I always figured there would be no pain in the Eternal. But since my entire body still aches, it seems my death has much in common with my life. At least for once I'm not cold. Wanting to burrow further into the warmth, I shift and get hit with what feels like a dagger to my skull.

"My lady? Let me bring you some water."

I stiffen, suddenly unsure of my surroundings. Cracking an eyelid reveals a dark room lit only by a small fire off to my left. *Where am I?* A woman comes to the side of the bed holding a wooden cup, and because I have no energy to even question her, I allow her to support my neck and give me water. It's the most delicious thing I've ever tasted.

When I finish the contents, I don't protest when she retreats with the cup no matter how much I want to. To my relief, she reappears out of the darkness almost right away. "Now some broth," she says gently, a long, blond braid hanging over her shoulder. "Elsy says you have to eat or you won't heal."

We repeat the process, this time with a bowl that she holds to my mouth. After a swallow, I try to speak. "Who . . . who is Elsy?" My voice is scratchy with disuse.

"Elsy is the healer," she says, and over the rim of the bowl, I watch her expression become mischievous. "She was most displeased with the deve."

It dawns on me that I'm not dead at all, but alive and among the barbarians. My sluggish mind wants no part of the realization, so I focus on the young woman. I don't feel any animosity from her . . . in fact, she seems to exude kindness, something that begins to unravel the ball of nerves in my stomach.

"Who are you?" I ask.

She smiles. "I'm Yvette, my lady."

Trying to shake my head ignites a bolt of pain, so instead I whisper, "Please don't call me that. My name is Rina."

The smile dims slightly, but she nods. "As you wish. Do you need to use the bucket?"

I blink.

"To relieve yourself?"

"Oh." I've never heard of a chamber pot referred to so crudely. "Yes, I do need . . . the bucket." Before the thought of how much it will hurt to move can overwhelm me, Yvette comes around to the other side of the bed and throws back the covers.

Shivering, I look down at myself in the low light. I'm wearing a long linen shirt that's stained with blood along the hem, but it's the bandage wrapped around my thigh that brings everything rushing back; the attack, the cart . . . the dungeon, the old woman with the knife. Then there's just flashes of half-formed images.

I'm weaker than a newborn kitten and my thigh screams through the whole ordeal, but with Yvette's help, I make it back into the bed. "Thank you," I whisper as I fall back into sleep headfirst.

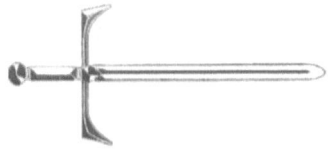

Days pass in a haze of feverish sleep, pain, and healing. Yvette is sometimes with me, coaxing me to eat and drink, but most of the time I'm alone. I also meet the healer, Elsy, who's a stern, old woman who doesn't put up with nonsense. She's not cruel or abusive though and I take an immediate liking to her as well.

Once I'm lucid enough to prop myself up in bed, I assess my surroundings more closely. I may not be in the dungeon anymore, but neither am I in a sleeping chamber. Though the room is quite large, there's no proper hearth, and the one window doesn't have shutters. It's just open to the air and serves as a vent for the iron brazier that's been placed next to it. Other than the brazier and the bed, there's me – that's it. Not that I'm complaining. I could still be in that pitch-black room.

"My lady! You're awake," Yvette says happily as she comes bustling through the door with a tray of food. "That's wonderful! Elsy says you must eat something more substantial today."

My rumbling stomach agrees.

"You can't survive on broth alone," she announces, placing the tray carefully on my lap.

"Thank you."

Though my thanks is probably premature. The tray only contains a wooden bowl of watery gray mash and a cup of water. I look up to find Yvette radiating expectation.

"I know it's not much, but –"

"No," I interrupt. "I'm very grateful. Thank you." I reach for the . . . "There are no utensils."

"Pardon?"

"There's no spoon."

"No, there's not," she agrees, shifting slightly on her feet. "I'm not to give you anything that could be used as a weapon."

"A weapon?" I repeat slowly, unable to keep how ridiculous I find that statement from my voice.

"Well, yes. I had much the same reaction, but my brother overruled me."

With a hand still weak from fever, I lift the roughly hewn wooden cup of water to my mouth, giving myself a chance to organize my still fuzzy thoughts. Instead of asking who her brother is, I go with, "May I ask how long I've been here?"

Yvette visibly relaxes. *Did she think I would berate her?* Surely not.

"You've been here for seven days."

Shock cuts through me like a knife. "Seven days?" I set the cup back down.

"Yes, you had a high fever for the first while and then you mostly slept."

"And you've taken care of me all this time?" I press my palms to my chest and then show them to her, displaying my gratitude.

She waves away the gesture, quite rudely to my mind, and says, "Well, Elsy said you would either die or you wouldn't. There wasn't much we could do to sway the outcome."

Her plain speech is jarring, but I do my best to keep my expression neutral. "Regardless, I'm very thankful. I can't imagine you were happy to be assigned the task."

"Oh, I wasn't assigned, I volunteered. Now eat up."

The finality in her tone tells me there won't be any more questions, so I lift the bowl to my lips. The contents slide toward my mouth and I force myself to swallow a tasteless bite. My stomach rebels but I manage to keep it down. Wanting to postpone the next bite, I say, "Seven days would explain why I smell so terrible."

I mean it as a joke, but Yvette seems distressed. "My brother is very mulish."

Again *her brother* and I can't head off my curiosity this time. "So you would have been my sister-in-law?"

She looks at me blankly, then laughs like the idea is outlandish. "No, Luka is not my brother."

Much to my disappointment, she doesn't give me any more information and I'm forced to go back to my breakfast. The next mouthful includes an awful, chewy lump and inspires me to throw caution to the wind. "Do you know what will happen to me?"

Yvette carefully sits on the edge of the bed, arranging the blue woolen skirt of her dress. "I don't, my lady. No one does. Nothing has been said publicly."

"I see." I want to ask if she has knowledge of what's been

said in private, but the glutinous mess in my bowl speaks volumes on the matter, as does the lack of a spoon. I may not be in the dungeon, but I am a prisoner, one who will most likely lose her head – literally. If I wasn't so exhausted, I might pity myself.

After forcing myself to lick the rest of my breakfast from the bottom of the bowl, I fall back into a heavy slumber. When I wake later in the evening, there's a tray on the floor next to the bed with my dinner. Instead of gruel, there's a watery stew more fit for swine consumption than human. I consider not bothering with it since I don't have much of an appetite. But ultimately, I decide that while there's still a chance my life may not be forfeit, I'll do what I can to come back from this nightmare. At least this time, I'm the only witness to the mortification of eating like a pig from a trough.

The next morning after some more of the gruel, I feel better in both body and mind. Yvette's chatter about her eight-year-old son, Rionnon, buoys my spirits and distracts me from the low throb of my headache, and the persistent ache of my thigh, ribs, and ankle.

It's not long, however, before our peace is breached, first by male voices on the stairs, then by the door to the room crashing open. Yvette stands from the bed, where she was attempting to braid my filthy hair.

"What is the meaning of this?" She looks down her nose at the four men, even though they're all easily an entire head taller than she is. They're dressed alike in the familiar vests, two of them with shirts underneath and two of them without, leaving their massive arms on display. My stomach falls as I recognize Noé.

"Wait in the hall, Yvette," he demands.

"I won't," she fires back and Noé's face twists with annoyance.

"Do as I say, woman."

"You're my brother, Noé, not my father, and I'll have you use a civilized tone in this room."

Noé is her brother? That saddens me. Yvette has been incredibly kind and I'd hoped we could be friends if I come through this.

The man beside Noé jerks his chin toward the hall and Yvette almost immediately inclines her head and whispers, "Yes, Deve." She leaves, flashing me a look of sympathy from the door.

So this is my intended. Wishing I could have at least met him fully clothed, I pull the fur more securely over my chest and proceed to greedily take him in. Of the four men, he's the tallest and the broadest, with a light brown beard and –

"Affix the chains," he orders.

My heart stutters. *Chains?*

The other two men come forward, one to each side of the bed, dropping what are indeed chains onto the stone floor. They pull large hammers from their belts and do exactly what they were ordered, they affix chains to the thick wooden legs at the head of the bed. Each hammer blow jolts the entire structure and vibrates through my body, taking my headache from a dull throb to excruciating.

When they're done, the deve orders them out, his cold voice echoing in the mostly empty room. I didn't think anyone could be more imposing than Noé. Maybe under different circumstances, I'd find the strength of my betrothed's jawline pleasing or the easy symmetry of his features handsome, but the emotionless expression he wears does nothing but scare me. And like always, fear presses iron into my spine.

He breaks into my thoughts with a loud declaration. "I have questions."

I battle back the sneer that wants to surface on my lips. He may have questions, but the chains have told me that he believes he already knows their answers.

"How old are you?"

Surprise hits me first, then doubt. I thought I was the only one being kept in the dark. "Uh, I'm twenty-one. How old are you?"

His glare of superiority doesn't falter as he ignores me. "What is your name?"

"You don't know my name?"

"Answer me." To my dismay, the harshness of those two words causes me to jump.

"Rina. My name is Rina." And though I've heard his name from others, I return the question. "And you are?"

"Your full name."

He has not a smidgeon of warmth toward me and I make a conscious effort to shore up my defenses to meet him head-on. "Amarinata Valentirnan D'heilar." His lip curls at my southern pronunciation, snuffing out the last of my patience. "Do you have a name or am I to call you Deve?"

His eyes flash at my sarcasm, but he chooses to press on with his next question. "Who gave you the scars you wear on your ribs?"

A tremor of dismay rocks me. I should have been prepared for anything from this barbarian, but instead he's gotten past my guard with only his third question. I want to rant and rage about the sanctity of my own body, about the –

"What did you do to earn them?"

My stomach bottoms out. "Earn them?" I whisper, not taking my eyes from his. Horror takes root inside of me, followed closely by repugnance.

"Answer him," Noé orders.

Such a question will get no response from me. Even when Noé takes a few aggressive steps toward me, I don't flinch.

"Leave us," the deve intones, earning him a scowl from the man. "Now, Noé."

With reluctance, he does as he's told.

I brace myself for the worst, my new-found strength almost no match for the rising dread. I'm in no shape to take a beating . . . or worse, and I send a silent prayer to the Mother, asking for this man to be satisfied with a verbal attack instead of a physical one.

Once the door is shut, I watch my fiancé fold his arms over his massive chest. "I am deve here. I will be obeyed."

"Or what? You'll add to my scars?"

His beard isn't so thick that I miss the way his jaw clenches. Then his arms drop to his sides and his big hands curl into fists. Terror, real terror, sluices through my veins. I think I almost faint with relief when all he does is turn to the window, looking down on what I know is a walled courtyard below. Without facing me, he says, "I want to hear your version of the events surrounding Carson's death."

He doesn't use the word *murder,* but the bloom of hope in my chest is quickly extinguished when the rest of what he said registers. "My version?" Not the truth, but my *version.* A huff slips from my throat. "Are you saying you would take my word over that of your men's?"

Over his shoulder, his gaze lands on me, heavy and considering. It tells me I'm right.

"Let's not pretend," I say, sounding as resigned as I feel, "that my word is anything more than worthless to you. Just get on with whatever it is you're going to do with me."

Now he doesn't bother to hide his frustration and seems to cast about in his mind for something as he turns to lean against the wall. He comes up with, "I could have your belongings brought up to you." He gestures around us at the bare walls.

Belongings? He mistakes my confusion for interest, clearly believing he's found something with which to bargain. "Or," he intones ominously, "if you won't talk to me, I could have everything piled in the courtyard and set ablaze."

Apparently, the deve missed his lessons in the art of negotiation. *What kind of a dolt goes into a discussion unarmed with even a basic set of facts?*

While I want to gloat over his folly, I realize that his preference for threats over careful deliberation will undoubtedly not work in my favor. "Well, *my deve,* if I'm not shackled to the bed, I'll be sure to watch it all burn from the window."

His temper finally breaks. "You think this is a game?" he yells. "One of my men is dead and I need to know what happened. Most are calling for your blood."

Infected by his bellowing, I match it. "My blood?!" I flip the covers aside and swing my legs over the side of the bed. Elsy removed the bandage from my thigh this morning, saying the wound needed air. Forcing myself to my feet, I almost collapse with the wooziness of being vertical and the horrible strain on my ankle and my leg, but I lift the shirt and show him the aftermath of someone wanting my blood. "You mean this was not enough?" I stumble forward, wanting to be sure the light from the window shows him every gruesome detail.

He doesn't even wince on my behalf. Bastard.

"When I say they want your blood, I mean *all* of it."

"Then what are you waiting for?" I demand, though my voice has lost half of its volume. "End this right now." My head spins, but before the blackness swallows me, I give him my truth. "I'm ready."

CHAPTER 4

LUKA

tupid girl. Or I suppose at twenty-one, she's a woman, albeit a very small one. "I'm ready," I mimic in a high voice for no one's benefit but my own as I put her back on the bed. I should have let her dash her skull against the stone, but something compelled me to catch her. "You're not *ready*," I grouse. "You're stupid."

I lift the shirt to check the leg, pointedly not looking at her cunt. The wound is red and swollen, but it's knitted and there's no obvious sign of festering. It's not pretty though and it must hurt like a devil. Next I check her wrist, which is mostly a crust of scabs, and then her ankle, which is the same but with the added color of fading bruises. At least the swelling has gone down enough that she doesn't appear to have a club foot anymore.

My gaze settles on her face, almost wishing she were

awake to get another glimpse of her intriguing amber eyes. And her raven-wing hair, which Yvette was braiding, has fallen loose. Even greasy it's a beautiful color.

Yanking the fur over her, I yell for Yvette. She and Noé shove at each other to enter the room first and I pin them with a flat look. I don't know why I took Noé's advice to set such a harsh tone with the chains when my gut was telling me otherwise. I need to trust my own instincts more.

"What happened?" Yvette accuses more than asks, rushing forward. I grew up with Yvette. We're the same age and I might have considered her for marriage if she hadn't popped out someone else's child at sixteen. This understandably blurs the lines between us sometimes, but I'm not feeling particularly generous at the moment.

"Watch your mouth," I snarl. "And tell me again why you volunteered for this duty?"

There's a flash of hostility. "As a man, I doubt you'd understand."

Noé waves his sister's nonsense away. "What did the woman have to say?"

"She said nothing," I grit out, heading for the door, then go back and rip the fur off of her body, leaving her with only the woolen blanket that she's lying on.

"Nothing?" Noé sputters. "She d–"

"My deve!"

I ignore Yvette.

"Luka!"

That pulls me up short and I turn to glare at her.

Does she heed the warning? No. Instead of shutting her mouth, she adds a pinch of pleading to her next words. "Where are you going with that? And she needs clothing and water for bathing."

"She gets *nothing* until I have her cooperation."

I don't wait for a response. I can't. The thought of having to punish Yvette for insolence turns my already sour stomach.

"You can't let her get away with that," Noé says, following me out.

"Your sister is —"

"Not my sister," he says with disgust. "The girl."

At the stairs, I stop in front of the recruit on duty. "No one but Yvette comes up or down these stairs. Am I understood? No one."

"Yes, Deve."

Noé and I make our way down and he continues to henpeck me. "You can't let it stand."

I stop off at my chamber and pitch the fur inside before I head back for the stairs. "And what would you have me do? Pull out my future bride's finger nails? Or perhaps you'd have me tether her to a whipping post in the courtyard?"

"That's where she's headed anyway."

At the bottom, my arm shoots out to stop him, and when I see he's being serious, something in me snaps. My fist is against his jaw before I even realize what I'm doing. And that first crack is so satisfying that I go back for another. And another. There's a reason that I'm deve and no one has dared challenge me in the past year and a half of my rule. All of my elite warriors are strong and skilled, but it takes a very singular mindset to fight like your life depends on it every single time. My father instilled that in me from a very young age. Some see it as savagery, I see it as survival.

Noé doesn't allow the fourth shot to connect, but he's on the defensive in the small space of the hall.

"A little old for brawling, aren't you?"

Somewhere underneath my anger and sick satisfaction, I recognize my uncle's voice.

"He's right," Noé pants.

Getting him against the wall, I shove my forearm across his throat, trusting that he won't pull a dagger and sink it between my ribs. Unwise, really. Suddenly it comes to me that Rina's *I'm ready* isn't as crazy as it sounded. Sometimes life is beyond exhausting.

My Uncle Teo's wry inquiry of, "Are you finished yet? I'd like a word with you, Luka," echoes against the stone.

Noé tenses at my uncle's lack of respect and just like that we're back on the same side. As my arm falls, I turn to my father's brother and Eldon's sire. Teo was my father's Second for many years and he despises that I don't come to him for advice, that he's been made irrelevant by the younger generation. Short-sighted or not, I refuse to taint my rule with anything related to my father.

"Pardon?" I ask, redirecting my savagery into the question.

"My deve, I'd like a moment of your time."

With the heat of violence still running through my blood, I doubt I have the patience for Teo right now, but he'll continue to seek me out until he gets what's on his mind out in the open.

"If you can keep up, you have until we reach the stables."

His mouth tightens at the corners, but he follows me into the Great Hall. "I'd like to meet the woman," he says and I almost scoff aloud.

"No."

"Why not?"

"I said no." Even if I could fathom a reason for such a meeting, I still wouldn't allow him anywhere near her.

"The First Deve expects you to marry the woman. Crossing him should not be done lightly."

I roll my eyes. "Whatever would I do without your counsel, Uncle?"

He doesn't appreciate the mockery, and for a moment, there's only the sound of our boots on the stone floor as we cross to the main doors, which are propped open as they always are during the day.

"He may cut off trade if you don't go through with the union, or worse, he may –"

"You're not telling me anything I don't already know."

Squinting against the brightness of the overcast sky, I hop down the steps. My uncle, whose knee doesn't do well with stairs, remains on the landing to yell, "What are you going to do, then?"

If only I knew.

The courtyard is busy. Winter is coming and though the crops have all been harvested and stored, there is still much to do if we're going to make it through the long, dark months ahead.

A team of horses arrives, pulling a cart of freshly cut trees from the forest and a few warriors emerge from the barracks above the stables to begin the process of chopping it into firewood. One of my first changes as deve was to mandate year-round work for the men. All men. In the past, everyone pitched in during the harvest, but otherwise if the warriors weren't training or out on patrol, they were loafing about and drinking ale. Now, every day, every man puts in a few hours of communal work. There've been objections aplenty, especially from the older warriors, and it hasn't completely stopped the drunkenness, but I've been adamant. Teo has warned me that I'm straining their loyalty, but I tell him the same thing I tell everyone: you don't like it, challenge me for leadership. It's that simple.

Entering the quiet of the stables, I let the soothing smell of horses replace the worry that during the dead of winter the men will have nothing but time to talk over their ale. And by *talk,* I mean complain and bitch not only about my leadership, but also about the First Deve's ever-increasing taxes.

Down the long row of stalls, Nightshade lifts his head. "Hello, boy," I whisper, ducking under the rope of his paddock. He tries to sniff out my hands, so I show him they're empty. "Sorry, my friend. I've got nothing for you this time. It's been a shit morning."

My giant war horse snorts, unhappy with me. "Yeah, I know, a poor excuse. But if you met her, you'd be more understanding." I run my hands over his whole body, sweeping away any dust or debris, watching for any flinching or discomfort. A warrior's horse is his greatest asset, and honestly, besides my mother and cousin, there's no one who I'm closer to than Nightshade.

As I saddle him, his ears swivel in the direction of the entrance and once again tension gathers at the base of my skull. A few stalls down, Jackanapes snickers as Noé arrives. "Ahh, you sweet bastard," Noé coos to his horse. "Has Luka invited you along?"

"He has not," I say and Noé nods. Most know that I like to ride alone to clear my head.

"Anything you need me to do while you're gone?"

My thoughts drift to the route I'll take on my coming ride as I tell him absently, "Not that I can think of."

"You sure? I could pry the answers we need from her faithless lips."

I grit my teeth. "Stay away from her, Noé."

"At least let me shackle her to the bed. She's going to take our threats for empty."

Lifting my attention from the girth buckle, I size up my Warrior Commander over Nightshade's back. "What is your obsession with chains? I still don't understand why you felt it necessary to use them on her in the first place. I doubt she weighs more than seven stone."

"She killed a man," he deadpans.

"And you believe Cayson when he says she tempted his twin into the woods with false promises of sexual favors?"

He shrugs. "All I know is that it sounds exactly like something a woman from D'heilar would do."

"That is true," I concede half-heartedly, unsure if I believe it. "Tell me, where do you have her belongings stored?"

"What?"

Something in his tone has me looking up again. "Her belongings. What she brought with her."

"She didn't bring anything."

My hands still. "What do you mean? Are they sending them later? To the river?"

"I don't know. Maybe the answer is in the letter."

I brush thoughts of the letter away. "What did *she* say about it?"

"I didn't ask. The bitch delayed our departure by almost three full days and then we got a late start. We were told she couldn't get her spoiled ass out of bed on time."

I frown. *Why didn't I know this?* "You left three days late, but you arrived only a day behind schedule?"

"Well, I pushed us hard to make up the time."

"And she bellyached the entire way?"

"Not really. She was mostly silent, but when she tried to lure Bron in, I put a stop to their talks."

I turn back to Nightshade. "Seems you were focused on the wrong brother."

"Seems so," he agrees ruefully. "Seven stone can add up to more trouble than one would expect."

Pulling my bow and quiver down from the wall, I strap them across my back and mount my horse. "I'll be back before nightfall. And Noé?" I wait for him to acknowledge me. "Leave the girl alone."

He inclines his head.

Riding northeast in the direction of Nadore Lake, I'm pleased when not long after leaving, Vennatrix joins us. "Where have you been, Venna?" I ask my usual hunting companion. Three summers ago, I found her as a wolf cub next to her mother's dead body, half-starved and dying of thirst. On a whim, I nursed her back to health and didn't discourage her from following me around.

She usually stays within a few miles of the stronghold, probably because she never found a pack of her own. My warriors and I are her pack now. She rides into battle with us and has proven her worth more times than I can count, as a hunter, a tracker, and a warrior.

With Nightshade and Venna with me, I'm able to clear my mind of the events of the past week. There's nothing but the cool, pine-scented air, the squeak of the leather saddle, and Nightshade's hoof steps on the worn forest path. It takes a good hour before Venna lifts her nose in the air and heads more directly north. Following, we come upon the deer she's tracking in a clearing that I know well. I spent summers as a young child running wild over the land surrounding the stronghold.

As quietly as possible, I dismount and nock an arrow. We're downwind and the huge buck gets no warning before the arrow slices deep into his ribcage behind his shoulder. When he doesn't go down right away, Venna takes off after him, but by the time she catches up, the buck is dead on the ground.

I go back for Nightshade and lead him into the clearing where Venna is nosing the buck's wound with intent. She bares her teeth at me in a low growl. She's never bitten me, but that doesn't mean I don't treat her like the wild animal she is. "That's mine," I tell her in my most commanding voice. "Go get something else." Still growling, she obeys, slinking off into the woods to find herself a rabbit or a fox. An unexpected grin has my lips twitching. Venna's not the only female to give me that look today, or even the second. Both Rina and Yvette made their displeasure known.

But my good humor is short-lived. The buck is a big fucker and there's no way I can lift it onto Nightshade's back. Pulling my hatchet from my belt, I seek out two saplings to make a sledge. The task is time consuming and turns out to be the perfect thing to keep my mind busy. Though it's cloudy, I'd say the sun is well past its zenith by the time Venna returns, her muzzle stained with red. Not long after that, I finally get the buck loaded onto the leather lattice I keep for such occasions between the two poles.

Dark is coming on fast when I arrive at the butcher's cabin. Leaving the buck in his care, I let him know what I want done with the hide.

It's been a long day and I'm tired and hungry. But that's all forgotten when I come in through the front gates and my gaze is drawn up to the northeastern corner of the stronghold. Amarinata Valentirnan D'heilar is sitting on the window ledge of her room, wrapped in the blanket, watching the courtyard below. And I swear, across the distance, I feel her amber eyes meet mine, kindling a glow low in my gut.

It's time to pay the princess another visit.

I've washed, put on a clean shirt, and eaten dinner before I take the steps to the tower. I put her in the turret to keep her isolated, but by the time I come to the guard stationed at the top, I'm irritated.

"Is Yvette with her?" I ask sharply.

"No, Deve," he stutters. Another recruit. It seems Noé is not as worried about her status as a cold-blooded killer as he'd have me believe. "She left before midday."

Midday? Then I notice a tray of food on the ground near his feet and he hurries to explain. "I was told no one may enter except Yvette and since she's not here . . ."

I don't know whether to commend or pummel him. "Give it to the pigs," I say, gesturing at the congealed mess that's obviously been sitting there for hours. "And bring a new tray up."

He hurries away and I go down the short hall. There's no latch mechanism on her door, reminding me that this isn't an appropriate place for a prisoner. If only she were an ordinary captive so I could lock her up downstairs and forget about her.

Pushing the door open, I squint into the almost complete darkness. Directly across from the door is a wall and to the right is the outline of the bed, but it appears empty. I step into the room to check the gaping maw of the window. She's not there either and my stomach swoops. Shit. *Has she escaped?* But then I spot a darker heap behind the brazier. She's curled up on the floor, dangerously close to the hot metal. I stomp forward, intending to yank her away from it, but she must sense me coming because she panics and desperately tries to scramble free of the blanket.

"Stop," I order and she freezes, still prone on the floor, only having managed to get an elbow under herself.

She pushes her loose hair back as I glare down at her. "What in the name of the Mother are you doing? One wrong move and you'll burn yourself, or a stray ember will set you ablaze."

Her panted breaths are accompanied by soft whimpering noises as she sits up slowly, favoring her thigh and her ribs. She leans her back against the wall and re-wraps the blanket around herself, angling her bare feet carefully under the brazier bowl. "It's cold," she mutters as if that explains her recklessness.

"Have I been too generous by providing you with a bed?"

She only stares back at me, seeming to be over the fright of my sudden appearance and now radiating contempt. Aware that threats and antagonism haven't worked with her so far, I decide to change my line of attack. Lowering myself to the floor, I sit across from her, my back pressed to the side of the

58

bed.

Long moments of uneasy silence pass while I study her shadowed features in the low glow of the coals, wondering how to start a conversation with her.

"Did I miss the torching of my possessions earlier?" she finally says. "Or has it been postponed until the morning?"

She comes out swinging and I have to smother the urge to laugh. *Who is this brave little slip of a woman? Does she have no sense of self-preservation?* I could crush her skull with my bare hands and yet she openly challenges me. I find it . . . not unappealing.

"How is it you've arrived with nothing to your name?"

She's not impressed. "You mean in your infinite wisdom, you haven't worked it out for yourself?"

I narrow my eyes. She piques my interest, yes, but my patience is already coming to an end. "Do you ever give a simple answer?"

"Actually, compared to you, I was very obliging this morning."

Scratching at my beard, I suppose she's right . . . if we were coming to this union on an even footing. Which we're not. We never were. This is my home, not hers.

"If I ask again will you tell me about yourself?" Her tone morphs from slightly mocking to interested. "May I ask how old you are?"

I guess there's no harm in giving her that much. "I'm twenty-four."

"And your name is Luka?"

For some reason, talking about myself is distasteful. It feels like I'm letting her win some kind of undeclared competition.

She breaks into my thoughts. "Do you find some advantage in keeping your name from me?"

"I don't need an advantage," I retort. "This is my stronghold."

Her expression closes off, and she nods like I've confirmed her worst suspicions. This is not going how I'd like. I try to change the subject. "How's the leg?"

I startle a humorless laugh out of her. "Why do you care?"

"I had nothing to do with that if that's what you're thinking."

Her brows lift, showing me how skeptical that statement makes her. "I thought this was your stronghold."

"It is. But that doesn't mean I can control a mother's grief." My words are weak even to my ears, but I refuse to admit to any wrongdoing. "And what about your ankle?"

The way she's taking my measure is reminiscent of my father's scrutiny when I was a child. He was always looking for cracks in my armor that could be exploited. In that context, I easily wait her out.

Finally, like I'm inconveniencing her, she lifts the blanket and extends her foot in my direction. "Still bruised, but I'll live."

It's improved even from this morning, though the skin is still a mottled yellow and green. "Be sure not to baby it or it will never be as it was."

Her amber eyes flare. "I will never be as I was."

It's clear she's not referring to her physical injuries and I suddenly feel like a fish out of water. I don't like it – at all . . . so intensely that I start to heave myself off the floor.

"I . . ." she begins and I hesitate. "I saw you riding a horse earlier. Was it one of the famed northern war horses?"

Discomfiture battles with my common sense. *Do I accept or reject her peace offering?* I've never run from anything in my life, so I plant my ass back on the floor. "He *is* a war horse," I say, sounding peevish. "As solid as they come."

"How many hands does he stand?"

"Almost nineteen."

"Nineteen?" she breathes. "That's huge."

I nod. "I call him Nightshade."

Her brows lift with surprise. "Like the poisonous plant?"

"Exactly. It gives him an extra edge of menace, I think." I don't tell her that Nightshade doesn't have a menacing bone in his body. He's the very definition of steadfast.

"Did you raise him yourself?"

"I did." I like her questions now. "He's been mine since he was born."

She looks almost wistful at my answer, then surprises me with, "Was it hard to break him?"

I'm not sure what she means by *hard*. "You mean hard work? No more than any other horse."

"Oh, no," she says, wavering for a moment. "I'm mean hard on you. I imagine it would be unsettling to take the wild out of an animal, to force him to be other than he is."

I almost laugh. What a ridiculous notion.

"You must think me fanciful," she goes on, sheepish now. "Ignore me. I'm not myself." She looks away and I watch her nibble at the side of her mouth. I think *fanciful* is probably her being exactly herself.

Before I can say anything, she turns those amber eyes on me again, causing my stomach to clench. In the glow of the coals, they're almost otherworldly. "The, uh, mare," she begins. "The one you allowed me to ride after the river . . . I . . ." Hesitantly, she lets go of the blanket she has clasped around her and presses both palms to her heart before she shows them to me. It's a gesture that marks her as distinctly southern. "I thank you for the experience," she whispers earnestly. "I hope you won't hold my actions against her."

I cock my head. "Hold your actions against who? The horse?"

She holds her tongue, forcing me to interpret her meaning for myself.

"The horse is fine," I tell her and she visibly relaxes.

"She has food and water?"

I almost scoff at the suggestion, but then I remember that I haven't fed or watered her and something very close to shame hits me.

"Yes, I'm sure she has food and water, but I'll check on her tomorrow to be sure."

Her lips start to form what I think is *thank you* when she stops herself and only nods.

CHAPTER 5

RINA

He takes up space; not only physically, but in spirit too. His presence is like a living force, pressing up against me, poking and prodding, searching out weaknesses and flaws. It's a good reminder that whatever angle he's playing with all this slightly awkward, civilized talk, is just that, an angle. I can't see what he's trying to gain though, not through the dull ache in my thigh or the gnawing hunger in my belly.

Even though I'm sure my fate has already been decided, I try not to rebuff him. After the loneliness of the past year, not to mention the past day, I'll accept any overtures of company that aren't accompanied by violence or threats. And right now, he seems mostly curious. I don't delude myself that the violence won't come. It always does. But until then, I'll pretend that my hunger and the cold aren't by his design.

"You have some knowledge of horses?" he asks.

"Some." The need to keep the conversation going gets the better of me and I add, "The horse I rode, Glory. She's a northern breed as well?"

In the low light, his head tilts. "You named her Glory?"

My cheeks heat, but I bite my tongue to stop an apology from leaving my mouth. At the time, I couldn't have known things would degenerate like they have, and the warrior at the river had said the horse was a gift. So no, I won't ask to be forgiven for naming her.

"A fitting name," he finally says. "She's a beautiful animal."

Surprise sparks some warmth within me. "She is. Her gallop is graceful and quick, like riding the wind."

He nods with approval. "Over short distances, she easily outpaces a fully-bred war horse." The pleasure in his voice adds fuel to the new heat inside of me.

"And to answer your question," he goes on. "She's a crossbreed of north and south. I believe her southern sire's bloodline is used to produce racehorses."

"She has R'hanian racing blood?" I can't hide my shock. R'hanians are incredibly expensive.

"That sounds right. The First Deve was gifted a stallion by your cousin, and Glory is the offspring."

The mention of the King douses everything, and from one heartbeat to the next, I'm back to being a bruised and battered woman, starved and forced to sit on the floor in an icy room.

Tension begins to creep up around us when I remain silent, keeping my gaze firmly on the floor.

"I've heard your cousin can be a very generous man. Is that true?"

Bile rises in my throat. How such an ignoramus could become the ruler of this realm is beyond me.

"Rina?" He sounds annoyed, something that's confirmed after another swollen pause. "I asked you a question."

I'm saved by a male voice calling hesitantly from the hall. "My deve?"

Frowning at me, Luka gets to his feet and comes back with a tray of food. He appears put out when he can't find anywhere to put it.

He holds the tray out to me. I should accept the offering with a smile and a thank you. Even if I very much doubt I'll become his wife, perhaps my life will be spared. But my fingers refuse to let go of the blanket, my lips don't curve, and the gratitude doesn't form on my tongue. Foolish, I know, but I can't bring myself to scrape and bow in exchange for the barest of necessities.

His expression hardens. Leaning down, he drops the tray the last few inches to the floor. To his satisfaction, the clang of it against the stone makes me jump. He stomps away and I expect that to be the end of it. But at the door, he turns to me. "I could return the fur I took from you this morning," he offers, and if I'm not mistaken there's a hint of shame in his tone.

"In exchange for what?"

He huffs. "In exchange for your civility."

"Civility? You withhold the basics of life yet it's me that lacks civility?"

He's mostly hidden in the shadows of the room as we stare each other down. It goes on for so long that he finally sighs loudly and starts to pull the door closed before I break. "Wait."

He turns back.

65

"There is something I'd like to have."

I almost can't summon the fortitude to swallow my pride, but the thought of never seeing it again gives me a hard shove forward. "My mother's ring was sewn into the waistline of the dress I was wearing. If I could have it back . . . I would be grateful."

He gives me a curt nod and leaves.

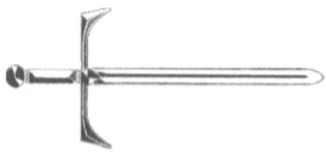

The stew warms me enough that I can move back to the bed where I'm blessedly able to sleep for a few hours before the cold wakes me and forces me to return to the brazier. Yvette finds me curled around its pedestal on the floor in the morning, miserable, trying to absorb what's left of its almost non-existent heat.

"Oh, my lady," she cries, rushing forward, dumping a bundle from her arms onto the empty bed. "I'm so sorry." She reaches for my hand to help me up. "Yesterday, my mother wasn't feeling well and by the time I settled everything at home, it was dark and I didn't dare make the trip back to the stronghold."

I hobble to the bed, my muscles stiff with the cold.

"But I thought the dimwits guarding the door would at least replenish the firewood. Father's tit, it's cold in here."

I don't have it in me to laugh at her profanity, but I do manage a weak smile when I see Bron in the doorway. "Good morning, Rina," he says, looking for somewhere to place the tray of food he's holding. "You look . . . better."

"Is that a question?" I tease half-heartedly.

"Give me that," Yvette says, bustling forward to take the tray. "Make yourself useful and empty the bucket." She lifts her chin at my toilet and I grimace. "And then get some wood up here."

Yvette doesn't even notice the exasperation in Bron's jerky movements as he obeys her orders. She calls out to him when he gets to the door. "Oh, and if you catch his holiness, the deve, in a good mood, be sure to press for whatever you think he'll allow."

Stifling a snort, he tells her, "You're going to get us all in trouble, Yvette." He has to go around a woman hovering in the hall.

"Good morning, Kata," Yvette says. "Come and hold the lady's tray, will you? I need to make up the bed."

The new woman cautiously shuffles forward. She's short, not much taller than I am, with dark hair and the same pale complexion that everyone seems to share here. Her blue eyes blaze in the natural light from the window, but there are dark shadows under them and the drab homespun dress she wears washes her out. Though *dress* is a bit of a stretch, it's more of a sack.

Yvette hands her the tray. "This is my cousin, Kata. She doesn't speak. But she's volunteered to help us out. Kata, this is her ladyship."

I shake my head. "There's nothing *her ladyship* about me, Kata, as you can see. My name is Rina." The woman, or maybe she's still a girl, shifts nervously on her feet and only chances a peek at me before she bows her head in greeting.

Yvette is all energy today and quickly unties the bundle she threw on the bed. My gasp echoes in the room, and she nods with approval. "Yes, I was most heartened by the deve's generosity," she says, arranging the furs over the straw-stuffed mattress.

My late-night visitor has replaced the one fur with three and I can't repress the gratitude that rushes through me. The cold is so debilitating, both physically and mentally, and the thought of being done with the unending shivering makes me dizzy with relief.

"Come on, in you get. You can eat your breakfast and then get some proper rest." Yvette holds the edge of the top fur for me and I do as I'm told.

Kata places the tray on my lap as Yvette breezes from the room, calling, "I'm going to make sure the wood is delivered."

On the tray, is a cup of water and another bowl of gray mush, except today it's much less watery. Again, there's no utensil of any kind. Kata, who must decide my reticence is over the quality of the food, nods encouragingly, seeming to indicate that it's not as bad as I think it is.

Pressing my lips together in a parody of a smile, I hold out my hands. "I just wish I could wash first," I explain and she lights up with understanding before she gently shakes her head. "Good thing I had my vanity stripped from me long ago," I tell her as I lift the bowl directly to my mouth and do my best to get the food into my stomach. It's messy and humiliating, but I manage. When I'm done, I pull the corner of the shirt out from under the fur and very carefully wet it with a small amount of the precious water and attempt to clean my chin and nose. Then I drink down every drop.

I notice Kata staring at me and something pricks at my supposedly non-existent pride, especially when she raises her hand and makes to touch me. Pulling away, I watch her shake her head vehemently. She reaches out again and gently touches my cheek bone and then my wrist, the wrist which still bears the scabs and bruises of the shackle. From there, she places her hand over her mouth and kisses her fingers as if wishing me a speedy recovery.

"You don't have to feel sorry for me," I tell her, my dignity still sore.

Again she shakes her head, but this time she also squeezes my hand. I get the impression that she's thanking me for something. Though for what, I don't know. Sensing my discomfort, she lets my hand go and takes the tray, heading for the door.

"Kata," I call and she turns. "Thank you," I say sincerely. Prickly pride or not, I've learned not to take anyone's kindness for granted.

She gives me a parting smile, and I burrow down into the furs and finally get some sleep.

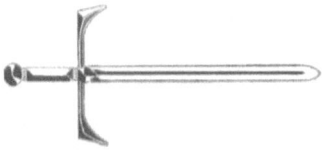

Over the next few days, the regular food and sleep help immensely with the healing process. The wound on my thigh no longer wakes me with its ache in the middle of the night and though I can't take regular steps without my ankle twinging, I feel almost human again. If only I were allowed to bathe. I'm filthy and I can barely stand the smell of myself.

I'm grateful for Yvette's visits. She's prone to chatter and her happy stories about her son leave me in good spirits even after she's gone home for the day. Kata comes too, but her silent regard feels heavy at times.

Otherwise, I sit on my window sill. The stronghold is built

around an enormous rectangular inner courtyard. The main building occupies the back wall and from my turret, three stories up, I have a bird's eye view over everything.

From what I can tell, the stables run along the entire right wall and the warriors' barracks are on the floor above, and the stronghold staff live on the left. Directly across from me, at the other end of the courtyard are the main gates, and in the center, lies a big ornamental sundial that lets me mark the time. And if I crane my neck, I can see the well, which is always busy, tucked close to the main building below the other turret.

But there's only so much to see, and with nothing to keep me busy, my mind churns. I fear that because the deve hasn't returned to ask any more of his questions, I'm officially living on borrowed time. Though Yvette still claims nothing has been decided, I've resigned myself to my fate.

It's too bad that resignation doesn't equal inner peace, because in the quiet, when it's too dark see anything, I begin to think of *him*. Curiously, my mind chooses to avoid the realities of my situation and instead focuses on the little details that I find pleasing; his rumbling voice, his passion for horses, his graceful movements despite his size. It's all a fantasy of course, but one I can't seem to shake. At my lowest, I even try to imagine what it would feel like to have him put his hands on me, not in violence, but with careful desire, or even love.

I figure there's no harm in it if it eases some of my despondency. It's better than imagining his huge fists twisting my head right off my neck.

On one such night, not long before sunrise, I've been awake for hours, and to hold the melancholy at bay, I've resorted to imagining his smile. It's purely fictional since I've never seen it, but it's the most soothing thing I can come up with.

Unfortunately it causes me to miss the flare of the coals in the brazier as the air in the room shifts.

I experience a split second of terror between realizing there's a figure looming over me and when a hand slams down hard on my mouth and jaw. Before I can even begin to fight, he's on top of me, pinning me to the bed. Panic surges and my muffled screams fill my mind. With my arms trapped under the furs, I buck and twist and thrash, but he's so heavy that I can barely breathe.

Reeking of alcohol, he hisses next to my ear. "The deve has sent me to loosen your tongue, you disgusting whore." Trying to get his hands on me, he gropes at the furs. I thank the Mother that his body is holding them down, shielding me.

He's finally forced to shift his weight to rip the fur back, and I take my chance to push against him. "Bitch," he accuses, rebalancing himself.

I keep fighting, keep screaming into his palm, my blood raging.

His frustration boils over and he bites down where my shoulder meets my neck with so much force that I see stars. What little breath I have left freezes in my lungs for a moment before my muted screams double themselves.

He chuckles. "That's the least of what you deserve." His hand slips down off my mouth and I immediately jerk my head forward and feel his nose crunch against my forehead.

"Fuck!" he howls and I shove him with all my might, once, twice, three times until he tips over the side of the bed.

Scrambling blindly in the very low light, I kick off the furs and immediately seek out the only thing in the room that could be used as a weapon: the tray. I raise it like a bludgeon, bringing it down over my attacker's back. One of the handles breaks off and I almost lose my grip as the man slowly straightens, his bleeding nose creating a horribly macabre image in the glow of the coals.

Cayson.

He snatches at me, but misses in his inebriated state as I make a break for the darker outline of the door. Flattening my back against the wall right outside the room, I wait for him to come barrelling out, then strike him with the tray again, using every ounce of strength my muscles can summon.

With a shriek of pain, I hear him go down onto the stones and for a second my mind blanks. *What do I do? What do I do? What do I do?* The question beats in time with my staccato heartbeat, so loud in my ears, so fast in my chest.

The hall is black. If I want to hit him again, I'll only be able to guess at his exact location. If I want to run, I'll have to pass right by him. But the door. I know where the door is. I stumble back into the room and wrench the door shut. There's no latch, but I run the broken edge of the tray down the hinge side of the door, frantically searching for a space large enough for it to fit between the door and frame.

"You cursed cunt," Cayson screams just as a corner of the tray sinks in by a fraction. He shoves at the door, but it only opens by a sliver before springing back closed. I shove the tray as hard as I can and more of it sinks in – and stays there, wedged solidly.

He screams again, pushing at the door, but the tray holds.

"I'll kill you. Do you hear me?! I'll fucking kill you!"

I back away slowly, my trembling hands held out in front of me, expecting the door to come crashing inward at any second.

"Who's there?" someone yells from somewhere down the

stairs and I almost faint with the reprieve.

"Dearest Mother," I whisper. "I thank you for your strength. Dearest Mother. I thank you for your strength." I repeat the mantra over and over until the backs of my knees hit the bed and I jump like a terrified cat away from water. Over my ragged breaths, I strain to hear any sound coming from the hall. I very much doubt Cayson is done with me.

CHAPTER 6
LUKA

It's been three days.

I've been telling myself that without the ring, there's no reason to seek Rina out. The excuse, however, is beginning to wear perilously thin with her hovering in my thoughts almost non-stop. Our late-night conversation left me . . . aggravated. I don't like that she's turned out to be *more* than I was expecting, that she's made some kind of an impression on me.

And if it's not her directly I'm thinking of, it's the problems she's brought with her. Last night there was a village meeting, during which I'd sat on the dais in the Great Hall and listened to the back and forth, mostly between Zola, Carson's mother, who was calling for my bride's blood, and Teo, my uncle, who was calling for calm.

While the killing of a Range Warrior is serious, I'm unimpressed with Zola, and two of her sons, Cayson and Crion, who've been trying to sway the collective opinion against Rina. Admittedly hatred for the D'heilar kingdom is not hard to rouse . . . but I can't say I like it directed at *her*. When preferred methods of punishment had begun to be shouted at the meeting – *stone her, 50 lashes, cut a limb off, brand her, bury her alive, take her head* – stirring the crowd to a fevered pitched, I'd stood to stab my dagger into the tabletop and roar, "Enough! I will decide what happens to the princess. No one else."

Now, this morning, my mood has not improved. I tell myself it's because I only managed a few hours of sleep, but I know time is running out. I must make my decision soon and for some reason I can't bring myself to do that without hearing what *she* has to say on the matter.

My father would have had a grand time with this if he were alive. In fact, I'm sure he's mocking me from the Eternal this very moment. *I always knew you were a weak-minded fool. How do you expect to lead if you can't even make this one, simple decision? Locate your spine and use it.* I force myself to block his imagined jeers from my mind. I will not rule with an iron fist that comes down randomly and without mercy . . . no matter how much self-doubt it causes.

"My deve," I hear in an urgent tone as I'm arriving at the baths.

"What is it Bron?" My voice is barely more than a growl, but that doesn't deter him.

"I need your assistance. It's urgent."

"It'll have to wait until after I've washed."

"Please, Yvette says it's an emergency."

I stop, letting him catch up. "Yvette?"

"Yes," he says, hesitating at my angry expression.

"Spit it out."

"It's about Rina."

Turning on my heel, I head back in the direction of the stronghold. "What about her?"

To the sound of our boots on the beaten path, I file through the scenarios that would need my attendance. I can't come up with anything. Unless . . . "Is she hurt?"

"We don't know. The door has been barricaded somehow."

"Barricaded . . . *what?*" That doesn't sound the least bit plausible. "How?"

"We don't know," he starts, but I hold up my hand to stop him from wasting my time.

"What *do* you know?"

"Only that Yvette is quite upset that she can't get into Rina's room."

I suddenly wonder if the woman has managed to escape, but I quickly discard the idea. She has no clothing and the temperature dipped below freezing last night. She'd be an absolute fool to run. Then another thought comes to me. *Has she jumped?* But I discard that too. A body in the corner of the courtyard would have been discovered by now. That leaves only two possibilities, that she's hurt herself or that she's being a spoiled child. I despise both scenarios and my mood plunges into darker and darker territory.

By the time I'm climbing the stairs, I've decided the woman is more trouble than she's worth. Those bewitching eyes notwithstanding, if she hasn't already done herself in, I'll throw her from the window myself. I ignore the wiggle in the pit of my stomach when an image of her body, twisted and broken against the cobbles fills my head.

The recruit on guard duty at the top of the stairs is surprised to see me. "What's going on?" I snarl.

"Uh, just a problem with the door."

"Useless," I scorn as I pass him by. I'm now convinced that this is a stunt to get attention. Well, if she wants attention, I'll give it to her.

Yvette is pacing outside the door. "My deve," she starts, but I don't want to hear it. Testing the door, I find it is indeed not opening more than a fraction. I push harder and the wood creaks but doesn't give. And now I'm officially livid. Putting my shoulder to the door, I use all my strength and slowly one of the hinges gives way with a squeal. Standing back, I kick until it crashes down, arcing awkwardly on its remaining hinge against the wall behind it.

The room is empty. "Son of a Mother's twisted womb!" I'll kill whoever was on watch last night.

But when my curse stops bouncing off the bare walls, I hear a soft whimper. Yvette tries to push past me, but I hold her back. "Go," I tell her. "I'll handle this."

"But –" she protests, looking stricken.

"I said leave." My icy glower leaves no room for discussion, but she does volley a parting shot.

"Luka, please treat her with care."

"Now!" I shout, making her jump.

She flees and I get a flash of Bron's disapproval before they're gone.

Rina is in the same place she was the last time I was here; on the floor on the far side of the brazier. Well, what I assume is her is buried under the furs that I provided.

"I should have let her freeze," I mutter as I rip away the cover . . . to find her curled into a pathetic little ball, her arms covering her head, her legs pulled up into my shirt. "Get up," I order. All I get are tremors that run through her body. "Get up now or you'll regret it."

She whimpers pitifully and disgust wells up inside of me as I grab her forearm and wrench her upright. The way her whole body cringes away from me doesn't even register when I get a look at her. Her jaw is swollen and covered by a nasty blue and purple bruise, but it's the bite mark on her neck that chills me. It's bloody and deep and repulsive.

A new storm swells inside of me. I give her a rough shake. "Who did this?" She only cowers, panting in short jagged bursts. Taking hold of her nape, I force her to face me. Her expression is eerily blank.

I freeze. I've seen this look before. My mother used to wear it after my father had gotten his hands on her. Fits of rage against her were his speciality until I got old enough to redirect his ire and take his fists. That I'm seeing it again, on any woman, let alone a woman I'm responsible for, sends my temper soaring. Someone is going to pay for this.

My instincts and experience kick in. Lowering myself to the floor, I ignore her panic as I pull her onto my lap. "Hush now," I soothe, cradling her against my chest, ignoring the reek of her body. "I'm not going to hurt you." That she doesn't put up much of a fight is strangely gratifying even if I know it's probably due more to exhaustion than trust.

It suddenly occurs to me that maybe not only fists were used on her. *Mother above, was she raped?*

Her teeth start chattering and her skin is cold and clammy

under my palms. I cover her back with a fur, and slowly, her small body starts to relax against mine.

But while she calms, all I can do is imagine meting out justice in its most primitive form. *Who would have the nerve to do this under my very nose?* As soon as the question enters my head though, I know the answer. What a fucking idiot. That I've known him all my life doesn't stop every ounce of my fury from funnelling down into that cold, dark place inside my soul that my father fostered so effectively.

When Rina fidgets in my arms, trying to find a more comfortable spot against my chest, I take the opportunity to sit her up. I'm satisfied to see there's some life back in her gaze . . . until she shies away from me and the damnable mewling starts up again.

"Stop that," I grouse. "I told you I'm not going to hurt you and I meant it."

"Please let go of my arm," she whispers, and I realize my grip is hurting her. I loosen my hold and she slumps forward, her forehead landing on my shoulder. She's clearly not ready to talk yet so I let her rest against me again for long minutes.

"Are you okay?" I finally ask even though I know she's not. "Did he rape you?"

She hauls in a shaky breath, then shakes her head with tiny jerks. "He tried," she rasps.

I can barely think around the relief. *Relief that she's only been beaten?* Fuck. I want to kill him. Attacking a woman is bad enough, but attacking a woman who is quite literally my property has earned him a world of pain.

"Did you send him?"

"What?" I'm still imagining all the damage I'm going to do.

"He said you sent him to do this to me."

Her words finally pierce my violent thoughts, and I almost shake her again. Keeping my tone as level as possible, I say, "Look at me."

A soft noise of fear fills my ears.

"Gather your courage and look at me, Rina."

It doesn't take as long as I expect. She sits up, and when her lashes lift to show me the golden amber of her eyes, something shifts and settles inside of me. It feels possessive and tender all at once. I've failed to protect her and whatever I need to do to make this right will be done. I vow it to myself.

"I didn't send him, little raven."

Her chin starts to dip, but I carefully place my index finger under her injured jaw to stop her.

"First, I have never, in my life, hurt a woman." I ignore her blatant skepticism. "And second, I would never send another man to do my work." That she seems more willing to believe.

"Do you swear it?" she whispers.

"Yes. I swear it." Once I'm satisfied that she believes me, I pull her back against my chest and I hold her for a little longer. I like how her small frame feels in my arms, but soon the smell of her gets to be too much.

"Rina," I say softly, encouraging her to sit up. My hands go around her waist and I hoist her to her feet. She squeaks with surprise, but steadies herself as I follow her up and head for the door. "Come. We have business to attend to."

"What?"

I turn and hold out my hand to her. "Come. You'll want to see this."

Her wariness doesn't deter me and I make an impatient

come here motion, which she responds to by hobbling forward. She looks like she's been through the fiercest of battles and I can't help but feel a surge of pride. She's so small, yet she's survived an attempt on her life by one of my warriors by cunning alone.

But that doesn't stop my impatience with her turtle's pace. She shrinks away from my advance. "Do not fear me," I order as I scoop her up in my arms and head out into the hall.

"That is easier said than done," she murmurs, never without a comeback to anything I say. Pride once again flares in my chest. Her mettle is so very pleasing to me.

The recruit on guard duty steps back in shock at the sight of her in my arms. "Find the healer," I bark. "And get that door repaired." He jumps to obey, rushing down the stairs ahead of us.

She lays her head on my shoulder. "You can be quite frightening."

I snort. "Apparently, not *everyone* takes me seriously." Even though I already know, I decide to ask. "Do you know who did this? Was it Cay–"

"It was him," she declares, cutting me off as if she can't bear to hear his name. "Where –" She exhales sharply when I jostle her at the second landing. "Where are we going? I am barely covered."

"Don't worry, their attention will all be on me."

That statement turns out to be only partially true. The hum of voices in the Great Hall is loud as we enter, but it drops off into a dead silence by the time I carry Rina the twenty feet to the dais.

Mounting the steps, I carefully set her on her feet, waiting until she's steady to let her go. Her eyes are wide and I don't know what comes over me, but I reassure her with a wink. "Stay here for a moment."

Making my way along behind the head table and chairs, I feel anticipation come over me. I'm going to enjoy the fuck out of this. I plant my boot in the middle of the long table and shove it with all my might. It makes a gratifying amount of noise as it crashes to the floor below. Those closest scatter to avoid injury.

"No one leaves until I'm done here," I proclaim loudly and a few of my warriors get to their feet to block the exits. The atmosphere in the room turns wary as I proceed to make a show of kicking the chairs off the dais as well. One by one, they take flight and clatter to the floor. From my periphery, I watch Noé and Eldon rise from their table and saunter forward, their excitement at the mayhem that's to come surely matching my own. When only one chair remains – mine, the more ornate one – I position it to my liking in the center of the stage. Turning to Rina, I snap my fingers and point to it.

Defiance flickers in her eyes. She doesn't appreciate being ordered around, but lucky for her, it doesn't stop her from limping across the platform and taking the seat I've offered her. Gasps break out in the crowd. Though I can't say if they're in response to her shocking appearance or my offer of the traditional seat of our leaders to an outsider.

"My deve," Eldon drawls, loving every second of this spectacle. "May I –"

"Shut up," I growl, not in the mood for his jokes. Jumping down, my boots hit the floor with a muffled whomp. In the Great Hall, there are three long tables that stretch like fingers toward the main doors. I choose the one on the left, using the bench to step up onto the tabletop. A ripple of alarm sounds as people grab their food and lean back as I start to walk. "It seems," I roar, "that some in this realm think my rules do not apply to them." I kick a bowl of morning porridge down the table, causing a few short screeches. Surveying my audience, I soak up their astonishment. I've never done something like this before. "Some of you seem to believe that I am deve in name only." I begin walking again, the table groaning under my bulk. "But we all know that's not how it works."

I hold out my arms so they can get a good look at me. "Have I somehow missed the challenge to my leadership?" The sarcasm in my tone brings out a few nervous titters as I finally stop and stare down at my prey. "Have I, Cayson?"

Keeping his head down, he pushes to his feet and steps back over the communal bench. When he lifts his chin, I laugh loudly in disbelief. "Shit, did she do that?" Undoubtedly, his nose is broken and he's well on his way to having two black eyes.

He points to the stage. "That whore –"

That's all he gets out before I lunge, my fist landing on his face in a hammer blow. He staggers back and people rush to get off of the benches to avoid being caught up in the melee. I don't let him recover and I don't hold back. With the crowd becoming more and more raucous in the background, I show him exactly why I'm in charge. With blow after blow, I dole out a beating he'll never forget. He barely gets any shots in at all before he goes down. He gets back up. Twice. He is a Range warrior after all.

When he shows no signs of being able to rise, I heave in a breath and rake my bloody fingers through my hair that's come loose from its queue.

"*I* am deve here," I roar. "No one else." I meet the bright eyes of those around me, then, to the entire crowd, I shout, "Do you understand?"

Laughing assent rings out. They've enjoyed the show. But that's not good enough.

"I can't hear you!"

"Yes, Deve," echoes back to me, clear and strong.

Satisfied, I reach down and hook my hand into the neck of Cayson's leather warrior's vest and haul him toward the dais. People scurry out of my way, clearing a path. A glance ahead shows me Eldon sitting on the arm of Rina's chair, chatting with her like nothing out of the ordinary is going on. Though it doesn't quite penetrate the haze of my savagery, I'm grateful to him.

Heaving Cayson up onto the dais further knocks the wind from his lungs and he wheezes pathetically. When he's laid out in front of Rina like tribute, I leap onto the nearest table. "Hear me now," I shout. "The D'heilar princess is mine. Mine to wed. Mine to discard." I raise my voice to a bellow, "Mine to punish however I see fit. No. One. Else's."

A collective gasp sounds as I draw my dagger from its sheath on my belt. I swing the blade in a wide arc around the room until I find Zola. "Approach the dais Mother Cyrun." More gasps, along with some protests, ring out, but to Zola's credit, she doesn't hesitate.

"There's fine," I announce when she's close enough for me to easily see the hatred lining her every wrinkle.

Jumping down, I walk to the dais and offer my dagger to Rina, hilt first. She's stunned, though not as stunned as our audience. I'm sure the sound of a single piece of straw being snapped would be heard in the now dead silence.

Rina's gaze lifts from the knife to me, seeming to search for whatever trap I'm laying for her. But when I don't renege my offer, she slowly slides from the chair to her knees next to Cayson and reaches for the blade. I watch her expression darken as her fingers curl around the hilt.

Hungrily, she scans Cayson's prone body as if deciding where the dagger will do the most damage. "Just the leg, my little raven," I caution, unable to hide my amusement.

Her eyes snap to mine, narrowed with defiance. And then she lifts the knife, two-handed, to bring it down right in the middle of Cayson's thigh. The man screams and Rina immediately pulls the blade free; not to save him from further pain, but to stab him again. I grab her wrist just as the dagger is about to pierce the skin for the second time. She tries to use her weight to drive it down and I'm forced to turn the blade sideways.

"Rina," I warn. "It's done." Her frustration blazes out at me, and I swear she wishes she could turn the knife on me. "You can bite him if you'd like," I say in an attempt to appease her bloodlust.

Her disgust is so acute that I laugh as she finally surrenders the dagger. "I don't blame you," I tell her. "I wouldn't want my mouth anywhere near him either."

Sheathing my blade, I raise my voice and address the crowd again. "Next time, there will be no mercy."

I hear mumbles of both approval and disapproval, but for once I'm not hounded by doubts. This is my realm and I'll run it how I see fit.

Reaching for Rina, I lift her down off the dais by the waist. "Come," I tell her, entertained by the resulting scowl. The woman will just have to get used to following my orders.

When she takes a limping step, I make to sweep her up, but she stops me. "I'll walk," she hisses, her vexation a living flame as she scans the room. Evidently she's been rejuvenated by events and now wishes to re-establish a sense of herself in front of all these people.

"Fine," I mock, though my tone is only for our audience. I rather like these sharp edges of hers and have no desire to see them blunted. I'll likely have to file them back eventually, but until then, I'll enjoy every scratch and nick she brings to bear. I turn on my heel and stride for the main doors, people parting in my wake. I have no objection if she wants to do this on her own, and I trust Eldon to protect her if there's trouble.

Waiting for her on the landing outside, I breathe in the cold air, reveling in the deep satisfaction of my actions. If this conviction was a regular part of my role, I would embrace my duties without a second thought.

Rina arrives a minute later, supported on either side by Yvette and Kata, with practically the whole of the village gawking from behind.

"My deve," Yvette says brightly. "Can I be of assistance?"

I shoot her a wry look. "You can bring a clean blanket to the hot springs."

"Oh? Anything else?" She's plainly hoping I'll ask for clothing.

"No." I quite like Rina half naked, and I'm now convinced if I provide her with the essentials, she'll attempt to run.

This time I ignore her insistence that I put her down as we cross the courtyard. "Hush," I admonish. "It's too far for you to walk with no boots."

"Well, maybe it's time you returned my slippers."

"Please," I scorn. "If you're referring to those flimsy leather coverings I found on your feet when you arrived, you'd be better off barefoot."

From such close proximity, the gold of her eyes practically sparkles with her dislike of me. "Where are we going? What is this *hot springs*?"

The warriors on guard duty at the gates try not to gape at us, but they fail miserably as we pass by. "We're going to bathe you. Your stench is making my eyes water."

"And whose fault is that?" she grits out. "It's inhumane not to let a person wash."

I shrug. "Fortunately, my inhumanity has worked in our favor."

"What?" Her tone is still acerbic, but I can tell some of the wind is dwindling from her sails. She's coming down off of the high.

"Well, now that everyone has seen you at your worst, they won't dare suggest I've been too lenient with you."

"Why would that matter?"

"A warrior is dead," I clip, suddenly annoyed with her again. "That has to be answered for."

When she offers no barbed comment in response, I'm oddly disappointed . . . and baffled. *Why does she not protest her innocence? Or at least explain the circumstances of Carson's death?* Surely they're similar, if not the same, to what happened to her last night. But no, for a long while, I walk us along the path in silence. It gets to the point that I start contemplating some insult that will re-ignite her ire. I much prefer her feisty to morose. But before I can think of something, she puts me out of my misery.

"I saw the wall," she says hesitantly.

"What? What wall?" But then, of course, her meaning comes to me.

"The, uh, wall of skulls."

"Ahh," is all I say. Around the hearth in the Great Hall, in Northern tradition, the skulls of our ancestors are arranged to cover the wall.

"It's quite . . ."

I wait for her to insult my heritage.

She clears her throat. "It was quite fear-provoking."

Huh, I was expecting something more along the lines of *sickening.*

"It's meant to be," I tell her, but then immediately back-track because that's not true. It has nothing to do with outside perception. "Well, it's meant more as a show of strength and unity. As a reminder that we belong here on this land just as our ancestors did. Every man, woman, and child is entitled to be added to the collective upon their death."

"Entitled?" she asks. "So it's an honor?"

"It is. Together we are stronger."

She mulls that over before she says, "That actually sounds very comforting. I'll have to look upon it with fresh eyes."

Every time we interact, she surprises me. If I'm honest with myself, she's absolutely nothing like I thought she would be. There doesn't seem to be a haughty or judgmental bone in her bod–

"Is that a dog?" she whispers urgently, her arms stiffening around my neck.

At first I don't know what she's talking about, but then I see the wolf. "No, but you can stop strangling me. It's only Venna."

Rina doesn't hear me. "It's too big to be a dog."

With surprising strength, she levers herself higher in my arms as Venna draws near. "Relax. She won't hurt you. I raised her from a pup."

Venna, always cautious, is now suspicious . . . if a wolf can be described in such a way. I pause on the trail. "Do you wish to give her a sniff, Venna? I don't recommend it. She reeks."

Rina freezes as Venna lifts her muzzle to scent her bare thigh. Giving a low whine, the wolf licks at the exposed skin.

"She likes you," I announce, continuing our trek, but Rina doesn't answer, only trembles with fear. Or maybe it's with the cold. It's hard to tell.

Venna goes on ahead and there are a few shrieks of surprise from the bathers in the pools. "That's my girl," I say with a smirk. Yes, today is definitely my day.

We go in and I ignore everyone to make my way to the furthest pool. "Out," I order the woman and her two children, who beat a hasty retreat to avoid not only me, but also the wolf.

When we're alone, I set Rina on her feet and Venna takes up a defensive position facing the only entrance to the space.

Unstrapping my leather vest, I toss it aside and pull my linen shirt over my head before I notice Rina's attention is strung taut between the wolf and the hot water. "We don't have all day, princess," I say blandly.

"She truly won't hurt us?" she asks, lifting her chin toward Venna.

"No one should ever trust a wild animal."

Despite her exasperation with my answer, the allure of the warm water is too much for her to resist. She dips her toes in, then turns an excitement-filled expression my way as I unlace my boots.

Not the bruise on her jaw, not the gruesome bite mark on her neck, nor the limp, greasy hair hanging in clumps around her shoulders can detract from her beauty as that smile appears. She's pure joy and wonder and I'm almost taken aback by how it kindles something inside of me, something that's warm and heartening, or even grounding. What a morning.

CHAPTER 7

RINA

I shiver, but for once, it's not from the cold or fear or panic. The water is wonderfully warm. And it raises my spirits like nothing else . . . except maybe being handed a knife to take my revenge on a scum-licking attempted rapist. I wonder if my lack of sleep on top of last night's trauma are starting to take their toll, because I'm light-headed and overwhelmed and . . . happy.

"You're not just going to stand there, are you?" he asks, stepping down into the shin-deep pool as bare as the day he was born.

With his back to me, he wades into the deeper water, and I take the opportunity to soak up the sight of him. If he strikes an impressive figure fully clothed, he's magnificent naked. From his broad shoulders to his tapered waist, the defined muscles shift under his skin, and further down, his backside is . . . I swallow hard. Unlike most men in D'heilar, there's not an ounce of fat on him anywhere.

He lets out a groan as the water swallows up that delectable body. Turning, he looks me over, pausing on my hand which I've pressed to the scars that run down my left side.

"I've already seen them," he informs me. "Along with the rest of you. You needn't play at modesty."

Vaguely, I nod. He's right. And since I'm sure he has his pick of women, I can't imagine my too-thin, scar-ravaged body would be of much interest to him.

Carefully pulling the grimy shirt over my injuries, I let it fall and step into the warm pool. I also let out a groan at the unadulterated bliss of it as I shuffle forward and sink down to submerge every inch of my aching body in the water, including my head. If only I didn't need to breathe, I'd stay cocooned here forever.

I hold out for as long as I can, then resurface to suck in a huge breath, unable to repress the smile that promptly becomes a grimace. Cupping my very sore jaw, I locate him off to my left. "What's it like?" I ask, watching as he pulls the leather thong from what's left of the queue of his hair and throws it over my head to land near his pile of clothes. "To go through life not having to worry about attack?"

His fingers pause in their efforts to detangle his shoulder-length hair. "You don't think I could be attacked?" The rumble of his low laugh tells me what he thinks of that statement.

He's missing the point of course. But I imagine it would be liberating to live life as the strongest member of a pack. Something I would know nothing about . . . which has me thinking. *How does a woman survive here?* I suppose she depends on her family if she has one. And if she doesn't? "So, here in the Realms, how does marriage work?"

His brows pull down in confusion.

"I mean, are spouses here expected to support and protect one another like in D'heilar?"

"Believe it or not," he intones derisively, "*barbarian* is not a word we apply to ourselves."

I shrink back slightly, taking his statement to mean that *spouse* has the same meaning on both sides of the river. "I'm sorry, I don't mean to offend you. I only want to understand."

"Understand what? Speak plainly." His mood is rapidly deteriorating.

"It's just," . . . I'm nervous now, but I press on if for no other reasons than to soothe my sanity and plan for my future if I have one. "I wonder if you would have preferred it if I hadn't fought back against Carson. If I had let him violate me."

"What?!"

If I hadn't offended him before, I have now, but this has been weighing heavily on me. "I get the impression that all these problems could have been avoided if I'd let him have his way. At the time, I couldn't have *not* fought back, but . . . I just wonder about it. After it happened, I held on so tightly to the idea that you would approve of my fighting, but –"

"How would you know what I approve of?" he spits, standing to reveal his powerful shoulders, anger vibrating from every inch of him.

"Of course," I say quickly, backing up and lowering my gaze in an attempt to appease him. "You're right. I couldn't know that."

My heart racing, I try to pretend I'm not afraid I've severed the tether that holds back his temper. Relief washes over me when, from my periphery, I see him ease back into the water. I bob around for a bit and realize that I may never get another chance to ask my questions, so I risk poking the bear anew. "I ask because –"

"I don't care why you ask," he growls, raking his palms down his face.

I sigh. "Will you not allow me one more question? Please?" Not that he's answered any of the others.

"Fine. But this is the last one."

I dip my head in thanks. "I ask because Yvette told me she cannot come to the stronghold after dark. And she has no husband. Is it not safe for women in general or is it because she has no one to protect her?"

"How should I know?" he grits out, glaring daggers at me. "I'm not a woman, am I?"

It's my temper that flares now. "You're being purposefully obtuse. You know what I mean and why I ask. I know you don't want me anymore, but perhaps –"

"I *never* wanted you."

It shouldn't hurt. I can't imagine any man, let alone one of his standing, would welcome a woman being foisted upon him, especially one like myself. But regardless, his words lance right into the parts of me that keep the loneliness at bay and allow the pain to spill free.

Realizing that the heat is becoming too much for me after my horrific night, I hurry to finish cleaning myself, lifting my feet to get in between my toes, swiping a hand between my legs and under my armpits. My fingertips are exploring the tender edges of the bite mark when he brings me back into the present.

"Perhaps what?"

"Pardon?"

"Before." His eyes shift away from me before coming back hard and steely. "You said perhaps . . . something?"

"Oh." Feeling raw and exposed, I consider not marshalling the emotional energy needed to answer him, but in the end, I acquiesce. "I was going to ask if perhaps there would be a place for me here, under your rule, when all is said and done. Maybe a farmer who needs a wife or –"

He scoffs loudly and with so much scorn that I rub at my chest as if to soothe the invisible wound he's already inflicted.

"I can work," I tell him seriously.

"Don't make me laugh, *princess.*"

I should have known better. I have lived under a cursed sky my entire life. Why would this northern version be any different? Slowly, my heart heavy, I move to the pool's edge and climb out. The filthy linen shirt I've been wearing for the past thirteen days sits in a heap against the rocks and the thought of putting it back on is more than I can bear.

A cold, wet nudge at my hand doesn't even startle me. The deve has all but admitted that I will not survive this, effectively draining every ounce of self-preservation left in me. So I let the wolf lick at my fingers. It tickles and I smile down at her mournfully. If I pretend she's a dog, she's really not so scary.

The noisy splash of water behind me reminds me that he's still here.

"Here," he says, his voice gruff. He's holding the shirt he was wearing out to me, his knuckles bruised and torn up from earlier.

Slowly I shift my gaze to his from the ground up. Even

95

his calves are heavily muscled, and they're dusted with light brown hair until I reach his thighs where, closer to the groin, years of riding has worn his skin baby smooth. His cock hangs heavy and long between his thighs and when it begins to respond to my scrutiny, my eyes jerk up along the defined ridges of his torso. As a testament to his warrior status, there are scars and nicks and burns scattered across his skin, as well as a large tattoo of a simple mountain lion across his left pectoral. The sandy brown hair that dusts his wide chest is the same color as his thick beard. He's so tall that my head doesn't even reach his massive shoulders. For a fraction of a second, I imagine what it would be like to skim my fingertips over such a masterpiece of human flesh and bone, and for him to welcome that touch. When my eyes finally meet his, a frisson of want slides down my spine.

The shirt gets pushed into my hand and my mouth opens to say *thank you*, but the words stall in my throat as he gathers up my wet hair and squeezes the water out. The brush of his calloused fingers along my shoulders turns the frisson into a full-fledged quiver.

While he pulls on his clothes, I stand there stupidly, watching him, not sure what's more shocking, the intimacy of the gesture or the care it shows. Either way, it's left me off-kilter.

The thick leather of his vest creaks as he pulls the buckles tight over his chest. "Put the shirt on or don't, but we're leaving."

He advances on me and I scramble to get it on before I'm lifted into his arms once again. The wolf, Venna, goes first, creating as much panic on the way out as she did on the way in. She pays her audience no mind and when we step out into the early winter sunshine, she takes off into the trees.

I want to question Luka further about the wolf, but with my head resting on his shoulder and the heat of the hot springs still keeping the cold at bay, I don't want to disturb this peace between us. Plus there are better things to concentrate on like the bulge of the bicep on his bare arm. I reach out and trace a vein that stands out against the muscle and skin. "You should never wear a shirt," I announce dreamily, not caring if he knows I find him attractive. *Why shouldn't I take pleasure where I can in my last days?*

His low chuckle resonates in my chest and my lids sink shut.

"Rina," is whispered at my ear and I wake to unfamiliar surroundings. The light is dim and the air is fragrant with . . . horses. I straighten up in his arms, and there, in front of us, is Glory, her soft brown eyes filled with curiosity.

"Oh," I breathe, squirming for Luka to put me down. The cold, hard-packed earth under my bare feet scarcely registers as he relents and I reach out to pat Glory's forehead.

"Are they treating you well?" I ask as she lowers her head to snuffle at my hand. I show her my empty palm. "I'm sorry. If I had anything, I would give it to you." I step closer and stroke her neck. "Do you like apples or carrots? I once knew a horse who loved potatoes, but I imagine you're much too refined for such nonsense, aren't you?"

I prattle on to her for a short while before the deve appears at my elbow with a small apple. Glory tries to take it from him, but he blocks her. "Don't be grabby, beautiful girl," he admonishes gently, handing the apple to me.

There's something akin to fondness in his tone and Glory only has eyes for him as she delicately takes the apple from my palm. "I understand completely," I whisper, unable to repress a soft giggle.

Without warning, I'm being lifted into his arms and Glory shifts in her stall, stamping her feet at the unexpected movement. "Come on, it's too cold for you out here."

"But –" I cut myself off, hoping if I don't make a fuss, he'll bring me back to visit again. I watch Glory over his shoulder until we exit out into the courtyard. "Will someone exercise her today?"

"I'm sure the stable master knows how to do his job." He must not like how my shoulders sag because he huffs with annoyance. "I'll mention it to him. Happy?"

"Yes. I know it's a special kind of distress to be cooped up all the time," I say, paying no heed to the people who stop and openly stare at us. "Is that Yvette?"

She is indeed standing on the stairs to the Great Hall, holding a small bundle, which turns out to be a woolen blanket. "Elsy is waiting upstairs," she says to the deve, her smile faltering a bit when she sees the bite mark on my neck again, but her tone remains cheerful. "Rina, I barely recognize you without the layer of grime."

The deve sweeps us past her before I can respond.

"Do you not want the blanket after all?" she calls after us. He only quickens his pace as I stare over at the wall of skulls. It's not ghoulish at all now that I have some context.

As soon as his foot hits the first stair on the climb to my tower prison, my stomach bottoms out and all fuzzy thoughts disappear. I really don't want to go back.

Two steps later, he says, "I need something from you." The words surprise me enough that my impending doom flies from my mind.

"You do?"

He grimaces. "I do. There's a letter."

"A letter?"

"Yes, I need you to tell me what it says." We come to the first landing.

"What? Why would you . . ." *Is he admitting that he can't . . . read?* Shock vibrates all the way to my toes. *How can he lead an entire realm of people and not be literate?* And to lower himself to ask *me* must mean . . . *what?*

He mistakes my silence for defiance. "I'm not asking," he says peevishly and it suddenly becomes clear that he took me to see the horse to gain my cooperation. Betrayal bubbles in my gut, but maybe I can use this to make the remainder of my days more bearable.

"Okay."

But he doesn't seem to hear me. "You won't eat a single bite of food until it's done."

"I said okay," I snap, resentment welling at how precarious my existence is. "In fact," I buck in his arms, "put me down."

"Settle," he gripes, trying to keep a hold of me, but in the end I force him to release me. We glare at each other.

"You," I say too loudly, making the word echo off the stone around us. "Are an ass. Do you know that?"

I turn my back on him and limp for the last flight of stairs.

"Rina."

"Don't you have food to withhold?"

"Rina." His tone harshens, but I don't care.

"Or a ring to find?" I taunt, reminding him that he hasn't found my mother's missing ring. Five stairs up and I'm already feeling winded, but I press on, using the wall to steady myself. Anything to get away from this man.

I don't make it up another step before he grabs my arm and half spins me around. "Can you n– ahh!" He gives me a tug and presses his shoulder to my hips, hauling me up like a sack of potatoes. "What are you doing?! Put me down. Right now, put me down!"

"Quit your whining, woman. If I don't carry you, you'll topple over and crack your head open." He then has the gall to smack my ass, sharpening my rage into a dangerous point.

"You bastard," I grind out, blood rushing to my head, making it throb in time with my heartbeat. "I demand you put me down!" Pushing up on his lower back, I get a glimpse of the stunned guard at the top of the stairs before my reality goes from upside down to right side up in a rush of vertigo. My legs fold under me as soon as my feet make contact with the floor and he has to hold me up by the armpits like a toddler.

"I was *not* born out of wedlock," he says smugly as I blink the light-headedness away. "You'll have to find a better insult than that."

I poke at his granite chest with my index finger. "How about unscrupulous reprobate?"

He scoffs. "Those fancy words mean nothing to me."

"Oh? Let me translate for you. You're a vile brute and a manipulator."

He pretends to consider, then leans in closer. "Better. But vile brute or not, you're still going to help me, *princess.*" The last word is unmistakably meant as an insult. How original.

"Hah! You better inform the cooks not to send up any more of their pitiful rations."

It's then that he notices something over my shoulder. Straightening, he lets me go. I wobble but manage to stay upright as he turns on his heel and heads back down the stairs.

"Yes, you'd better hurry," I call. "They may be sending up breakfast as we speak."

A throat clears behind me and I turn. "A'Deve," Elsy greets with a deferential nod and an amused quirk to her mouth.

A frustrated noise claws its way out of my chest. "Elsy, if you'd be so kind as to not use that term, I would be very obliged," I say, mincing my way past the mangled door to sit on the edge of the bed. Exhaustion weighs like a mountain on me now.

The healer follows me in. "I hear it's been an eventful morning," she says with humor, then exclaims, "What is *that?*"

I assume she means the bite mark, so I don't respond. Elsy sets her woven basket down next to me and picks out a clay jar filled with some kind of ready-made healing concoction. As she smears it over the raw edges of the wound, I smell honey. "I assume your jaw isn't broken since you're able to bicker with the deve."

"Yes," I say wearily, sliding my jaw from side to side. It hurts but it's not serious. "I got lucky, I guess."

"Let's see the leg."

I pull the shirt up to show her the wound on my thigh and she sighs. "You shouldn't have been in the baths, but it's coming along. It's not festering anyway." When I can only muster enough energy to shrug, she pulls aside the top layer of the furs that have been moved back onto the bed. Probably by Yvette. "Get some sleep before you keel over."

She tucks me in and I'm grateful. Sleep is coming on quickly when an idea pops into my head. "Elsy?" She looks back from the door, her long, gray-streaked braid swaying. "How many tutors work in the realm?"

"Tutors?" Her countenance couldn't be more incredulous.

101

"I don't know about where you come from, but around here, no one has the luxury of free time to be collecting the useless knowledge provided by *tutors.*"

CHAPTER 8

LUKA

Bron is at the bottom of the stairs, waiting, and I feel the abused flesh on my knuckles pull as my fists clench.

"Before you say anything," he says, making a quick survey of our surroundings. "I've got the ring."

That stops me in my tracks. "Really? Where was it?"

"A boy lingering around the burn pit had it. It took a bit of convincing to get him to give it up."

I shake my head and mutter, "Really, Bron?"

"Never underestimate the value of diplomacy, Deve."

"What did the kid extract from you?"

"So cynical you are. I hauled some wood for his pregnant mother."

"What?" My head jerks back in surprise. "Where is the

husband?"

"Dead of a fever going on two full moons now."

I blow out a resigned breath.

"And now the boy will grow up with a sense of loyalty to you since I threw a chicken into the bargain at your insistence."

"My insistence?"

"Oh, yes," he says, repressing a grin. "You can be quite generous. I'm hoping the boy returns to me if he hears anything of interest around the village."

Bron may not be able to match his brothers' brute strength, but he easily runs circles of intelligence around them. "Are you forming a band of spies, Bron?"

"What can I say? Nobody overlooks a child of six or seven years like a fully-grown man."

I grunt with agreement. "Keep an eye on the family."

"Of course."

"Well, let's see it."

He pulls the silver ring from his tunic pocket and hands it to me. It's unremarkable in every way; plain, scratched, and small. *This is what Rina is so desperate to have returned?* It can't have much value, silver or not. Nothing about this woman makes any sense.

I never wanted you.

I almost wince at my earlier words as I stare at the ring. Her expression had gone disturbingly vacant, as if my comment had erased her presence, leaving behind a hollowed-out shell. I'd taken her to see the horse in the hopes of re-filling that shell with what makes her *her.* My plan worked too, up until I blurted out the bit about the letter, not realizing how the horse would be perceived as a bribe until too late. But by then, I was well on my way to planting my foot in every pile of manure imaginable. If Elsy hadn't run me off, I'd probably still be up there, ankle deep in horse shit, exchanging barbs with the infuriating woman.

Which reminds me . . . "Go over to the kitchens and find out what Rina's being fed." If she's on prisoner's rations, I'm going to be pissed. I didn't even notice what was on the tray the other night.

"Fed?" Bron repeats like he has no idea what I'm talking about.

"Yes, fed." I move to peer into the Great Hall and spot Eldon across the room. He's sitting at a table with his wife, Daysa, while his youngest son tries to bounce on his lap with his pudgy legs. When I turn back, Bron is still there. "Go. Make sure she's getting enough to eat," I tell him before heading for my cousin.

"Daysa," I say, sitting next to her and planting a kiss on her plump cheek. "Are you still putting up with Eldon?"

"I am." She gives me one of her shy smiles. "You know he makes me unbearably happy."

"Well, I wouldn't argue your word choice. He is definitely unbearable."

She laughs, tucking a piece of her blonde hair that's come loose from her braids behind her ear. "Twisting my meaning? Soon you'll be a politician to be reckoned with." At my sour reaction, she changes the subject. "Will you be gracing us with your presence at dinner this week, my deve?" Almost every week, I go out to their home for a few hours where I'm able to shed my title and simply be Luka.

Their small son shrieks with happiness, his legs pumping furiously. "Anton seems to think I'll be there, so it must be true." I reach across the table and offer him my finger, which he immediately grabs onto and tries to cram in his mouth.

"Maybe you'll bring our new a'deve with you," Eldon says innocently.

I'm about to tell him to shut his mouth, but Daysa speaks first. "Oh, yes. Please do."

"She's hardly the a'deve," I say, my voice tightening.

Eldon must sense my mood because he stands to leave, handing the baby over to his wife. "My darling, I'll see you later this afternoon at home." She blushes as he leans over the table to kiss her mouth before yelling a farewell across the room to his two older children who are playing by the hearth.

Following him outside and over to the stables, I decide to leave his comment about Rina alone. With his ability to make light of almost anything, it's impossible to argue with my cousin. He's such a cheerful bastard . . . or what was it that Rina called me earlier, a brute? I feel the beginnings of a smile start to pull at my lips.

As we saddle our horses, however, my conversation with Rina in the pool starts to nag at me, spoiling my good humor. Her questions had made me uncomfortable and I'd dodged every single one of them.

Is it not safe for women?

I'm not sure I've ever considered the question. I know my mother was never safe, but that was only from my father. The idea that Rina needs the same protection as she did serves to scratch and pick at old wounds.

Once we're on our way out to the warrior training grounds, I ask Eldon something I'm not sure I want the answer to. "Would you let Daysa walk from your home to the stronghold after dark?"

"What? Alone?" *Alone* comes out sounding like I've lost my mind.

"I'll take that as a no." After a moment of silence though, I press him. "To my knowledge, not a single eastern savage has penetrated our borders in more than two years."

"So?" But then what I'm getting at clicks with him. "Luka, you were Warrior Commander of the Range for two years before you took charge. You cannot pretend to be clueless about how *your* men are immune to the consequences of certain actions."

"Are you saying there are rapists in my ranks?"

"*Rapist* is a very ugly word, cousin. I doubt even the old deve could have ignored it. He did, however, ignore words like *predator* and *opportunist* for over twenty years."

I rein Nightshade into a full stop. "What are you saying, Eldon?"

"I'm saying," he turns back to me, "that you can't deny that the word of a woman would never be taken over that of a warrior's. Ergo women do not speak up, they adapt."

Frowning, I watch Eldon turn his horse, Fearmonger, around and come back to me.

"Luka," he says gravely. "You have the opportunity to make a real difference to the women of this realm, and that starts with righting the wrongs committed against our new a'deve."

My gaze sharpens on him. "You make it sound simple. A Cyrun brother, a Range warrior, is dead at the hands of a woman from D'heilar. What would you have me do?"

His face pinches. "I don't care where she's from. You've basically announced that no woman may defend herself."

"I've done no such thing!"

"Haven't you?" He raises his brows in a way that strikes me as irritatingly superior. "I'm sorry, Luka, but she did this realm a favor by removing a man who caused more trouble than he was worth, and you should have let her finish off another this morning."

"I would have a mutiny on my hands," I exclaim, throwing up my hands in disgust. "And it is not my job to police the morality of my warriors."

"Isn't it? Your father was weak, Luka. And so far, you're not proving much better."

"I never wanted this Mother-forsaken title," I grit out from between clenched teeth.

"So you've said. But it's yours now. I suggest you embrace it."

And he has the audacity to set his heels to his horse and leave me behind.

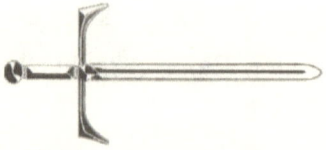

While my talk with Rina had unnerved me, my cousin's words leave me stewing in a foul mood for three days. The nerve of him. Calling me weak, comparing me to my father. Perhaps he'd prefer to return to the days of watching the unfortunate – men *and* women – being beaten in the Great Hall for some imagined slight? *Not much better than my father, my ass.*

Eldon should know better. Eldon *does* know better. Even if he's two years older than I am, we spent much of our childhood and adolescence protecting one another from our respective sires. Nothing solidifies a relationship like taking a beating for someone. No Cyrun brother ever did that for me, that's for sure. Eldon and I have had each other's backs from the beginning – which makes his pronouncements all the more cutting.

Except, by day three of my great sulk, deep down, I acknowledge what I've always known – that my usually good-natured cousin has spoken the truth. There *are* problems and I *should* be doing more to correct them. But according to my Uncle Teo, change that comes too quickly will thaw the rule of law faster than the snowpack in a spring heat wave. I'm inclined to agree with the old man even if he did have a close relationship with my father.

The possibility of a revolt against me is very real.

I'm too young, some say.

Or too soft.

Or too stupid, especially after the First Deve cornered me with this fucking marriage contract.

Admittedly the men who are vocal in their opposition to me came up in the ranks under my father. They're all older. Even before I made my coup, they resented my rise to the position of Warrior Commander. Could they beat me in one-on-one challenges? Not bloody likely. But a village-wide revolt led by them could tear this realm right down the middle. After three generations of peace, the thought of my people taking up arms against each other is incomprehensible.

A fact that re-ignites the old mental tug of war in me. *Am I worthy to lead? And if I am, shouldn't I be doing more? Why do I dither? Why can't I find a straight-forward path, one where the cost of doing the right thing isn't so high?*

Perhaps I *am* just another version of my father.

I admit I've turned a blind eye on occasion to questiona-
ble circumstances that I didn't want to deal with. In fact, Eldon
is right about Rina. Though it took his rebuke to realize that
my knee-jerk reaction to Carson's death was exactly what my
father's would have been. And that fills me with shame.

Plus, on top of everything else, there's my unreasonable
behavior regarding her and the letter to contend with. As I
trudge up these never-ending stairs to see the woman in question, I'm not feeling particularly hopeful that this encounter
is going to go well. If I were in her place, I would send me to
the bottom of a lake, weighed down by a boulder. At least I'm
not empty handed since I've got her ring in my vest pocket.
But truthfully, I'm hoping to keep the ring in reserve for future
contingencies. She did already agree to read the letter for me
after all . . . even if I didn't realize it at the time.

Maybe I should give her the ring as a gesture of goodwill?

The idea has a bark of laughter launching itself from my
chest to echo off the stone walls around me. I really would
deserve the brands of *too young, too soft,* and *too stupid* if I
did that.

The memory of Rina stabbing Cayson in the Great Hall
appears unbidden in my mind, sending a jolt of lust through
me. The woman is a witch, I swear. Because, over the last few
days, if I wasn't bemoaning my cousin or replaying our talk,
I was trying not to think about Rina's blood-thirsty penchant
for revenge . . . or her insightful observations, or her barbed
insults of my person, or her languid perusal of my body at the
baths.

I'm more than halfway to my destination when I realize
my memories have slid into daydreams of a very carnal nature.
Shit. I give a quick scan of the rolled parchment in my hand to

re-center my thoughts. The simple sketch of a mountain lion is the only thing visible without unrolling it, but I know that inside, beyond the recognizable crest of the D'heilar family, the page is filled with the baffling interconnected lines that somehow convey meaning. That immediately cools my ardor.

At the top of the stairs, I breeze by Ion with a nod, satisfied there's now a proper guard rotation in place. But my stride stalls out when I come to her room and find there's still no door. *What the fuck?* Self-recrimination rears its ugly head. While I've been in a childish snit, she's been left exposed. Dammit. It's one more thing that, as deve, I should have checked on.

Stepping into the room, I find her sitting on a fur on the window ledge, with another wrapped around her. She trains her amber eyes on me . . . resulting in a staring contest I could do without.

Her brimming reproach, either about the door or maybe my extended absence, announces that she has no intention of making this easy on me. I'm torn between cowing her into submission and continuing to gawk at her still-bruised, but beautiful face, which I notice has lost some of its gauntness since I saw her last. The tension between us becomes so uncomfortable that I'm forced to speak first. "You look much better."

No response. Just a bland stare.

"The door should have been fixed by now," I say, toeing at the wreckage, which has been neatly piled against the wall.

Still nothing.

This woman.

As if to dismiss me, she goes back to staring out the window.

"I took Glory out yesterday." Her head swings back

111

around and I almost cringe at the memory of her accusation of *manipulator.* "I don't think she appreciates having to haul my extra weight around."

She scans down my body like she's taking my measure, stalling for a moment at my groin . . . and my cock twitches. Then I feel like an idiot because it's the parchment in my hand she's interested in, not my manhood. "N–" Her voice catches as if it hasn't been used in a while. She tries again. "No, she wouldn't. I'm sure you hold her back from her true speed."

We go back to silence.

My victory at getting her to interact with me shrivels. "You're going to make me ask, aren't you?"

"Yes," she says stonily.

After another bout of staring each other down, I raise the letter up in defeat. "Will you tell me what it says?"

Surprise blooms across her face as if she never expected me to actually do it. Holding out her hand, she chides me with, "I said I would."

I cross the short distance and deliver it to her. She unrolls the parchment and skims it briefly, before surprising me by asking, "How did you get this?"

"What do you mean? It was sent with Noé from D'heilar."

"It's not addressed to you."

"What?" I hesitate. "How do you know that?"

"Because it's addressed to Kharon, First Deve of the Bear Realm."

Excuse me? "You're sure?"

"Well, of course, I'm sure. It's written right here." She points to a line of squiggles.

"But our emblem is on the outside," I counter.

She turns it over and brings the letter closer for a better look. "Is that what it is? A rendering of a mountain lion?"

Irritation begins to boil in my gut. "Well, it's certainly not a bear."

"No, I suppose not. Should I read it anyway?" she asks, sounding intrigued.

To her mind, that would be wrong? Because it's not addressed to the correct person? "It wasn't *our* mistake," I say, the one chiding her now. "I have no doubt we should read it."

She brightens. "Okay, then." She clears her throat. "My dear friend," she starts, then snorts. "Well, this wasn't written by the King himself, that's clear."

At my frown, she clarifies. "My cousin has no *dear friends*. He has people who fear him or people who pander to him. That's all."

I scratch at my beard. *She doesn't have a favorable opinion of the King?*

She goes back to her task. "I hope this letter finds you well. I would have you know that the whore has been sent north . . ." Her voice peters off as we realize she is the *whore* being referenced. *Definitely not a favorable opinion of each other, then.* I watch her skim down the page, her obvious fury gaining ground until she reaches the bottom and crushes the parchment between her hands.

"What are you doing?" I demand, seizing it from her as she leans over to toss it onto the simmering coals in the brazier.

Throwing the fur off her shoulders, she stands and tries to snatch it back, but I lift it over my head. "You will burn that immediately!" she orders.

"I will do no such thing! What does it say?"

"That repulsive, parasitic sycophant. That swiving, rat bastard. That disgusting –"

Some of the words she spews I know intimately, the others I can guess at by their context. "Who?" I interrupt her tirade. "The King?"

Her rage-filled tone matches her expression perfectly as she spits, "No. Not the King. Mattice Dulat."

The name rings a vague bell, but I'm forced to ask, "And he is?"

"A monster." Her hand presses to her side where the burn marks mar her skin.

"He did that to you?" I ask, shock hitting me like a sledge-hammer. *Who is he?*

Her only response is to glower at the letter that's still held out of her reach. When it becomes obvious that I'm not going to let her destroy it, she retreats to the other side of the brazier where I see she has her other fur again arranged on the floor.

"No," I say, taking hold of her arm. "First you'll answer my questions."

I swing her back around and am caught completely off guard as she thumps me on the chest with her little fist. "Let go of me!"

I tsk. "Settle down." But she has the nerve to hit me again, twice, forcing me to drop the letter to capture her wrists. This only incites her to fight harder.

"Let me go," she shrieks, yanking against my hold. "Let go! Let go! Let go!"

"Enough," I thunder. But she continues her litany of rage, jerking more and more violently against my grasp until I'm able to get her twisted around so her back is to my front. I pin her to me by banding my arms around her torso, trapping her arms. "Are you finished with this little tirade?" I hiss at her ear.

She squirms against me, her breaths like a bellows.

"I can see you're upset," I go on, trying to ignore how my cock swells with her movements. "But you need to calm down." It takes another minute before she realizes the futility of her struggle and the tension in her small body begins to drain away. "Better," I say, lowering my voice. "Now, can I trust you to remain calm?"

She relents with a shaky nod and I loosen my hold enough for her to turn in my arms. Her eyes flash with mutiny, but beneath that, there's sorrow radiating from her very soul. It leaves me fumbling with the urge to fend it off for her, to protect her from whatever demons haunt her.

She pulls in a breath that sounds suspiciously like a precursor to sobs. "Hush now, little raven," I whisper, sliding one hand down to the small of her back and the other up under her hair. "Whoever he is, I'll see him dead before he hurts you again. I vow it."

What am I saying?

Her only response is another shaky inhale as her hands drop to my hips and her forehead to my chest. Then slowly, like honey spilling from a dipper, her entire body settles against mine.

The utter rightness of the feeling makes my thoughts hazy. Her shoulders relaxing, her cheek coming to rest over my heart, her belly providing a warm place for my now heavy cock, it's all perfection.

Shit. This isn't supposed to be happening.

Just a minute longer, I tell myself, gently massaging the

base of her skull. Except that draws a contented sigh from her, one that's laced with longing, one that sets off a wave of desire so strong my hard-on goes from reveling in her proximity to out-right craving her. Behind my closed lids, images spark to life . . . tasting her full lips, tracing her nipples, holding her steady as I sink in deep. They're so vivid that my arms tighten around her until a loud caw sounds.

It's a crow.

It's landed only an arm's length away on the ledge of the window. "Get," I tell it, unhappy with the interruption. Or is it relieved? *Because what in the Mother's name am I doing?*

We watch as the bird gracefully jumps from the sill, its brilliant black wings glinting in the winter sun. With the spell broken, I let her go and retrieve the letter from the floor. "Come and sit down."

She complies, more, I suspect, because she's feeling un-steady than any real inclination to obey. But I'll take what I can get. I hold out the letter to her. "I need to hear all of it, each and every word." Her features twist, but I head off her protests by uttering something I don't think I've said in years. "Please?"

A stare-down begins once again but this time the still-sim-mering heat between us melts it away and she finally says, "Fine, but must you loom?"

"Loom?"

"Yes, loom. You tower over me even when I'm on my feet. Please sit down."

When she refuses to take the letter from me until I do as she asks, I sink down on the edge of the bed beside her with a muttered, "I'm supposed to be in charge."

Taking it from me, she unrolls the parchment again. "My

dear friend," she reads, restarting from the beginning. "I hope this letter finds you well. I would have you know that the whore has been sent north to that unsuspecting upstart in the Mountain Lion Realm."

She must feel me tense at the unknown word – *upstart* – because she pauses, but I jerk my chin at the page, indicating she should continue.

"I have arranged for some unfortunate violence to befall her along the way." She's reading it in a monotone and it takes a second for the words to register with me. *Unfortunate violence? Father's tit.* My mind scrambles to follow because she hasn't stopped. "But even if that doesn't come to pass, I have hopefully done enough physical damage to her already that the new deve will reject her outright."

"What?" I hiss, unable to keep silent any longer. Pushing to my feet, I start to pace. Whoever this man is, he is as good as dead. "Carry on," I say tightly, my rage barely contained.

She finds her place. "If not, her shrew's tongue will surely peck and tear at his undoubtedly monumental arrogance. Taken together, these factors should cause enough of a rift between them that the marriage will be an impossibility, serving both our purposes. Whether the nuptials happen or not, we will meet in the spring as agreed. Your ally, Mattice Dulat."

"Son of a twisted womb! Does that letter look genuine to you?"

"I . . ." She's taken aback, but she considers my question, examining the D'heilar seal and what I take to be the man's mark at the bottom. "Yes."

"And what is the word used to describe me, *up* . . . something?"

"Upstart. It's a person who rises in rank unexpectedly.

One who isn't deserving."

I want to tear someone's head off for this. "Who is this Mattice Dulat?"

She flinches at my strident tone, but answers. "The King's advisor."

Skepticism begins to take root as I try to make sense of what she's telling me. *Why would the King's advisor personally maim a girl and then arrange to have her raped?* "Did you read that letter true?" I demand harshly.

Her amber eyes go round. "What? Yes, of course I did. I read it word for word." Her voice gains in volume. "Just like you asked me to!"

Shaking my head with disbelief, I pace. Something doesn't add up.

"You think I invented *this?*" She brandishes the letter like a weapon. "Have someone else read it to you then!"

"How convenient for you," I practically sneer, "that our scholar died last month."

Setting her jaw, she slowly gets to her feet and stands tall in front of me despite her slight stature. "Take your letter," she says, enunciating every word. "And get out."

"This is my stronghold, woman."

She shoves the letter into my chest. "Get! Out!"

CHAPTER 9

RINA

The gall of the man. Forcing me to read about my own torture, and then accusing me of fabricating it all? The sheer gall.

Watching his retreating figure, broad shoulders and firm backside included, doesn't bring any satisfaction though. I'm once more alone, trapped within these four icy walls. That I already regret his leaving has a strangled cry forming in my gut. I have to fight to keep it in, but he won't get anything from me. Not a thing.

Wretched man.

And now that he's gone, Mattice Dulat rises like a serpent in my mind. No! Sweat breaks out on my brow. No. I mustn't think of that. In a panic, I turn a circle and my attention catches on the chains that are still attached to the bed posts. Rushing forward, I take hold of the closest one and begin wrenching it up and down, back and forth with all my might. The clinking of the metal against the stones is my only focus. There are no memories of burning flesh or endless pain. No taunts or threats or terror. None of it.

When the spike embedded in the wood gives by a fraction, I pause in my efforts. It's coming loose! I start up again, tugging harder.

Without warning, I fall back on my ass, staring at the chain in my hands. Jubilation crashes through me as I scramble to my feet and lug the heavy iron links to the window. Looking out, I can't believe my luck as I spy the man himself, huddled with Noé and Eldon in the middle of the courtyard near the sundial.

"My deve!" I yell with as much sarcasm as I can muster. His head lifts, hunting for the source of the call. When he spots me, he pushes Noé aside and stalks closer. Planting his hands on his hips, he glares up at me, striking the most handsome picture of domineering arrogance I can possibly imagine.

"I have something for you!" I announce and fling the chain from the window.

He doesn't even flinch when it lands with a loud, clanging thump against the cobbles not far from his boots. At first he only stares down at it, but then he throws his head back and laughs, a deep, raucous belly laugh that bounces off the walls of the courtyard, mocking me with its mirth.

"You'll pay for that, princess," he shouts, except his tone lacks any kind of rancor. He sounds amused rather than angry. Bewildered, I watch him turn on his heel and head for the stables. *For the love of all that is sacred. Did he not just accuse me of being a liar? To my face?*

The high of the moment starts to fade, my indignation burning itself out and leaving me with nothing but a depressing sense of resignation and four walls. The cold creeps up from the floor, weaving itself into the very bones of my bare feet. I retrieve my fur from the window ledge and limp around the brazier to the one on the floor. With no door, I can't bear to sleep on the bed in the open, so this is my pallet. During the day, I usually relocate to the bed, but today, I had no energy for it and now I simply burrow myself between the furs where they lay.

To keep Mattice Dulat and the horrors of that terrible day at bay, I give my encounter with Luka free rein in my imagination. Yes, he's infuriating and overbearing, but he's never hurt me and I can't deny that being in his arms has been my only real respite. There's nowhere I feel safer than when he's hauling me around . . . or holding me. And if I'm not mistaken, I felt his arousal against my stomach earlier. The idea that I affect him like he does me is intoxicating. I'm not a virgin, but somehow I doubt being with the deve would be anything like being with Roland. Roland, who in hindsight, abused his power over me. But the me of today doesn't regret allowing him to take advantage of me any more than my nineteen-year-old self did two years ago.

The six years I spent at the remote outpost in the far south of D'heilar after my mother was hanged were formative. I arrived at thirteen as a grief-stricken, informal prisoner, but I gradually became a valued member of the domestic staff. I worked in the kitchen or the fields or the stables. I didn't have any close friends there, but they became a kind of makeshift family that allowed me to heal somewhat after being orphaned. There weren't many luxuries, but there was food to eat and books to read and the climate was pleasant.

I met Roland in my last year there. He was the new commander of the outpost garrison and double my age. I never loved him, but I didn't mind his attentions. In exchange, he took me under his wing and taught me many useful things; to use a bow and arrow, to camp, and to start a fire with a flint rock. Besides my life as a very small child, my time with him was the happiest of my life.

It didn't last of course. Word of our relationship got out and from one day to the next, Roland was gone. Not long after that, I was summoned to Salandar City in the north where I was promptly introduced to Mattice Dulat, and then held for a year in my chamber with very little interaction with anyone.

My hand presses to the burns on my side, and my mind again scrambles to avoid re-living the nightmare of Mattice Dulat's one visit. He'd started out by announcing that I was being sold to a barbarian in marriage, and when I'd shown interest rather than fear, he'd upped the ante. After reading the letter, I realize he'd come to get a feel for my reaction to the marriage and my *interest* hadn't been acceptable. So he'd scarred me. To make me unattractive. My stomach turns. The way he'd stood back and considered my naked flesh as if I was a blank canvas still haunts me, not to mention the heated blade and the agonizing singeing of my flesh. Maybe I should count myself lucky he didn't mutilate my face. But that sick fuck probably wanted it to be something that only Luka would discover.

I'd like to say I escaped with only the physical scars, but some days the lingering fear and paranoia overwhelm me, forcing me to curl into myself . . . like now as I stare blankly at the wall on the other side of the room through the tunnel created by the underside of the bed.

I have no idea how much time has passed when I startle at a hand nudging my shoulder. "Rina?"

Blinking away the past, I find Yvette looking down at me with concern.

"Why are you on the floor?"

"The door," I mumble, almost rubbing my eyes but the smell of iron on my dirty hands stops me. She helps me into a sitting position and the cold slithers against my skin, making me shiver.

"What about the door?" she asks.

"It's broken. Anyone can come in."

I don't miss the pity on her face, but I choose not to acknowledge it while she reassembles my furs on the bed. It's then that I notice a boy standing near the door. He waves awkwardly.

"This is my son, Rionnon," Yvette says.

I attempt a smile as the last of the fog rolls away. "Hello. I'm Rina."

Again, he gives a little wave.

"Your mother talks about you all the time," I tell him, wanting him to feel at ease. "You're twelve, right?"

Yvette's brow knits, but the boy is pleased. "No, I'm eight."

"Ahhh," I say like I'm just realizing my mistake. "You're quite tall for eight, aren't you?"

He takes a few cautious steps into the room. "I want to be as tall as my Uncle Noé one day."

"Oh, yes, that's quite tall."

Little by little, he comes out of his shell and it's not long before he's telling me all about his uncle. Though I find the topic distasteful, it's clear he worships the man. I suppose Noé is not the worst role model he could attach himself to. Yvette has never mentioned the boy's father, and I didn't want to be rude by asking about him.

By the time Rionnon is telling me all about the bow his uncle gifted him this past summer, he's moved further into the light of the window. "Uncle Noé hasn't taught me how to use it yet, but he claims he will one day soon." His slightly bitter tone says otherwise.

"Well, I'm not doing anything if you want me to show you."

"You?"

"Yes, me." I repress a laugh at his dismissiveness. "Don't be fooled by my lack of height. Depending on the size of the bow, I'm an excellent shot."

He looks so skeptical . . . and it hits me. I've seen that look before. Maybe it's more innocent than the original, but it's eerily similar. And the paleness of his eyes . . .

"Are you really?" Yvette asks. In an ironic twist, I now pity her. Because like me, she was attacked by either Carson or Cayson Cyrun, but unlike me, she wasn't able to fend him off and was left with a child.

"Rina?" she prompts.

"Oh, uh, yes." I shake the thought away. "I can hit a hare from the back of a moving horse."

"Can you truly?" Rionnon asks with swiftly rising enthusiasm.

"Absolutely." I gesture for him to join me at the window and we discuss distance, accuracy, and the direction of the wind.

By the time the sun is starting to set, he's cajoled Yvette

into the promise of bringing him back in the next couple of days for his first lesson. Though I suspect he simply wants me to prove that I'm not embellishing my skills.

After they leave, my nightly meal arrives on a tray, the guard down the hall yelling for me to come and collect it. Since the deve kicked my door down, this has become the new normal. The rules pertaining to my imprisonment have loosened; being allowed in the hall, more visitors, more and better food, and one of my guards even introduced himself as Ion two days ago.

He's the one who offers me the tray now. "Thank you, Ion," I say, appreciating that he doesn't ogle my state of un-dress.

He dips his head with a bit of deference. "You're wel-come."

Limping back to my room, I first rearrange my furs back on the floor next to the brazier. I simply don't feel safe on the bed in full view of anyone entering the room. Then, in the growing dark of sundown, I sit with my back to the wall and eat my meal.

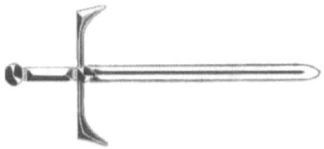

Overnight, winter comes with a vengeance. The moon is at its zenith when I wake shivering, knowing the temperature must be well below the freezing mark. With stiff fingers, I fill the brazier with the last of the wood, noticing the layer of frost that coats my window ledge. For a while the fire fends off the cold, but its icy tendrils eventually sink like claws into my flesh without mercy.

I fear the night will never end, and by the time the pale light of dawn is creeping over the horizon, I'm too exhausted to move. It's too cold even for the sound of male voices on the stairs to rouse any kind of reaction from me.

"Princess," the deve clips, all business today. He says more, but it flows off of me like water from a duck's back as I watch the plume of his breaths in the air. His lips are moving and I can hear him, but I only deduce that he's angry. Of course he's angry. He's usually angry.

When he grips my arm and shakes me gently, it feels like it's happening to someone else. I know I should snap out of it, but the will to gather my wits isn't there. Vaguely, I watch the stairs slip by, then the Great Hall. Next, the whole of my vision is filled by the bluest of skies. I ponder its vast beauty until it disappears. Wanting to protest, I open my mouth, but nothing comes out.

Reality makes an excruciating reappearance in the form of a thousand stinging nettles. Panic swamps me as I come back to myself, splashing in the water of the hot springs. I cry out and push against my bonds. "I know it hurts," he rumbles at my ear, pulling me closer to his chest. "But it will pass."

My breaths saw in and out of my chest as the prickling sensation in my limbs worsens. I shake violently, my teeth clatter. "It'll pass, little raven. It'll pass." My eyes find his and I grab on to the tenderness I find there like it's a lifeline. "There you go. You'll feel better soon."

And he's right. Slowly, the pain ebbs, allowing my thundering heartbeat to settle and the heat of the water to provide comfort instead of agony. And all the while, I study him; the slope of his nose, the texture of his long beard, and the small scar that's left an indent on his cheek. When I can, I snake my uncoordinated arms around his torso and hold on, never wanting to be alone again. He rests his cheek against the top of my head.

"This cannot continue," I whisper minutes later.

"I know."

He knows? He knows what? That the last threads of my sanity are worn so thin that they're about to give way?

The arm under my knees lowers my feet to the pool's floor, but I refuse to let him go. "Come now," he coaxes. "Lean your head back. We'll rinse your hair."

But as if my life depends on keeping myself pressed to his chest, I refuse.

"Take a breath then," he says and we start to sink down in the water. The muffled quiet eases some of the strain while he awkwardly works his fingers through my hair.

He's here and I'm not alone.

When he stands, with water pouring down my face, my grip loosens, and he takes the opportunity to grasp my shoulders and set me away from him.

Convincing myself not to glom back onto him takes almost more effort than I can summon. But the small sliver of self-respect left to me makes itself known and I manage to turn away. He lets me bob and paddle about the pool for a time while I attempt to reassemble the tattered pieces of myself.

"We need to talk about the letter," he finally says.

"No," I whisper.

"What?"

"I said no. I cannot continue as I am."

"Meaning?"

"Meaning if you want to leave me to freeze to death, I cannot stop you, but –"

"I didn't –"

"I don't care. All I know is I'm not sure I wouldn't welcome your holding me under the water until my life bleeds away." A flicker of something appears in his expression, but I press on. "I want clothes. *Proper* clothes for the cold. And boots." The surprisingly unyielding tone of my voice helps to further bolster my will.

"Rina," he says like I'm daft. "That would mean having to lock you in the holding cells. If I don't, you'll make your escape the first chance you get."

"Escape?" I laugh, a sound verging on manic. "To go where? I have nothing. I have no one."

"I'm not a fool," he claims. "You're resourceful. You'll –"

"I'll what? Live in a cave? Alone for the rest of my days until you or my cousin's men find me." I shake my head. "No. If you want my help, I want recompense."

He's going to refuse, I can tell, so I quickly continue before he can close the door on my fantasies. "I want water for washing. *Warm* water. And I'm not eating with my hands anymore."

His face contorts with what might be disgust, or confusion. "What?"

"You heard me. I want something to eat with and –"

"I'm not giving you a knife," he interjects.

"I don't need a *knife*. A spoon will do. But I refuse to eat like an animal out of a trough any longer. And I want to ride Glory one more time before . . . the end. And," I rush to think of more. "And maybe eat some kind of cake." I take a deep breath and cross my arms over my breasts under the water before I dare face him again.

He rubs a wet hand across his beard as if in thought, then says, "Fine."

"Pardon?" I whisper, because there's no way I've heard him correctly.

"I said fine. You can have those things if you help me with the letter . . . first."

My elation withers. *"I'm* not a fool either," I tell him. "After all my demands have been met, we'll talk. Until then, you can confer with your dead scholar through the Mother."

He makes a valiant effort to keep a straight face, but in the end, he can't smother a soft chuckle.

I should probably keep my next comment to myself, but somehow it comes out anyway. "How is it possible that you can't read that letter for yourself? You have, or *had*, a scholar, but he didn't teach the deve's son to read?"

He's suddenly wary. "It is forbidden."

"Forbidden?" I can't hide my shock. "Why on earth?"

"By order of the First Deve, Kharon . . . so we are not polluted by the ideas of D'heilar."

"But the letter was addressed to him. You can't tell me he would trust someone to interpret the information for him." I scoff with disgust. "Typical autocrat, wanting to control the information so he can fit it to his own narrative."

His heavy brows draw together.

"He controls what you see and hear," I explain. "So he can convince you to do as he wishes."

His mien grows darker until he starts to forcefully wade to the edge of the pool. "Come. You're warm enough."

"You're upset?"

"I said get out of the water. We're wasting time and your *needs* are many."

Watching him pull his pants over his powerful thighs, I can't resist taunting him a bit. "You see how that works? I control the information and you do as I want."

The hard glare he turns on me sends an unexpected pulse of want right to my core. *What . . ? Shouldn't it scare me?* Except I no longer believe he would hurt me, so I'm not afraid . . . a truth that channels itself into even more heat.

"I could teach you, you know?" I blurt, not wanting to consider my reaction too closely. "To read and write. That way you wouldn't have to depend on anyone."

He straightens from collecting his shirt, a mixture of suspicion and alarm on his face. But he's clearly considering it. Slowly, he arranges the shirt as if to pull it on over his head.

"No!" I say, wading forward to step from the pool. "That's mine." If he thinks I'll put that same, three-day-old shirt on again, he's got another thing coming.

He doesn't hand the shirt over right away, but that's fine, because the view of the man's torso is magnificent. Mother save me, but I can't dislodge my gaze from the ridges on his abdomen that lead down . . .

"Do you think it's possible?"

My eyes snap up guiltily. "What?"

"For me to learn to read," he says, exasperated now, holding the shirt out to me.

Right. I take it, ignoring the delicious scent of him on the fabric as I put it on. "Anyone can learn," I tell him, adjusting the drawstring around the neck before I squeeze the water from my hair.

Mulling over my announcement, he shrugs on his vest, the thick leather creaking as he tightens the buckles. When he shoves his feet into his boots, I get a sense of having lived this scenario before. *Is this to be our new routine? I come close to death and he revives me here in the baths?*

As he scoops me up and we head back, I hope not.

"Are you certain?"

"Pardon?" I try to curl more tightly into his chest to preserve the warmth of the hot springs.

"Are you certain I could learn?"

"To read? Yes, of course. It's the same as any goal. The more time and effort you put into it, the greater your skill."

Silence descends and it's not until we're heading up the tower stairs that I realize the sway of his gait has lulled me almost to the point of sleep. Straightening up in his arms, I ask, "Can I walk from here?"

He just grunts and continues up the stairs to the landing.

"Please?"

Frowning, he finally stops and puts me down.

"Thank you." Putting my foot on the first step, I start the climb. "I need to re-gain my strength," I explain, and I'm so pleased that compared to my last attempt, this one is much easier. I'm still a bit winded, but definitely stronger. The sense of celebration is promptly muted however by the sound of male voices coming from my room down the short hall. Sidling closer to Luka, I let him lead, then peer around his chest through the door.

I have a door!

"My deve," an older man booms jovially. He's wearing

a thick leather apron that covers his protruding belly and his flowing white beard reminds me of a grandfather. "Your door has been delivered."

"I asked for it days ago," Luka growls.

"Yes, well, these things cannot be rushed or they won't fit." The man, who must be a carpenter, notices me and his head tilts with interest. Grandfatherly becomes predatory and I move closer to Luka, tucking my fingers into one of the buckles on the side of his vest. He allows it, but I must startle him, because I almost get hit with an elbow.

He turns back to the man. "If it's done, get gone."

Luka's harsh tone has the carpenter's smarmy countenance faltering and whatever he was about to say next is cut off by Ion who appears behind him with an armful of the ruined pieces of wood. "He *is* done now, Deve," the young warrior says, his tone surprisingly stern as he crosses to the window. By the dull clatter, I assume he's throwing everything to the courtyard below.

The older man takes the hint and hurries out without another word.

Our attention is drawn back to Ion. "I had the fire wood brought up."

"Good," Luka says, jerking his head toward his post down the hall.

"Thank you," I say as he passes us.

Luka ushers me further into the room to close the door, inspecting its fit. "I don't like the man, but his skill can't be denied." Then without a backward glance, he opens it, grumbling something that sounds like, "I'll be back later."

The door bangs shut and I'm left on my own again. At least with the daylight, the temperature has warmed up to a tolerable level.

I breakfast alone when my meal is delivered. I watch the sun make its journey across the sky alone. I nap. The hours pass. I count the people in the courtyard. I count the stones that make up the wall around the window. I feed wood into the brazier. It gets colder and I lie under the furs on my bed.

By mid-afternoon, I begin to lose hope that the deve will hold to his word and an irrational sense of despondency works its way into my bones along with the cursed cold. I try to chase it off by jumping about to warm my blood. I'm breathing hard by the time I sit on the window sill again, feeling somewhat better. A bird's caw sounds from above me and I lean out to see what must be the same crow as yesterday perched on the battlement about fifteen feet up.

"Have you come to visit?" I call, but he screeches and hops back, out of sight. I sigh. "Fine, don't talk to me."

To keep my mind occupied, I try to count the stones on the outside wall as far up as I can without falling. Losing count twice, I start over . . . and all the while, in the back of my mind, an idea begins to take hold. Soon I'm not counting, but analyzing the way the blocks have been fit together. Unlike in D'heilar, they haven't been filed smooth and I can see a great many handholds. Reaching out, I run my fingers along the wall. The blocks are cold, but my window faces south so they're not slippery with mold or moss.

"That would be stupid, Rina," I say aloud, glancing down at the three-story drop to the cobblestones below. But . . . looking up again, I plan out my ascent, because I simply cannot be *still* any longer. I need to do *something*. If I don't, I'll lose my mind, especially now that the seed of adventure has been planted.

The sun is sinking swiftly toward the horizon, so if I'm

going to do this, it has to be now. Climbing up onto the window ledge, I reach out and test my idea for the first handhold. It couldn't be more perfect and a heady wave of possibility surges through me. This is the point of no return. If I swing myself out, I won't be able to maneuver myself back inside. There will only be up. Or down. Luka flashes in my mind's eye, and idiotically, I worry who will help with the letter if I fall. But right there, I find the greatest reason to do this . . . my life has been reduced to almost nothing and my future is filled with much of the same.

I slowly ease myself out and a huge smile spreads across my face. I send my bare foot out to find a solid place to rest and then take the greatest risk of my short life. I let go of the window casing and transfer my weight.

And start to climb. *Holy shit!*

The first few transitions go well. The hand and foot holds are solid. When I hear exclamations from below, I almost laugh at the idea I'm exposing my private parts for all to see. But I block my audience out and concentrate on the burn of my arm muscles as I pull myself higher.

Reaching for my next hand hold, I'm forced to stretch up on my toes, and I get a very real shot of fear. My wounded leg is weaker than I expected.

Do not look down.

A strong breeze tries to pry me from the wall and my fingers squeeze the stone with all their might. With my heartbeat thundering in my ears, I continue climbing. The fatigue in my muscles worsens, but I'm doing it. Fear and jubilation mingle, more potent than any wine I've ever tasted.

Do not look down, Rina.

Near the top, my arms and legs quake so badly that I suddenly worry I'll make it, but won't be able to pull myself over the edge. Light-headedness assaults me.

Focus, Rina. Focus.

I lift my leg, my now numb toes searching for somewhere to land and I push higher.

Yes! I'm able to throw my hand over the battlement . . . but my fingertips barely clutch at the far edge. Panic shears through my overworked heart. I don't quite have enough leverage to pull myself up, but my arms and legs are close to seizing up. Time is running out.

Fuck it.

I trust my grip on the edge and heave with what little strength I have left. My toes scrabble for purchase. They find nothing. Horrified acceptance begins to take hold just as my toes connect with a tiny outcropping and I push upwards. My chest hits the ledge and I crawl over, falling in a heap onto the other side.

My mind blanks, and for a moment, there's only the sawing of my breaths in and out of my chest. Unexpected laughter slips out of me, softly at first, then with more feeling. I'm not too proud to recognize its sharp maniacal edge and embrace it.

"Wooooo!" I scream to the darkening sky and its echo sets off another round of giggles.

A bang has me rolling my head against the stone to see a trap door flip open and Luka's head pop out. A triumphant smile stretches across my lips. I don't care that his glare is meant to instill terror. Nothing can pull me down from this high.

I'm not empty. I'm not only existing. I'm living.

Fully emerging onto the parapet, he stands over me, looking murderous. "What the fuck?"

All I do is smile up at him. I have no energy left for anything else.

"I asked you a question," he growls.

This has another burst of laughter leaving my throat, which only serves to enrage him further. He crouches down, closing his big paws over my upper arms and hauling me up. My feet dangle as he holds me at eye level like I weigh no more than a doll. Studying me with fierce disapproval, he finally pulls me close and presses his forehead to mine. "Rina," he breathes.

"Luka." I'm loopy and exhausted, but it's accompanied by joy, which has me using the last of my strength to wrap my legs around his waist. I don't want him to put me down. I only want him closer.

A low rumble comes from his chest. Though I'm unsure if it conveys approval or not, with me braced against him, he's able to slide one arm under my ass and the other across my back. I manage to lift my jelly-like arms to his neck. "Luka," I whisper with another giggle. "I'm alive."

He pulls back to see me and I'm seized by the impulse to stop the censure that's surely coming. I kiss him. In my haste, I only catch the side of his mouth. But I kiss him.

"Wha–" He tries to pull his head back, but I follow and this time manage to make full contact with his mouth, his beard tickly against my skin. He freezes but doesn't protest.

I kiss him again, and this time, his lips come alive under mine, sending triumph into my blood. It's wonderfully sweet and gentle until his mouth opens and our tongues meet. Then my heartbeat explodes, sent high by the glorious jolt of decadence. The kiss becomes hungrier, the give and take of our lips building until there's only him and me and the ache between my thighs. I've never felt anything like it and I arch my breasts into his chest, getting my first real taste of passion in years.

His hold on me tightens, pulling my core more firmly against the hard plains of his torso. The zing that radiates out from my clit fractures my thoughts and pulls a moan directly from my soul. My head lolls to his shoulder, stalling the kiss. I press my nose into the soft skin below his ear, the smell of him amplifying the pleasure and . . .

Without warning, everything tilts. I clutch at him to steady myself, but my feet meet the ground. My legs wobble as he steps back, allowing the frigid air to scrape against my hot skin and reality to crash back in.

His scowl is fierce. "Don't *ever* do that again."

My armor almost cracks with the impact of his words. They hurt. They make me want to pierce *his* heart with my own attack, but he doesn't give me the chance.

"Do you hear me?" he rants on, turning his back as he throws his hands in the air. "I almost shit myself." He whirls back and points an accusing finger at me. "If I'd had to watch you fall to your death . . ." He shakes his head as if he can't think of a way to end that sentence.

All thoughts of hurling insults at him burn up in the renewed coals of my arousal. He's mad, yes. But not about the kiss.

CHAPTER 10

LUKA

The woman is infuriating. Absolutely infuriating.

"Are you listening to me, Rina?" I demand, not liking how her expression goes from crestfallen to . . . sly. *Is that a smile curving her lips?* I may strangle her on principle alone at this point. Though I won't need my hands to choke her, just my rock-hard cock.

Damn her.

"You think this is funny?"

It's then I notice her nipples, pebbled against the linen of my shirt, and the memory of her moan echoes in my head. The pulse it sends to my already-swollen member enrages me further.

"Because I assure you, it wasn't funny – *in the least* – to watch you cling to the side of this stronghold about to drop to your death." With every man in the vicinity gawping up at her bare cunt. My fists clench. They were lucky she was so high up.

I watch her sway slightly in the wind and I realize maybe her nipples aren't poking through the shirt to taunt me, but because it's freezing.

"Come," I say in a gentler voice, holding out my hand to her. "It's cold."

She blinks owlishly at the abrupt change in my demeanor, but takes my hand. As I reel her in, I warn, "Don't think this changes anything. We're still going to talk about your recklessness."

She has the nerve to smile. "I very much look forward to this talk, Luka."

My name on her lips causes another visceral surge of desire. "I didn't give you permission to use my name."

She shrugs. "We can add it to the list of things that need to be *discussed.*"

This time the suggestion in her voice isn't as subtle. "I am not a man you want to trifle with, little raven."

Her smile widens and I curse under my breath.

"Let me go down first," I tell her snappishly at the trap door. I don't want those fuckers getting even a glimpse of her coming down the ladder.

At the bottom, I make the men step back, then help her down on her unsteady legs. Once she's back on solid ground, she crowds closer to me at the sight of Noé, Eldon, and Ion. "I'll meet you downstairs," I say, dismissing my Second and Warrior Commander.

Noé's face pinches up like he's bit into a lemon, but Eldon

gives me a knowing smirk that I immediately want to smack him for. He hands me the large bundle we were on our way to deliver when we came upon her climbing the wall like a spider. Taking Rina's hand, I lead her to her room, where I pitch the bundle onto the bed. "Here are the requirements for your cooperation. Get dressed."

I pace the room while she fumbles with the twine that keeps everything together. Her shaky hands are a sure sign that she needs rest, but it's also irksome. Pulling the dagger from my belt, I cut the rope for her. "When was the last time you ate?"

"This morning," she says absently, then inhales sharply. "Are these boots for me?"

"It's *all* for you," I grouse, though I'm pleased by her re-action. I had the skin of the buck that Venna and I hunted down made into boots, leggings, and a vest for her.

Stroking the soft hide that lines the boots, she sighs. The cursedly erotic sound stretches my patience even thinner. Her climbing act about did me in, and that kiss . . . and my reaction to it. How I hate the feeling of being off balance. I need to move this along.

Striding to the door, I tell Ion to have a plate of food sent to the map room downstairs, then I sit next to her and help her dress.

She attempts to smack my hands away when I become too pushy, but mostly she accepts the help. She claims to love the soft buckskin leggings that slide up her thighs. They're not a perfect fit, but the tie at her waist keeps them up. When I remove the shirt from this morning, I have to force my greedy eyes away from her small breasts. Instead, I scan over the scars that run along her ribs and shake my head.

That still makes no sense.

I get her into the new, soft linen undershirt that actually fits her, then the thick woolen overdress. "The weave is lovely," she says, fingering the light blue fabric.

"As long as it keeps you warm." I frown at the too-long sleeves, but she's smiling, so I grudgingly push the imperfection from my mind. The fur-trimmed, leather vest and the matching boots further light her up and all the turmoil of the past half hour finally settles into a warm glow in the pit of my stomach.

"How do they fit?" I ask as she stands to test out the boots.

"Like a dream come to life. But all this will cause comment, won't it?"

"I am deve," I declare with satisfaction and . . . a touch of hunger. "I'll dress you as I please." And pleasing she is, looking very much like a Northern a'deve. My a'deve.

Mother above, maybe she could be mine if she weren't so different from the people of this realm. If her hair wasn't as black as night, or her skin the soft brown of a white-tailed deer, or her eyes the golden hue of a summer sunset . . . all of which add to her appeal for me. But dammit, it's that she surprises me at every turn that's the real problem. I could surely resist her physical charms if I didn't find her mettle so fucking alluring. If only I could explain *that* to my people.

Or maybe that Abyss-dammed kiss has turned my mind to mush.

"Luka?" she says, startling me back into the present. I almost wrench myself away when she lifts a hand to my shoulder and draws me down. Pushing up on her toes, she kisses my cheek. "Thank you."

I clear my throat, not appreciating the need to swallow

back a nonsensical rise of emotion. Mush indeed. "They're waiting," I say gruffly, snubbing her thanks.

"They?" Her voice rises with concern as she follows me from the room. "Who are *they?*"

"Not to worry, just Noé and Eldon."

"Oh." She hurries to keep up with my pace down the stairs. "Are we not going to talk about the kiss?"

"No," I growl. "We are not. At least not right now."

She makes a little harrumphing noise and I have to repress a twitch of humor.

"That is last on our list."

"But it *is* on the list?" she asks, sounding cheered. "Because I'd like to experience it again before the end."

I pull up short in the middle of the hall. "The end? Is that what your stunt was about? *The end?*"

Though she recoils slightly, her answer rings with resolve in the torchlight. "Everyone has an end. I know that."

Huffing, I take her hand and practically drag her down the hall. She's not only infuriating and reckless, she's also ridiculous.

In the map room, Noé and Eldon sit with their feet up on the big table in the center of the room, drinking ale. "Is her highness finally ready to talk?" Noé complains. "Has a bit of clothing loosened her tongue sufficiently?"

I'm about to tell him to shut his mouth, but Rina beats me to it.

"Noé, let's not pretend you'd last longer than five minutes, naked, with your balls frozen to your thigh."

His boots drop from the tabletop with a threatening thud

and he gets to his feet.

"Oh, sit down," Eldon laughs. "She's right. You wouldn't last, and neither would I. She's been through a lot."

I pull out the chair for her across from them and point to it. I'm not sure if it's her newfound disregard for her own safety or courage she's always had, but even with Noé trying to intimidate her, she takes her place. That glow in my gut gets a little warmer as I sit next to her.

Noé sinks back into his chair, grumbling, "Let's get on with this sham. We've already wasted a day."

Pulling the letter from where it's been folded between my shirt and my vest all day, I toss it down in front of her. "Read it again."

Her eyes narrow.

"Can it not be read more than once?" I ask, not having considered such a thing. This act of reading *does* seem like it belongs to the dominion of the supernatural.

"Yes," she says tightly. "It can be read as many times as one wishes. But you could ask nicely."

My jaw clenches. "You cannot be serious."

"Why not? It costs you nothing to be polite."

Leaning forward, I take hold of her chin and pull her toward me. "Oh, it costs me. It costs me time and patience. I suggest you remember who I am."

"How could I forget, my deve?" she says sweetly, not cowed in the least.

Tamping down on the urge to have another taste of those full lips, I let her go. "Get on with it."

"Fine." She picks up the letter, trying to hide her little smile. *Is she baiting me? On purpose?* She starts reading and

143

I close out everything from my mind except the business at hand.

"To Kharon, First Deve of the Bear Realm."

"You're sure that's what it says?" I ask, watching her for any sign of deception.

Pursing her lips, she puts the letter flat on the table and uses her finger to indicate the words as she speaks them. "To Kharon, First Deve of the Bear Realm."

"But that's definitely not a bear on the outside," Noé accuses.

"No, it's not," she agrees, turning it over for us all to review the mountain lion symbol. "Maybe the person who drew it mixed up the letters." She flips it over to the squiggles, then back to the lion. "It seems like the ink used to draw the figure is darker than the ink used for the script."

There's a knock at the door as I pull the letter from her hands. Ion enters with her tray of food, so I take the paper over to the fireplace where the light is better. Noé joins me and we examine it together.

"She's right," he says, surprised. "The ink isn't the same, is it?"

I blow out a heavy breath. "No, it isn't."

The door closes and we go back to the table where Rina is beaming happily at me. "Thank you for the spoon."

I dismiss her thanks with a wave, my mind on the letter. "So, the question is, was this error intentional or accidental?"

"Why would it be intentional?" Eldon asks. "It gives us vital information about their plans."

Rina swallows a bite of her stew. "Maybe it's not real information."

Now there's a thought I could do without. How I hate political intrigue. "Here," I say, thrusting the letter at her again. "Read some more."

She puts her spoon aside, but doesn't get far before I stop her.

"There, that word, *upstart*. You say it means this advisor doesn't like me?"

She nods. "And in my opinion, it's phrased to imply that your First Deve doesn't like you either. Like they've discussed you before."

"That I believe," Eldon says. "It's no secret that Kharon was livid when you ended your father. Those two were thicker than thieves for going on twenty years."

"No," Noé says, drumming his fingers on the table. "No way. No deve would stoop to plotting with D'heilar. If his people found out –"

Eldon interrupts. "How would they find out? He's got everything and everyone tied up tighter than a virgin's quim. He has for decades. No one would dare say a word against him."

"Still," Noé insists, "I can't believe a man as great as Kharon would betray the Realms like that."

"Great?" Eldon disdains. "Let's be real, shall we? The man would sell his own flesh and blood if he thought it to his advantage."

"What?" sputters Noé as I notice Rina struggling to balance a large piece of meat on her spoon. While Noé and Eldon debate Kharon's honor like old biddies, I pull my dagger from its sheath and hand it to her handle first.

In the candlelight, her amber eyes sparkle as she whispers, "I thought I wasn't to be trusted with knives."

She takes hold of the handle, but I don't let go. I draw her closer to me with it. "Just this once."

"Very unwise of you." She runs her tongue across her lips . . . those sweet-tasting, full lips that I can't stop obsessing over.

"No. Do you know what is unwise, little raven?"

The delight on her face makes her quite possibly the most beautiful woman I've ever seen. "What?" she breathes.

"How you think it's okay to provoke me." I jostle the knife between us, and it suddenly occurs to me how vulnerable I've made myself to her by almost resting the point on my chest. She could plunge it right into my heart if she wanted to.

Eldon breaks into our bubble. "Is this some kind of herald to sex? Because I'm strangely aroused right now."

Surrendering the dagger to Rina, I consider knocking my cousin's teeth from his head when Noé makes a noise of disgust. "Is this a strategy meeting or not? Let's just get on with the letter."

He's right. Dragging my glare from Eldon, I watch her pick up the parchment again. Her good mood quickly disintegrates as she reads about the *unfortunate violence* that will befall her and the hope that I will reject her.

The rage I felt yesterday surges back to life and I shove to my feet, unable to sit still.

"Why," Noé starts, "would they want you to reject a woman they're forcing you to marry? It makes no sense."

"No, it doesn't." I scratch at my beard, frustrated and restless and horny. "But I think Kharon knows that he's put me in an impossible position, that this marriage will likely trigger a challenge."

146

"But if he wants to rid the Realms of you," Noé says. "He should *want* you to marry her, not reject her."

"What will happen if I'm rejected?" Rina asks.

"I guess," Eldon says slowly. "We would be penalized in some way."

"Possibly they would cut off our shipments of ale," I tell them. While we do brew some of our own hops and distill some grain here at home, the quality is close to rot-gut level. Nothing like the smooth ale we trade for with the Bear Realm, where ale is their speciality.

"What?!" Noé exclaims. "That's impossible. The men would revolt."

We're all quiet for a moment. "So," Rina says. "There will be discontent if I'm rejected and discontent if I'm not."

"Which is what Kharon wants, surely," Eldon muses. "But maybe we can use this as a rallying cry, Luka. Taxes for the Bear Realm have increased every year. We could create an us-against-them kind of scenario."

"We can't do that!" Noé is appalled. "That's treasonous."

"Relax," I tell him. "We are discussing our options, nothing more." I tap the parchment that's brought us nothing but difficulties. "Let's finish."

Rina takes a breath and reads to the end, finishing with, "Your ally, Mattice Dulat."

Rina lowers the letter to her lap, and Eldon and Noé proceed to quiz her on everything she knows about the King's High Advisor. Her personal involvement with him is not known to them, and I find myself unwilling to spill her secrets. Though it may not be the smartest course of action, dredging up her past with the loathsome pig feels unnecessarily cruel, especially when she's doing so well at keeping her answers succinct and unemotional.

"What I don't understand is why this man is involved at all?" Eldon says, baffled. "Is he speaking for the King himself?"

"And if he is," I continue the thought. "Why would the King want to destabilize the bonds between north and south? Surely a united front against our common enemy to the east is of more importance."

Lifting his cup of ale, Noé states the obvious. "It *has to* be of more importance. The savages are relentless."

"Or perhaps," I say. "D'heilar wants to move north. To conquer us once and for all."

Both Eldon and Noé laugh, but Rina nods. "Speak, little raven."

"That sounds exactly like something my cousin would want. If Gaden is a peacock, the Realms are mud, marring his extravagant feathers."

We all stare at her.

"What? That's what most of D'heilar thinks of the Realms, Gaden most of all. And my death at your hands would simply reinforce the idea that you are not to be trusted."

Eldon leans forward, planting his elbows on the table. "But that would mean your own cousin has sent you to your death."

"Oh, there's nothing he'd enjoy more." Noé makes a harsh noise of disbelief, so she continues. "It's not uncommon in D'heilar to eliminate those in contention for the throne. I was seven when my father and two brothers were put on trial and hanged. And the same happened with my mother when I was thirteen."

Shock hits me, and I realize how very little I know about the D'heilar kingdom or my intended bride, and my mind conjuring an image of Rina, alone at such a young age, isn't to my liking at all.

"And they call us barbarians," Eldon scoffs.

Rina shrugs. "That he's found a way to use my death in a political move doesn't surprise me at all."

I watch her brush her fingers over the last part of the letter. "Tell me."

Her head comes up. "What?"

"Tell me what you're thinking."

"Oh, just the way it says *your ally* . . . it makes me think that maybe he *isn't* speaking for the King. That maybe the partnership is only between Dulat and Kharon."

"If that's the case," Eldon says, "what does Dulat have to gain that the King does not?"

I mull this over. "If your cousin is overthrown, who is next in line for the throne? Does he have children?"

"He's married, but they don't have any children that I know of. I've heard he has two illegitimate daughters, but no sons."

"Is legitimacy a big thing in D'heilar?" Here in the Realms, it's not. If a man is strong enough, he can rule no matter what his parents have or have not done.

Rina laughs. "The Mother's sanction of a union is sacred in my homeland. Legitimacy is almost as important as being male."

"So, you would be next in line?"

She shakes her head. "Like I said, a woman cannot sit on the throne."

"But your son?"

Dread slowly steals over her. "No," she whispers. "Never. I'll never allow any child of mine to return to D'heilar. I'll die first."

Eldon, always the level-headed one, says dryly, "That's not a likely scenario, Luka, since her children will be Northern-born. And unless this advisor is some long-lost distant cousin, he wouldn't profit from removing the crown from Gaden's head."

"But he may be positioning things in his favor for the future," I muse. "Just like Kharon."

Noé and Eldon open their mouths to voice their opinions, but I hold up my hand to stop them. "Right now, we don't *know* anything. But there's someone who might."

"What? Who?" Noé asks.

"Cayson. Someone approached him while you were in the south and I want to hear all about it."

CHAPTER 11

RINA

They talk long into the night, and though I'm desperately tired, I couldn't be happier to listen to them. I have a full stomach, and the room – named for the large map tapestry on the wall – is warm and inviting with its roaring fire. Plus, my mind is engaged.

I learn much about the Realms. There are six of them that cover the vast expanse to the north of the Colundra River. According to the map behind me, running from the relatively peaceful shores of the west to the vicious wilds of the east, they are Eagle, Bear, Stag, Snake, Mountain Lion, and Wolf. Learning that we are so close to the great, open savage lands sends a chill into my heart.

Also disturbing is the knowledge that Luka's rule is not as solid as they'd like it to be . . . though I'm not so sure I agree. Luka is under the impression that the people accept him by default, because there's no other immediately obvious candidate, but I saw the admiration on their many faces in the Great Hall when he asserted himself. His confidence and sheer strength energized them, one and all.

Along with me.

He's *more* than I ever expected him to be; more intelligent, more reasonable, more handsome. Luka, in whose presence I feel safe. Luka, who is rude, but not cruel. Luka, whose kiss sent my heart soaring.

Do I mourn what we could have been?

Maybe.

Okay, yes. Of course I do.

But there's no point regretting something that was impossible from the start. Not only can I not imagine a man like Luka allowing outside forces to manipulate the course of his life, but I think I'm the only person – literally – who ever wanted the union between us.

That's not to say that I've given up entirely. After the exhilaration of today's events, I plan to make the most of what's left of my life.

I must fall asleep at the table because the next thing I know I'm being carried up the stairs. I nestle into his neck and breathe in his divine scent. It's all man and wood smoke and ale and *Luka,* and when he puts me down on my bed, I protest with a quiet, "Stay?"

But he only arranges many more furs than I'm used to over me. "Go to sleep, little raven. I'll see you tomorrow."

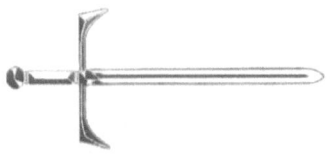

When I wake, I'm pleased to find that my quest for *life* still lingers . . . and that I'm not frozen solid. Though there's frost around my window again this morning, I'm warm under all my new furs.

But by late morning, loneliness, along with the inactivity, is once again crushing down on me. At least now, I can pace the room in my new boots. I briefly consider making another climb, but discard the idea as taking a step too close to madness. There's no way the Mother would grant me another victory and I don't particularly want to meet with death today, not while there are still things I want to experience.

Finally, Yvette shows up with a tray of food, followed by her son, Rionnon, whose smile couldn't be bigger, probably because he's carrying his bow and quiver of arrows. It appears to be the perfect size for him. And me.

"You have clothes," Yvette says cheerfully. "You're a new woman."

Grinning, I turn a circle, so relieved to have company. "Yes, I'm ready for the world now." I hold my hand out to Rionnon for the bow. "Let's take a look." Checking it over, I marvel at its quality. "It's exceptional."

"Is that good?" he asks with excitement.

Laughing, I ruffle his hair. "It's better than good. Do you have a bracer to protect your wrist and a finger guard?"

He digs into the leather pouch that's tied at his waist and pulls out the items. Helping him tie the leather bracer around his right forearm, I ask him if he's ready to begin and his enthusiasm warms my heart.

It quickly becomes apparent that the boy has never been shown a single thing about archery. My opinion of Noé falls a little further. What kind of uncle, the boy's father figure from what I understand, dumps such a weapon into a child's hands and doesn't give him any instruction? But Noé's failure turns out to be my gain.

After we've gone over all we can without actually loosing an arrow, I tell him the lesson will have to end here and his face falls.

"What about from the window?" he begs and I laugh.

"And shoot some poor sod in the ass by accident? The deve would have my head."

I can almost hear the workings of his young mind. And as sure as thunder following lightening, he comes up with, "What if I can get a target to shoot at? And someone to make sure the people stay clear?"

I'm loath to crush his excitement, so I turn to Yvette for help. "Well, if you can accomplish what you claim, Rionnon, I don't see why not."

"Thanks, Ma," he yells, racing from the room.

Yvette and I share a smile. "He's a very quick study," I tell her.

"I'm so very grateful to you, a'Deve." She inclines her head in a show of respect and I snort.

"Don't let the clothing fool you, Yvette. I'm still a prisoner here."

"I'm still grateful. Noé is always busy and his grandmother and I know nothing of archery."

I move over to the bed, where my tray has been carefully balanced, and take a seat. Discovering a spoon in my now congealed gruel absurdly adds to my good mood. "Well, I can't tell you how wonderful it is to be useful." I point, offering her a seat at the other end of the bed.

"May I ask how you learned to shoot a bow?"

I tell her of my affair with Roland in between bites of my breakfast.

"I've never had a serious beau," she says wistfully when I finish the tale. Before I can point out that Roland wasn't really a beau, she adds, in that same contemplative tone, "I got pregnant when I was so young."

Though it's indelicate, I decide to take the opening she's provided me with. "Will you tell me about Rionnon's father?"

She's suddenly cautious. "His father?"

"I don't want to assume, but Rionnon's eyes are quite unique."

"Yes," she admits. "They are."

"He," and I use *he* because I can't bring myself to utter either of the twins' names, "refused to claim his child?" I ask gently.

Her head gives a tiny shake. "I did not ask him to. I will *never* take anything from Cayson Cyrun for as long as I live."

I nod, her vehemence putting another piece of the puzzle into place. "Were there really no consequences for him?"

She looks away. "He is a Range Warrior."

"You say that like it's the beginning and the end of everything."

Her laugh is brittle. "Because it is. The last deve –"

155

"Luka's father?"

"Yes. The last deve never disciplined a warrior for such an offense."

My face screws up and it's not the gruel that has offended me. "But I thought he ruled for more than twenty years. How can a group of soldiers never be disciplined?"

"Oh, no, you misunderstand. They are held to the highest standards when it comes to their duty. But a crime against a woman is not really seen as a crime at all."

The gruel curdles in my belly. "This continues under Luka?"

Yvette is distinctly uncomfortable now. "No . . . well, sort of. Girls are still taught to always have a care for the risks."

I think my jaw may hang open. "And what are the boys taught?"

"Oh, it's not what you're thinking. The majority of the men in this realm play no part in such things, but there are a few snakes who take advantage of their station."

Thinking that over, I pluck the apple from the tray and consider it. This is something new that I would not have received a few days ago.

"Rina?"

I look up, surprised. Yvette usually avoids using my name.

"You should know," she says, "that Luka is nothing like his father."

I sigh. "But Luka changes nothing."

"Change takes time, my a'deve. And the old deve probably would have put you in a cage in the courtyard and watched you starve to death. Luka has never shown such cruelty."

"Yes, I suppose he is not all bad."

"I'm back," Rionnon exclaims, bursting through the door. He's out of breath as he gestures to the window. "I got everything. Come and see."

We join him. "Well done," I say. There is indeed a target set up on a wooden pedestal in the courtyard. "Are those your friends?" I ask, indicating the five little urchins jumping around, waving up at us.

"Yes," he says proudly. "They'll make sure we don't shoot anyone in the ass."

"Rionnon!" Yvette scolds, but I laugh.

"Let's do it then."

While the boy catches his breath, I yell down and have his friends do their best to adjust the target. Everything about this is outlandish; the angle, the distance, the height . . . the chances of pissing Luka off. But whatever. It's part of my new zest for life.

Rionnon's first ten shots are terrible, but I explain that archery is about practice and trial and error. I'm impressed with the way he fights through his embarrassment in front of his friends, and keeps trying. After another ten shots, he improves.

"Much better," I say, though there's some ass down in the courtyard now who's laughing up at us.

"It can't be done," he pouts.

"It can. Let me show you."

Nocking the arrow sends tingles to my fingertips. It's been a long while since I've done this, but the muscle memory comes back to me like it was yesterday. My first shot hits the target, but not the center. The boys down below cheer though, which brings a smile to my lips.

"Bring them up," I yell down and they start scrambling to collect the spent arrows. "Carefully!" Turning to Rionnon, I ask, "Are you too tired to continue? Your muscles must be getting sore."

He looks appalled. "No! I want to hit the target."

I nod, and we go over everything again.

The boys spill into the room, full of excitement and wonder, and I notice two of the five are actually girls. I smile back at them all as they bombard me with questions until Yvette shoos them away.

Three shots later and Rionnon finally hits the target. The crowd that's gathered in the courtyard sends up a cheer and the boy preens. "Now the princess," someone yells and Rionnon gladly hands over the bow, stretching out his tired arms.

I consider refusing the request. Everyone below is more than likely expecting me to fail . . . which of course pushes me to do it. I hit the center of the target this time and a cheer goes up. Pride fills me. "Make it harder," the same voice yells and a man pulls the target back by ten feet.

I hit that one too and I get another round of cheers. The quality of this bow is quite extraordinary.

"One more," a woman calls as the man again moves the target back.

Laughter in my voice, I yell down, "You'll keep pulling it back until I fail."

The same woman cups her hands to her mouth. "You can do it!"

I'm about to nock the next arrow when a group of riders comes in through the gates. I recognize Luka right away and my enthusiasm wavers. But maybe *living* doesn't mean retreating every time there may be consequences for my actions.

I pull the string back, take aim, and let the arrow fly. A huge cheer rings out when I hit the bull's eye. Luka doesn't have much reaction, but beside him, Eldon is clearly entertained.

The ruckus lasts longer this time before the same man pulls the target back again, almost to the far wall now, and the woman calls out, "Again!"

So there's *living* and then there's being stupid, I think to myself. "Only with the deve's permission," I call down and half the crowd starts petitioning him for just that.

"By all means," he bellows. "I need to see this."

His tone isn't angry, is it? I don't think so. Slightly mocking maybe, but there's a touch of amusement too. An unexpected case of nerves assaults me. *What if I miss?* I'll look like a fool. *But does that really matter?*

As soon as I aim, the usual sense of calm steadies me. The arrow flies and lands true, hitting the target right next to my last shot. Jubilation surges through me, especially when Eldon puts his fingers to his mouth and lets out a loud whistle that sounds over the cheers.

I sketch a self-mocking bow and the crowd gets louder.

A knock sounds at my open door and I turn to see Bron standing there, grinning. "The deve wishes to see you downstairs, my a'deve."

"Pardon?"

"Downstairs." He gestures to the hall. "He wants to see you."

"I can show you the way," Rionnon says eagerly. "I have to collect my arrows."

With a touch of trepidation, I follow Bron down the stairs,

while Rionnon races ahead. I envy his unending energy. "Is he angry?" I ask Bron softly as we come out into the Great Hall. The few people milling about turn to stare and I suddenly feel as naked without Luka by my side as I did walking around in only his thin shirt.

"I don't think so, but I'm still not able to gauge his moods very well. I only became his aide a few months ago."

"Aide?" I quicken my steps to keep up with Bron's long strides.

Glancing back, he gives me a wry look. "Yes, my job involves being constantly at his beck and call. And you should have told me to slow down, Rina." Waiting for me, he offers me his arm. "I didn't mean to tire you, only to avoid his accusations of my loafing about."

How like Luka. "Do you loaf about often?"

He laughs and I feel my apprehension lift. Bron has always been good to me. But as we come to the open main doors, I remember how many people were in the courtyard. Passing a self-conscious hand over the long mass of my unbraided hair, I swallow hard. "I'll walk on my own from here," I tell Bron, slipping my hand from his elbow.

He gives me an approving nod. "Of course."

We step out and everyone turns. I do my best to pretend their stares don't weigh on me, but when I'm halfway across the seemingly vast distance to the gate, the first of a series of insults is hurled at me. I flinch slightly, but keep my head held high, focusing on Luka sitting tall atop his horse. I take heart that interspersed with the slurs, I hear support as well.

Luka remains carefully blank, so I follow suit. "You asked for me, my deve?"

He motions toward the stables where Glory is being led

out, saddled and ready to go. My heart leaps. He's granting my wish.

"This way, a'Deve," Bron says, touching my elbow. I follow him to the mounting block. Gathering my skirt, I get my foot in the stirrup and ignore the ache in my thigh as I throw my leg over Glory's back.

Glory shifts her footing and I find Luka has manoeuvred Nightshade over to us. "Are you well, princess?" he asks in a low voice.

"Yes, I am very well. Thank you."

Pulling Nightshade around, he says, "Let us depart, then. We have business to attend to."

Business?

There are more riders than I first realized, and as we file through the gate two abreast, Glory and I end up around the middle of the group. Once we're on the road, the men give me a wide berth. "I hope you don't mind solitude," I murmur to Glory, patting her neck. Her ears swivel back as if she's actually listening to me. "Even if you do mind, I imagine being out and about is still better than being cooped up in the stables."

At the head of the pack, Luka and Noé urge their mounts into a canter and the rest of us follow suit. Thrilled to be out of my room, I soak up the new sights and sounds. The small houses with their steeply-sloped thatched roofs in the immediate village quickly thin out and soon we're surrounded by rolling farmland interspersed with herds of sheep huddled together to fend off the chill. From what I can tell, most of the crops have been harvested and the only thing breaking up the colorless landscape is the occasional home with smoke curling from its chimney. It's all mundane and uneventful, but I couldn't be happier. Glory is also in high spirits, and as the ride continues,

I have to restrain her from charging ahead numerous times.

I'm laughing at her latest attempt to take off when Eldon comes up beside me. "Noé told me that you ride well. He wasn't wrong."

I throw him a cautious glance. For lack of a better word, Eldon has been nice to me so far. In the Great Hall, while Luka beat Cayson to a pulp, Eldon sat with me, making pleasant commentary. Though I was in such a state that I don't remember much of what he said, his presence was welcome. And last night again, he was kind.

"Yes," I say. "Years ago, I spent a season herding cattle."

His incredulity is almost comical.

"There was a lack of men where I lived when the garrison wasn't replaced right away," I explain, but he's still clearly skeptical. Shrugging, I add, "It was better than kitchen duty."

This time he laughs. "Now that, I believe."

Luka slows our pace to take a much narrower path through a copse of trees and we come out at what can only be described as a large homestead. Half of the house is built to be two storeys and there are also quite a few outbuildings.

The noise of our arrival draws a man out from a barn, and an older woman from the house. My chest tightens. It's *her*. The one who stabbed me. The one who was called to witness me stab her son in the Great Hall, Cayson's mother, Zola.

She scans the half dozen warriors who are dismounting their horses. "Deve, what is the meaning of this?"

"Zola," Luka says, matching her derisive tone. "You will stay out of their way."

Zola's confusion turns to fury as Noé leads the men past her and into the house without invitation. "How dare you?!

Four of my sons are Range Warriors."

Luka looks down his nose at her. "You will submit to the search."

"Search?" she squawks. Turning on her heel, she stalks back inside.

"Come on," Eldon says and I follow him across the clearing to a very grumpy deve.

Eldon dismounts with a sigh. "If you need me, I'll be attempting to keep Noé in check."

Luka only grunts, watching instead the man who's now approaching from the barn.

"Deve." There's no scorn in the greeting, but neither is there any obvious respect.

"Gray."

He's a big man, and like Luka, he has a hardness to him that suggests if the idea struck him, he could crush a man. They both look to the house where a bit of a crash sounds. "You've not been making my life easy of late, Luka."

"Pity. The ease of your life has been my only consideration." The sarcasm hits its mark, but instead of anger, it gets a smirk from this man, Gray. "When will you be back?" Luka asks him.

"Not sure I'll ever return."

"You're not meant to be out here, playing at making barrels. The Range needs you. I need you."

"Eldon has your back just fine."

"It should have been you, not Noé, to make the trip south, and you know it."

"Noé will out-grow his self-righteousness eventually. He

163

means well."

Luka scoffs. *"Means well* doesn't fix this bind he's placed me in, does it?"

Gray's regard finally lands on me though his words are still for Luka. "I heard all the details of the display you put on in the Great Hall and I've seen the aftermath first hand. Seems your cock has resolved your bind just fine."

Luka kicks Nightshade ahead, forcing Gray back. "Watch your mouth. A cooper is not worth half as much as a warrior."

A woman storms out of the house, one who is not Zola, but one who's even angrier. "Gray?!" she calls. "They've broken the water jug. Aren't you going to do something?"

"Do not fear, my love," he returns. "The deve will replace anything his men destroy."

Before more can be said, a loud argument between men erupts from within the house. With a muttered curse, Gray heads that way as Noé strides out.

"My deve," Noé says, verging on gloating as he theatrically opens his palm to reveal four gold coins stamped with my cousin's likeness. "We found them in the brothers' room. They didn't even bother to hide them."

Zola bursts from the house. "The coins prove nothing!"

Luka glares. Noé continues to smile. Gray's hands land on his hips and his head drops with resignation to study the ground.

"What?" the woman who I assume is Gray's wife asks shrilly as the rest of the warriors file out of the house. "What of the coins?" The last two men half-drag a still black-and-blue Cayson between them.

"Cayson Cyrun," Luka says, his loud voice filling the

clearing. "You are charged with breaking your oath to me, the Range, and the Mountain Lion Realm. You will meet me in combat on the new moon."

"Oath breaking?" Zola screeches at the same time that Cayson protests with, "I didn't!"

"Those coins say otherwise," Luka says and I can tell he's trying to keep a lid on his temper. "You accepted them to carry out the will of another man. That is treason. Until the new moon, you are stripped of your honor and you will remain chained to the hearth in the Great Hall on display for all to judge you, along with the coins."

Zola is fit to be tied. "You thrice damned fool! You're not half the man your father was."

"Enough, mother!" Gray booms.

"And you?!" she spits. "You're a weakling. As firstborn, you should have challenged this pathetic excuse for a deve long ago."

"No, as firstborn, I should have kept my brothers in line. Now this family is in disgrace."

CHAPTER 12
LUKA

"N oé," I say over Zola's continued uproar, "take Cayson and the coins back to the stronghold."

"Certainly." His haughty tone repulses me. He may take pleasure in this, but I don't. In no way does this twist of events benefit the realm. Two of my sixty-eight elite warriors have been proven traitors.

Finally, I settle my gaze on my princess. She looks regal, sitting atop her mare with natural ease, dressed like a true Northerner in fur-trimmed leather. "Come, little raven. We ride north for the lake."

Not doubting that she'll follow, I urge Nightshade into a trot along the Cyrun's property line. It takes a solid few minutes to cross over to the road that snakes through the trees, but once we can ride two abreast, I notice that Glory is fighting to be given her head.

I can't repress a smile. "If you stay on the path," I gesture ahead, "it should be clear to tire her out."

"Yes?" she asks, appearing hopeful.

"Yes. I won't be far behind."

"Ha!" she yells, not needing to be told twice.

Nightshade wants to join in the fun, but I hold him back. Even if he's not saddled with the extra weight for battle, he's not built for high-speed sprints and the last thing I need is for him to strain a muscle.

Alone on the trail, I know I should be reflecting on Cayson and Carson's open and blatant betrayal. But the only thing with any traction in my thoughts is the image of Rina making those almost impossible shots with a weapon that women do not generally touch. I'm rather annoyed that there's now more to add to the long list of things she says and does that make me want her. And I definitely want her now – badly.

I come around a curve in the road, expecting to see her near the top of the hill where the trees taper off, but she's not there. My heartrate picks up. *Could she have already made it over the rise? Or –* and I search the forest around me – *she wouldn't run, would she?*

I'm an idiot. Of course she would run. *Didn't I say if I gave her clothes, she'd flee?* And only yesterday she risked her life climbing the wall of the stronghold. She's not some delicate, lily-fingered maiden. Of course she'd run.

I put my heels to Nightshade, and his every hoof beat punches my outrage deeper. *How dare she? After everything I've put up with from her.* By the Father, if the woman won't give me her obedience, I'll take it. I'll keep her on a leash so tight she'll choke with every breath. She won't move without my permission. I may not have decided what to do with her yet, but she's still mine. I own her.

But first, I need to get her back.

The idea of hunting her down blooms hot in my belly, and rapidly oozes down into my groin. Images of chasing her through the trees, of running her to ground and gaining her submission by any means necessary consume me like a wildfire.

By the time I crest the hill, my anger-ridden lust is at a fever pitch, and all I can think of is her writhing in ecstasy – under me, over me, on her hands and knees before me – pinned down by my cock, so it takes a moment for the sight of her riderless horse to register with me.

The fervor cools. *Has she been thrown?* A touch of panic pings behind my breastbone as I scan the shallow valley below. Son of a twisted womb. She's there, nowhere near her horse, with her hand outstretched to Venna.

What in the name of the Abyss is she doing?

More panic pings in my chest. Only a sliver of Venna is domesticated. The wolf could just as easily make a meal of Rina as let herself be scratched behind the ears. Not wanting to spook the wolf or the woman, I don't call out and I hold Nightshade to a slow descent.

Venna, who blatantly ignores me, pushes her head against Rina's hand, allowing herself to be fawned over like a lap dog. The beauty of the woman's answering smile only adds to my ire. She has no right to be so . . . *appealing.*

She speaks in a whisper as if not wanting to break the spell she's cast over the wolf. "This is incredible."

"Incredible, you mean, that you still have all your fingers? Yes, it is."

Venna, making a complete liar out of me, cranes her neck in an attempt to get the right spot rubbed. "You're not going to bite me, are you, Venna?" Rina coos. "She likes me."

"You're both fools," I grouse, trying to beat back the need to discipline my princess. Preferably before I lay her out and fuck her hard and deep . . . or maybe after. "The only one with any sense is your horse."

Grimacing, Rina puts her free hand to her brow and combs the landscape. "Yes, I may have underestimated Glory's reaction to the wolf." She looks up and my expression catches her off guard. "You're angry."

"I should be." I dismount and give Nightshade a smack on the rump so he jumps forward. "They will gradually drift together when Venna leaves and Glory is calmer. Until then, we walk."

"Gladly," she says, her smile returning as she gives Venna a final pat and we set off. "I never knew to appreciate such freedoms until I no longer had them."

Her simple sincerity isn't accusatory, but it banks some of my smoldering wrath. "You shouldn't have gone so far," I accuse.

She cranes her neck to see me, and the alluring contrast of her golden eyes against her light brown skin does nothing to settle me. Neither does the sight of her wetting her lips nervously under my scrutiny. I'd like nothing more than to pull her up against me and taste that mouth again.

"Luka, I told you I'm not going to run, and I meant it."

I grunt like the barbarian she sees me as, then I ask her what's been needling me for the last hour. "Tell me how you learned to shoot a bow so well. Do they teach ladies such things in D'heilar?"

"Not hardly. After my mother was killed, I was sent to a farming outpost in the far south."

I wait for more but it doesn't come, and I'm forced to prod. "And?"

"And I was put to work where work needed doing. I learned all kinds of unladylike things there; peeling potatoes, plucking fowl, emptying chamber pots, mucking stables." Then, as if realizing her opportunity to plead her case, she goes on with, "I told you I can work. I can be useful."

I ignore the appeal. "That doesn't explain the shooting. You were a prisoner and yet they put a weapon in your hand?"

"Oh, well, there were special circumstances in the case of the bow and arrow."

"Such as?"

She chews at her thumb nail as if considering her answer.

"Just give me the truth."

Tugging the hem of her dress out from under the toes of her boots before her next step, she sighs. "Yes, I suppose the truth will serve us best."

I see now that the dress is too long for her and I make a mental note to –

"I had a lover for a time."

My thoughts splinter. "You *what?*"

She arches a brow. "I had a lover. I'm twenty-one, Luka, not twelve."

I force my feet to keep moving even as my hands curl into fists with the absurd need to pulverize this so-called lover. "When was this?"

She has the nerve to laugh. "Two years ago, my deve.

There's no need for your jealousy."

"Jealousy?" I sputter." Surely you jest." Though any other plausible explanation is elusive. "Anyway, what does this lover have to do with learning how to handle a bow?"

"Oh, in exchange for my favors, I asked him to teach me."

Something catches in my chest. *In exchange for her favors?* "I thought women only did that kind of thing for love."

Gazing down at the ground, she shakes her head like I'm being silly. "If only the world were a gentler place." She leans over and picks a stem of long grass, twirling it between her delicate fingers.

"But it's not."

"No, it's not. Love never entered into my bargain with Roland."

I huff with disgust and she pins me with a suddenly hostile look.

"I wanted to be able to defend myself."

"You don't have to justify your actions to me."

"No, I don't," she slings back. "So you can keep your *disappointment* to yourself."

"What?"

She tsks. "What was that reaction, then? Horror? Revulsion?"

"Why would I be horrified by your intelligence?" This woman makes no sense. "You used a situation to your benefit. That's to be commended not condemned."

"Then why the –"

"Would you stop? It's the sordid details of your lover I don't need."

Her face pinches. "What details? There were no details."

"His name is definitely a detail."

Her tetchiness morphs into disbelief before finally landing on . . . smug. *Smug?*

"You *are* jealous," she exclaims.

I snort, but inside, my stomach flips. "No. I just have no desire to hear about a man who needs to *trade things* to entice a woman into his bed."

"Oh, we never used a bed."

My temper flares red-hot now. I'm on the verge of letting her have it when I catch her lip-twitch in my periphery. "You're toying with me," I say incredulously.

Laughter bubbles from her throat. "Yes, Luka, I'm toying with you. Who knew you'd be so easy to tease?"

The sound of her happiness blunts some of the sharp edges scraping at my mood, but still I mutter, "Insolent little wench. How many times do I have to warn you that I –" I pull up short, noticing her uneven stride. "Are you limping?"

She shrugs, not stopping. "It's to be expected when one is stabbed in the leg."

"You know, your sarcasm is not as delightful as you think it is."

"Are you sure about that, Luka?" She grins. "I think you might secretly like it."

This woman. "How is it you're the only person in this realm who dares to openly mock me?"

"I do not mean to mock you, my deve," she claims with a smile. "I'm simply making conversation."

Somehow, I doubt that.

"May I ask you something? Yvette mentioned that you cannot relinquish the title peacefully. Is that true?"

Relinquish? "You and your high-born words," I grumble. "But if I understand your meaning, then yes, it's true. Once a deve, always a deve . . . until death. Until someone challenges me and wins."

"Have you ever been challenged?"

"No."

"Do you expect to be?"

"Why all the questions?"

"Well, my fate is in your hands. It's not unreasonable for me to want to understand your situation, is it?"

"I suppose not." I pause, then come out with, "And every deve is challenged eventually."

A gust of wind lifts her long black hair, and she gathers it at her nape. "Do you know who it will be?"

"For now, there have been no rumblings from within the Range that I'm aware of."

"A challenge would only come from the warriors?"

I look at her askance. *How can she be so ignorant of our ways?* "Yes, of course. A mere farmer isn't likely to best me with a sword, now is he?"

"True." She ponders that for a bit before she comes up with, "Does this system not overlook those with weak sword arms but sharp minds?"

Something resembling a laugh rumbles out of me. "A sharp mind is wasted in a weak body since a deve must defend himself and the realm."

"I see."

She does? Then why does something about her tone suggest otherwise. I don't get the chance to ask her, though, because she's not done with her questions yet.

"How did you know to search the Cyrun house?"

"Oh, I didn't. We were going over our strategy to question Cayson when Noé suggested that maybe the brothers had been paid. I thought it unlikely, but I was . . . wrong."

Her giggle pulls my surprised gaze in her direction, where I find mirth written into every line of her beautiful features. "Does it actually pain you to admit such a thing?"

I feel so at ease that I almost chuckle along with her. "Maybe a little. My father raised me to believe a deve is never wrong."

Humming her understanding, she holds out her hand for me to steady her as she goes over a fallen log. "Yes, I've heard he was all softness and warmth."

This time, I don't hold back the laugh.

"You *do* like my sarcasm," she crows good-naturedly, sliding her fingers from my hand to the crook of my elbow. "Is it true, then?"

"What? About my father? Definitely."

Her levity fades. "Was he at least good to you if not those around him?"

"Fuck no. There was not a decent bone in the man's body."

"I'm sorry, Luka."

"Don't feel sorry for me. I learned to adapt. It was my mother who suffered most."

She goes quiet after that and I suddenly regret the serious turn in our conversation. Repressing a sigh, I reassure her by covering the hand that's in the crook of my arm. Her fingers are slightly chilled so I leave my hand there.

"I remember my father as a kind man," she says hesitantly after a time. "But most of my memories are second-hand because I was so young when he was taken from us."

The sadness in her tone almost has me wanting to pull her into my arms, or at least to say something comforting, but my mind can't come up with a single thing. I'm relieved when she finally keeps talking.

"My parents were very much in love." She stops walking and her stalled momentum brings me around to face her. "I can't imagine how my father's being violent would have changed the entire foundation of my life."

I make an attempt to do just that. Imagine how my life would have been different if my sire had been loving instead of abusive, or even rational instead of mad . . . and I can't do it. The whole idea is outlandish. My memories of him only involve fear and loathing.

I'm startled as she presses a warm palm to my jaw. "At least he didn't succeed."

"Huh?" I'm so disconcerted by her touch that I can't follow her meaning. "Succeed at what?"

She strokes my beard and my knees weaken. Her tenderness is almost more than I can bear. "Turning you into a man like him, without a decent bone in his body."

I blink, then disbelief rumbles its way out of me in the form of a guffaw. "You of all people should know that's not true." I take hold of her wrist and slowly pull her hand away to put a stop to the dizzying pleasure.

"Luka, I've known true malice and you don't even come close." The compliment has my gut quivering with even more pleasure.

"Yes," I say wryly, not wanting her to notice how she affects me. "I'm as pleasant as a summer stream."

She giggles some more and says something about me being as sarcastic as she is, but then a soft sound of pain draws my attention to her now more obvious lopsided gait. Shit. I let out a shrill whistle and Nightshade raises his head from where he's grazing on what's left of the summer's grass. Sure enough, Glory has joined him, and with Venna gone, she dutifully follows when he makes his way toward us.

"You need to rest," I tell Rina.

She balks at the idea. "No, I'm fine."

"Rina –"

"I'm *not* going back."

At her unyielding tone, my brows lift. "Ever?"

The mulish jut of her chin doesn't abate.

"All right," I concede. "We won't make it to the lake, but –"

"We'll make it to the lake fine."

"Would you let me finish?! We won't make it to the lake, but we don't have to go back to the stronghold yet. Will you ride with me on Nightshade or –"

"No," she says obstinately, reaching for Glory's reins. "If you help me up, I'll be fine."

"She'll be fine," I mutter. The woman is truly impossible. Her pride is prickly enough to rival a bramble patch. If I get any closer, I'll surely die of a thousand tiny cuts.

She lifts a foot like I'm supposed to lace my fingers together and boost her up. I shake my head with exasperation. I'd wager the resulting strain on her thigh would turn that slight sheen of sweat on her brow into actual droplets. Putting my hands around her waist, I simply lift her onto the horse's back.

Her surprise becomes a wry grin as, from her new perch, she says, "Being so big must often be convenient."

For a moment, I get caught up in her. *Why is it so compelling to watch her face come alive with whatever she's feeling?* I think I even look forward to the mystery of what will come next . . . I grimace. *What has come over me?*

"Perhaps Elsy has a tonic for that."

I shake my head as if to clear it. "What?"

"A tonic," she repeats. "My mother used to feed me a good dose of prunes when I was little. But maybe Elsy has a version that would serve you."

It takes a few heartbeats for me to grasp her meaning before my lips reluctantly tip up at the corners. "Is that so?"

"Yes, I think it may remedy all the scowling you do." Her contemplative tone only serves to tug my lips into an actual smile as she gathers her dress and carefully gets her leg over the saddle to sit astride.

Allowing her to continue to openly poke fun at me is probably a mistake. I should put her in her place. I should drain the piss and vinegar right out of her. I should. But I don't and it's for purely selfish reasons. The way she comes to life when she teases me is addictive.

I mount Nightshade and she follows me back the way we came, not complaining about our direction despite probably worrying that I'm taking her back to the stronghold. She'll eventually learn I'm not a man who goes back on his word. I worry, though, that time will run out. Despite the proof of the Cyrun brothers' betrayal, I know that either freeing Amarinata D'heilar or simply marrying her without some kind of retribution will breed serious discontent, discontent that I heard with my own ears only an hour ago in the stronghold's courtyard.

While I am mostly certain of the Range's loyalty to me, here in the Mountain Lion Realm, we can be a vengeful lot. Something tells me that if I want to keep my own life, I won't only have to make an example of Cayson, but also of the princess.

The very thought is abhorrent. And my mind begins to twist and turn to find a way around such a roadblock.

I'm grateful when we break through the trees and I spot Eldon and his oldest son inside the open doors of their barn, brushing down his untacked horse, Fearmonger. I dismount and Rina asks hesitantly, "Why are we here?"

"We're here for dinner," I say, reaching to help her down. "You're not too high-born to eat in a humble home, are you?"

She shoots me a quelling look and whispers, "Don't be an ass, Deve."

"Behave, little raven," I warn, though I'm sure my smirk ruins the effect.

The door to the house opens and Daysa appears with little Trudy at her side. The child comes running. "Uncle!" I catch her up in my arms. "Have you come to visit?" she asks, beaming at me. Then she notices Rina. "Who's that?"

"Her name is Rina."

Trudy continues to smile as Rina gives her a little wave. "Is she your intended?"

"Intended?" I laugh. "And where did you learn that word?"

"Mama. Mama says you'll be married by the new moon."

Daysa titters, stepping forward to take her daughter. "Children say such silly things, my deve."

"Only children?"

Trudy squirms out of her mother's arms to stand squarely in front of Rina, taking her hand in hers. Trudy studies their joined hands, probably noticing the differences in their skin tones before she finally says, "Would you like some goat's milk? I milked Patty myself."

There's almost a collective exhale. I think we were all waiting for something outrageous to come out of her mouth. But in her childish wisdom, Trudy has proven us all fools. If only everyone were as accepting as this four-year-old girl.

Rina looks first to me for permission, appearing to be at a loss for words for once. I nod as Trudy starts to pull her toward the house. Daysa jumps to follow them. "Or there's mulled wine, my lady," she calls.

CHAPTER 13

RINA

The little girl chatters excitedly as she tows me inside the house. Letting go of my hand, she runs past a large open spit in the middle of the room, where a pig is roasting, to pull out a chair from a dining table. "You can sit here, Rina," she announces.

"Trudy!" her mother practically yelps. "You will address the lady as *a'Deve.*"

"Oh, no, certainly not," I say quickly. "My name is Rina."

"But –"

"No, please. I insist. And you're Eldon's wife?"

The woman bows her head in deference. "Yes, I'm Day-sa."

"Thank you for having me to your home. I'm very pleased

to meet you." My eyes must bulge at the sight of the child struggling to pour a cup of something from a large earthen ware jug because Daysa lurches forward just in time to stop the spill.

At the very least I expect to witness a scolding, but am pleasantly surprised when she only helps her child complete the task. "Would you care to sit . . . Rina?" Daysa's tongue trips over my name, seeming uneasy with the informal address.

Smiling brightly, I limp my way across the hard-packed dirt floor to the table, ignoring the brutal ache in my leg.

"Are you hurt?" Trudy asks.

"I'm fine," I assure her, taking the proffered seat. "I just rode my horse a bit too hard and now I'm sore."

"Oh." A line forms between her brows, making her appear adorably grown-up. "Papa says I can't ride the pony yet. But *Donny's* allowed to," she informs me bitterly.

"Donny's your brother?"

"Yes. His real name is Eldon like my Pa's, but that's confusing, so we call him Donny. He's a whole year older than me. I wish it was the other way around. If I was older, I wouldn't lord it over him like he does to me. But Mama says that boys are sometimes very competitive. Do you have a brother?"

"Ah, no, not anymore."

The sweet girl nods gravely with understanding. "A brother of mine died last year. I don't much remember him, but Mama and Papa were ever so sad. Mama says sadness isn't bad, but that I shouldn't let it swallow me." She lets out a giggle, going from serious to light-hearted in a single heartbeat. "That sounds so silly, doesn't it? Like it's a monster under the bed."

From there she launches into a treatise on Patty the goat,

and I can't help but be completely charmed by her. I'm sure little Trudy would talk until the sun rose tomorrow if it weren't for a baby's squawk coming from a back room.

"Trudy, bring me the baby, please," Daysa says, and as soon as Trudy leaves, she exchanges the cup of milk in front of me with one filled with warm, fragrant wine. "This will help with the leg." She gives me a conspiratorial wink and my heart tugs at her kindness.

"Thank you," I say, lifting the cup. I allow myself a few sips of delectably strong and spicy wine while I take in the room, which has a homey, lived-in feel. The large, open stone hearth where the pig is roasting is the focal point of the room. I follow the trajectory of the smoke curling its way up to an opening in the thatched roof. It lets some light in, but with the only window shuttered tight against the cold and only a few lit candles on the table, much of the room remains in shadow. I can make out a spinning wheel and behind that, a large frame for weaving though.

Daysa sits across from me, taking up a knife to continue her task of cutting up carrots. "How can I help you?" I ask.

"You can stay right there," she tells me, wiping at a wisp of blonde hair that's come free from the braids she has arranged in a crown. "You're our guest."

Trudy emerges from the back of the house, struggling under the weight of an infant. Scared she's going to drop him, I get up to take the child. The baby stares closely at me, probably because my face is not one he recognizes, then grabs a lock of my loose hair and stuffs it in his mouth. I laugh, retaking my seat as Daysa comes for her son. "Oh, may I hold him?" I ask, hoping she doesn't hear the pleading in my tone. She doesn't know me and has no reason to trust me with her child.

"You *want* to hold him?" she says, sounding doubtful as

she pulls my wine out of the baby's reach.

"If I may."

Shrugging, she goes to a work bench set against the wall and returns with a bowl containing what must be mashed carrots and turnips. "He mostly likes to feed himself," she warns as the little boy reaches eagerly and fists some mash.

Trudy, not wanting to be left out, climbs onto the chair next to me and proceeds to list her brothers' shortcomings, the worst of which is their lamentable gender. Soon I forget my troubles and the pain in my thigh, and I enjoy myself more than I have in years. Daysa and her children are sweet and sociable and I don't remember being so readily accepted anywhere in my life. I learn that Eldon and Daysa have been married since they were eighteen and it's obviously a happy union. She speaks of Eldon with loving exasperation and I admit it sparks a twinge of jealousy in my heart. I very much wish I could claim such an experience for my memories.

It must be the influence of the mulled wine, but when Eldon and his son come in from the cold, followed by Luka, I smile at my betrothed with genuine warmth. I may not have someone who will greet me with a loving kiss like Eldon does Daysa, but I do have a grumpy someone who almost beat a man to death in my name. Things could be worse. Much worse.

And my smile only grows broader as Trudy runs for him again, yelling, "Uncle Luka!" He lifts her up high into the air, setting off shrieks of happiness from the girl. Once she's settled on his hip, he seeks me out as if to reassure himself I haven't run off. He doesn't get a chance to say anything, though, because the baby lets out a loud screech of joy at all the commotion.

"Well," Daysa says. "If little Anton thinks we should have more wine, I don't see how we can refuse." She pours the men their cups as Luka sets Trudy down so he can sit next to me.

From his spot at the head of the table, Eldon takes a long swallow, then gives his youngest son, who's still on my lap, a once over. "Ah, Anton, messing up the ladies already, I see."

I giggle, re-directing the baby's mash-filled fist to his own mouth. "He just likes to share, don't you, little man?"

Luka pulls a clump of squishy carrot from my hair and, his expression softer than I've ever seen it, offers it to Anton.

It becomes apparent that Trudy's penchant for talk comes from her father. Eldon ultimately takes over the conversation and has us all laughing with his jokes and affectionate banter. Much to my delight, Luka isn't safe from his cousin's teasing. And even better, Luka not only allows it, but needles Eldon right back. I barely recognize him as the man I've gotten to know over the past almost three weeks. He's relaxed and open . . . and his laugh. Mother help me, but his laugh is rich and deep, which makes it almost impossible to keep my eyes off of him. And every time he catches me staring, I blush. I can only hope that the wine and the low lighting camouflage the effect he has on me.

By the time dinner is ready, I'm on the other side of tipsy and inordinately pleased that Daysa lets me help her serve the food. It's wonderful to feel included.

Placing a trencher filled with roast pork, potatoes, and carrots in front of Luka, I lean into him subtly. "My deve." Our eyes meet and I swear I see want there.

"Princess," he rumbles, "are you well?"

"Yes," I reply innocently. "Why do you ask?"

He quirks a brow. "No reason. Get your food and come and eat with me."

Goodness but the man is handsome. "Okay."

Eldon's booming laugh fills the room, scaring me.

"You can keep your mouth shut," Luka tells him, his voice all jagged edges.

"I haven't said a single word, cousin," Eldon shoots back. "Actually, I think I've held back so well all evening that you'll be sending over another jug of this fine drink we've been enjoying."

"We'll see."

I'm not sure what they're talking about, but I smile anyway, happily muddled by the wine. When I finally sit with my food and take my first bite, I moan. "Ohhh. This is so good."

Eldon lets loose another half-drunken laugh. "Does the deve not feed you, Rina?"

"Oh, you know," I say with a slight wave of my hand. "I'm sure I eat better than the pigs themselves, but this," I take another bite, "is divine."

Through gritted teeth, Luka says, "I found out Noé had her on prisoner's rations."

Eldon winces. "Remind me never to get on that man's bad side. He can be a right bastard when the mood strikes."

Dinner is a boisterous affair, one I enjoy more than any other in my life. Even when Luka says I've had enough wine. Even when Eldon makes fun of my southern accent. Even when Trudy asks when we're to be married. I love every moment.

Later, after the children are put to bed in the back room, Eldon pulls Daysa down onto his lap and begins to whisper sweet nothings to her.

I turn away to give them privacy, but Luka chokes on a laugh. "Are three children not enough for you, cousin?"

"Not nearly." He doesn't bother to lift his head from Day-

---

sa's neck. "You'll see."

"See what?" Luka swirls the last of his wine in his cup.

"See that there's *nothing* better than fucking a baby into your woman's belly."

My mouth falls open and the low-level arousal I've been feeling all night ratchets up a few notches.

"Well," Luka drawls. "As much as I'd like to stay and watch this play out, I'll take that as our cue to leave."

Daysa's intoxicated titters are overshadowed by Eldon's possessive growl as he pulls his wife closer. "You weren't invited to watch. Though I'm sure you'd learn a thing or two."

Luka pushes to his feet as he laughs, and again, I marvel at the sound. "Cousin, I suppose if I were to take lessons, it would be from you since there's so much proof of your expertise."

Clearly pleased, in a drunk, glassy-eyed kind of way, Eldon reaches for the hem of his wife's dress. Daysa swats at his hand good-naturedly, saying, "For the love of all that is sacred, go and saddle the horses, while I fetch a cloak for our a'deve."

My protestations that I don't need one go unheeded as Eldon and Luka slip out into the night to ready the horses and Daysa disappears into the back room. When she returns, I'm studying the half-finished fabric on her loom. She's woven a clever pattern into her work. "This is beautiful," I tell her, skimming the wool with my fingertips.

"Thank you."

"I can spin like most women, but I haven't had much opportunity to learn to weave. Do you think you could teach me if the opportunity presented itself?"

"Oh, well I, I wouldn't –" she stammers.

My stomach sinks as I hold up my hand to stop her. "I'm

sorry. I presume much."

"No, it's not that. It's just you are the a'deve and," she lowers her voice, "a princess. Such work is beneath you, is it not?"

Under the wine's influence, I sway a bit, smiling ruefully. "Everyone is under the impression I've come from a life of luxury. But I assure you, I've worked every day for most of my life."

Once her surprise fades, she lifts a hand to squeeze my arm as if in solidarity. "Then, I'd be honored to teach you all that I know. Now, let's not keep the men waiting. I don't wish to bank Eldon's passion." She gives me a saucy wink and my heart leaps with the knowledge that we have a chance at becoming friends.

The cold air greets me like a slap as we step outside, but my steps falter for another reason. The night sky. It's as if the Mother herself has painted it with swathes of blue and green.

"It's an auspicious night, indeed," Daysa says from beside me, "if we're to be graced with the northern lights."

"It's incredible," I breathe as the light slowly shifts across the sky. "Does this happen often?"

"No, not often. A few times each winter season maybe." I startle as she takes my elbow. "Come. They grow impatient."

With my eyes glued to the sky, I'm not sure how I make it to the barn without stumbling.

"We bid you a good night," Daysa says, handing me the cloak.

"Oh, thank you for the offer, but I'm fine."

Luka steps forward. "Give it to me."

"I'll see you tomorrow, Luka," Eldon says, then gives me

an incline of his head. "A'Deve."

They start back to the house and my manners come back to me in a rush. "Thank you for a wonderful evening," I call and Daysa gives me a final wave. The thump of the bar being lowered on the inside of their door echoes through the clearing, but I'm too busy gaping at the sky once again to give it much notice.

"You've never seen this before?" Luka asks, drawing my focus back to his solid, inimitable presence.

"No, it's magnificent." *Like you,* I think, taking in his broad frame.

His nostrils flare. "You've been looking at me like that all night," he accuses.

I swallow hard. "And how's that?" I whisper.

His brows lift ever so slightly as if daring me to continue with my charade, but I refuse to back down even when he prowls forward, throwing the borrowed cloak over Nightshade's back. "You know exactly how." He comes so close that I have to keep raising my chin until I can feel the warmth radiating from his chest on my throat.

He runs a single, callused finger from my temple down over my cheekbone to my jaw, causing a shiver that has nothing to do with the cold. The caress doesn't end there, but continues down the side of my neck and skims along the fur collar of my vest. The thick leather creaks as his fingers hook into the neckline and slowly pull me forward until I'm flush against him. "There it is again . . . that look." The low pitch of his voice settles like a warm weight between my thighs.

My heart beats madly as his other hand wraps around my waist to pull me in more tightly, letting the obvious ridge of his length come to rest against my belly. "Do you feel that, little raven?" He curls his hips into me. "That look of yours does things to me."

Feeling completely overwhelmed, I can barely breathe as the hand at my collar slides around my neck to the hair at my nape. He holds me there, vibrating with need, just staring at my lips, for what feels like an eternity before his mouth finally descends on mine. It's worth the wait. He's hungry and insistent as he plunders my mouth. I revel in the aggression which is in stark contrast to the softness of his lips and the lush taste of the wine. My knees turn to water and my mind spins endlessly on the thrill of it all.

Luka is kissing me.

After long moments, we settle into delicious nips and grazes and nibbles and my fingers dance their way up his arms, tracing each muscle and tendon through his thin shirt, until they reach his neck.

Then our tongues meet and the shimmering desire explodes inside of me. I become desperate for him, needing him closer. I'm not sure if I mean to pull him down or pull myself up, but I pull. And my efforts are rewarded as he hoists me up with an arm under my bottom.

Our lips break apart and his dark, lust-drenched expression comes into view. *Is he . . . angry?* I want no part of that, so I nuzzle into his neck, filling my lungs with his scent.

"Damn you. I –" His words cut off when I suckle at the spot below his ear, letting my tongue taste his skin.

"Hmmmm, damn me for what, you big brute?" I bite him gently, causing his breath to hitch. "You can't deny you want me just as badly as I want you."

"This isn't right. You –"

Not wanting to hear a list of my inadequacies, I re-seal

my lips to his. And this time, the kiss escalates quickly. We're soon panting into each other's mouths, sucking on tongues and bruising lips, completely lost in each other. The heat in my core becomes so insistent that I attempt to get my good leg around his hip. If I don't get some friction to my clit, I'm going to be devoured by the heat of our own making.

He bites my lip. "Quit your wriggling."

"No," I rasp. I can feel his throbbing erection against my thighs. "You promised me a *discussion.*" Struggling against the skirt of my dress to get my leg up only aggravates him more. Suddenly we're moving and he plants my ass on a rung of the ladder leaned up against the side of the barn.

He barely gives me a second to find my bearings before he's gathering up the material of my skirt. "Wha . . ." I grab onto his shoulders to steady myself.

"You're right. I did promise you a *discussion.*" His fierce tone sends a pinch of misgiving all the way to my toes. *He wouldn't hurt me, would he?* But once my skirt is hiked up over my lap and he presses his hand to the apex of my thighs, my worries disintegrate.

"Oh, fuck," I breathe.

The pressure turns into slow, languorous circles. Without the ladder to hold me up, I'm sure I'd melt into a puddle at his feet. The soft surface of the buckskin is perfect to drive me mad.

He leans into my ear. "Is this what you've wanted all night long? Me with my fingers on your cunt."

I curl my arms around his neck, burying my nose in his neck as another slow circle has me almost coming out of my skin.

"I think it is," he taunts. "Your eyes have been begging

for this." His wicked fingers slide up to the laces. "Or maybe you've been begging for my fingers *in* your cunt?" He slowly unties them to push his way in between the leather and my curls.

He makes contact with my clit and I cry out, my heart rate soaring with how good it is.

"Oh, shit. You're wet. So fucking wet."

He works his big callused palm further into my leggings, cupping me, almost sending me right over the edge. Never have a felt anything like this, like the Mother has set me on fire and now she's waiting for me to burn up. I rock into his hand, seconds away from doing just that.

"No," I whine when the pressure lets up.

"Hush."

"No, I – ahhh!"

A blunt finger explores my folds and I become a mess of unintelligible ecstasy as he slowly pushes it into me. "Oh, yes," he rumbles. *"Exactly* what you've wanted from me."

The feel of his finger inside of me is beyond divine. There's not much room for either of us to maneuver but my hips twist and buck, desperately trying to urge him on. "Stop squirming," he orders, wrapping a hand around the front of my throat to push me back so he can look me in the eye.

"Please, Luka," I plead, faint with desire.

"Please, what?" he demands, his expression intensifying as if my begging is to be enjoyed or even savored. It sends a tremor rippling through my core. He must feel it because he applies a bit more pressure to my neck. Sweet bliss. I arch. "Yes, I need –"

"No," he announces hotly. "You *need* whatever I give

you. Nothing more. Nothing less.""

The objections on my tongue disappear as he pushes the heel of his hand hard into my clit, driving his finger deeper. *Yes!* Another squeeze to my neck. The animal need to chase down my climax consumes me. He squeezes again and I take hold of his forearm, dying for that last final bit of something that will set me off.

CHAPTER 14

LUKA

In the glow of the northern lights, she's magnificent; wanton, desperate, about to dip her toes into a very deep pool of rapture. Her tight cunt is slippery and spasming at even the slightest movement of my hand – either the one with the finger inside of her or the one wrapped around her neck. Vaguely I recall Eldon's hell-cat comment and feel a smirk tug at my lips. Hell-cat, indeed. This side of her is too good to be true.

"Be still," I order when she continues to roll her hips, but with her eyes at half-mast and her breathing heavy, she pays me no mind. I give her a shake. "I said be still or you'll get nothing."

Finally acknowledging me, she grips my arm more tightly. "Fuck you," she gasps as another twinge squeezes the finger I've got tucked up inside her. My cock throbs with the insult. So defiant at every turn, my delicious little raven. Though there's not much room in her pants, I partially withdraw my finger from her depths.

"No," she wails, but it dies off as I add another finger to the first and shove them both into her. We both revel in the stretch. "Fuuuuck," she moans.

Dammit, why did I choose to do this here? I need her sprawled across my bed, naked and completely at my mercy, where I can play with her, bringing her to the edge over and over before I drive into her in every imaginable position, in every possible hole. The prospect causes heat to swamp me from head to toe. I quit playing around. Squeezing her neck a little tighter, I thrust my hand up into her again and again until she topples over into oblivion.

It doesn't take long. She was ripe for it and I devour the sight of her body shuddering and her features going slack. As she comes down off her high, looking small and vulnerable, the need to protect her buds to life. My palm slides from her throat to the back of her neck and I cuddle her against my chest. Over my shoulder, I scan the yard, but it's empty of any movement except for the horses. A little aftershock clutches at my fingers and I realize I'm still buried inside of her. Reluctantly, I pull free, setting off a succession of whimpers from her.

"Sshhhh," I soothe, stroking her hip under the dress. "I've got you."

She lifts her chin to nuzzle into my neck and I shiver with the sensation it sends to my painfully hard cock. I am not looking forward to sitting my horse with –

I grunt as she runs a hand over my groin. "Rina," I warn.

"Yes?" Her voice is husky and with her tracing the outline of my very sensitive length along my thigh, I almost give in to what she's suggesting. But this can't happen here. I grab onto her wrist.

"Enough."

She lifts her head, giving me a glimpse of disbelief. "You don't want me to . . ."

"No."

My stony response kindles a flash of hurt before she wipes it away. "Suit yourself." She draws herself up and reaches for the laces of her pants.

When I swat her hands away, her prickly temper renews itself. "Luka, I can do it."

"So can I."

Retying the strings, I watch her shoulders sag as if I've punctured a hole in her fiery demeanor and now it's all draining away. I don't like it.

But if I don't like it, I should explain.

But explain what?

That a hand job will leave me unsatisfied? That I won't have her on her knees in the dirt, blowing me out in the open? That I'm scared I'll *fuck a baby right into her belly* and then have to live with the consequences?

I hold my tongue as I pick her up off the ladder and set her down.

She limps toward Glory and I frown. "You'll ride with me," I tell her, throwing Daysa's cloak around her shoulders.

She trains a weary expression on me. "Can you stop? Not everything out of your mouth has to be an order. It's tiresome."

"As is your wilfulness." I consider her, trying to remember which of her legs is the injured one. "Now –"

"Luka!" she screeches as I lift her up onto Nightshade's

195

saddle without warning. "Luka, I can ride my own damn horse."

Ignoring her, I pull a length of rope from one of my saddle bags and tether Glory. Rina's still carrying on, examining the ground as if it's a solution to her predicament. I wouldn't put it past her to jump down for no other reason than to spite me, but at least I've stoked her fire again.

Planting a foot in the stirrup, I heave myself up behind her and get us situated, arranging both her and my erection into the least uncomfortable position. Her complaints finally settle into a simple glare so I flip the hood of the cloak up over her head and cradle her more fully in my arms.

We set off in peaceable silence, her bow-string taut body slowly relaxing against mine with the sway of the horse. I should have guessed the peace was too good to last.

"Aren't you cold without a cloak?" she asks.

"Wouldn't you prefer the quiet of the night?"

She fiddles with the sleeve of my shirt. "Humor me? The effects of the wine are wearing off and my leg is sore. I need the distraction."

I let out a put-upon sigh. "No, I'm not cold."

The blessed silence lasts but a minute when she tries again. "These northern lights, are they a presage of good or ill?"

Presage? Where does she come up with such words? Though I suppose her meaning is clear enough with *good or ill*. "It depends."

More quiet until a noise of disgust spoils it.

"Really, Luka. Can't you even try?"

"What, woman?" I demand, exasperated. "What do you want me to say?"

Tipping her chin up, she becomes annoyed when the hood blocks her view of me so she shoves it back. "I just want to know if these lights bode well for us or not? Is that too much to ask?"

"And I told you, it depends."

"On what?!"

"On whether you believe the souls of the dead wish us good or ill."

"Oh."

"Yeah, oh." I guide Nightshade into the forest and the blue and green of the sky fades to an ethereal glow, filtered through the evergreens' branches.

"Do you think they wish us well?"

I resign myself to this conversation she's determined to have. "Maybe. If they're not snickering with the Fates for creating our problems in the first place."

She lets out a cross between a sigh and a hum, something that doesn't tell me if she agrees with me or not. I'm sure she's planning out how to prove my answer is flawed . . . and oddly enough, I'm not opposed to hearing her clever comeback. Except, when it finally comes, it's not a retort at all.

"Luka?"

The hesitant note in her voice has me glancing down to check that she's all right. "Hmmm?" I coax when she doesn't speak, better arranging the cloak to cover her legs against the dropping temperature.

"What do you think happens when we die?"

I snort. "What do I *think* or what do I *know?*"

"Since corpses don't generally share their experiences with the living, nobody can *know,* can they?"

Her sarcasm pulls at my lips and I press my cheek to her temple. I really do love her fire.

"According to the Mother," she starts. "We live on in the Eternal, but what if that's only a fable to comfort the dying and the grief stricken?" Her voice drops. "What if we're just gone?"

My little raven fears death. But don't we all? "Well, if we're just gone, then we're just gone. There's nothing to fear in that, because fear itself would cease."

She seems to mull that over. "You're a wiser man than I took you for."

I laugh, and Glory tosses her head, pulling on the tether. "Flattery? Really, Rina?"

"I mean it! What you say makes sense. Even if I won't be with my family again, I won't be without them either."

A shadow eases its way over my soul as I realize she's applying my *wisdom* to herself in a very specific way. My mouth opens to quiz her further when the sound of loud voices in the distance weaves itself through the trees. Rina stiffens in my arms.

I halt Nightshade in the shadows well before the main road to the stronghold. Though I doubt there's any danger, there's no sense in throwing ourselves out into the open without knowing more about the situation. From what I can tell, there are more than two men, something that has my right hand checking that my dagger and my axe are on my belt where they should be. Not ideal to take on multiple men, but –

I halt this useless thinking. I am not going into battle. I realize it's Rina and her skittish unease that have my instincts on high alert.

"Rina."

It's like she can't hear me because all her attention is fixed in the direction of the advancing men. She's scared.

"Rina," I repeat, this time more forcefully, startling her. "I want you to look at me." Reluctantly, she turns, giving me an eyeful of pure dread. "You have nothing to fear. You're safe with me."

Doubt shines back at me. I think I'm offended. "Don't you remember my speech? I am deve here," I say, mimicking myself in a low whisper. It gets a small smile from her. "Well, I *am* deve here. If I say you're safe, you're safe."

A burst of drunken laughter makes her jump and she cranes her neck back around, trying to locate the source. I place a finger under her chin and pull her gaze back to me. "Whoever they are, they'll never lay a hand on you. Okay? They won't even come close."

She gives me a jerky nod and we go back to watching the road through the trees.

When they come around the bend, I count four of them. They're all Range warriors and from what I can tell, all well into their cups. As they draw nearer, I recognize them individually. They all came up under my father and tend to be the ones who grumble the loudest about my rule. Scanning the group, I pick out their weapons, noting they're armed as I am, with daggers and hatchets, except one man who carries his sword. *Within the realm? During peaceful times?* But Dumfries isn't the oldest active member of the Range for no reason. He's wily and always ready.

I've decided to let them pass when I spot a woman riding pillion behind one of the men. She's wearing nothing but a night rail, her long brown hair unbound, her bare shins and feet reflecting in the blue-green light. She looks miserable.

"You will remain silent, Rina," I tell her in a quiet, no nonsense voice as I kick Nightshade forward, coming out on the road behind the men. They may be inebriated, but they're still Range warriors and the noise of our horses has them turning in their saddles as one.

"Deve?" Gore asks, squinting at us, his dagger already in his hand.

"It's me," I confirm as their horses come to a stop.

"Is there something we can help you with, Deve?" Dumfries asks, tacking on my title like he always does, as if it's an afterthought. I don't miss the way he surveys Rina with interest.

"You," I call, lifting my chin to the girl. "What's your name?"

"Me, sir?" she squeaks, visibly shivering. On closer inspection, she's even younger than I thought. "Farrana, my deve." She inclines her head deeply in respect.

"How old are you?"

"Uh, sixteen, sir," she says and Rina makes a noise of disgust. I can't say I disagree with her.

"So we'll be on our way," Dumfries says, and then adds, "The ale is flowing in the barracks tonight. Will you be joining us?"

Ignoring them, I continue with the girl. "How did you come to be with these men?"

She ducks her head. "They said if I don't want to share their ale . . ."

"Go on," I insist.

The girl cringes but finally comes out with it. "If I don't want to share their ale, my family's barn may catch fire."

I set my jaw. "Is that right?"

When no one says anything, I survey the men with contempt. "That would be quite a coincidence, wouldn't it?"

Dumfries shrugs.

"Have you no shame?" My rebuke hangs in the frigid air as they exchange uncertain glances. "You'll return her to her home immediately."

"What?" Dumfries sputters. "You have no right!"

"Don't I?"

Like they're boring me, I turn my attention down the road to where the torches light up the waiting gates of the stronghold. I loosen the reins and Nightshade starts forward. When it becomes apparent, I don't plan to go around them, they grudgingly make way. "If the family's property suffers the slightest damage, you will answer to me. If the girl suffers the slightest injury, you will answer to me. You are men of the Range. Act like it."

I can tell Rina is holding her breath as we pass among them, and honestly, I almost expect to feel the bite of a dagger in my back. But fuck them. To kill me without challenging me formally would be the height of dishonor. And Eldon, Noé, or even Gray coming to power in my wake wouldn't change that after they were dead in a one-on-one challenge.

Allowing Rina to peek around my arm, I whisper, a laugh in my voice, "Watch the one with the sword. He'll be the first to make a move."

"How can you think this is funny?" she hisses back.

"I told you, I am deve. And that means something."

It takes another minute before she finally reports, "They've gone back the way they came. How did you know they would

201

abide by your orders?"

I blow out a breath. "There is much to consider before a man moves against a deve. And every one of them is older than thirty. It's only the young who loose an arrow with a half-cocked arm." I laugh outright now. "Like I did with my father."

Her scrutiny practically scalds me it burns so brightly. "How old were you?"

"Twenty-two."

"Riders approaching!" is called from the ramparts and I lift my free arm in greeting.

The men on guard duty allow us through the open gates, bowing their heads. "Welcome back, my deve," one of them says, then after a slight hesitation, he adds, "And you, my a'deve."

When I ignore them, Rina feels compelled to answer. "Thank you." I don't reprimand her . . . or the guard. Though I'm still unsure how I feel about this a'deve business that's going around.

The clop of the horses' hooves on the cobbles has the two stable boys on duty come running.

"Grab onto my elbow," I tell Rina, holding my arm high to carefully lower her to the ground while the boys take the reins.

"My deve," one of the boys says as I dismount. "May I speak to the lady?"

In the torchlight, I give him a once-over, but Rina comes forward before I can respond. "Of course you can."

The boy bows his head . . . possibly with more reverence than he granted me. The little shit.

"A'Deve," he says with bemusing excitement. "My brother saw you shoot today from your window and said it was a feat worthy of the Father himself!"

I barely hold in a scoff.

The boy's not done yet though. "My brother also said you were ever so kind to him when they returned the arrows." He gives her another deep inclination of his head.

"Oh?" Rina replies. "Is he one of Rionnon's friends?"

The stable boy nods vigorously. "My mother wishes to thank you for your kindness."

Rina presses her palms to her heart, and in her custom, offers a blessing. "I return the thanks and wish much fortune to you and your family . . ." She pauses. "I'm sorry, I don't know your name."

"Baron, my lady."

"Well, I wish you and your family much good fortune, Baron." She says it with sincerity, like she actually means it, and the boy humiliates himself with all his gushing thanks.

"Just take the horses," I gripe. "And be off."

He snaps to attention. "Yes, Deve." And they lead the horses away.

I offer Rina a dry, "Will her ladyship, the a'deve, need carrying tonight?"

Rolling her eyes, she reaches for my arm. "She will not. But she might need a bit of support." We start across the courtyard to the main doors. "You know, I've tried to discourage everyone from using the title. It wasn't my idea."

When I just grunt at her, she goes on with, "Do most boys' names end in *–on* here?"

"What?"

"Baron, Eldon, Bron, Rionnon, Ion . . . even Carson and Cayson, the bastards. Luka's not short for something, is it?"

I laugh. "It is actually. My name is Lukaron."

"Really?" The blue-green of the sky has faded by now, but her smile, akin to the sun in the dark, seems to light up our surroundings.

"It's better than Amarinata," I grumble, waiting patiently for her to climb the steps.

"If you say so."

Pulling the heavy door open, I watch her pass into the Great Hall under my arm, her smile becoming a giggle. Mother help me, but the sound pulls something very pleasantly taut inside of me.

"Well, well, well," comes from off to our left. "How very touching, the deve and his intended whore."

Rina startles and moves to my back, using me as a shield between herself and Cayson, who's chained to the hearth like the faithless animal he is.

"Shut up, brother!" sounds from the other side of the room and Rina starts again. I turn to send Bron a glare and find him sitting with his oldest brother, Gray, in the almost deserted Great Hall. I don't remember the last time Gray was here.

What happened to Gray a year and a half ago haunts me. Even if he was the victim of my father's crimes, in a sick and twisted way, he committed those crimes for my benefit, and there's no question that I was altered to my very core because of them.

Images of that grisly night do their best to swim to the surface as I head in the brothers' direction, but I shut them down. I have to. Gray already knows how I feel about what happened to him. He doesn't need any reminders.

I throw my leg over the bench and sit beside Bron, my back to the room. "Here to visit the traitor?" I drawl and Bron rubs a hand across his brow, looking stricken. I feel like a heel, but distracting Gray from what may be showing on my face is more important than Bron at the moment.

"Deve," Bron starts, "I want you to know that I played no part in my brothers' scheme. And I wish I'd done more to protect the a'deve, but Noé –"

I lift my hand to silence him. "I never suspected you did, Bron, so stop planting your seeds of doubt in my head and go get me some ale."

"Of course," he says, getting up, relieved to be let off the hook so easily. But it's true, it never crossed my mind that he was involved.

"Oh and a half cup of gut-rot," I call as he slips away to the kitchen.

With no other choice, I finally turn to Gray. He's watching Cayson over my shoulder. "What's going on there?" he asks, lifting his chin. "Why are you not currently balls deep in that? I would be."

"Since I doubt you're referring to your brother, I assume *she's* over there."

"She is. She's looking at the skulls on the wall. So far she's staying out of my brother's reach."

"Yeah, she's not stupid, that one."

"You like her," he accuses with what almost passes for a chuckle.

"Fuck, I don't know. Things are . . . unclear."

He sips from his tankard. "Most of the village hates the idea of an outsider ruling next to you, and they've seized upon

Carson's death as a way to prevent it." He shakes his head. "And this thing with Cayson . . . I don't know, Luka. It's even less popular than she is."

"Surely the bloody coins are proof enough of your brothers' betrayal."

"The coins don't mean much to people. Sure they're interesting, but the idea that they hold value isn't well understood here. It's all foreign manipulation to them."

I scratch at my beard, self-doubt rearing its ugly head. "Fuck. This is why you should have been deve. You never would have let yourself get roped into an arranged marriage to some unknown princess."

"Don't be stupid, Luka. First of all, I was already married, and second, despite my mother's plots, I was never aiming for the title."

If only my father had believed that, I think darkly. Aloud, I say, "Can I count on your support? This will all come to a head sooner or later."

He takes another slow sip of his ale, but remains mum because we're interrupted by, "Disgusting whore!" which echoes off the stone walls.

"I should go over there and finish that filthy rapist right now," I grit out. "Touching what's mine, trying to undermine me instead of facing me like a man. I don't know how you're related to him."

Tankard paused halfway to his lips, he pins me with a scathing look. "The same way you were related to your sire, Luka. The same fucking way."

Shame immediately cools my wrath, and I'm grateful when Rina appears at my side to provide a distraction. I watch her incline her head to Gray in greeting, then say, "My deve?"

She waits for my full attention before she goes on in what I'm sure is her most pleasant tone. "I was wondering if you'd be so kind as to loan me your dagger."

A grin tugs at the corner of my mouth. This woman. "And what would you be needing it for?"

She sits beside me, her back to the table so she can continue to size up her prey. "It seems I've grown weary of the word *whore* this evening."

"And you think a knife is going to cure you of this weariness?" I ask wryly.

She swings her head to face me. "Maybe not, but I doubt it will make it any worse."

I concede her point with a tilt of my head. "I hate to disappoint you, my little raven, but you'll have to wait to watch him suffer. These things must be seen to be done in the proper way."

Huffing with annoyance, she pivots on the bench, carefully getting her wounded leg over to sit facing the proper way.

"A'Deve," Bron greets, returning with the requested tankard of ale and a wooden cup of spirits. He circles the long table to sit next to his brother.

"Here," I say to Rina, plunking the cup down in front of her. "Drink this. It will help with the leg."

She sniffs at it. "What is it?"

"Woman, can you not just do as you're told? Not even once?"

"Probably not." But she takes a drink anyway.

Over her choking and sputtering, I tell Bron and Gray about what happened on the road with Dumfries and his cronies. "So I'll need you to get Elsy to check on the girl tomorrow," I tell Bron. "Her name was Fanny something."

"Fanny?" Bron says doubtfully. "Never heard of a girl with that name."

"Her name was Farrana," Rina rasps, leaning against my arm, still recovering from the rot-gut.

"The candle maker's daughter? Dark hair?"

Rina nods and Bron pulls a face.

"She's still a child practically."

Gray finishes off his drink. "That band will be a problem if you're not careful," he says, pushing to his feet. "Now, I bid you all a good night."

"I'll see you tomorrow at the training ground, Gray," I try, but he walks away without answering. He may never come back to the Range, but it will always be worth the attempt to convince him. "Come, Rina, let's put you to bed."

The stairs prove too much for her and when I sweep her up in my arms, she nestles against my chest. "That was a wonderful thing you did for that girl tonight," she murmurs. "It made my chest swell with pride. Don't let anyone tell you that you're not a good man, Luka. You are."

I snort, though her praise is soothing. "You're too tired to think straight. In the morning, you'll reconsider."

Her soft sigh peters out when I don't continue to climb the stairs. "Where are we going?"

"It's too far into the cold season for you to stay in that room," I tell her, not mentioning how unacceptable it is to me now not to know for sure that she's safe.

Nudging the door open with my boot, I carry her in and find Kata sitting next to the blazing hearth with a needle and thread. She immediately stands, setting her sewing aside.

"Kata, hello," Rina says, lifting her head from my shoulder. "Is it not late for you to still be up?"

The mute woman shakes her head.

"Did you get the things I asked for?" I demand.

She nods vigorously and walks to the bed to show me where a night dress has been laid out, along with woolen socks and another shirt.

"Good. You can go."

Inclining her head, she goes to the bed and throws back the fur cover and the feather-stuffed ticking to show me the heated bricks she's placed in the bed to warm it up. Then she retrieves her sewing and skitters away.

"Luka?" Rina whispers. "Whose room is this?"

"Mine."

"Yours?" She sounds aghast as I set her down on the bed.

"Yes, like you."

She's suddenly much more alert. "Like me, what?"

"You're mine."

Expecting her to blow up at me, I'm taken aback when tears well on her lashes. "You mean that?"

A painful twinge behind my breastbone takes me by surprise. "Are you so disappointed?"

"No, I'm not disappointed!" The tears brim and spill down her cheeks. "I, I'm just . . ."

"Sad?" I provide flatly. *Why did I think she'd be pleased?*

A hysterical little laugh rattles out of her throat. "Sad? No, Luka, I'm so very grateful."

Oh.

Well, grateful is not happy, but it's miles away from dis-appointed or sad, so I guess I'll take it. I take it until she begins to scrabble at the buckles of her leather vest. "What are you doing?"

"I know you said you don't want me like that," she says, giving a hard, frustrated tug at the new leather which is stiff and uncooperative. "But surely there's something I can do for you . . . maybe if you close your eyes and imagine . . ." She abruptly stills and lifts her chin to show me the most tortured expression I've ever witnessed. "Unless you already have someone? Of your own choosing?"

She looks positively ill, which perversely eases some of the conflict raging in me. I even consider letting her believe that I really do have someone. But I think that may actually crush her. She's such a paradox, my little raven. So strong one moment, so vulnerable the next. I gently move her hands and undo the buckles myself.

"Luka," she whispers. "I didn't realize –"

"I don't have a woman."

She sniffles, wiping at her tears with the back of her hand before I push the vest off her shoulders. "You don't?" Her voice is heartbreakingly small.

"No, I don't." I get her to stand and I pull the dress over her head.

"Maybe after I've eaten some more meals?"

What is she on about? I'm more interested in the desire that's re-seeping into my bones. And the need to take care of her. Because she's small and lovely and mine. I crouch down to unlace her boots and toss them aside.

"Maybe," she hesitates, "maybe I'll be more agreeable to you then?"

I get her shirt up and over her head, and she immediately clasps her hands together against her chest, effectively hiding the scars on her ribs and her breasts.

"Agreeable?" I ask, dousing the word with skepticism as I go to work on her soft leggings, reveling in the lingering smell of sex on her skin. When she's naked in front of me, I take hold of her throat and force her chin up with my wrist. "You think you are not *agreeable* to me?"

She keeps quiet, but the gold of her eyes begins to recede with her arousal. She loves my hand on her throat, and frankly, so do I. "I asked you a question." I give her a gentle shake. When she remains mum, I use my free hand to slowly pry one of her arms away from her body and bring it to my groin.

"Does that not feel agreeable to you?"

I use her little hand to follow the thickening length along my thigh. Up and down, our fingers intertwined, I make her stroke me. "This is how fucking hard you make me, little raven." I apply some pressure and I almost moan. Damn it all, after everything that's happened tonight, I need to come like I need air in my lungs. "Now, don't move."

Releasing first her neck and then, more reluctantly, her hand, I set about divesting myself of every stitch of clothing. She re-covers her chest, but she's too busy watching my skin be revealed to notice my disapproval. Once I'm buck naked though, my disapproval morphs into satisfaction when her lips part at the sight of my heavy, bobbing cock. To her credit, she reaches for it without hesitation.

But I'm quick to put a stop to that. Grabbing her by the throat once again, I push her away to arm's length, bowing her back against the bed. "No. You'll keep your hands to yourself. In fact, you'll lace them behind your head."

Her eyes go wide, seeming to assess my words and then her options. She'll soon realize she has none when she's with me. Waiting for her to obey, I take myself in hand. Fuck, am I hard. A situation that's not made any easier as she surrenders to my request and her hands meet at the back of her neck.

"Good. Now I can get a proper look at what's mine."

With her throat still in my grip, I let go of myself to touch her pillow-soft mouth. "These lips are mine," I say, slipping a finger between them, my lids drooping as she sucks on it. "That's a good girl, let me feel that tongue."

Moving on, I trail the wet finger down to caress the small swell of a breast. "This is mine," I tell her as I gently pinch a luscious, dark nipple, making her shudder. "And so are these scars." Ignoring the way she tenses, I drag my fingers along the ruined flesh on her left side. "They say a lot, little raven. How much of a survivor you are, how strongminded, how brave. They're mine and I can't wait to feel them under my tongue."

My hand drops further down. "And *this* is definitely mine." I slide my fingers into the triangle of hair at the apex of her thighs and tug, causing her to take a sharp breath. Letting go, I caress over her hip and down the back of her thigh to carefully lift her injured leg, placing her foot above my knee, opening her up to me. "Every last inch of this cunt is mine. Do you hear me?" She gasps as I use my fingers to spread her open, exposing her juicy little clit. "I'm almost tempted to make you come again," I taunt, letting a finger graze her sensitive flesh.

"Luka," she murmurs weakly.

"But no. This is about how agreeable you are to *me.*" I punctuate the word with a squeeze to her neck before I lean into her ear. "I want you watching as I come all over you."

I take hold of myself and begin to stroke. "Fuck, that's good. I don't know what I want more," I pant, not bothering to hold back. "To fill your womb or your mouth or your ass."

CHAPTER 15

RINA

Mother above. *What is he saying?* Heat is raging across my skin and I'm unsure if it's caused by his filthy words, the view of his sculpted chest, or his big hand roughly working his cock. His cock that matches the rest of him, his cock that's excessive and daunting . . . his cock that I wish he'd at least try to fit inside of me. It's irrational and messed up and hot as –

"Fuuuck. So close," he groans. "You watching?"

I nod, all my focus on how he's now pumping his hips into his fist.

"Oh, shit," he whispers ever so softly. My eyes jerk up in time to witness his entire visage slacken as warm splashes of his come land on my stomach and thighs.

I take a shaky breath.

UNDER A NORTHERN SKY

He slips the hand on my throat around to the back of my neck and leans down to nuzzle at my ear, carefully lowering my leg to the floor. "You see how beautiful you are? You couldn't be more *agreeable.*"

With a kiss to the corner of my mouth, he leaves me standing there naked, leaning against the bed on unsteady legs, his come dripping down my body in the firelight.

Overcome and vulnerable, I tuck my hands back under my chin to shield myself from whatever will come next. My swirling mind calms somewhat when I realize he's only gone to an earthenware pitcher that sits on a sideboard to pour some water into a bowl. He wets a rag before returning to me.

The cold, slightly rough texture of the cloth is not as shocking as his wiping at my skin himself. "You're cleaning me?"

He smiles softly, concentrating on his task. "Yes, I'm cleaning you." It seems an orgasm improves his disposition tenfold. I'll have to remember that.

Not wanting to read too much into his actions, I distract myself with his nakedness. It's not only his still partially-hard length that has my interest, but the muscles of his lower abdomen too. They're so defined that they make grooves in his skin. I reach out to touch them.

"Uh, uh, uh," he tuts to still my hand. "That's not a good idea. You need some rest." He chucks the rag aside and pulls the night rail over my head before tugging back the furs to get rid of the warming stones. "In you get."

Feeling completely disconnected, I blink up at him.

He graces me with another soft grin. "It's the rot gut kicking in," he explains, scooping me up and placing me on an exceptionally soft, warm mattress. Whatever fantasy this is, I want to stay here forever. That's my last thought as I sink into a deep sleep.

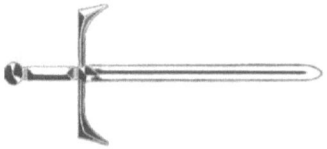

I wake to a screaming bladder and an unfamiliar room. With my head a bit muzzy from the wine, it takes a second for yesterday's events to come back to me, but when they do, I get hit with a deluge of happiness . . . and maybe a smidgeon of embarrassment.

"Luka?" I call hesitantly. No answer. I'm alone.

A soft thumping comes from one of the two windows. The shutter has been partially propped open with a wedge of wood, but strains against the thin rope that keeps it from flying open. There's enough light for me to take in Luka's room, which is more of a rectangle than a square with the bed at one end and the now-cold hearth at the other. The door is off to the left, along with a chest and a wardrobe, and the two windows to my right are separated by a sideboard. Evidently Luka has simple tastes.

Spotting a wooden panel-divider in the corner near the fireplace, I reluctantly slip from the warm furs to investigate. In between the rugs, the stones are icy under my bare feet, but I'm more than grateful to discover a chamber pot behind the screen, a proper one with a chair and a lid. No more buckets for this girl.

When I finish, I head for the jug of water on the sideboard and spot a tray of food next to it. My heart free-falls. *Am I to eat alone?*

A bit of hurt begins to weigh me down as I wash my hands and face. Then my mood plummets straight into despair when the search for my clothes and boots turns up nothing.

"No," I whisper harshly into the silence. It's not possible. After last night, he still plans to keep me half-naked and alone? "No," I deny again, because it can't be true.

You're mine. That's what he'd said. Does that means something different to him than it does to me?

Apprehension rising, I march to the door and tug on the handle. To my ever-lasting relief it opens.

"My a'deve? Can I help you with something?" Ion is standing across from the door in the empty hall.

"Have you seen the deve this morning?"

"Yes."

My eyes narrow when he says no more. "Do you know where he is? I'd like to speak to him."

"That's not possible."

"Not possible?" I say, the volume of my voice creeping up. I can't believe he'd slink away before I woke. "How very convenient for him."

Ion steps closer as if to corral me back into the room. "My a'deve, I –"

"Unless you're going to tell me exactly where I can find the insufferable man *or* my clothing, I suggest you stop talking." *Ugh, I'm such a fool!* I thought things had changed between us. I guess *you're mine* was meant in the literal sense. Mine to rule over, deciding where I go, what I eat, what I wear, who I talk to. Maybe I could accept that if he hadn't left me to do all of it *alone.* But after yesterday, I can't and won't stand the solitude anymore.

With barely a glance down at the night rail which only comes to my knees, I make for the stairs, but Ion steps in my path and my toes barely escape being crushed by his boots. "Where are you going?"

I glare up at him. "Get out of my way."

"I can't do that."

"Can't or won't?"

The difference appears lost on him. Either way, he's not budging. My desperate anger boils over. "Luka!" I yell, hoping my voice carries all the way down to the hall. Before Ion can react, a door down the hall opens.

Turning, I see an older woman in a doorway. "Your ladyship, princess of D'heilar," she says, respectfully inclining her head. "My mistress would like to invite you for refreshments." She steps further out into the hall and lifts her arm as if welcoming me into the room.

Ion all but sputters, "I can't allow that."

"I was not asking your permission Ion Welltorn," this new mystery woman says evenly.

Giving Ion a triumphant little smirk, I turn on my heel and cover the distance before he can think of how to prevent me. It seems not everyone bows and scrapes at the warriors' feet. "Thank you," I say primly to the woman as I pass her only to stall out right inside the door. It's like entering another world.

"Welcome."

My slack jaw closes at the greeting from a woman who sits next to a roaring fire. She puts her needlepoint aside and stands to incline her head.

"Oh, please don't stand for me," I say a bit stupidly, still thrown by the grandeur of the room. The stone walls have been covered with thick tapestries of colorful images and there are bouquets of winterberry holly sitting on ornate pieces of furniture throughout the large room.

"Please, have a seat," she says softly, re-taking her own. "Madeleine will pour us some tea."

I don't know who these women are, but tea sounds wonderful. "Thank you so much." I offer her the traditional southern gesture of pressing my palms to my heart, and then want to kick myself. Reminding people I'm a foreigner is foolish, but she only smiles kindly as I take the chair across from her. The heat coming off of the fire and the luxurious sheepskin rug beneath my feet are more than welcome.

"Your room is lovely," I tell her, trying not to gawk at an incredibly elaborate candelabra that sits on a nearby table. It doesn't resemble anything I've ever seen.

"Yes, my life has improved considerably since my son took power."

My head whips around. *Her son?* I study the woman more closely. She's older, maybe fifty or so and there's an air of fragility about her. Worry lines bracket her mouth and her light-brown hair – though artfully braided into a crown about her head – is noticeably streaked with gray.

"You're Luka's mother?" I blurt, immediately getting to my feet to incline my head. "I'm sorry, I didn't realize." She brushes the civility away with a casual wave as I sink back down into my chair. "I thought maybe you were a priestess."

This amuses her, making her appear years younger. "No, not a priestess. Not even close. My name is Niri."

I feel a genuine smile come on. "I'm Rina."

The other woman, Madeleine, brings Niri her tea in a true southern tea bowl made of ceramic and my smile widens.

Once I have my own bowl cupped in my hands, I shiver with delight at its warmth.

Niri says, "I must admit I've never hosted a Southerner before. I hope the tea's flavor will meet with your approval."

Not caring if it tastes like mud, I dutifully take a sip. "Oh," slips out of me and I'm pleased I don't have to lie. "It's wonderful. It reminds me of home."

"And where is that for you, Rina?"

My stomach clenches. "Home?"

She nods.

Why did I use that word? I don't have a home. But I suppose she means where I was raised. "Uh, I was born in the capital, but I . . . moved to an outpost in the far south as an adolescent." Wanting to change the subject, I ask, "Have you travelled south before?"

"Goodness, no, child."

I feel myself flush. Of course she hasn't. Tentative peace accords notwithstanding, D'heilar has been at war with the Realms for decades and decades.

"I hope it doesn't shock you too badly," she goes on, "to know that my grandmother got this tea set when she accompanied my grandfather on a raid across the river."

"Really?" I say, my mortifying gaffe almost forgotten. "How exciting. Your grandmother sounds like a woman to be admired."

"Indeed."

Niri's approval of my response gives me the courage to add, "I, too, would raid alongside my husband if given the chance."

She laughs. "You're a brave young soul, then. I hear you

are keeping my son . . . off balance, Rina. Is this true?"

Feeling a kinship with this sweet woman, I take another soothing sip of the tea, hoping it's not inappropriate to continue with our banter. "Nah, your son is too big to be pushed off balance."

As if we've summoned him, Luka's angry voice sounds from the hall. A second later the door crashes open. I have no idea what he was expecting to find, but it's not this cozy image of us drinking tea.

"Luka?" Niri says with concern, setting her tea aside. "Is something amiss?"

His accusing eyes briefly touch on me before moving on to his mother. His expression gentling, he approaches her in the slowest, most tempered manner I've ever seen him adopt.

"Mother," he greets, carefully crouching down before he kisses her cheek. "You are well?"

He throws a suspicious glance at me over his shoulder, and I roll my eyes. *What did he think I would do? Stab her with her own needlepoint?*

"Of course I'm well, son. I'm getting to know your lovely bride."

I'm not sure which I enjoy more, his skepticism or her reaction to it.

"I was thinking," Niri says, "to attend supper tonight in the Great Hall with my new daughter-in-law at my side. It'll give me a chance to get to know her more fully."

"What?" he chokes out. "That would be . . . unwise."

"Why on earth? She has been here for almost an entire cycle of the moon."

Luka couldn't be more obvious as he wracks his brain

for an excuse before coming up with, "I'm sure Madeline has informed you of the warrior chained to the hearth downstairs. It will be unpleasant for you."

"Nonsense. I could do with a little excitement."

"It's also market day, Mother."

"That's right!" she says, even more enthused now. "Maybe Zola will be there and I can look down my nose at her from our table."

My strangled laugh gets me another dagger-laden look over his shoulder, something along the lines of *shut up or else.*

"It's settled, then," Niri says, patting his big hand. "We will walk down together." Before he can argue, she changes the subject. "Now, you must feed your bride. I can hear her stomach rumbling from here."

From between clenched teeth, he mutters, "Yes, Rina, let's get you fed. Good bye, Mother."

Even if he is an ass, it's still sweet that he carefully kisses her cheek again and gets to his feet, deliberate and slow so as not to scare her. Of course, he's not so tender when he holds out his hand to me, making a snappish come hither gesture. I make him wait, pretending to consider his offer. Finally, when his temper is on the verge of swallowing him whole, I set my tea cup down and rise to make my farewells.

"I thank you for the tea," I say, pressing my palms to my heart, this time not caring that I'm being foreign. It's the only way I know how to show the depths of my gratitude and I'll damn well show it. "It was very nice to meet you."

"And you, my dear."

Luka makes a little noise of what can only be interpreted as displeasure as we leave. Then out in the hall, he hisses, "Of all the underhanded tricks, I can't believe you would attempt to use my mother."

I feel my brow furrow. "What?"

He stomps down the hall and swings open the door to his room. "Get in here."

I cross my arms over my chest. "No."

"Rina," he warns.

"Luka."

His jaw shifts, telling me he's not fooling around. But I don't care. Neither am I. Then he seems to really see me. "Why are you not dressed?!"

My annoyance becomes rage. "Is that some kind of twisted joke?"

Ion, who's trying to disappear into the stonework, shifts on his feet and Luka turns his wrath on him. "Get gone."

"I'm talking to you, Luka!" I erupt, not caring if the whole stronghold hears me. "If you don't want me wandering your halls in my underclothes, I suggest you provide me with adequate clothing."

The space between us crackles with animosity. "What is the use of providing you with it, if you don't wear it?!"

"What's the use of providing it," I mock him, "only to take it away at your whim?!"

"What?" he snarls, storming into his room only to return two seconds later. "Kata!" he bellows toward the stairs, making me jump.

"Don't scream like that! You'll scare her."

"Just get in here."

"No! I won't be locked up anymore. If I must be treated like an animal, you can chain me to the hearth downstairs with

Cayson. At least I'll have some company, then, no matter how rotten."

"I don't know what you're playing at, princess, but I'm not buying this bullshit."

The viciousness with which he delivers that cryptic remark feels like a slap. It's like I've woken to an unrecognizable world. *Hadn't we turned a corner together yesterday?* Because this man is like a stranger. I'm forced to swallow back a horrible lump of disappointment.

"What?" he scoffs. "No comeback?"

My eyes flip up to his. "Sorry, turns out my well of bullshit isn't as deep as you thought it was. I have nothing left to say to you."

He's already opening his mouth to insult me further when Kata comes barrelling around the corner from the stairs, her arms full. She pulls up short when she sees us, then cowers when Luka turns his ire on her.

"Where have you been?" he thunders and I scurry to put myself between them.

"Enough," I seethe at him. "Go be an ogre somewhere else."

Kata juggles the clothing in her arms, lowering her head again and again in respect or apology to Luka, trying desperately to show him . . . the bottom of my blue gown?

"Oh, Kata," I say, surprised. "Did you move the hem on my dress?"

She nods so vigorously I fear she'll strain her neck.

"Thank you." I finger the material and find it slightly damp. "Did you wash it too?" More nodding. "But when?" I ask. "Have you been up all night?"

Kata only shrugs her slender shoulders, shifting the heavy bundle in her arms. I spot my boots in the pile and pull them out to lessen the load. They're much cleaner than they were yesterday.

I curl my arm around her shoulders. "Come," I say, guiding her around the giant, brooding barbarian in the middle of the hall.

Undoubtedly not used to being ignored, Luka follows us into his chilly room. "The high and holy princess needs companionship, Kata."

I turn to send him the dirtiest look I can muster. "What is wrong with you today?"

"Me?"

"Yes, you," I tell him, planting my hands on my hips. "As far as I know you went to sleep beside me last night as satisfied as you'd allow. Now, you're acting like a bear with a thorn in its paw. A thorn that I didn't put there."

His lip curls as he turns his back on me. Oh, no, he doesn't. I cover the distance and get myself in front of him. "Just tell me what's happened."

Huffing, he meets my gaze. "My lady mother –"

"Luka, I did *not* seek out your mother. I didn't even know you had one. And now that I've met her, I'm not convinced that sweet woman had a hand in raising you. In truth, the possibility you were hatched," I wave my hand up and down the entire length of him, "fully formed, right from an egg is becoming more and more believable to me."

That stops whatever's about to come out of his mouth. He blinks. And then a soft rush of air distracts us both and we turn. Kata, who's thrown open the other shutter to flood the room with light, is trying to hide her silent laughter, and suddenly, I can't hold back a smile of my own.

Luka's expression loses some of its tetchiness too. "Can we go to the hot springs?" I ask him.

He goes back to looking constipated. "No."

"Please, Luka."

"No," he intones like I'm daft. "I'm in the middle of a council meeting."

"Is that what's got you in a temper? Can I come with you?"

"No."

I re-cross my arms over my chest. "Can I be given a task? In the kitchen? Or in the stables? Or –"

"Absolutely not."

"Why not?!"

"I won't have my intended bride plucking chickens or mucking stalls."

Frustration boils over. "But you'll have me rot, alone, within these walls?"

"Outside these walls, it's not safe!"

"Who cares? If someone puts a knife between my ribs, all your problems will be solved." I hit on inspiration. "And as an added bonus, you'll get to run the culprit through with a sword afterwards. Obviously you could do with a spot of violence."

He steps closer, anger emanating from every inch of him. "Oh, I'll give you violence."

"Is *violence* another code word like *discussion*?"

We're almost toe to toe now and I have to crane my neck back to keep him in sight. Again, I'm struck by how wide his shoulders really are, by how much I love his big frame towering over me. I almost embarrass myself by sighing, but Kata saves me by trying to slip from the room.

"Kata," I call without taking my eyes off of my barbarian. She pauses. "Get some sleep, please. The deve excuses you from any work you're expected to do today."

Luka's lips tighten, but he doesn't contradict me. When the door shuts behind her, he watches me lick my lips and I hurry to press my case. "So, about that job . . ."

He takes hold of my throat and sparks ignite inside of me. "You're seriously trying my patience." His voice has lost its edge though, smoothing out into more of a honeyed cadence.

Pressing closer, I rest my hands on his hips. "I can be useful, Luka. Please let me prove it to you." I'm not sure I'm still talking about him assigning me a task anymore, but I love the way his eyes heat. After a second of hesitation, I let my hand wander from his hip to his groin where he's already growing hard in his pants. It almost has me melting to my knees on the hard stone. But all the erotic imaginings of taking him into my mouth evaporate when he takes a big step back.

"Do not manipulate me!"

I barely allow the shock or the hurt to register before I snort out a derisive laugh. "You're not serious. Are you saying that I cannot want you without it being manipulation?"

His cold façade doesn't alter so I shove my disappointment down and march to the bed where Kata put my things. As I go through them, I inform him of my plans. "Ion will take me to the hot springs and to the stables to visit Glory."

"I did not –"

"I'm not asking. You have two options, Luka. Chain me up downstairs with my would-be rapist or let me go with Ion." When he makes to argue, I cut him off. "If you lock me in this room, I will simply climb out the window. I will not be caged anymore."

"Rina," he growls.

"Luka," I growl right back.

With an angry curse on his breath, he wrenches the door open. "Ion!" he shouts, pulling the door closed behind him with a crash.

My shoulders slump, but I can't help but be pleased. I've won this battle. Maybe. Then I realize there's an entirely new set of clothes mixed in with the slightly damp ones that Kata washed. By the Mother, how my heart swells in my chest. I'm one step closer to having a real life.

Laying the damp items over the chairs to dry, I quickly dress in my new linen undershirt and thick overdress. This one isn't blue, but a mossy green that I love. The new pants are made of wool, not buckskin, but they fit better and slide easily into my boots.

With new optimism running through my veins, I happily eat my congealed porridge and apple before heading for the door, grabbing my vest off the bed on the way. When I give Ion a bright smile, he reluctantly grins back. "Shall we?"

CHAPTER 16

LUKA

I'd slept. Actually slept. And the dawn hadn't brought with it the usual impending dread I've been feeling since Rina arrived. True, I'd drunk a lot more than usual last night. I'd also laughed and socialized and forgotten about my title. But if I'm honest with myself, the reason was the woman whose ass cushioned my hard cock when I woke.

I'd watched her sleep, marvelling at her small, shapely form that fit so well against me . . . the one that I jacked off on and marked as mine. It was a good thing that a soft knock had come on my door. Otherwise I'd have woken her to relive the whole experience instead of letting her get the sleep she needed.

Unfortunately, the knock had sent my morning straight downhill with my uncle requesting my presence to voice his concerns about Cayson and the treason charge. It pissed me off. Thankfully, Eldon was there to act as a buffer.

When Ion interrupted the discussion, slightly out of breath, to notify me that Rina was with my mother, my first instinct was panic. After almost twenty-five years of enduring my father and his various forms of abuse, she's not well. Her emotional state often deteriorates to the point of suffering shaking spells, which in turn, can lead to long bouts of being bedridden. I've been trying to shield her from the details of my up-coming marriage, but of course her maid, Madeline, brings her all the gossip.

My panic had escalated into rage, however, as we climbed the stairs and Ion described Rina's ill-tempered outburst. *Who knew what she'd do to my gentle, long-suffering mother?*

Of course, I had nothing to worry about. *Did I realize that right away?* No, I'd had an outburst of my own and said some stupid things. I wince internally. She'd been right to call me an ogre. And now I'm back in this meeting, listening to my uncle . . . and he's just repeating himself at this point.

"To take the side of this, this woman," Teo blusters, his graying beard flapping, "over that of a Range warrior is unheard of."

"Have you not listened to a word I've said?" Eldon says, becoming exasperated. "Cayson and Carson Cyrun took coins to work against this realm. They broke their oath. Plain and simple."

The old man hums and haws over the exact nature of what he calls 'misplaced loyalty' and all I can think of is Rina; Rina arguing with me, Rina mocking me, Rina not afraid to stand up to me, Rina naked and half-lost to passion with me. *Where is she now? Still at the hot springs?* I trust Ion implicitly, but if he's beset by multiple men? That's not very likely, but still. It should be me escorting her. She's mine. My responsibility. *I*

230

cannot want you without it being manipulation? I shiver. My little raven *wants* me.

Fuck, how long do I have to listen to this drivel? My father never would've put up with it. His word was law, end of story. Which is why, I remind myself, I'm listening instead of pretending I'm all-knowing. But I think I've had enough for one day.

I slam my hand down on the table. "Enough. Cayson will die on the new moon by my hand as any oath breaker would. That is final." Not a shred of doubt assails me as the words slide off my tongue.

"Nephew, the people will not like it!"

Standing, I lean forward on the table and meet the man's eyes. "That's too bad."

I'm at the door when my uncle calls me back. "Luka, that woman will be your undoing if you're not careful."

I don't bother to acknowledge him. A different man would take that as a threat, but I know my uncle. He's not stupid. And he and my father schemed and connived to *ensure* I would one day rule. Just because it came to pass years in advance of their plans doesn't mean he wants to bring me down now. Besides, what he says is true. She very well may be my undoing if I'm not careful. But the more time I spend with her, the less I fear a challenge from any quarter.

It's certainly true that some factions in this realm don't like me or what Rina represents. And then there's Kharon, the First Deve, who wants me gone. And the King of D'heilar, who's meddling as well.

But let them come. Let them try to remove me. I'll be ready for them.

I wonder at how Rina's presence has brought about this

much-needed clarity to my thinking. Before her, my mind would constantly circle itself, doubting, overthinking, re-considering. This new confidence is energizing.

I still need to be wary though, I think as Eldon and I head downstairs. Getting complacent or too comfortable is the real danger. Things are still very much uncertain and allowing myself to become wrapped around her little finger . . . or around her lithe body, while I piston into her sweet cunt . . . is a bad idea.

Great. Now I'm uncomfortable in my pants – again.

As we enter the Great Hall, I clap eyes on Cayson, sitting with his back to the skull wall, looking decidedly dejected. The scene is satisfying, but it also brings on a nice hum of low-level fury. For betraying me and this realm, he'll die. But for touching what's mine, he'll die slowly and in agony. First, though, I must know who gave him the coins.

Noé is already waiting for us, but Cayson's interrogation turns out to be a waste of time. He claims that no one paid them to attack the princess, that he and Carson won the coins in a game of chance. That might be believable if we didn't have the letter. Taken together, the coins and the letter are too much of a coincidence. I wish I could torture the truth out of him, but it would be dishonorable to weaken the man before I face him in combat.

I spend the rest of the day – on the training field, or meeting with Bron, Elsy the healer, the cook, or in the stables – preoccupied with Rina, hoping to catch a glimpse of her on her first day free to roam, but she remains elusive.

Finally climbing the stairs to my room before dinner, I get a nice jolt of anticipation. She better be there, safe and sound and whole. If I have to hunt her down, I'm not going to be happy.

I shove the door open too hard and it bangs against the wall, scaring her and her little maid. But once Rina's alarm passes, she graces me with a smile that can only be described as dazzling and I'm momentarily struck dumb by it. She's painfully beautiful, sitting on a stool in her new green dress, having Kata braid her hair.

"My deve," she chirps.

For some reason, I feel awkward.

I don't like it. This is my room, in my stronghold, in my realm, so I shut the door with another bang, then grouse, "I see you made it through the day."

"Yes, I'm alive and well." The bright smile doesn't dim. "Not a single person raised a hand to me today, or even insulted me."

Giving her a brooding hum, I make my way to the sideboard to pour some water into the basin to wash my face. Although I just came from the hot springs, it gives me something to do that doesn't involve me demanding she kiss me hello.

"I even received a gift," she goes on as I dry myself with a piece of linen. "Two actually."

Suspicion blazes to life in my gut. Chucking the linen aside, I prowl toward them. "And who, exactly, is gifting things to *my* bride?"

Kata touches her shoulder. "All done?" Rina asks and Kata nods. "Thank you for your help today." Kata inclines her head and makes herself scarce as I fold my arms over my chest.

"Rina?" I prompt. "Who's giving you things?"

At my tone, she has the audacity to allow a small, knowing smile onto her lips. *What is it she thinks she knows?* "Well, first, the cook . . . Dagmar, right? She's certainly a woman to be contended with, isn't she? I heard her deliver a tongue lashing to a maid before she presented me with a slice of her mouth-watering mincemeat pie."

I feel the tension between my shoulder blades ease. Sure, Dagmar rarely gives out treats, but it's not unheard of. "And the other?"

She lifts her hand to her chest where what appears to be a small flower is pinned to her dress. "One of Rionnon's friends brought his mother to meet me and she gave me this. Isn't it lovely? It's made of little scraps of wool." She waves me closer.

Humoring her, I crouch down for a better look. I'm unimpressed. My attention shifts to her face and I'm surprised to catch her watching me. I almost jerk back when she reaches out and runs her fingers into my still slightly damp hair that I've left loose around my shoulders.

"Thank you, Luka," she whispers.

"For what? I didn't give it to you."

She leans in and something in my chest leaps with the quick kiss she places at the corner of my mouth. "For allowing me some freedom today. I truly savored it."

I want to dismiss her thanks, but her golden eyes, so filled with emotion, hold me transfixed.

A knock at the door startles me. "My deve?" a female voice calls. Madeline.

"We should go," Rina says. "I'm more than a little nervous."

Straightening, I offer her a hand up off the stool. "Nervous? You think I'd let someone harm you?"

"What? No."

I pause at the door. "Then, what?"

She blows out a slow breath. "Well, whether I have one day or fifty years left in my life, this dinner will set the tone for my future."

Frowning, I stop her from opening the door. "You must know there will be some hostility. It's possible my lady mother's presence will stifle some of the worst of it, but they can be an unruly bunch . . ." I trail off as she stands taller.

"I know."

"Okay."

In the hall, my mother mostly fusses over Rina, but she spares me a nod of approval. When I extend my arm to her, she chastises me. "No, my son, you will enter with your bride."

"Fine, whatever," I grumble. "Let's get this done."

I take Rina's hand, liking how her small palm fits into my bigger one. It feels familiar and . . . right, except that by the time we get to the bottom of the stairs, it's trembling enough that I notice. I stop and lean down to kiss her forehead. "You're with me. That's all they need to know."

She nods, then repeats my words from upstairs. "Let's get this done."

For a quick moment, I consider how my people will see her. Though I like her better in her fur-trimmed vest, the green of her woolen overdress suits her, and with the top half of her hair braided in a northern style, I'd go so far as to say she's elegant. Not at all *puny* like Noé first described her. She may be small but she's not fragile. My chest expands with a surge of pride as we go in.

A hush falls over the room until my mother comes into view and a ripple of murmurs breaks out. It distracts everyone enough that I'm able to get Rina settled in the chair next to mine on the dais without incident.

"Don't you worry, darling," my mother tells Rina softly. "They're all staring at me since I rarely come down for dinner."

I don't register Rina's reply because Lorna appears, ale jug in hand. The possibility she may not *just* be unwelcoming occurs to me. *What was I thinking, bringing Rina downstairs like this? And on market day of all days?* So far the crowd is more curious than hostile, but that doesn't mean things won't devolve. I pull my dagger from my belt and set it on the table with a thump.

Rina's hand finds my thigh, her thumb beginning a soothing motion as Lorna pours the ale. "You're to be our a'deve?" Lorna asks her, not unkindly.

"I am."

A wide smile breaks out on the serving girl's face as she dips her head. "I'm most happy to hear that. I saw you hit the bull's eye yesterday. Very impressive."

"Thank you. What is your name?"

"Lorna. And don't you listen to any of the men out there," she says, indicating the tables behind her. "Unlike our deve, some of them don't deal well with change."

She turns to go but not before she winks in my direction. My grunt of disapproval gets lost in the clamor as the food is brought out, the platters stacked high and the baskets filled with freshly-baked bread. To my surprise, Dagmar, our bad-tempered head cook, serves the dais personally.

"Dagmar," I say dryly. "Since when do you leave your kitchen?"

Her hard aspect firmly in place, she directs her helpers with where to put each platter. "If the welcoming of a new a'deve is not reason enough to show myself, I don't know what is." She has a platter of carrots and turnips plunked down right in front of me and turns on her heel to go.

Leaning down to Rina, I murmur, "Have you bewitched the entire village?"

As if in response, Cayson launches a loud insult into the room. "You let that whore from D'heilar eat at the head table?"

There are a few hisses of agreement, but then someone hurls a boiled potato that hits him square in the chest, and the hisses are drowned out by the uproar of laughter and catcalls.

"My bewitching skills still need a bit of work apparently," Rina says, spearing a large piece of meat. She looks it over before biting a chunk off directly from the knife. Chewing, she still manages a grin which almost makes me forget where we are and kiss her delectable, grease-stained lips.

We're interrupted by Yvette and Rionnon. "May we approach, my deve?" Yvette asks deferentially and instead of rolling my eyes like I want to, I motion them forward. Rionnon springs up onto the dais, his smile only for Rina. "I wanted to thank you for the archery lesson yesterday." He places a small quartz rock on the table in front of her plate.

"Is this for me?" Rina asks, visibly delighted as she picks up the white, semi-transparent crystal. "Wherever did you find it?"

"Over by the baths," he proudly announces. "I found it last year and I was saving it for a special occasion. I want you to have it."

"How incredibly kind of you, Rionnon, thank you. I'll treasure it always."

"You will?" The boy is both thrilled and astounded, and I rub at my beard to stop myself from chuckling. Rina wields charm almost as well as I wield a sword.

"Certainly. I haven't received many gifts in my life." She

237

sets her knife aside and presses her palms to her heart and offers him her gratitude.

Though he's a bit unsure of the gesture, his adoration of my intended couldn't be more obvious. In the end, he inclines his head deeply before jumping down off the dais to go back to his seat with Yvette.

Rina turns her happiness on me. "It's pretty, isn't it?"

"They're common enough around here."

Her lips press into a disapproving line. "But it becomes rare when it's combined with his consideration. Just like . . ." She trails off and instead of finishing her sentence, she picks up her cup and drinks deeply.

"Just like what?" I prompt, taking the cup from her hand.

"Just like my new dress. Thank you, Luka."

"You're welcome, my little raven."

A throat clearing interrupts us. "My deve, a'deve," a thin woman says, her body almost bent double with her show of respect. I don't recognize her or the raggedly-dressed child beside her.

"Yes?" Rina inquires politely.

"I wonder if my daughter and I may present you with a gift, my a'deve?"

"Oh, ah, I . . . yes, of course you can."

The woman chooses to focus only on Rina as she lifts the girl onto the dais, probably because I'm irritated with another disruption. With shaking hands, the child places what appears to be a woven circle on the table before retreating to her mother's arms.

"Oh," Rina says, another one of her smiles breaking like the dawn. "Did you crochet this yourself?"

"Yes, my lady." The woman peeks furtively in the direction of the hearth, then in a low voice that barely carries, tears welling, she adds, "I thank you with all my heart."

I feel Rina about to rise to go to the woman, but I clamp my hand down on her thigh to keep her in place. "Luka," she says through gritted teeth. "Let me up."

Despite my grip on her, she manages to slide her chair back and force me to either make a scene or do as she wants. This woman! She listens about as well as a deaf mule, I think darkly, watching her go around the table and embrace the woman. They talk in soft undertones while I scan the room like a hawk, not liking one bit that Rina's opened her flank to attack. Eldon gives me a nod and so does Noé, telling me they're monitoring the situation as well. It doesn't ease my mind in the least because already the ale is flowing and the room is getting louder and more raucous. When she returns to her seat, I'm ready to let her feel the sharp edge of my tongue until I see there are tears on her lashes.

"That poor woman," Rina seethes, glaring daggers in Cayson's direction. "How many more days until you end that despicable excuse for a man?"

"Four," I say from between clenched teeth. "But that does not excuse your disobedience."

"Children," my mother says in low voice. "That's enough. Eat your dinner before it gets cold. You can make up later in your room."

I lean down to Rina's ear. "Oh, you'll be making it up to me, guaranteed."

She's on the verge of lobbing a retort at me when she notices something in the room. I follow her gaze to where Bron and Ion have their heads together.

"You," Rina accuses me, drawing the word out. "Well, I see now why you so readily agreed to let me go to the baths with Ion."

"I let you go because Ion is a loyal, well-trained warrior."

She laughs, and I'm not at all sure I like the way she's appraising me now, as if a new light is showing her things she's never seen before. "It has nothing to do with those eyes he's making at Bron, then?"

"Don't be crude, princess. As far as I know, they have a long-standing relationship." I stab at the meat on my plate. "And don't think you can distract me from your careless disregard of my wishes."

"I'm sure we can work on fulfilling your wishes later," she says sweetly before we're interrupted again by more of her admirers, this time the two stable boys. By the end of the night, she's collected a motley assortment of junk and Lorna has to bring her a small basket to carry it all.

Overall the night turns out to be like any other. The drunken laughter is loud, the warriors are vulgar, and a couple of scuffles break out, but other than Cayson in the very beginning, no one openly disrespects Rina. Except maybe our ancient, dour priest, but he'd been mostly indifferent when he'd presented himself at the dais and I'd introduced Rina. But whatever. With one foot already on the pyre, he's long had limited influence in the realm.

Despite the evening being a success, it leaves me inexplicably irritable; horny, jealous, possessive. Even I'm surprised by the depth of my need for her attention, for her smiles to be for me, not to mention her consoling embraces and her tears – all of it should be mine.

As soon as the door to my chamber is shut behind us, I

have her against it, my palm splayed against her breast bone. Seizing the basket from her, I drop it to the floor and shove it away with my boot.

"Do you have something you need to say, Luka?" she has the nerve to ask. I wonder if there's as much fire in my expression as there is in hers.

My jaw works from side to side. "I wouldn't be so quick to challenge me."

Her hands go to work on the buckles of my vest, adding weight to my already raging hard-on. "Or maybe," she whispers, biting at her full bottom lip as her hands slip beneath my shirt. "You love it when I challenge you."

I shiver as her fingertips lightly trace over the muscles of my abdomen. Leaning down to her neck, I inhale her scent and my cock jerks as if it's starving for her, because it is . . . I am. The thought beats back my lust. I cannot be burying myself in her cunt. What if I'm forced to put her aside but she carries my child? Or what if I end up dead in a challenge and can't protect her or a child?

Backing away from her, I ignore her hurt and confused expression and situate my favorite chair to my liking next to the hearth where the crackling fire burns brightly. I shrug out of my vest and my shirt before I take a seat. Leaning back, I snap my fingers and point to the sheep skin at my feet. To my relief, the coarse gesture renews her spirit. As always when I demand things of her, she seems to deliberate her options. This time, instead of denying me like I expect, she saunters forward.

Trying to make some room in my pants, I spread my legs wider and order, "Strip."

Her chin lifts, but I get a flash of apprehension in the firelight. There's that paradox in her again, this time emerging as stubborn shyness. She's going to do what I ask despite being unsure, if only to show me that she can, and it couldn't appeal to me more.

Dragging the stool closer to the fire, she sits to get her boots off. When she stands to pull her overdress off, I again snap my fingers and point to the space between my boots. "Right here, little raven. I don't want to miss a thing."

Her throat works, but she complies, pulling the dress over her head on her way to me. I take it from her and toss it aside so I can concentrate on the points of her nipples that show through the thin fabric of her shirt. Absolutely mouth-watering. Sitting up straighter, I grab hold of her hips and yank her forward to fit my mouth around one of the tempting buds. She gasps, threading her fingers into my hair, holding me to her breast as I suck and nibble through the material. The delicious sounds she makes send my arousal sky-high. I repeat the process on the other side, wishing I could do this all night, but the uncomfortable throbbing in my pants insists I move things along.

I flip the shirt over her head and tug her pants down, getting her to step out of them. When I'm done, I settle back in my chair to look my fill. I don't think I've ever wanted her more; those incredible full lips, parted with her soft panting, the pert breasts with their tightly puckered nipples, the sexy scars marring her side, the swell of her hips, and that thatch of dark hair covering what I want most. *Fuck. That's the one thing I can't have.* "Turn around," I demand and she blinks at me, uncomprehending. "Now." I make a twirling motion with my finger.

Wobbling a bit, she does as she's told. Good grief, this view is possibly more arousing than the front. The long, heavy fall of her black-as-midnight hair has me groaning out loud. It reaches halfway down her back, and as I run my hand down the sleek length of it, I imagine what it would feel like wrapped around my cock. The best part of the view, however, is her ass. Despite her small stature, it's round and plump. "Bend over for me."

Her body stiffens and over her shoulder, she graces me with so much confused innocence that I almost come in my pants. "You heard me," I say in a gentler, coaxing tone. "Bend over. You're mine and I want to see you. All of you."

Still she hesitates.

"Let me help," I tell her. "Clasp your hands behind your back."

She's suspicious it's some kind of trick, but ultimately obeys because it's a much less confounding task for her. I caress her delicate wrists where they sit at the small of her back before taking hold of them in one hand. She doesn't fight me as I urge her over. "That's my girl," I say softly and she whimpers. "A little more." Her hair falls forward, exposing her back, but I barely notice that, not with her ass right in my face.

Holding her steady by her wrists, I let my free hand slide over her hip and down her thigh to her ankle where I compel her to widen her stance with some tender stroking.

"There we go." I run my hand back up, along the inside this time, and her breathing picks up. "Just look at you. Spread open. Dripping wet. Incredible." I can smell her arousal as I lightly trace the seam of her cunt to find her clit. She twitches in my hold. "Easy. I just need to get a feel for what's mine." I circle her swollen bud and she mewls.

In the back of my mind, behind the raging lust, I acknowledge that she's everything I could ever hope for; beautiful, intelligent, sensual . . . willful yet willing. As I tease her entrance with my index finger, awareness hits me: I'm not going to want to give her up if things fall apart. But then I push into her slick flesh and all thought is obliterated.

CHAPTER 17

RINA

What is he doing to me? I'm going to come undone around his finger. Just his finger.

"Luka," I pant, uncaring that I sound desperate as he starts up a molasses-slow rhythm. I *am* desperate. "I need more."

Last night he went on a rant about me needing what he gave me, but tonight, he takes a different tack. "More?" he purrs, holding me steady by my wrists when I try to rock back. "Not sure this sweet little cunt can take more. Like you, my little raven, it's so small."

"No, I mean, yes," I babble, arching my back, hoping to give him a better angle. "She can." *She? I mean it. I mean,* "Oh, Luka, please," I whine as that finger slides forward again.

"You think? I don't know." He bends me further over and

I suck in a breath of surprise. "I wouldn't want this to be uncomfortable for you."

"It won't." The last word comes out as more of a protest than a reply because he withdraws from me to trace my opening again.

"No?"

"No," I whine, then freeze as I feel another finger being notched.

"I guess," he says casually, pressing down on my tail bone to hold me more firmly in place, "there's only one way to find out."

The slow invasion of two callused fingers is sublime. I can barely hear him over all the noise I'm making. "Look. At. This. You should see this slippery little cunt take my fingers. It's tight though, isn't it?" He stalls out and I feel faint with how much I don't want that.

"Wha . . . no, Luka, I –"

His wrist rotates and an incredible wash of heat sweeps me from head to toe. "Ohhh, yes," I groan as he presses forward again, giving me slow stroke after slow stroke. This new angle is . . .

"Yes? You think? I don't know."

I have no clue what he's on about, only that he's stopped again, but this time he's lodged in deep and brushing against some spot inside of me that's making my entire being coil tighter and tighter. A long, drawn out moan falls from my lips.

He pulls his fingers away. "I'm not sure."

The coil begins to ease. "Luuuukkaaaa."

He uses his wet fingers to explore my cleft, tugging gently, pulling me wider on one side and then the other. "Hurting you is the last thing I want to do." He sinks deep again and a full-body shiver crashes through me as he finds that place inside of me again.

Oh, fuck, I'm panting hard now, so close to completion, so dizzy, so –

"No," he announces, pulling out.

"No! Luka. No, what –"

"I don't want to hurt you."

"Hurt me?" My hips push back searching for his fingers again, but all he does is trace along my opening. "Luka." Nothing. I squirm. "Fuck! Come on."

"Such language," he taunts, glancing over my clit. I shudder in his hold.

"Don't be a bastard," I practically wail. "Come on. Fuck me already!"

He gets to his feet without warning and my heart skips several beats. His hand slides from my wrists to loop around my waist, holding me snugly against his thigh. "Well, you just had to ask."

An oath dies on my tongue when he spears his fingers deep, stretching me wide.

Pleasure re-surges.

This time he doesn't let up. Again and again and again, he thrusts into me with firm strokes. I barely register the sheepskin below me through the long strands of my hair that sway back and forth as he fingers me mercilessly.

I push up on my toes, I squirm, I whine, but I can't quite get close enough to touch the oblivion I need so badly. At least not until he uses the fingers of his other hand to press down on my clit. Now with every thrust, he's jerking me against that sweet bundle of nerves. The pressure quickly sets me off and rapture rushes over me in powerful waves.

Delirious and worn out, I feel myself being lowered onto the sheepskin. He arranges me to sit on my heels, facing him. With a grip in the hair at the nape of my neck, he forces me to look up at him. He's so broad and big and looming, I think dazedly. And that smirk on his lips is divine, smug in all the right ways.

"Did you like that?"

"Yes," I breathe.

"I'm glad." He sounds sincere, which fills me with even more satisfaction. Pulling me up by my nape to my knees, he presses my face to the solid length of him that's still trapped behind his pants. I snuggle the bulge as if I were a cat.

"Take it out," he orders, setting off a little aftershock in my core.

I peer up along the sleek muscles of his torso to find his smouldering gaze above his beard, framed by his loose hair and the flickering light of the fire. What an incredible view. With another nudge of my cheek, I go to work on the laces of his pants, anticipation making my movements jerky.

My fingers have barely gotten their first feel of him when he pulls his hips back. "Change of plans. Keep your hands behind your back. Otherwise this will be over before it starts."

"But —"

His hand tightens in my hair. "No buts. Just your pretty little mouth open and ready."

He cuts off any further protest by leaning down to my ear and whispering, "Next time you can do anything you like." His tone grows harsher as he continues, "But right now, I want your fucking hands behind your back."

If it's the growl in his voice or the words themselves, I don't know, but with a nervous lurch in my stomach that adds to the warm glow between my thighs, I do as I'm told.

Watching him reach into his pants erases all of my objections. Even though I saw him yesterday, I'm still taken aback by the size of him. My core clenches, sending a tremor through my entire body. "That's right," he croons, painting my lips with his leaking cock. "It's all for you. Now open up." He places the tip on my tongue, sliding forward so I can close my lips around him. "Yeessss," he hisses. "Like that." He holds still while I swirl, suck, lick, and nibble to the sounds of his approval, happy that my past experience has prepared me for this, if not the mind shattering orgasm he extracted from me earlier.

Soon he becomes restless. Soon the hand at my nape draws me a fraction closer and his hips involuntarily inch forward. Soon my jaw is stretched wide and he's flirting with my gag reflex.

"Look at me," he whispers thickly.

My mouth full of him, I do as I'm told. He doesn't say anything, just seems to assess my state of mind. He sweeps a thumb under my eye. "Are you going to cry for me, little raven?" Before I can answer, he presses forward into my throat by an inch, gagging me. He holds remarkably still as my throat contracts around the intrusion and water begins streaming from my eyes. "That's it," he groans. "Swallow for me, let me feel it." The 'swallowing' is not voluntary and the unfamiliar sensation sends a zing of aroused panic to my core. I try to pull back against his hold. "No." The single, hard syllable causes another zing, this one laced with more arousal than panic. "A little longer," he says and the overpowering need to please him has me relaxing by a fraction.

He lets out a guttural, "Fuck", then sinks deeper, setting off another fit of silent choking and lightning strikes of desire. The need to please him wars with the need to breathe. I'm on the verge of unclasping my hands to push him away, but again his sharp, "No," stops me. "Settle and I'll let you off."

Settle? Settle?!

I beg him with my eyes, but he's not moved, his sternness only serving to tighten the knot of excruciatingly aroused panic. My throat finally loosens a bit and he pulls out.

While I choke and cough, and suck down air, he holds me against his thigh, petting my hair, praising me, telling me how beautiful I am, how much he loved it, and I cling to him. I'm a mess of tumult and trust and raging hunger, and when I turn my head and find him still hard and right there, I wrap my lips around him again without hesitation. I want him so badly, and this time he allows me to do as I will, letting me use my hands to pump the shaft while I suckle the tip.

It doesn't take long to send him over the edge, and he chants whispered, filthy curses as he does it. I do my best to swallow everything he gives me, but when his softening length slips from my lips, it's accompanied by some of his seed. His knees hit the rug on either side of mine and he takes hold of my jaw with both hands. Without a word, he kisses me, long and deep, his tongue cleaning every bit of his seed that I wasn't able to swallow. It has me feeling like I'm floating, weightless and content.

"You're so perfect," he whispers into my mouth when he's satisfied. "Now I'm going to need you to be a good girl and lie back."

Huh? I grab onto his shoulders as he pushes me back and lays me out on the sheep skin. Before I even have an inkling of his intention, he's spreading my thighs wide and feasting on my core.

"Luka!" I gasp, gripping his hair tight, pushing him away. Or am I drawing him closer? Either way, I'm drowning in a deluge of pleasure I've never known. It's shocking and intense and exquisite . . . to the point that my body has no idea what to do with it all. He forces me to ride the edge of my orgasm for what feels like a lifetime before his fingers breach me once again and set off a long, drawn-out, flare of white-hot ecstasy.

I come back to myself as he lifts me from the rug and places me on the bed. For the second night in a row, I'm wonderfully wrung out and I couldn't be happier.

Morning comes with a horrible sense of déjà vu. Sitting bolt upright, I scan the dimly lit room for Luka as the covers slide to my waist and the cold air bites at my exposed skin.

"You okay?" he asks gruffly and my head whips around to the sideboard where he's pouring water into the basin.

Relief tugs at my heart. "You –" I clear my throat and try again. "You're still here."

Unimpressed with the obviousness of the statement, he turns back to his morning ablutions.

Already searching for my clothes, I throw my legs over the side of the bed. He doesn't have a smile for me this morning, but he hasn't left me to wake alone either, so I'm counting it as progress. "Can I break my fast with you?"

He gives a non-committal grunt.

"Are you going downstairs?" The parts of the floor that aren't covered by rugs are cold under my bare feet as I scramble to collect my strewn articles of clothing. Rushing for the chamber pot, I notice he's already fully dressed . . . and that he hasn't answered me. "I can be ready quickly."

Relieving myself while pulling on my shirt, I ignore my dismay at his silence. If he thinks he can rid himself of me, especially now, he's delusional. I get my pants on and jam my feet into my boots, then while turning my overdress right side out, I come out from behind the partition – and stop dead.

He's seated, casual as can be, in his hearth chair. The now fully-open shutter on the window behind him brightens the room considerably and I don't miss how he's subtly tapping a tortoiseshell comb on the arm of the chair. "You have time to wash."

"I do?" I say stupidly.

He jerks his head toward the sideboard over his shoulder, letting me know that his patience isn't endless.

"Thank you." I breeze past him with a bright smile. "Will I be allowed some freedom again today?" I ask, washing my hands. "To go to the hot springs?" Wetting a cloth, I scrub it over my face. "Ion was very respectful and he kept everyone at bay, not that many wanted to speak with me, but . . ." I lower my pants and carefully wipe at my tender flesh. "Anyway, did you know he doesn't like Venna very much? Is it not general knowledge that she's quite friendly once you get over the initial fear?"

He sighs. "Woman?"

"Yes?" I set the cloth aside and pull my green overdress on before heading back in his direction.

He gives me a withering look. "It's early. Must you chatter? Just bring the stool and sit." He indicates the space in front of him.

"Uh, okay," I stammer, more than a little confused. *Bring the stool?* Returning with it, I sit facing him, which only earns me more frowning disapproval as he twirls his finger. "You want me to . . . oh, right."

Turning around, I begin to question my sanity. Surely he doesn't mean to –

The first touch of his fingers in my hair startles me. "Easy. I'm not going to hurt you." He works at loosening the leather strips holding the braids that Kata arranged yesterday, then unravels my hair and starts with the comb.

For the first couple of minutes, I sit in stunned silence as he carefully detangles my locks. A touch self-conscious, I finally whisper, "Luka, you're combing my hair."

He snorts. "You're very observant in the mornings."

"And you're very grumpy," I retort pleasantly, keeping things light. He doesn't take the bait though and reverts back to his tight-lipped self.

What feels like another eternity passes, and I have to admit that his attentiveness is far from unpleasant. It may even be even arousing . . . or soothing, or . . . Mother help me, is he taking care of me? I could get used to this. When he uses the comb to apportion a section of my hair and begins to rebraid it, I can't keep silent any longer. "You've done this before?"

He lets out an audible noise of irritation, but he answers. "Yes, for my mother when I was a child."

The irresistible urge to press him for more almost gets the better of me, but I manage to hold my tongue.

"She . . ." he pauses as if considering his words, and I hold my breath. "She didn't like having other women around her.

My father was known to compel them into the nearest bed."

He must pick up on my grimace even though my back is to him, because he goes on with, "Oh, yes, I knew from a very young age what kind of man he was." Gesturing for me to hold the end of the braid, he ties it off with one of the leather strips before gently tilting my head to start work on the other side. "I've been swearing to myself for as long as I can remember that I'll never become him."

My welling compassion doesn't overflow because he hastily changes the subject.

"So, I have a job for you."

"What? Really?!"

After a short, disbelieving laugh, he mutters, "Only you would be excited about being given work."

"Luka," I protest, half-turning my head until the motion tugs at the braid. "Tell me."

"Keep still, woman. And hold onto that enthusiasm. You might need it since Bron can be surprisingly headstrong."

"Bron?"

"Yes, with the scribe dead, I need you to teach him the writing and reading thing."

"Oh . . . not you?"

I feel him shrug. "Not for now. Maybe when winter sets her claws into us more firmly." He gets me to hold the second braid while he ties it off. "You'll start after breakfast."

He stands and heads for the door, leaving me to scramble after him, checking his work with my fingertips. It's not as intricate as Kata's, so my joy is probably out of proportion, but I couldn't care less. I'm thrilled with the two simple braids that will keep the hair off my face, yet leave most of it loose how he seems to prefer.

He yanks open the door to reveal Kata and Ion waiting in the hall. "Morning," I sing song as I rush to keep up with Luka's long strides which already have him down the hall.

Kata smiles, passing into the room with a bucket of water and a bundle of something, but Ion remains stoic in the presence of his deve and follows in our wake. On the stairs, the stiff, morning ache in my thigh forces me to slow and Luka outpaces me entirely. Ion offers me his sturdy arm, and between him and the wall, I manage to hobble to the bottom.

Both Ion and I are so absorbed in my progress that neither of us see Luka backtracking to shove Ion away from me and take his place. It's not violent, but it has Ion putting his hands up in surrender.

"Was that necessary?" I ask wryly as he covers the hand I wrap around his forearm, petting me.

"Is it not healed yet?" He sounds disgruntled of all things.

"I'd remind you, my deve, that I didn't stab myself just to annoy you."

Our arrival in the Great Hall stifles the urge to tease him further. Instead, I lift my chin and concentrate on minimizing my limp. Like yesterday, the room quiets down with our entrance, but unlike yesterday, it starts back up again almost right away. Though I can still feel some stares as Luka leads me to one of the long tables instead of the dais, evidently we're old news.

We sit across from Noé, who appears to be his usual ray-of-sunshine self.

"Good morning to you, too," I say with enough sarcasm that Bron, who's seated down the bench, has to repress a laugh.

Lorna, the serving girl, distracts Noé from his retort by

coming up behind him, ale pitcher in hand, to press her body against his back. "Would you like ale, my a'deve, or tea?"

Is she . . . staking her claim to Noé? In front of me? Ewwww. "Uh, tea, please," I croak.

She must understand my expression loud and clear because she grins devilishly and says, "You don't know what you're missing."

"And I never will," I announce with a grimace. Luka explained to me that the 'beads' in Noé's hair are actually the molars of his savage kills.

"I appreciate that." She gives me a low incline of her head and rushes off to fetch me some tea.

"Hey, she didn't leave the pitcher," Noé protests, then narrows his eyes at me. "What's wrong with the bloody ale? Not good enough for you?"

Bron guffaws. "No, Noé, it's not the ale that's not good enough for her."

A soft giggle escapes me, igniting the combined suspicion of Luka and Noé. "Clueless, right?" Bron says, sending me a wink, while Ion, who's settled himself across from him, smiles.

"Clueless about what?" Noé is definitely cranky, but before he can force an answer out of anyone, a girl I've not met yet sets plates of food in front of me and Luka.

"Eggs! I haven't had eggs in . . . I don't remember how long. And sausages!" I take up my spoon and groan at how good the first bite is.

More plates have been delivered, but no one is eating. They're all staring at me. I swallow what's in my mouth. "What?"

"Nothing," Luka says, his glare making a round of the

table, forcing everyone's attention to their own plates. "Just make sure you eat it all."

He doesn't need to tell me twice. Lorna returns with my tea and the pitcher of ale, and something about her sparks an idea about Kata. "My deve," I say in between bites. "Is it all right if Kata joins Bron's lessons?"

"What? Why?" he asks dismissively, scarfing down a piece of sausage.

"Isn't it obvious? She's mute. She has no other way to communicate."

"What lessons?" Noé grouses.

Ignoring Noé, Luka tells me, "She's your maid, do with her what you will."

"She is?" Delight infuses the question. "I've never had a maid before."

"As long as she gets her work done."

I can't stop myself from half-rising to kiss the side of his mouth. "Thank you." I turn to Bron. "You don't mind, do you?"

"Not at all," he says, reaching across the table to take Ion's hand. "Ion can learn, too."

"Learn?" Noé sets his mug down hard. "Lessons? You are asking for trouble. If Kharon finds out –"

"How would he find out?" Luka challenges. "Besides, our scribe is dead and Kharon hasn't seen fit to replace him."

"That doesn't excuse –"

"You've made yourself clear, Noé. When Kharon comes to kill us all, I'll be sure to let him know you voted against me."

Noé has more to say on the subject, but Eldon arrives at the table, crabbiness written into every line of his body language. There must be something in the air this morning. "Here you are. We have shit to do before mediation this afternoon, Luka." Then he notices me and his voice warms. "Rina."

"Hi, Eldon." I gesture to the open spot on the bench beside Noé. "Would you like some ale while you wait for Luka to finish breaking his fast?"

He grumbles something under his breath, but takes the seat. I signal Bron to pass me his unused cup, so I can pour the ale.

"Did you know about this *learning* thing?" Noé demands of Eldon.

Taking a deep breath, Eldon turns to him and very seriously asks, "When are you going to pull that stick out of your ass?"

"Fuck off. It's my job to be the voice of reason."

"Yeah, reason, not constant, nagging disapproval."

I can feel Luka becoming agitated beside me, like he's preparing to use his dagger on his men instead of his breakfast. Placing my hand on his thigh under the table, I distract them all. "What's mediation?"

Eldon swings his head my way and raises a brow, telling me he knows exactly what I'm doing. But that doesn't mean I don't want to know the answer to my question.

"It happens at the end of every cycle of the moon."

With a huff, Noé adds, "It's where every idiot whines about his problems to Luka, who –" He seems to search for the right word.

"Mediates?" I supply. "Finds a solution?"

Eldon makes a face. "Exactly. They can't solve their own daft problems, so they make Luka do it for them."

"Why don't you appoint a magistrate or a justice of the peace to do that?" I suggest only to be greeted by horror-stricken expressions. "What? You don't have anyone you can trust? Or . . . or is the decentralization of power forbidden?"

Eldon looks impressed, Noé like I've sprouted a second head, and Luka just shoves the last bite of his eggs into his mouth before he stands. I grab on to his arm to stop him. "May I go to the baths later?"

He shakes his head. "We'll go together, after mediation. Stay in the stronghold."

"Does that include the stables?"

His patience at an end, he takes hold of my neck and leans down to my ear. "Do you ever stop, woman?"

"That doesn't answer my question."

He makes a growly noise of disapproval that arrows its way directly between my thighs. "Fine, you can go to the stables." He pulls away but not before he breathes in the scent of my neck, making me quiver.

"Oh, Luka?"

"What now?"

"Thank you."

He brushes a gentle thumb across my bottom lip as I smile up at him.

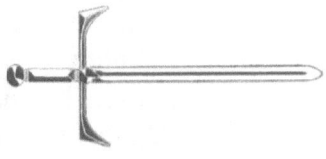

In the beginning Kata only reluctantly agrees to the lessons, but after the first hour of instruction, she's in high spirits. Both she and Bron take to the concept with ease, and even Ion, who only watches in the beginning, can't resist learning how to spell his name.

In the map room, with the supplies that Bron found in the scribe's chamber, we make good progress. The quills are of decent quality, as is the ink and the parchment. Bron also brings along documents he found lying on the desk of the dead man. While we're eating lunch, which we had sent upstairs, I scan them.

"What the . . ?" I mumble.

"Pardon?" Bron asks.

"Well," I say slowly, skimming one to the end. "It seems the scribe was in the process of writing some kind of report to this first deve person, Kharon."

Bron nods. "Yes, we pay taxes based on the scribe's reports. It's about such things as apple yields and wool production, is it not?"

Shaking my head, I focus in on the names that I recognize. "No, this is about specific people."

"What?"

"Yes, it reads like gossip almost. For example, it mentions that Luka has decided to go through with the marriage contract even though he's against it. And here," I squint at the page, "he speculates about the chances of Gray challenging Luka for leadership because he's the only man with a chance to beat Luka." Turning the parchment over, I find the other side blank. "Sounds like he was a spy. Is that normal?" Poor Kata fidgets, like she doesn't want to be privy to such information, but Bron is thoughtful. "Can I keep this? Show it to Lu–"

The door is shoved open without a knock and Ion is immediately on his feet. In one fluid movement, he has his chair twisted around to be used as a barrier and draws his dagger. The rest of us just startle in our seats.

The old man in the doorway halts. Curiously, he ignores Ion's weapon in favor of taking in what's on the table with what I think is revulsion. I assume it's the writing paraphernalia, and not our lunch, that has his hackles up.

"Can I help you?" I ask, barely masking my instant dislike. Whoever this guy is, he thinks he has the right to judge us. He's going gray at the temples, but is dressed in a warrior's vest, the mountain lion burned into the leather on his left breast.

Apparently the dislike is mutual because he skewers me with a haughty look. "You must be *her.*"

"I must be," I agree. "And you are?"

He takes a step forward, but Ion stops him with, "That's far enough."

The old man's nostrils flare. "Since when do warriors not respect their elders?"

"I'm sorry, but *no one* is to approach the princess by order of the deve." Ion lifts his dagger another inch when it seems like the man is about to disregard him.

Our visitor plants his hands on his hips. "Bron, Luka says I must speak to you about Varron Haddend speaking at this afternoon's mediation."

"Apologies, sir, but there will be no more additions at this late hour. If you like, I will consider his name for the next new moon."

The man scoffs, then again examines the contents of the table. "You dare flout our ways?"

261

Only the Mother knows what possesses me to open my mouth, but I can't let his comment pass unchecked. "When your ways are meant to weaken the realm, yes."

His eyes bulge. "You insolent little whore."

"How original," I say drolly. "I've never heard that one before."

"I would ask you to take your leave now, Teo," Ion says, moving to put himself more directly in the man's path, the tip of the knife leading the way.

With a twist of his mouth, this Teo person turns on his heel and leaves, not bothering to shut the door behind him.

Sheathing his dagger, Ion closes the door.

"Please tell me that wasn't someone Luka loves and respects," I plead. "I don't know why I can never keep my mouth sealed."

Bron grins. "He's his uncle."

"No!"

"But don't worry. There's no love lost between them. Teo was the last deve's second for close to twenty years."

We get some more practice in before Bron is needed downstairs for the mediation and Kata indicates that she has work to catch up on. That leaves Ion and I to go out to the stables to visit Glory.

The Great Hall is much busier than usual as we pass through. Bron is there in the thick of it, directing warriors to move tables and benches to the edges of the room. There are a lot of unfamiliar faces, and I'm grateful for Ion's reassuring presence since Luka is nowhere to be found.

Outside, the air is cool, but the sun is shining as we cross the courtyard to the stable entrance. Glory is happy to see me, probably thinking I'm going to take her out for a run. "No such luck, my beautiful girl," I murmur to her. "Maybe our big bad barbarian will have time for us tomorrow."

I turn at the sound of clomping hooves. Stable boys are leading in a group of the giant war horses that need to be untacked and brushed down, Nightshade among them. Glory and I watch and listen to the activity from her stall. Ion, not liking to be idle, helps them work and I giggle at their bawdy, adolescent jokes.

When Ion returns for me, I ask him, "How long do you think the mediation will take?"

He jogs a shoulder and peers down at me. "Why?"

"Do you think we can slip in and watch from the back?"

Chuckling, he leads me out. "Just remember if your presence starts a riot that it wasn't my idea."

"A riot?" I trot along behind him, happy to note that the damaged muscle in my leg isn't as sore as it was this morning. "That's hardly likely, now is it?"

"We'll see." He pushes back a lock of his dark hair that's come loose from its queue. "If the deve wasn't going to be there, I wouldn't be taking you into a room full of possibly hostile people."

"Ion?"

"Hmmm?"

"Thank you."

"What?" He sends me a confused glance. "What for?"

"For caring, even if you do it because Luka would kill you if you didn't." We mount the stairs to the entrance to the Great Hall and I put my finger to my lips, telling him to stay quiet if we don't want to get caught.

We do indeed slip inside unseen. Everyone is facing the dais, where Luka sits alone, sprawled in his chair, an elbow planted on one of the arm rests. He's the very image of casual arrogance and power, wearing that look of impatience I know so well. In front of him, a man pleads his case.

"My deve," he says respectfully. "I've lost seven sheep and one of my own dogs since I was here at the last new moon."

"At which time," Luka drawls, "I told you to pierce the mongrels' hides with arrows when you catch them on your land."

"But I'm not a good enough shot. And if I get too close, I fear they'll attack me."

Luka sighs heavily.

"I'm but a sheep farmer, my deve."

"Arkon Addir step forward," Luka orders and a man saunters into the circle as if he doesn't have a care in the world. "Your mutts are getting on my nerves. If you cannot control them, they'll be put down."

"My brother is a member of the Range, and he assures me that –"

"Ralton is your brother?"

"He is."

My stomach dips when the man doesn't add the required honorific at the end of his sentence. Luka's head tilts ever so slightly at the insult. Though his features remain blank, I know

Luka's moods, and his temper is on the brink of getting the better of him.

To my surprise, he only lifts a finger, beckoning a warrior forward. "Since Ralton is on rotation at the river and he can't be ordered to put the dogs down himself, I want you to take three men and ride out there. Talk to the neighbors. See what's going on. But get this solved."

"Yes, Deve."

The dog owner begins to sputter something, but Noé emerges from the crowd, drawing his dagger. Silence falls and the man melts back into the throng without another word.

"Bron," Luka gripes. "Who's next?"

Over the course of the next hour, my respect for Luka grows with every case he hears. He doesn't lose his temper, he doesn't insult anyone, and though I can tell nothing would make him happier, he doesn't maim a single person.

CHAPTER 18

LUKA

Halfway through this torture session, I catch sight of her, standing near the main doors with Ion. Yes, I'm annoyed on principle by her presence, especially since the crowd could turn on her, but curiously, her presence is also grounding. Often I lose my shit during mediation, but this time, I keep my head throughout the entire process. It might have to do with hating the thought of her thinking less of me. Or it might have to do with having every intention of using her sweet mouth as a reward for my good behavior.

"Bron?" I ask when another complaint is dealt with.

"That was the last one, my deve."

"Thank fuck."

I jump down and march into the crowd, murmurs of surprise rising up around me. Rina's smile triggers some kind of primal instinct in me as I dip down and carefully press my shoulder to her middle, hoisting her over my shoulder, uncaring of the ramifications.

"Luka," she shrieks, her voice ringing with laughter. "What are you doing? Put me down!"

I head outside and her protests continue, filling the courtyard. Not even the agog expressions coming from every direction are enough to dull my enjoyment. I think I may even be wearing a smile.

She pushes up on my lower back, and still giggling, insists, "At least tell me where we're going."

"To the hot springs. I wish to bathe." We pass through the main gates and take the worn foot path heading east. Out here, the absence of stares loosens something in my chest and I haul in a very satisfying breath of crisp winter air.

"Really, Luka," she says. "I can walk. Please. Your shoulder is like a boulder."

Not wanting to hurt her, I set her back on her feet. She's off balance and red in the face, and I can't repress another smile. Good grief. Holding her steady with one hand, I rearrange her long black hair that's in complete disarray with the other.

"What was that?" she asks in the gathering dark.

That's a very good question, one I'm not able to answer. So I deflect. "Did I hurt your leg?"

"Nah, not much," she says, though she takes my proffered arm as we start walking. An unheard of apology is set to leave my mouth, when she announces, "I was impressed with how you handled everything back there."

I laugh, allowing more of the tension of the day to slough away. "I thought you objected to being thrown over my shoulder."

"Haha, you lout." She whacks me lightly on the belly. "I meant the politicking."

"Politicking?" I grumble, though I'm pleased she liked the restraint that definitely cost me. "Where do you come up with these words?"

A soft noise of pain sounds from her and I slow my pace. "Thanks," she breathes. "I'm sure it will be healed soon."

She wants to reassure me, but all she does is remind me that I have to do a better job of keeping her safe. "How did it go today with Bron . . . and Kata?" I'm still unsure about allowing the mute girl to have the forbidden knowledge. Bron is one thing. I can claim I needed a scribe, but if things go badly, the girl could end up at the end of Kharon's sword.

"It went well. Actually all three of them have an aptitude for it."

"Three of them? Ion too?"

"Well, he was there with us," she explains, rushing to smooth my ruffled feathers. "And it was better than him staring at the wall, pretending he couldn't hear us."

I exhale heavily. Hopefully this doesn't come back to haunt me.

"What I could have done without is being called a whore. Does no one in this realm have any original insults?"

"Who called you that?" My dander is immediately up. "Ion? I'll kill him."

"What? No, of course not. I had the pleasure of meeting your uncle. He's a real charmer."

"Teo?"

"Yes, he came looking for Bron and didn't like what was going on. Ion had to ask him to leave with his dagger drawn."

"Fuck," I mutter. "He's a pain in my ass."

"But not as much as I am, though, right? I *must* be your number one pain in the ass by now."

I bark out a laugh as we arrive at the entrance to the caves. "Oh, you're at the top of one of my lists, all right." I grab myself suggestively through my pants. "Now, pass me one of those candles from the crate."

From the fire pit that's lit at nightfall, I light the candle she hands to me. Shielding the flame with my palm, I lead her through the deserted caves to the last pool and drip some wax onto a stone ledge to affix the candle. It doesn't give off a lot of light, but it keeps the total darkness at bay.

We rid ourselves of our clothes and slip into the hot water. "This is truly a divine luxury," Rina says on a sigh before she dunks her head under the water.

Despite the lush heat tempting me to relax, I quickly scrub at all the important nooks and crannies on my body. There's something much more tempting to be had.

"Little raven," I call softly and she turns from where she's paddling about on the other side of the pool. I heave myself out of the water and sit on the stone with my legs dangling. Gesturing at my hardening cock, I tell her, "I've got another job for you."

She giggles. That she not only gets my crude humor, but also finds it funny intensifies my need for her. She's *everything* except Northern. And she only adds fuel to the fire by slowly making her way to me and asking, "Are you going to hold me down again?"

I try to gauge her, but in the very dim light, I can't get a sense of her feelings on the subject. I go with the truth. "Yes." I stroke myself. "Will you object?"

She's close enough now that I see her bite her lip. "Probably. It scares me a little, but . . ."

I lift my brows in question.

"But I like it."

In my hand, my cock jerks. She comes to stand in front of me, the water not quite deep enough to cover her breasts. Perfect. I move my hips closer to the edge and lean back on my hands. "Come, then. I've been thinking of that beautiful mouth of yours all day." I watch her eyes slide down my chest, hungry and devouring, until they hit their target and linger for a long moment.

When she takes me in her small, warm hand, a bolt of pleasure lances through me. It's no matter that she's not able to completely encircle the girth with one hand, she uses two. Her mouth envelops the tip. Father help me, it's divine. In-fuck-ing-credible.

I endure the blissful little licks and sucks, fascinated by the stretch of her lips and her enthusiasm for her work. Reaching a hand up, I brush my thumb along her brows, her cheekbones, her nose. "You can do better than that," I whisper. Her gaze flips up to mine and the intimacy of the moment sizzles along my spine. She slides deeper and a drawn-out groan rips from my lips, my entire torso tensing. I want to press her straight down until her nose is buried in my groin. But that would undoubtedly end things too quickly, and I want to enjoy this. Fuck, I want *her* to enjoy this. So I take a steadying breath instead and trace her upper lip, shivering as I caress myself in the process. "That's it. That's so good."

I hear it then, a scuffle on the stone floor of the cave, and it's close.

I turn, instinctively pushing Rina back, and I get a glimpse of a raised club coming straight at my head.

Shit!

The candle flickers with the movement, then snuffs out. Momentarily distracted, my attacker misjudges the blow and it glances off my forearm as I slide into the water.

Rina squeaks with fear in the sudden, inky dark, but my sharp, shushing hiss silences her. Urging her back, I curse the noise of the water as I strain to listen. I'm almost positive there are two of them. With the new moon so close, the light from the sky is almost nil through the cracks in the ceiling, but as my vision adjusts, the darker shapes of the men become discernible against the stone. There are two; one at the entrance, one where I entered the water.

"Want woman," the one with the club growls in a thick accent.

My blood runs cold. *Eastern savages? In my realm? After my bride?* And me naked, weaponless, and without the high ground. I search out Rina's hand and point her index finger in the direction I want her to go. Thank fuck she doesn't argue.

Hoping fury isn't clouding my judgment, I weigh my options. There aren't many. I decide the one with the club will have to die first and I start back in his direction.

A low snarl sounds. It doesn't come from nearby, but carries through the cave system. Venna. I silently laugh as I reach out to grab the distracted man's booted ankle and yank. He topples over with a thud, crying out. His companion rushes forward, but I back away further into the pool.

"You want me?" I jeer. "You'll have to come in and get me."

"Jy! Jy!" fills the cave, and I wonder if it's a curse, a call for help, or the downed man's name. Whatever it is, the only answer comes from outside the caves in the form of Venna's attack and men's screams. After a bit of hesitation, he abandons his companion and stumbles away into the darkness.

The man left behind moans. I'll have to hurry. Cursing the dark, I haul myself from the pool and after a bit of fumbling around, I find his fallen form. Taking hold of his head, I twist. The sickening crack of his neck fills the space.

"Rina."

"Yes?" she whispers shakily from the far corner where I sent her.

"Get dressed if you can." I feel around for my pile of clothes, pulling on my pants and my boots. "I'll be back." Clutching my dagger tight, I listen to the ruckus outside begin to die down. Worry for Venna pushes me to pick up the pace despite the lack of light.

It's not long before the glow of the fire pit comes into view. Encountering no one, I cautiously make my way outside in time to witness Venna violently wrench away another chunk of a savage's neck.

Finding no other sign of the intruders, I give the wolf an ironic, "I think he's dead, Venna." She turns to growl at me, hunching over her kill. "Save it for our enemies," I chide, grabbing a new candle and lighting it.

I find Rina half-dressed, pressed to the side of the cave, clutching a knife that I assume she found on the dead man. "They're gone," I announce, pleased that she's resourceful enough to arm herself. Gently taking the weapon from her, I toss it aside. She's trembling and in the light of the candle, her fear is like a living shadow. "All is well," I soothe, curling her hand around the candle so I can help her with her boots. "Venna is here. No one will get past her."

"They were here for me," she says, her voice barely audible.

That's not something I wish to discuss right now. Straightening, I help her into her vest.

"Hhhow can you be so calm?"

I glance at the body with a burning hatred. "It's either that, my raven, or become sick with rage. Hurry. We must go."

Though I doubt very much the wolf would allow any of our assailants to linger, I stay vigilant as we come out into the night air. Kneeling down, I tell her to get on my back, and once I get a feel for her weight, I start off. "Come, Venna. We go for our warriors and then we hunt."

I set a ruthless pace that must be uncomfortable for Rina, but she doesn't once complain about the rough ride. As soon as the main gates are close enough, I holler for the men on guard duty. "Sound the alarm!"

Only when the bell is ringing do I let myself relax by a fraction.

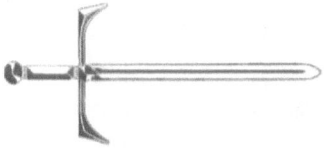

The night turns out to be a long and cold one, but my ire keeps me warm. My best trackers find evidence of four riders at the hot springs, which means I have two remaining fugitives to hunt down. Venna picks up their trail easily and we follow it for hours, far to the east, well into the Realm of the Wolf. I should probably alert Koda, the Wolf Deve, to our presence in his territory, but I don't plan to be here long. I'm determined to get my prey and be gone as soon as possible.

I don't care if I provoke Koda. I don't care if it's danger-ous to ride without the moon. I don't care if we risk ambush from more savages. I'll die before I let this incursion stand.

Dying proves unnecessary however.

When we finally surround them, there isn't even a skir-mish. One of the men has a badly wounded leg, courtesy of Venna, and the other sees the futility of resistance. Even if I'm the one to put my sword through the injured man's heart, it's all very anti-climactic and unfulfilling. We bring back two bodies, one dead, one alive.

Upon our return to the stronghold, I want nothing more than to seek out my raven and assure myself of her safety, but realm business must come first. Finding nothing out of the ordinary in the savages' possessions, I dutifully watch the surviving man's torture. Much to my vexation, it proves fruit-less because of the language barrier. The sun is finally coming up over the horizon when I beat on my barred bedroom door. When Ion opens it, he slips out without my having to say a word.

Rina, still half-asleep, is taken from the bed and spread out on the sheepskin in front of the fire where I eat her cunt out again and again. When I'm satisfied, I jack myself hard and come all over her splayed thighs. It doesn't sate my hunger for her, but it does take the edge off my restlessness enough that I'm able to get a few hours of sleep.

CHAPTER 19

RINA

Luka remains unforthcoming about what happened after he ordered Ion to bar us behind the closed door of our chamber. All he's willing to say is that the men sent after me will never be a problem again. What he doesn't shield me from, though, is the meeting that happens in the map room the following afternoon. He puts me in a chair beside him as he and his high-ranking men hash out how this happened and what can be done to prevent it in the future. He broods and glowers, but holds his temper in check while toying with his dagger. Even the normally easy-going Eldon is all business. I like what I see from his men, many of whom I've never officially met. They fear Luka, yes, but not so much that they don't openly voice their opinions. What strikes me the most is how Luka is the utter opposite of my cousin, the King, who operates via intimidation and coercion.

When they're done, Eldon and Noé stay behind with us, and they go over who they think would have the nerve to send eastern savages into Mountain Lion territory. The suspects are familiar; my cousin, King Gaden, his advisor, Mattice Dulat, and Kharon, First Deve of the Realms.

Noé objects to the last name, saying there's no way a Northman would deal with the savages, but Luka isn't convinced and neither is Eldon. They finally leave together, Luka warning me to stay within the stronghold's wall with a look that somehow has me blushing to the tips of my ears.

And over the next few days his *attentiveness* doesn't diminish. In fact, it only increases. Soon I can't even glance at his mouth without growing warm – all over. In public, he enjoys making me squirm in my seat without even saying a word. In private, his dirty words and his tongue drive me absolutely mad.

In between all the orgasms, we talk. We talk about our childhood adventures, our firsts, our favorites. Not surprisingly, Luka lives up to some of my preconceived notions of Northern men; he loves his war horse, his sword, and training. But he also loves his mother and has a weakness for sweets. This softer side of himself he only shares with Niri, and Eldon and his family . . . and now me. I'm honored and half-way in love with the big brute even if he shies away from anything that involves his emotions.

My only worry is that he hasn't given me the one thing I'm endlessly on the verge of begging for: his cock, sheathed inside of me, where it *belongs*. Since it's constantly in my mouth, his reasons for withholding himself in this way must involve getting me with child . . . something that would create a long-term bond between us. I won't lie. That he's not willing to risk such a bond hurts. It's possible that things have not progressed on his side of the equation in the same way that they have on mine.

And with everything else going on, I almost forget about Cayson Cyrun. But the day of his reckoning comes anyway.

"Tell me again how killing the deve would redeem this man," I ask Bron, disgust and nerves jockeying for the high ground inside of me as we wait for this farce to begin. From what I can tell, almost the entire realm's inhabitants are lining the demarcated area at the training ground. The atmosphere is fair-like and there are even a few jugglers in the center to keep the crowd entertained.

Bron scoffs, and Ion, from my other side, says, "No harm will come to the deve. Not even Eldon can best him at hand-to-hand combat."

I blow out a heavy breath. This morning Luka had dismissed my worry as unnecessary, stating only that Cayson predictably favors his left side.

"Only Gray would have a chance," Ion goes on, scanning the crowd for any sign of hostility toward me. I wonder how he's filtering them because there are undeniable glares coming my way despite the celebratory mood. "And he's left the Range."

That doesn't make me feel any better. Gray is Cayson's brother. What if he decides to defend him? "But you didn't answer my question. How would this spectacle redeem Cayson for his crimes?"

"Northern custom," Bron explains, "allows for any man to prove he has the Mother's favor by besting the deve in combat."

I want to keep arguing but a small girl and her mother have drawn near. The child graces me with a shy smile and

277

holds up a pink quartz in her grubby hand. She can't be more than four or five years old and I crouch down to accept the gift. "Thank you so much, sweetheart. I'll treasure it always."

They dip their heads in respect. "May the Mother condemn Cayson Cyrun," the woman whispers before she leads her child away by the hand.

"Indeed," I murmur, slipping the stone into the pocket of my vest.

A cheer goes up from the far corner of the field where the four eastern savages' heads have been put on display at the ends of pikes. A farmer is providing children with rotten vegetables, and one of them has hit his target, dislocating a decomposing jaw.

"Ugh," Bron chokes.

"Come now, dearest," Ion says with a chuckle. "If I remember correctly, you weren't above that kind of thing as a child."

"My brothers goaded me mercilessly," he laments, reminding me that not only is Gray Cayson's brother, but Bron is as well.

"I'm sorry, Bron. This must be hard for you."

He sighs. "Honestly, I'm not all that torn up about it. My brothers and I have never been of the same mind. Only Gray ever showed me any kindness." He arranges the cuff of his tunic as if in thought. "And that was only because our sire was dead by the time I was born, and as the oldest, he was duty bound to show me some guidance." He reaches across me for Ion's hand. "But now, I have you. You're my family."

I swivel my head in time for Ion's reply of, "Always."

Their emotion fills my heart with a heavy joy and I feel tears start to well. I've always wanted to find somewhere that I belonged. "That's so beautiful," I whisper and they're reminded of my presence.

"Are you going to cry?" Ion asks in disbelief.

"No, of course not," I sniffle. "That would be silly. It's just, I know the situation is different, but I don't have any family either."

Bron wraps his arm around my shoulder. "We are your family now, aren't we, Ion?"

"We are," he says, his deep voice tinged with solemnity.

"Thanks," I whisper, wiping at my cheeks. "You don't know how much I appreciate that."

Ion clears his throat as he goes back to surveying the crowd. "Enough now. We have appearances to maintain."

"He's right," Bron agrees. "Plus, we need to concern ourselves with the deve."

"But you said he'd be fine," I accuse, my voice rising in pitch.

"Physically, yes. But emotionally, it must be a special kind of torture to have to dispatch one of his best friends from childhood."

"What?" I breathe.

Bron nods. "I'd imagine it's part of the reason the deve's first reaction to your situation was so negative. The twins are of an age with him, and they were thick as thieves as children."

Feeling sick, I murmur, "I had no idea."

"Well," Bron says, winking at me. "These warrior types are not known for their open communication skills, are they?"

The sound of drums fills the clearing and the crowd parts, revealing my intended's arrival, flanked by Eldon and Noé.

My breath catches. He's magnificent. Dressed only in buckskin pants that fit him like a second skin and his boots, he walks with supreme confidence, his fists clenching and unclenching with pent up energy. His bare chest and broad shoulders scream of brute strength and power, and the gold torque of the Mountain Lion Deve that encircles his bicep glints in the winter light. He seems not to hear the crowd, as if all of his focus is turned inward, something that makes him appear all the more fierce.

They're followed by two drummers and a cart filled with weapons. Last comes a limping Cayson. He's flanked by his two other brothers, Gray and Crion, but on closer inspection I see his ankle is still shackled by a chain to the cart.

Eldon steps forward and a hush comes over the crowd. "People of the Mountain Lion, you are here to witness Cayson Cyrun's attempts to win the Mother's forgiveness for his betrayal of this realm and its lawful deve, Lukaron Djothar."

Loud cheers erupt, but a few shouts of contempt spear into my heart. The sudden and terrifying reality that Luka may be lost to me today hits me like a battering ram. As if sensing my distress, the man in question lifts his head in my direction. His gaze is so steady, so heavy upon me that I can't help but calm. He fears nothing and neither should I. *Trust in me,* those dark eyes convey. *I won't falter, I won't fail.*

When Eldon crosses between us, briefly interrupting the connection, there's almost nothing left of my trepidation. I give Luka a nod, sending him an echo of the strength he's given me. I can't be sure, but I swear his expression fleetingly warms for me.

Cayson is unshackled and the swords and shields are distributed. Considering a man's life is on the line, the ceremonial aspects are short and to the point. I'm coming to realize that actions carry so much more weight than words here in the north.

Without delay, the two men begin circling each other. When the blows start, the crowd erupts and almost drowns out the twang of sword on sword or the dull thump of sword on shield. Though the majority are there to support Luka, it's clear that a few want Cayson to put an end to his rule. Among them are the men who were on the road that night.

A loud cry rents the air and my attention flies back to the battle. Luka has landed a kick, sending Cayson flying onto his rump in the dirt.

"Get up!" Luka roars and the crowd goes wild.

Once Cayson's back on his feet, Luka doesn't let up. He drives him back with strike after strike, somehow managing to twist and spin and avoid Cayson's reach at every turn. I'm not ashamed to admit that my desire for him increases with every passing minute. He's physical poetry and grace personified.

There are a few close calls that send my heart lurching up into my throat, but it's obvious from the start that Cayson is outmatched. When Zola's tormented cry of, "Mercy!" rings out over the din, both sadness and satisfaction swamp me. Luka, however, doesn't hesitate. After a powerful combination of blows, Cayson finally goes down hard and has no time to react to the sword blade that spears right through the middle of his chest, pinning him to the ground.

A hush falls over the field, one that's immediately punctuated by Zola's wail of despair, then the roar of approval from the crowd. I can't pull my eyes from Cayson, who's still alive, choking on his own blood and feebly trying to pull the sword free. The only word I can think of to describe it is *horrifying*.

Luka once again advances on his opponent, this time carrying a very large poleaxe. With Cayson watching, Luka takes his time before bringing the weapon down with such force that the single blow is the only one needed to sever the head from its body.

Blood sprays everywhere much to the delight of the spectators. Luka chucks the axe aside and yanks his sword from the corpse, raising it in triumph. The noise of the crowd reaches a crescendo and Luka roars his own approval.

"Let this . . ." he bellows, then waits for the crowd to quiet down before he starts again. "Let this serve as a warning. *I. Am. Deve.* Accept it . . . or challenge, but I won't be intimidated. I won't be manipulated. And I will *not* tolerate betrayal."

With his people's raucous approval reverberating in my ears, I start forward.

"Oh, shit," Ion exclaims, scrambling to follow me.

As I close the distance, I watch some of the younger recruits get a stake and mount Cayson's severed head to display alongside the savages'. At twenty paces out, Luka notices me. The stare he levels me with almost brings me to a standstill. Savagery and lingering bloodlust cling to him like a shadow in broad daylight, and for a fraction of a second, I worry he'll lash out at me. But doubting him now would only taint what we've begun to nurture between us. It's worth the risk. *He's* worth the risk.

I forge ahead until he looms over me, his chest scraped and bruised and there's a spray of blood across his shoulder. I open my mouth to congratulate him on his victory when he simply takes hold of my upper arm and starts walking, hauling me along with him.

I don't make a fuss, just hasten my steps to match his pace. I do pry at his fingers, though, which earns me a snarl. I don't let up. First, he's hurting me, and second, we must be seen as partners – deve and a'deve – who rule together, something that isn't possible if he's dragging me around like a rag doll.

He stops unexpectedly, annoyed with my attempts to loosen his grip. Returning his glare, I pointedly look to where he's cutting off my circulation. Even though his lip curls into a sneer, he allows me to guide his hand down until our palms meet. Triumph soars in my blood at the compromise as we head back toward the stronghold.

As we near the edge of the crowd, Zola barrels toward us, mad with grief, her fist raised. Before she can strike me, Luka shoves her back, sending her to the ground. Gray immediately steps between them, animosity pouring off of him as he protects his mother.

I snake my free arm across Luka's waist, pressing myself into his side without letting go of his hand, willing him to forget about Zola. The aesthetics of beating an old woman couldn't possibly be favorable, and a brawl with Gray could be disastrous with Luka tired and his thinking clouded. To my relief, Luka ultimately lets it go and pulls me past the man.

The boisterous crowd straggles along behind us on the way back to the stronghold, without a doubt in the mood for a party. On the steps of the Great Hall, a collection of women awaits Luka's return, including his mother. She's plainly happy to see him whole, but he only spares her a curt nod, passing not only her by, but also Dagmar, Kata, Lorna and many others who work in the stronghold.

Up the stairs and down the hall to his chamber, he pulls me along. He doesn't let go of me until we're safely behind the door and that's only because he needs both hands to bar us inside. I head for the pitcher of water to get him cleaned up.

"I want you naked."

The water pitcher poised over the basin, I pause to glance at him over my shoulder. Everything I see tells me he's not going to negotiate, so I don't know why I try. "You're covered in filth."

"I don't give a *fuck* what I'm covered in." His hard tone raises goosebumps across my skin as I set the pitcher down.

Over the bed that separates us, I take in the thinly veiled violence in his posture, his fists clenching and unclenching, his gaze still flat and partially vacant. Half of him is clearly still back on that field fighting for his life. "My throat is still sore from last night," I announce.

His eyes narrow, though whether it's in response to my defiant tone or because he picks up on my dare to fuck me properly, I can't say. All I know is that he unwinds slightly as I reach for the buckles on my vest to do as he's asked.

"You fought well," I say and a flash of interest beats back some of his blankness. My boots join my vest and dress in a heap on the floor before I go to work on my pants. "Tell me, does such grace influence *all* your movements, my deve?" The tilt of his head tells me he's unsure of what I'm implying, though the ever-increasing bulge in his pants says his body doesn't care. As my shirt comes over my head, I decide to spell it out for him.

Completely naked, I hitch my knee up on the mattress and crawl toward him. "What I mean, Luka, is do you fuck as well as you fight?"

As if he's been let off of a leash, in two giant steps, he's at the side of the bed, his hand at my nape, hauling me up to my knees. "You're about to find out." His mouth crashes down on mine, and it's like we go to war. Our lips and tongues begin a drawn-out, frantic battle, igniting the now very familiar blaze between my thighs. He pulls me flush against his body and I grope and claw at his back. We explore each other until his hands drop to my ass and he curls his hips into mine. I gasp into his mouth.

"You're going to take every inch I give you," he declares. "Do you hear me? Every fucking inch. I'm going to bury myself so deep inside of you."

I want to agree, I want to consent, but his greedy lips are back to consuming mine. In an attempt to get him closer, I slide my own hands down to grasp his ass . . . his leather-clad ass. The barrier incenses me, and I start to scrabble at his laces, mewling my frustration.

"If you want my cock, you just have to ask for it."

If I wasn't drunk on him, I'd object to his condescending tone. If I wasn't ready to combust, I'd drag this out. But as it is, "I want your cock, Luka."

He tugs me back by the hair at my nape to study me while he undoes the laces and sets his beast of a cock free. It bobs between us, long, hard, and very erect before he reaches for the apex of my thighs and I almost come out of my skin. His rough, calloused fingers send streaks of pleasure careening through me until he pulls them away.

"Nn–"

My objection is cut off by a wet slap to my core. I freeze. *Holy shit.* It wasn't hard, but I felt it. Again, he jerks me by my hair, this time to hiss in my ear. "This is going to go my way. Not yours. I give. You take. Is that understood?" He presses his nose to my neck and inhales deeply. "Now be a good girl and lie yourself down."

He lets me go and I wobble, a bit dazed. He lifts his chin at the bed. Overwhelmed, I do as he wants. But as soon as my back hits the feather mattress, he seems to change his mind.

Reaching for my waist, he uses his strength to turn me over and arrange me on my hands and knees. Immediately he's dragging me back to the edge of the bed and notching himself into place.

"Waaaiiit," I cry as he starts to press into me. This isn't how I wanted it to go. "Wait. Please!" He hesitates and I take my chance to wiggle forward, dislodging him. I fall sideways and quickly flip over to stare up at his pissed off expression. "Please," I whisper. "Can we do it face-to-face?"

His jaw clenches, and it's as if he has my heart between his teeth.

"Just this once?" I bargain in a small voice, not telling him that I've never done it like that before, not wanting him to see how the hurt grows the longer he refuses to agree.

He finally huffs with irritation, but climbs onto the bed and settles himself between my thighs. Pushing my hair back from my forehead, he says, "You're not very obedient."

An exhale catching in my throat, I plant a quick kiss on the side of his mouth for granting me this when he doesn't want or need it. "Thank you," I whisper.

His only response is to reach between us and position himself. Anticipation races across my skin as he begins to push forward, watching every nuance of my expression. The first few inches are incredible. His girth stretches me in all the right ways. But when the inches keep coming, I tense up a bit. I twist my hips, trying for a momentary reprieve that he doesn't grant me. "Uh, uh, little raven," he tuts, seeming to soak up my discomfort. "What did I say?"

He feeds me some more and my chin lifts as if that will create more space inside of me. He's not forcing it, but he's not letting up on the pressure either.

"What did I say? How much of me will you be taking?"

"All of it," I pant, completely uncertain if the fullness of him is the best thing I've ever felt or the worst. "You said all of it."

"That's right," he chokes out as I cede him further ground. "Oh, fuck."

I whimper, my inner muscles rippling along his length in protest. Or is it approval?

"You are paradise," he breathes, stalling his invasion to lean down and take my mouth. The languid kiss goes on and on, so gentle and sweet that when he starts pressing forward again, I'm nothing but a moaning, wanton mess.

Just when I truly don't think I can take any more, his mouth slides to my ear. "There we go," he whispers, sounding delirious. "Almost didn't think we'd make it."

Something about his use of the word *we* sparks a burst of emotion and I bury my nose in his collar bone. Withdrawing almost to the tip, he pushes back in, forcing a feverish, "Oohhhhhh," from my lungs. The slide of him is truly glorious. Advance, retreat. Advance, retreat. I lose myself in the slow, divine rhythm.

When the pace becomes more demanding, my eyes fly open and I find his ablaze, his jaw set, and something inside of me lets go. I love him so much. The thought comes as a tell-tale tremor in my core eclipses it.

"Yes," he groans, interrupting the strokes to bear down on my clit. "Come for me."

I cry out, my entire world contracting then expanding as I burst into a million tiny pieces.

Though I'm scarcely lucid, I do feel him pull out of me, which triggers a mournful, little whimper. I wish he'd stay and cuddle me for a –

A tug at my ankle shocks me back to myself. He's out of bed, dragging me along the mattress. "Luka!"

"Hush," he admonishes, arranging me at the corner of the bed, my ass on the edge. "You had your fun, now it's my turn."

Still standing, he positions himself at my core. He doesn't mess about, just pushes straight into my sensitive flesh, sending a hard shiver down my spine. Wrapping my legs around his hips, I watch him tip his head to the ceiling and inhale deeply as if to center himself. Then his big palm lands beside my head on the bed, startling me. While I adjust to the new angle of him inside of me, his other hand slides under my shoulder to cradle the back of my neck. He lifts me slightly, pulling my body more tightly onto his length. Mother have mercy, but I am full, and with him curved over me like a predator about to devour its prey, every muscle in his torso tensed, he is a sight to behold.

"Hold on, little raven," he whispers as he slides out until only the tip is poised at my entrance. After a second of hesitation, he shoves himself back in deep and begins the process of drowning me in ecstasy.

CHAPTER 20

LUKA

I'd forgotten. *Fuck, how had I forgotten?*

Since I became deve, I haven't dipped my cock into a single cunt. It was the responsible thing to do. I didn't need a bunch of bastards running around, and I was already bound by the title so I certainly didn't need a wife further weighing me down. But this . . . *fuuuuuck*. This tight, slippery cunt is beyond anything I remember. It's like fucking into the best fantasy I've ever had and then some.

I should have turned her over though. I should have taken her from behind so I couldn't watch her come. Now the image of her lost to nirvana while stuffed full of me has been seared into my mind – three separate times. Three fucking times I've felt her cunt squeeze me with its vise-like contractions.

The slap of skin on skin is loud in my chamber. I'm riding

her hard and relishing every stroke that gapes her swollen cunt and bounces her tits. I wish it could go on forever, but eventually it all overpowers me. And when I empty my balls into her, I swear I almost black out. It's sublime.

I come back to myself slumped over her small frame, her chest struggling to pull air into her lungs under my weight. One of those sweet, protesting noises she makes when things aren't going her way comes out of her as I push up. I'd probably chuckle at her ridiculousness if my extremely sensitive cock wasn't being pulled from its new favorite place.

With her legs splayed on either side of the corner of the bed and her head lolling to the side, she's done-in . . . and gorgeous. How has this woman gotten around my defenses? Now I can feel her warmth and comfort inside of me, like she's somehow managed to seep into my very soul. But instead of panicking and trying to siphon her back out as I get my boots off, followed by my pants, all I want to do is care for her.

Her full lips push together, offering me a lazy, well-satisfied smile. "Luka," she murmurs.

I crawl back on the bed, straddling her. "Yes?" I ask, scooping my arm under her shoulder again before I haul her up the bed to the pillows. She giggles as I maneuver us under the furs.

With her safely in my arms, every last ounce of strain in my body melts away.

"That was wonderful," she informs me, her hand lifting to caress my bearded jaw. I'm sure my dead-pan look would be more effective if I weren't leaning into her touch.

"Are you going to start prattling on about the obvious now?"

More giggling. "I don't prattle. Though," she pauses as if

to think it over. "It's true that I'll probably be mentioning, days from now, again and again, how no one has ever brought me the stars like that."

I snort. "Is that supposed to be poetry?"

"Oh, yes," she says, adding to her sweet grin by lifting her wrist to her brow in dramatic fashion. "As soon as the opportunity presents itself, I'll commission a bard to commemorate your aptitude for gifting the stars."

At that, I laugh. "Gifting the stars, huh?"

She nods. "It's a perfect fit . . . almost as perfect as hearing you laugh."

I sigh, then unexpectedly come out with, "There's not a lot about being deve that lends itself to laughter."

She hums with reluctant agreement. "I suppose." Her nails start stroking through my beard and my lids sink closed. "Bron told me that Cayson was your childhood friend. Today must have been difficult for you."

I grunt, not liking the turn of the conversation.

"I understand," she says gently, "why you wouldn't want to talk about it, but if you ever do, I'm here to listen."

Dipping my chin, I search her gaze. "There's nothing to talk about, little raven. It needed doing, and now it is done."

With a level of awareness that makes me uneasy, she concurs. "Okay."

Okay? Since when does this woman ever let anything go so easily?

"Can I ask you something?"

I laugh for the second time in as many minutes. "You can't stay quiet, can you?"

"It's about something else," she claims.

Leaning down, I kiss her mouth. "Fine. Ask your question."

"I want to know why you call me that . . . little raven. Is it because my voice is grating to the nerves? I'm never sure if I should be offended or not."

My whole body shakes with silent laughter. "No. It's not because you get on my nerves. Though that does –"

She whacks my chest, which makes me laugh all the more. Grabbing her hand, I pull it to my mouth and kiss her knuckles. "Do you really not know, *little raven?*"

Shaking her head, she attempts a pout, but her wide, expectant eyes betray her innocence. She really doesn't know.

"I call you that because your hair is the exact shade of a raven's wing. In the sun, it gleams, and in the moonlight, it shines."

She blinks and sudden tears appear on her lashes. "Now who's the one with the poetry?"

"It wasn't meant to make you cry."

"I'm sorry. I'm being silly. I've been doing that a lot today." She pushes forward against my hold and I let her lips meet mine.

The kiss starts innocently enough, but soon heat re-ignites between us and my mind starts serving up progressively more and more explicit ideas about sinking back into her still seed-filled body. Rolling more of my weight onto her breaks our lips apart, and I let my mouth roams down her neck and across her chest to latch on to an erect nipple.

"Luka," she breathes. "Even if it's not forever, thank you for giving me these moments. They mean so much to me. *You* mean so much to me."

Distracted, I hear the murmured words but don't actually process them. All I can think about is how I'm going to make this incredible woman mine all over again.

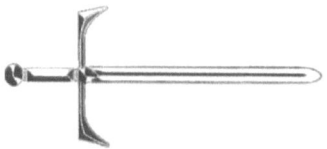

The banging of the alarm bell wrenches me from a dead sleep. For an instant, I can't identify what's sprawled across my chest and I'm at the point of heaving it away when Rina's sharp inhale penetrates my muddled thoughts.

She lurches up. "Is that . . . what is that?"

"Light some candles," I order, swinging my legs over the edge of the bed, already searching for my pants in the dim light of the hearth embers.

She obeys for once, and we work at our respective tasks to the continued clanging of the bell. I get my boots on and notice Rina's hands are trembling. "You're safe here with me," I remind her.

She swallows hard. "Is it the savages? Have they returned for me?"

Three loud thumps sound on our door. "We're about to find out."

"My deve!" Bron says through the door. "The Wolf cauldron has been lit."

The knot in my chest eases by a fraction. The savages are not here, but in the Wolf Realm to the east. As I raise the bar, all the noise comes to an end and I exhale with relief. On the other side of the door, however, Bron is still a bit manic, reminding me that this is only his third go round as my aide in a high-pressure situation. My palm lands on the smaller man's shoulder, steadying him. "Are preparations underway?"

"Yes, Deve."

I nod. "Eldon has been sent for?"

"Yes."

"Good. Have the kitchen prepare rations for three days as well as breakfast for . . ." I pause, glancing back at Rina who's gotten her dress on. "Thirty men. Inform Noé, and send Ion up."

"Okay. Uhhh, only thirty?"

"That's what I said." I shut the door in his face, the old self-doubt that used to plague me nothing but a flicker. I'm not leaving the stronghold with minimal defenses when this week saw savages on our doorstep. The Wolves will accept half of us or none at all.

"What's the Wolf cauldron?" Rina asks, now slipping her boots on.

"An emergency beacon to the east. The Wolf Realm is asking for our help to repel the savages."

That's clearly not what she was expecting me to say. "Does that happen often?"

I move to the weapons chest and flip open the heavy lid. "Not usually this close to winter, but yes, a number of times a year."

"And . . ." She hesitates as if choosing her words carefully. "And the deve answers this appeal for assistance himself?"

Rummaging through the contents, I grin to myself. "I do, yes." I don't mention how my father never rode or fought with his men, or how, even before I came to power, these forays into battle as Warrior Commander forged a bond between me and my warriors. It has proven an incredibly valuable means of breeding loyalty in the ranks. The dagger I'm seeking is at the bottom of the chest and I pluck it out. "Come here." I pull the knife from its leather sheath and hold it out to her handle first.

"What's this?"

"This was mine when I was a boy. Do you know how to use a dagger?"

"Not as well as a bow, no."

"We'll work on that when I return. But for now, I want you to keep it on you at all times." While she turns the blade over in her hands, I loop the sheath's belt around her waist, satisfied to see that it fits her nicely. "Do I need to tell you that this is for defense purposes only?" The wry tone of my voice brings a quirk to her lips. "I'm trusting you, Rina."

"Thank you," she says simply and I squeeze her shoulders before I make my way to my clothing cupboard. Digging out my warmest shirt, I'm grateful that she took a wash cloth to me earlier. Going into battle already covered in blood and grime isn't appealing in the least.

"When will you return?" she asks.

"No idea. It may be a week, it may be three." My thickest long-sleeve leather battle tunic goes on over the shirt. I have Rina adjust the laces until I'm satisfied with my range of movement. My vest also needs adjustment before I move on to arming myself. My battle sword has probably been cleaned and put with my things in Nightshade's stall, but I strap my short sword to my thigh, my long dagger to the outside of my boot, and thread the handle of my axe through its loop on my belt. My regular dagger is already in place.

She watches me as I swing my fur traveling cloak over my shoulders. "Will you be warm enough?" she murmurs.

Her concern is like a shot of rot-gut, warm yet fierce. Besides my mother, no one's ever worried for my well-being. It's oddly settling, though the buzz of anticipation I always get before embarking on these missions isn't dulled in any way. "Don't fret. I'll do everything in my power to come back to you in one piece." I set my palm against her cheek. "And I expect you to obey Ion while I'm gone. Don't leave the stronghold for any reason except to bathe." She's on the verge of arguing, but I cut her off. "I mean it. If I come back to a stolen or dead bride, I will be more than angry. Let's keep things on an even keel while I'm gone, all right?"

Her lips purse but she nods.

I seal our agreement with a kiss as someone bangs on the door. "My deve?" Ion calls.

"Ready?" I ask Rina, taking her hand and heading for the door.

Downstairs, the Great Hall is abuzz with activity. The stronghold servant girls are already set up at their usual table, braiding the warriors' hair and applying the charcoal war paint. When I sit, Lorna immediately leaves what she's doing to attend to me, but Rina stiffens, her gaze sharpening with raptor-like intensity on the woman.

Lorna misses nothing. "My a'deve," she says, dipping her head. "Perhaps you could work on the deve's hair, and then I can show you how to apply the paint for next time." Handing over the strips of leather and a comb, the woman makes a hasty retreat.

Rina's little harrumph forces me to stifle a chuckle. "Do I

need to take that blade away from you already?"

Her head swings in my direction and she pins me with a look of such possession that my exhausted cock twitches. She ignores my taunt, though, and instead demands, "You want your hair braided?"

"I do." Though I have no idea if she's capable of the somewhat intricate braids that keep a warrior's hair close to his scalp, I tip my head at another warrior whose hair resembles what I want.

Eldon arrives, obviously displeased. "Fucking savages," he mutters. "They have no respect for my beauty sleep."

Trying not to grimace as Rina tugs roughly at my hair with the comb, I welcome Eldon's daughter Trudy onto my lap. "Uncle," she says. "You're going to kill savages?"

"I am."

"Will you tell me again about the Wolf warriors that are girls?" Trudy is fascinated by the existence of the Wolf Realm female warriors. She's more open-minded than I am. Despite knowing it's my father's disdain for them that influences my attitude, I'm not sure what I'll do when a woman shows interest in becoming a warrior here in our own realm.

"Maybe next time," I tell her. "Don't you have duties to attend to?"

"Oh, yes!" She jumps down and scampers away as if she's just remembered.

I don't know who started the tradition, but the youngest daughters of the warriors paint a mark on each warrior's palm when his hair and face paint are complete. It usually resembles a squiggly line, but it's meant to represent the long body of a mountain lion.

While Rina finishes my hair, Eldon and I go over a few

things. As usual, he'll remain behind and in command while I'm gone. I'm not worried. He knows what he's doing. Though it's usually done in reverse – the second takes control of the men in battle and the deve stays behind – Eldon has a family to care for, and I . . . I can't imagine staying behind. Battle is what I was born to do.

Lorna arrives back with a pot of charcoal paint and shows Rina how to apply the vertical lines that bisect the left eye from brow to lip, explaining the thickness of the main line denotes rank.

"Sounds like a cock-measuring contest to me," Rina announces, making Lorna burst into peals of laughter.

"That's exactly what it is. And it's good for them." She runs the horse-hair paint brush down my face with a steady hand. "It keeps them striving to do more and be more, so they can wear their lines proudly into battle."

I only grunt at her assessment, which is pretty accurate. Earning my lines certainly motivated me as a younger man. I watch as she trades brushes to continue painting the three thinner lines that will run parallel, each one closer to my ear than the last. As she's finishing, Noé shows up and throws himself on the bench beside me like an overly dramatic adolescent. "You're set on only taking half of the Range? There's been a ton of bitching."

"Anything that needs my attention?"

"Nah," he grumbles. "Sometimes I feel more like a den mother than a commander though."

I laugh. And everyone in the vicinity turns to stare, but I ignore them and clap Noé on the shoulder. "Now you know exactly how I felt when I was Commander."

"Uncle?" interrupts us. "Are you ready for your lion?"

Trudy is holding a small clay pot in one hand and a thin brush in the other.

"I am," I tell her, holding out my palm.

Setting the pot on the table, she dips the brush, and with a firm grip on my thumb, she applies the line with a flourish. "Now you will have the best of luck, Uncle!" Then she turns to Rina. "Would you like one too, for fun?"

Rina lets out an exaggerated gasp, much to Trudy's delight. "I would love one, thank you."

With another dip of the brush, Trudy gives Rina a mountain lion on her palm. I don't think Trudy realizes how much her small gesture means to Rina, who's staring at her hand with a lot more emotion than is called for.

"Oh, Trudy," I call. "I need another one on my other hand. I need a raven."

"A raven?! But I don't know how to draw a raven."

I sense Rina's regard, but I keep mine on Trudy. "Well, imagine a bird in the sky. How would you draw that?"

The little girl bites at her lip. "Like this?" She dips the brush and makes what appears to be two hills on my hand. They're wings.

"Yes!" I kiss her on the cheek. "Exactly. You're my favorite niece."

She gives me a little giggle. "I'm your only niece."

"Which makes you even more special."

She continues down the line of warriors as I get up to make space for the next man.

Rina is quiet despite all the nervous boisterousness, and while we eat a quick breakfast, I catch her peeking down at her palm a few times. I want to reassure her that all is well, but if we're to *be* together, she'll have to get used to me having to leave at a moment's notice.

Dawn is breaking over the horizon when we assemble in the courtyard. Nightshade is brought to me saddled and ready, and he nibbles on an apple from Rina's hand while I double check my gear and supplies. Sheathing my broad sword on my back, I mount my horse and send Ion a quick nod, which he returns. He's aware of the seriousness of the task I've assigned him. Then I meet Rina's sad eyes and reach down to her. We clasp palms briefly, raven to mountain lion, and without a word, I lead my men out of the gates and to the east.

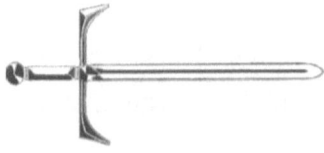

I set a hard pace, one that my warriors and their mounts are used to. It hasn't rained in recent memory and the day is clear, if cool, and we make excellent time heading east by northeast. Noé has taken our best scouts ahead, but they've found nothing out of the ordinary.

Koda, Deve of the Wolves, is not a man who's easily rattled; he deals with the savages day in and day out. If he's lit the cauldron, there's no question of his need for reinforcements.

By late afternoon, we're well into Wolf territory. Their stronghold, along the eastern shores of the vast Lake Nadore, is far-removed from their border with the savages, so unless something catastrophic has happened, the incursion will be further to the east and I'm reluctant to run us so far north only to have to retrace our steps.

With the light fading, I order a halt in a copse of trees

we've used as shelter before. It's colder than the Father's tit, but a fire would give away our position, so cold rations it is.

My guess proves correct and only an hour into our stop, the first perimeter watch signals the approach of Noé, our scouts, and four Wolf riders. In the dark, the only rider I can distinguish is Noé, but he's not the one to address me.

"Luka, you have my regard."

I couldn't be more surprised to see the Wolf Deve himself dismount his horse. We clasp forearms in greeting. "Koda." He's a big, intimidating fucker, and not just in size. His presence would be impossible to ignore even if he never said a word. Eight years ago he took over the Wolves by sheer strength and cunning, deposing the realm's founding family, something that reminds me how precarious my own rule is.

"I wasn't sure you'd come," he says, his breath pluming in the cold.

I feel a tick of aggravation. "Since when have I not come when you've called?"

"I meant you, personally. You have a lot going on at home, do you not?"

I scan the men around us and imagine they're all listening closely. I change the subject. "Are we moving on or camping for the night?"

"We camp. First light will see us move out. Light your fires," he allows, letting his voice carry. "The enemy won't be on the offensive tonight."

"You heard the man," Noé says loudly. "Get set up."

An hour later, the smells of roasting meat and the low hum of conversation fill the forest. Koda and I have made a fire away from the men to talk privately while we eat.

301

"I heard you had a savage incursion," he says in between ripping chunks of meat off of a rabbit leg.

I blow out a breath. "More like an attempt on my life . . . and the life of my new, intended bride. They mentioned her specifically."

His chewing pauses and his eyes meet mine over the fire, his bald head gleaming in its light. "Mentioned her?"

"It seems someone doesn't want us to go through with the contract."

"Any idea who?"

Ever since I was named Warrior Commander at nineteen, Koda and I have been trading information and building a working relationship. At least, that's my hope. It's a risk to trust him, I know. But a calculated one.

I shrug. "Either Gaden . . . or Kharon. Or both." I tell him about the letter.

"I heard your scribe was dead." He chucks the clean bone into the fire and takes up another. "He's been replaced already?"

Shaking my head, I take a bite of my own dinner to give myself time to consider how much to tell him. "My betrothed," I start slowly. "Has pointed out the folly of depending on others in this regard."

"About time you put those pieces together."

I scowl at him. "Are you saying you have men who can read and write?"

"Of course."

"You don't worry about Kharon's wrath?"

"Kharon is a pampered weakling who sits in his castle like he's the Father himself."

Hearing this from Koda's lips has my stomach turning over. My whole life, two things were beaten into me; loyalty to my sire and loyalty to Kharon. I'm not sure I appreciate Koda's taking a sledgehammer to the one remaining foundation of my life.

"Tell me about her," he says, pulling me from my thoughts.

"Who? My intended?" My lips twist with irony. "You mean you haven't *heard* everything you need to know?"

He shows me a flash of teeth from behind his long, blond beard. "I wish to hear *your* impressions. Have you decided to go through with the marriage, then?"

"I don't know. It's complicated. Her presence is . . . disruptive."

"Don't fool yourself, Luka. The dissent was already there. Either you consolidate your rule or you perish. It's that simple."

I sigh. "I suppose you're right."

"Of course I am. And my question remains. Will you go through with the marriage? Not for Kharon or D'heilar. But because she's an asset to you and your people."

"Not because I like her?"

He huffs incredulously. "That's already obvious, young Luka. And I respect that you're not letting your cock make your decisions, but you have to boil it down to whether she makes you stronger or weaker."

I break out in a cold sweat, not only because he's right, but because I know the answer to his question. I'm relieved when Venna takes that moment to interrupt the conversation with a soft rumble of her vocal cords. She creeps up on my left, her maw full of a large rabbit.

"Fucking shit," Koda mutters.

"Where have you been, Venna?" I ask her. She's either finally caught up with us or was staying out of sight today and has deigned to join us.

Dropping the dead rabbit in the dirt near my thigh, she butts her head to my shoulder. "Thank you, my friend," I murmur, letting her smell my grease smeared fingers. "But I've already eaten."

After allowing a few scratches to her ears, she retrieves the rabbit and withdraws to a spot outside the light cast by the fire.

"That shit is unnatural," Koda informs me.

"She's saved my life many times . . . and taught me much of loyalty. But enough about that, tell me why we're here."

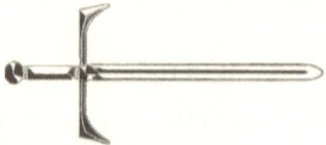

It turns out Koda's problems with the savages have become more complex. Instead of their usual hit and run looting raids on farming outposts, they've been encroaching on Realm territory in a more permanent way. An actual savage settlement was found on Wolf land a couple of weeks ago.

What Koda should have done was gone in and massacred the whole lot of them, women and children included. But like I would have, he gave their vulnerable the opportunity to evacuate. Now the men left behind have entrenched themselves in the surrounding area, making them harder to root out.

It's a long, tough week of ambushes and close-quarter

fighting that results in Koda's losing two men. By the end, I'm banged up with scrapes, bruises, and a small gash on my calf that needs to be cauterized, but generally unharmed. I'm more annoyed by the cold than anything else, and I spend the nights when I'm able to lay my head down, dreaming of Rina. I'm not sure if I'm surprised by how much I look forward to returning to her. But I won't deny that I am, especially when I keep rubbing at the raven on my palm long after it's worn off.

Day eight sees us heading back, though to my supreme irritation, a heavy rain storm forces us to make camp with only half the journey complete. It's not until around noon of day nine that we're close enough to the stronghold that Nightshade perks up and willingly picks up his speed. He wants to be home as much as I do.

With only a few miles to go, I spot a group of six riders in the distance. They're ours and on a well-established patrol route. Their presence isn't out of the ordinary, but their number doesn't sit well with me – at all. Whistling loudly, I get their attention and they rein in and wait for us.

Eldon is with them. Eldon. Eldon who should be in the stronghold.

"What's happening?" I demand.

"We've had a report of savages, my deve," Eldon reports.

"Here?" My chest tightens. "When?"

"Not long ago. I've got four patrols out."

"How many savages?"

"That's unclear. But no more than six we think."

"In the middle of the day?" That strikes me as odd. The savages are not stupid. I survey the men with him. "You said four patrols? Of six?"

He nods.

"That's twenty-four men, Eldon," I snap.

"Yeah, I can count, Luka."

We're usually careful not to treat each other as cousins in front of the men, but the sinking feeling in the pit of my stomach tells me that something is very wrong. "That doesn't leave many men in the stronghold."

"Don't worry. The gates have been shut against attack."

Still, I don't like it. "Come," I order, urging Nightshade into motion. "We return immediately."

CHAPTER 21

RINA

When Mama was taken from me, all my prayers went with her. I'd been taught that calling upon the Mother in one's own name was improper, and with no one left to pray for, my relationship with Her mostly withered. But now, every day that Luka is gone from the stronghold sees my rusty prayers making a reappearance. To say that I'm concerned about him would be wholly inadequate. I truly miss his gruff, moody self. Some days the longing for him is almost a physical thing.

To distract myself, I try to stay busy. Bron, Kata, and Ion are making good progress with their reading and writing. It's particularly rewarding to see Kata's wonder grow every day. And in the evenings, I sit with Eldon and Daysa and their kids for dinner here in the stronghold, and sometimes Yvette comes with Rionnon. Also, Luka's mother, Niri, invites me to late morning tea every day. She's very sweet and I love the stories she shares about Luka as a child.

There are those, however, like Teo, whose hostility has become more evident since Cayson's demise and Luka's departure. Their frowns and their thinly-veiled recriminations have become frequent enough that worry over the situation is forever lurking in the back of my mind like a spectre attempting to crawl out of the Abyss. If these people never accept me, what will Luka do? With the two men who orchestrated our union – Gaden and Kharon – not even interested in seeing it through, what kind of a chance do we stand?

I sigh. *Please come home to me, Luka.*

"You wouldn't have a certain warrior on your mind, would you?" Niri asks, the slight tilt to the corner of her mouth telling me she finds my pining charming.

"Maybe," I admit, taking a sip of my tea to hide my embarrassment. "That savages have been sighted here in the Mountain Lion Realm again doesn't bode well." The alarm bell rang earlier and when Eldon ordered all warriors to report to him, Ion had dropped me here with Niri. I'm a bit surprised he hasn't returned for me yet, but I did see the gates being closed.

"No, it doesn't. But Eldon knows what he's doing."

"Yes, of course," I answer vaguely.

"And my son knows how to take care of himself wherever he is."

I nod, but it must not be very convincing because she goes on.

"Luka is a great warrior, Rina." She pauses, then as if she's finally figured out what's bothering me, she adds, "And an even greater man. I have every reason to believe he'll do what's right when the time comes."

My grip on the teacup tightens as she gets right down to the heart of the matter. "I worry that what's right for the realm won't align with what's right for me . . . for us."

"My sweet girl," she says, reaching out to squeeze my hand. "You have no –"

The door bangs open and Bron spills into the room, panting as if he's run a great distance. "Rina, we must go."

Setting my tea aside, I rise to my feet. "What? The savages are here?"

"No, not the savages. But we must go. Come," he orders, coming forward and taking hold of my upper arm.

He's pulled me almost out the door by the time I wrench myself out of his grasp. "Bron! Tell me what's going on."

"They're moving against you."

"What? Who?!"

"Teo, Dumfries, Gore . . . we have to hide."

The only name I recognize is Teo's. "Hide? I will not hide."

"The deve will not forgive any of us if something happens to you, Rina." His hand slashes through the air between us, startling me. Bron is not as big as some of the warriors, but he's certainly bigger than I am.

"Child," Niri says softly, coming up behind me. "You should listen to him. Teo is not to be trifled with."

"But what does he want?"

"Most likely your head," Bron says.

My head jerks back. "Surely not. Like you say, Luka will not forgive."

Bron checks the hall, his movements jumpy and frantic. "We have no time to argue."

"Teo would not risk his own life to take mine," I insist. "So what does he want?"

"At a minimum, he wants a pound of flesh, Rina."

Niri gasps, but my mind turns. *A pound of flesh?* "He wants to see me punished?" Maybe this is what's needed to earn a place for myself here. "And that would appease him?"

Bron's horror almost has me doubting myself. "No," he says fiercely as he grabs my arm again and pulls me out into the hall. "Don't even think it."

"Bron! Stop. Please. Listen to me."

"No! You listen to me." He tugs us to a halt and turns on me. "It won't work."

"But if I don't face them, they will never accept me," I say, the idea taking root. "Not ever. Even if Luka goes through with the marriage, I'll forever be waiting for the blade that lands in my back."

The hesitation bleeding into his countenance is enough to convince me I'm right. "I've suffered much in my life, Bron. Almost none of it on my own terms." Loud male voices sound from downstairs as I go on, "But now I have the chance to choose my fate."

Boots echoing on the stairs have him losing his nerve. "No, Rina. You are the a'deve. You –"

"But that's just it, Bron. I'm not. Not yet. This may give me a real chance at it, though. What's the worst they can do to me?"

"You don't want the answer to that." He re-takes my arm, this time hauling me in the other direction, toward the back stairs.

"Bron," I plead, twisting and turning against his hold, but he's too strong for me.

"No, you were left in my care."

He pulls up short as two warriors cut us off at the top of the back stairs. They don't even hesitate; one of them punches Bron full in the face, laying him out flat, and the other clamps an iron grip around my wrist and yanks the dagger Luka gave me from its sheath at my waist.

"Wait," I screech as the man starts pulling me down the stairs. "Let me make sure he's okay."

"He's fine," says the one who hit him. I realize it's Crion, Bron's own brother.

"How could y–"

"Shut up," growls the one dragging me along.

"I'm coming willingly," I grit out as we arrive at the Great Hall, which is unusually empty. "There's no need to be harsh."

"Isn't there?" Crion sneers. "It's not like you showed any mercy to my brothers."

"What?!" I have to rush to keep up with their steps. "Your brothers attacked *me*."

Outside on the steps, the man with the grip on me comes to an abrupt halt and I stumble into his back and almost fall. The sounds of murmurs rippling across a crowd register as I right myself.

My already racing heartrate increases to a wild thump in my chest. Below me, the courtyard is packed with people. What must be the entire village is assembled and silently staring up at us. Somewhere a baby wails pitifully. In the distance, a dog barks. *Mother help me, this is to be a public indignity?*

The pounding in my chest becomes painful. *Have I've miscalculated?*

A throat clearing off to my right is jarring in the eerie quiet. Teo. He's radiating enough officious smugness to last a lifetime.

"What is this?" My voice is strong despite the quaking behind my ribs.

"This is you paying for your crimes."

I lift my chin. "By whose authority?"

He hesitates briefly, but forges ahead anyway by turning to the crowd. "People of the Mountain Lion, in accordance with our laws, Amarinata D'heilar will give restitution to the Cyrun family for the death of their son, Carson."

This sends a much louder ripple through the crowd. It seems that this is as much news to them as it is to me. Teo motions to my captor and I'm dragged down the steps to where two waist-high posts have been driven between the cobbles about nine or ten feet apart, thin ropes dangling from each. The villagers have formed a semi-circle around the spot.

The man roughly turns me, putting my back to the crowd. I feel stupid standing there while he shoves up the long sleeves of my dress and binds my wrists with the ropes, but what else can I do? I've made my choice, and now I have to accept the consequences. I'm almost grateful that the ropes are slack until he starts looping them around the tops of the posts to pull them taut. With my arms pulled away from my body to form inverted V's, the ropes soon begin to bite into my skin.

Are they going to leave me out here like this to suffer? For how long? Hours, days? Panic begins to well in my chest. *How long before Luka returns?* I'll freeze to death overnight. If only I was wearing my vest.

Teo comes down the steps and I twist in my bonds to track his progress over my shoulder.

"Restitution is a cornerstone of our society," he pontificates. "Without it we –"

"Are you really trying to justify this?" I ask loudly, disgust overcoming my fear. "A man tried to rape me. I defended myself. That is the end of it."

Teo only gives me a haughty lift of his brows as he gestures to someone. Before I can turn to see who it is, they've taken a hold of the collar of my dress and a cold blade touches the back of my neck before it slices down through the material of my dress, all the way to my waist.

Lurching against my bonds, I desperately try to face my assailant. "What are you doing?" The frigid air licks at my back when the dress and my shirt both gape open. My gorge rises as helplessness slithers up from my belly.

"Whore!" rings out from the crowd as if inspired by my exposed flesh. That's followed by, "Go back to where you came from!"

"Well said, my fellow Mountain Lions," Teo gloats.

"Stop this madness," yells a voice, a female voice. I think it's Daysa, but for all my yanking and twisting, I can't see far enough around. I can still see Teo though, and . . . *Is that a whip in his hand?* My thighs start to tremble. My fists clench, then jerk open. With the ropes pulled so tight, the blood trapped at my wrists makes my fingers throb painfully, and for a moment, I lose myself to the panic. But as I open and close my hands, I'm reminded of how I've been obsessively tracing the mountain lion Trudy drew for me since Luka's departure. I take a deep breath. I need to stay calm if I'm going to survive this. I can do this. For Luka. For a chance at love, and family, and community. I can do this.

More insults fly around me, but also more support. It heartens me somewhat to hear some women speak out against –

The first strike of the whip comes without warning, painting a line of fire across my shoulder blade and wrenching the air straight from my lungs. Shocked to my core, I can't scream or cry or thrash. There's only the pain as my legs threaten to buckle out from under me. Struggling for breath, I hear the snap of the whip after the fact, ringing in my ears like a crescendo.

"Kata, no!"

Kata?

Another snap jangles my nerves, but it doesn't bring any agony.

"Stop!"

I crane my neck around. Yvette is crouched down by Kata and murmurs in the crowd begin in earnest.

"Get out of the way!" Teo orders. "How can you be so stupid?"

From my periphery, I watch Yvette stand. "No."

"No?!" Teo turns to Crion. "Get them out of there!"

"No," comes again. I swing my head in the other direction in time to see Daysa join Yvette and Kata. Noise in the crowd increases.

When Crion begins shoving at the women, Elsy, the old healer, steps forward. Then Lorna joins them, creating an ever increasing barrier between me and the whip. Crion is left unsure as more serving girls line up.

A screechy voice fills the courtyard. "How dare you?" It's

Zola. "How dare you protect the whore who killed one of my sons and caused the death of another?"

"Your sons," Yvette spits, "were scum. The world is a better place without them."

That comment causes an uproar and my heart swells as more and more women join the fray, including the young girl, Farrana, and Niri, who must have followed us downstairs from her room.

"Enough!" bellows Teo. "The women will stand aside or be punished. Severely."

Shouts of condemnation and approval break out from every direction. Trudy starts to wail, but Daysa yells for her to stay back with her brothers. As the furor increases, I start to feel faint. The lash on my shoulder aches with the fire of a hundred suns and my hands pulse painfully from the lack of circulation.

Then I hear the most beautiful sound I can imagine, the deep roar of Luka's voice. "What, in the name of the Almighty Mother, is going on?"

I strain to turn far enough to see him as the crowd parts. There he is, the very embodiment of menace, prowling forward, his cloak swirling around him. He shrewdly takes in the whole scene and a jolt of mortification hits me at the predicament I've let myself fall into. But Luka's stride never falters, not even when Trudy runs out, sobbing for her Papa.

As he passes Teo, a dagger materializes in Luka's hand, and in the space between heartbeats, his uncle goes from standing there, holding the whip, to gurgling on the ground with a blade protruding from the side of his neck. Shock reverberates across the courtyard.

Crion stumbles back, away from the women, away from

the eerily calm deve, who stops at his mother's side. "You are well?" I hear him ask.

"I am now, my son. Please take care of your bride."

Luka lifts his gaze to me, but somehow I can't bring my-self to do the same. Shame, hot and potent, heats my skin as he approaches. From somewhere, he produces another knife and cuts the rope on my right and my strained muscles force a pained puff of air from my throat.

"You will not falter, little raven," he says in a low, uncom-promising voice only for me. It's an order, not a question.

"Yes," I whisper, locking my legs to keep myself upright. My shredded dress is plunging perilously low in the front and I clutch at it with my free hand, a foot of rope still attached.

He cuts the other rope, but when he tries to rip it away from my skin I can't hold back a whimper. I watch, feeling detached as he pushes my sleeve back and takes in the swol-len, almost purple skin of my hand. It's a bit gruesome and the tether holding back his rage snaps. "Lock this stronghold down!" His voice gains volume with each word until the last one feels like it shakes the very ground. "No one leaves until I know exactly what's happened here."

CHAPTER 22

LUKA

I feel like shit for making her walk on her own. But to show weakness, even after what she's been through, would be a mistake.

She trails behind me through the Great Hall. At least I hope she does since I can't bear to face her. Never in my wildest imaginings did I believe my own uncle would go to such lengths to subvert my will. Sounding a false alarm? Sending my warriors on a goose chase? Gathering our people to witness the humiliation of my bride? Unfathomable. All of it. And as a testament to his stupidity, he didn't even tense as I'd advanced on him. If the feel of the blade sinking into his neck wasn't so fresh, I'd be hard-pressed to believe any of it had actually come to pass.

What a disaster. The image will be branded forever into my memory. Teo, standing there, a bullwhip trailing from his hand, and my beloved restrained and stripped to the waist, a bright red lash across her shoulder.

I send a bench flying with a kick. "Damn him!"

Rina squeaks with fear, forcing me to make a good attempt at reining in my temper. "Come, I need you settled upstairs before I deal with this . . ." I feel my lip curl as my arm waves toward the door. "Debacle."

When I get no response, I finally set eyes on her. She's huddled in on herself, gripping the front of her dress to her chest. Rage surges once again in my blood. *How dare Teo do this? And what is wrong with her? Why is she so passive? Where the fuck is my little spitfire?*

I march toward her and sweep her up in my arms. "I don't have all day, princess."

She gives me nothing but a sharp inhale of surprise, and I'm already up the stairs and at our door before I remember that she's not a hardened warrior. That she probably needs soft words and gentle touches right now.

Setting her down on the bed, I ignore how battered and wary she looks. I have difficult things to attend to, so soft and gentle will have to wait. "Elsy will be up to tend to you."

I turn on my heel and head for the door.

"You're leaving?" she despairs in a whisper.

Without turning, I tell her the truth. "I'll be back later."

"Wait! Please check on Ion and Bron and Kata. I don't know what's happened to them."

That further incenses me. How like her to be worried about others when she should be worried about herself. I slam the door behind me.

Downstairs, as soon as I emerge from the Great Hall, I'm

inundated by questions, claims, and requests. "Silence!" I roar. There are a few lingering yammers but most take me seriously. I start with my most pressing concern. "Where are the men who stayed behind in the stronghold?" I search those around me, surprised to find Gray front and center.

"In the holding cells," Eldon says grimly, handing me the knife I gave to Rina. "I took this off of Dumfries."

"Son of a twisted womb." With so much fury riding me, I'm sorely tempted to go down there and end the man, but there are more important things to contend with. Namely, my cousin. Is it reasonable to expect Eldon to continue as my Second after I've ended his sire? He must follow the direction of my thoughts because he inclines his head more deeply than usual, causing a small flutter in my chest. His support is key to my rule *and* my sanity. It always has been and it always will be. I give him a terse nod and move on to the next issue. "The horses have been brought in?"

Noé, blistering with his own barely contained rage, grits out, "Yes, Deve." When we arrived at the gates, instead of forcing the guardsman – who was clearly relieved to see us – to begin the process of re-opening them, we came in the hatch door.

"Where's Elsy?" I demand.

A path is cleared, letting me see the woman crouched with Kata on the cobbles. "See to the a'deve," I order as the women stand. My eyes zero in on the little maid. *Is that blood along her collar?* The pitch of my gut at the realization that she took a lash for Rina is almost enough to make me wince. But I can't think about that right now, I have much to get through first.

And so the day goes. Piece by piece, what transpired in my absence is assembled into a grisly picture of betrayal and disloyalty. The need to do violence sits like a nagging crone on my shoulder, constantly pushing me to act out. But I am the deve, not a spoiled child. Plus the thought of Rina being disappointed in me is enough to keep myself under control. I've already failed her enough for an entire lifetime and adding to the tally against myself is unappealing in the extreme.

By the time we gather in the map room, the sun has long since set and my patience has dwindled to near non-existent levels. But I need to hear my men's thoughts before tomorrow comes.

"How is it possible that Dumfries *and* Gore were left behind when we headed east to answer the Wolves' call?" I grind out, pacing from one end of the room to the other, only stopping to throw a glare at Noé who, as Warrior Commander, is in charge of managing the men.

He's defiant. "It wasn't my idea to leave so many men behind. Dumfries and Gore were not among those clamoring to come along."

"This is not useful, Luka," Eldon says, sounding about as content as I feel. "If anything, it was my mistake to defer to my father's wishes this morning. He duped me into letting the three of them stay behind to defend the stronghold against savages that did not even exist." He pounds his fist on the table. "I was such a fool."

Bron, who is finally well enough to speak with some sense after the blow he took to the head, sighs. "None of this could have been foreseen. Teo actually supported the match with Rina. That he cooked up this scheme and then actually went through with it is beyond comprehension. And it was me who failed to convince Rina to hide. The blame is mine."

The word *hide* chafes, but Bron is right, he should have done more. "Tell me, how exactly, she managed to defy you." My sarcasm-laden tone has him smoothing a hand over his bruised face before he meets my eyes.

"She thought facing Teo might help to earn her a place here, that maybe –"

I snatch a candleholder off the sideboard and hurl it at the hearth. "Damn her into the Abyss! It's not her place to *think*. She should fucking obey."

The sudden quiet is broken by Eldon's sardonic, "Luka, you like her *because* she thinks. And so do the women of this realm. You saw how they lined up to defend her. That is true loyalty."

I throw myself into my chair at the head of the table as Noé sets his mug of ale down. "The women did make an impressive display today, but in general, they are . . ." His hand circles in the air, trying to find the right word.

"They are crucial," Bron supplies. "They make up more than half of our population."

"Not what I was going for," Noé fires back. "I was going to say they're of little consequence."

That sets Eldon off, and he and Noé get into an argument about the value of women to my rule. I finally cut them off with a much more pressing question. "What the fuck are we going to do with Dumfries, Gore, and Crion *bloody* Cyrun?"

Ion, who's been quiet up until now, pain-induced sweat on his brow from his recently-set dislocated shoulder, answers plainly, "They die." He was found unconscious and tied up in this very room. He'd been on his way back to Rina when he was attacked by the four traitors.

"Fuck me," I bitch, thinking we can't afford to keep losing trained warriors at this rate.

"He's right," Noé affirms. "They must die. There can't be any room to maneuver within the ranks. It's follow or challenge. Full stop."

Eldon is nodding. "Agreed. And this underhanded bullshit shouldn't be rewarded with a chance to restore their honor either. Fuck them. They go to the block."

My brows lift. "You're usually the most level-headed of us."

"They're nothing but cowards," he retorts. "If they wanted to challenge you to combat, they would have."

"You know it's not that simple," I tell him. "There are factors –"

"No," he cuts me off. "It's possible my sire thought he was doing what was best, but most likely, he was just a bitter old man who overstepped, same as Dumfries, same as Gore."

"What about my brother?" Bron asks miserably. "He's only twenty-one."

I rub at my temples. I'm so tired. All I want to do is wrap myself around Rina's warm little body and sleep until the next full moon.

A knock at the door sounds. "Who the fuck is that?" I mutter as Noé gets up to answer it. *Is it more ale? Or better yet, my raven, begging for my presence? No, it's another Cyrun male.*

"What do you want, Gray?" Noé snaps, not letting him into the room.

"I wish to speak with the deve."

"He's busy."

"Noé," I say wearily. "Let him in."

Gray is as exhausted as the rest of us, except he and I both know he carries more burdens than most, and it's obvious that today they're weighing particularly heavy on him. I gesture to Noé's chair on my right and he accepts the invitation to sit.

"I came to say a few things," he announces.

"You always have my ear, Gray, you know that."

He gives me a terse nod. "First, I want you to know I had nothing to do with the daft events of this day."

The possibility did briefly cross my mind, but I'd rejected it. Despite not being an official member of the Range, Gray had volunteered to go out on patrol and wasn't anywhere near the stronghold when Rina was taken.

"And second, I want to plead for my brother's life."

"You're out of your mind," Noé exclaims.

Gray ignores him, keeping his gaze on me. "He's young, Luka. Surely you remember what it's like to want to please your parent. My mother poisoned his mind, and he was so easily flattered by a man as important as Teo."

"Poisoned minds do not easily recover," I tell him. "And if he's such an easy target for flattery, what's to stop it from happening again?"

"I will. I'll stop it. I'll take full responsibility for Crion and his actions in the future if you pardon him."

Eldon laughs. "Pardon him? Just like that? I don't think so."

I hold up my hand for silence. "Have you spoken to him?"

Gray nods.

"And did he tell you what they had planned for my little bride?" I'd had the truth from Dumfries and Gore already, but I hadn't bothered with Crion.

Gray's expression somehow becomes grimmer. "Twenty-five lashes."

Renewed ire boils in my blood. "Imagine what twenty-five

lashes would have done to her."

"Believe me, I have."

"And yet," the volume of my voice rises, "you're here asking for mercy when Crion would have shown none."

Gray bows his head briefly as if to fortify himself. "I haven't come empty handed, Luka."

"Oh?"

"I'll return to the Range. You'll be short on trained men." He swallows hard. "But I have a condition . . . I'll only train the young recruits until I'm actually needed in battle. I do not wish to be interacting with the warriors on a regular basis."

A half-formed sigh comes out of my throat, but after the unthinkable betrayal he suffered at the hands of my father, I don't blame him. Obviously the night I'd found Gray in the dungeons, tied down and being raped by one of my father's men weighs heavier on him than me, but I'll never forget it. It was the catalyst for so much change in this realm. I'd put my dagger into the perpetrator's heart, freed Gray, and then gone upstairs to find my sire. He was merrily eating and drinking in the Great Hall as if he hadn't ordered an attack he hoped would mentally and emotionally destroy my greatest rival for the deveship. I'd challenged the despicable bastard in front of everyone.

Gray extends his arm to me and we clasp wrists. I don't, however, let him go. I pull him toward me and look him directly in the eye. "Crion will take fifty lashes before I agree."

"Twenty-five."

Every man at the table scoffs.

"Forty, and that's final."

Gray nods. "Is he expelled from the Range?"

"He'll be on probation, one that you will supervise."

"Done." He inclines his head before he stands. "Thank you, Luka."

"Oh, and Gray," I call. "Welcome back."

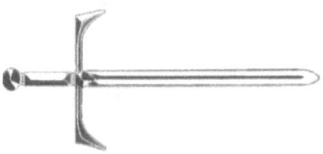

Rina is nestled in the bed and I can't help but stare at her in the light of the glowing embers as I strip my clothes. Tomorrow will be another long day and she has no idea of what's to come. She'll adapt though. She has to.

Slipping between the furs, I curl myself around her back, careful not to jostle her. She's left the tie at the neck of her night rail loose, allowing the material to hang down off her injured shoulder. It's not bandaged, and in the very low light, I can see that the lash didn't break the skin. *Thank fuck.* The area is bruised though. She'll be sore tomorrow.

"Luka?" she asks sleepily.

"Go back to sleep."

She tries to turn in my arms but I hold her in place.

"Is everything okay?"

"Everything's fine."

As she starts to relax, so do I. This is perfect, I think vaguely as I sink into sleep . . . not even her whispered, "I'm so sorry," can pull me back.

I wake before dawn with a heavy heart. Today will not be a good day.

Not wanting Rina's day to start before it has to, I'm careful when I rise from the bed. Though my reasons for slinking out probably aren't so noble in reality, that's what I focus on.

Her little maid is waiting in the hall, spots of blood marring the bandage she has wrapped around her neck. "Kata," I say, inclining my head. "Thank you for protecting her when I couldn't."

The skittish woman's eyes bulge as she returns the gesture, hugging the bundle she's carrying closer to her chest. She listens intently while I give her instructions for the day, barely managing to keep the surprise from her face. Understandably she has questions about my orders, but since she can't ask them, I'm spared the explanations.

Though I have much to prepare before the sun reaches its zenith, the morning passes by like molasses. When it's finally time, I enter the courtyard from the stables where I was readying Nightshade for the journey. I've made this affair mandatory for every man, woman, and child, so the space is packed, including the ramparts, and eerily silent. This is not a joyous occasion.

They part for me as I make my way to the Great Hall's steps, and for once, their heavy regard isn't intolerable. No, this time, it gives me strength.

I'm pleased to see that Rina and my mother have been installed in chairs on the landing, elevated above the rest. My mother glows with pride, but Rina appears extremely ill at ease. In stark contrast to yesterday, she does her best to seek out my gaze, but I purposefully avoid it. Until this is done, I need to stay the course.

Noé hands me the poleaxe on my way up the steps. Unlike my speech for Carson's death rites, I haven't practiced this one, or even thought much about it prior to this.

But since that farce of a funeral, my life and my role in it have crystalized. My purpose is clear to me now. Koda had laid it out for me in simple terms; consolidate or perish. Clear-cut, easy. It's about time I started acting like it.

"I'm not going to stand up here," I begin, my voice echoing off the tall walls of the courtyard. "And try to convince you that I'm worthy of being your deve. Because I *am* your deve. If, like these cowards," I gesture to Gore and Dumfries who are on their knees before their respective blocks, "you seek to plot against me, your head will also roll. No exceptions."

I let that sink in. "I have not been an unreasonable man so far. I've listened to your problems. I've listened to your grievances. I've been more than generous with my judgments." I twirl the poleaxe in my hands. "But if you're *still* unhappy with my rule, as is our custom, your first, *your only* course of action is to challenge me. Is that clear?" I hear a few mumbles of assent, but that's not good enough for me. "I said is that clear?!"

If I'm surprised by their enthusiasm this time, I don't show it. I just raise the axe in the air and let their cheers wash over me. When the noise begins to die down, I stroll down the steps and close in on my first target.

"Byron Gore, you are condemned to die for treason," I intone. "May the Father cast you into the Abyss."

Two men have to hold him down before I can get a proper swing in. With a horrible thunk, the blade goes through his flesh and bone and into the block. His head tumbles onto the cobbles, blood gushing from his neck.

I move on to the next. "Tarron Dumfries, you are condemned to die for treason. May the Father cast you into the Abyss."

Dumfries shows more decorum than Gore and shakes off the men trying to push him forward. He holds still on his own as the axe comes down.

I never liked either of them; they were my father's men through and through, sharing his vile beliefs and ideals. But that doesn't mean I wanted to be the one to take their lives in this way. Their deaths will now forever cling to my soul like dark, heavy shadows.

I turn to the steps and my mother inclines her head, a sign of respect that I return before I hold out my hand to Rina. When she just sits there, I make an impatient gesture for her to join me.

Her golden eyes slit like a cat's under the overcast sky. *She's angry with me?* Maybe she wants to know why Crion is tied between the same two posts she was, still in possession of his head. *Or is she horrified?* Either way, I don't know what I'll do if she makes a scene.

Thankfully, she chooses to very calmly rise from her chair and take my hand so I can help her down the stairs. At the bottom, she decides she needs both hands to lift her dress to avoid the carnage on the blood-splattered cobbles. When she makes no move to re-take my hand, I keep my displeasure to myself. Fine. She can follow me. Except, as soon as I enter the edge of the crowd, my protective instincts are set off, and I have to half-turn and lift my arm, forcing her to go ahead of me. Her soft huff of disapproval would be strangely arousing if people weren't pressing in from all sides.

But there's no hostility. "A'Deve," is whispered reverently again and again as we cross the courtyard, women and children reaching out to touch her. Men too, I notice, incline their heads for her as well as for me. Lucky for them they keep their hands to themselves. If they tried to touch her, I'd probably beat them to death with their own arms.

At the stables, my men hold the people back from following. Most have lost interest in us anyway since Noé has started with Crion's lashes. Did I delegate that particular task? Not exactly. Noé volunteered, so I'm not feeling guilty about it. My undivided attention is now for Rina, who's already rushing down the aisle to see her beloved horse.

"She's already saddled," she calls, sounding miffed. "Are we going somewhere?"

Two of my men, Baylor and Kersh shuffle on their feet, not sure what to make of her disrespectful tone. For my part, I can't stop a grin from tugging at my lips as I head in her direction. It's been almost a fortnight since she's dressed me down. How I've missed her.

She's already mounted Glory and, beside her, Nightshade is restless. "Do you like your new cloak?" I ask her, admiring her upon her mount, the white and grey fur pelts giving her a noble air.

"That's what you say to me after twelve days? *Do you like your new cloak?"*

Taken aback by her scorn, I hesitate for a second. "Is that a yes?"

"You answer me first. Are we going somewhere?"

No longer amusing, her attitude begins to gall me, and my

answer comes out as a terse, "Obviously."

Without another word, she lifts her chin and urges Glory into a walk, making her way to the stable door.

"Infernal woman," I mutter as I haul myself up onto Nightshade's back to trail after her.

"Yes, I do remember," I hear her say in a much happier tone. "Dion, right?"

"Yes, my a'deve," Kersh says, smiling at her like she's the Mother herself. "I'm honored that you remember me."

Suspicion flares to life. *They know each other? How is that possible?*

"Of course I remember. You were the only person who spoke a single kind word to me on my journey north."

"Oh, uh, I, uh, I'm sorry to hear that."

At my noisy and derisive exhale, everyone turns. I glare at all three of them.

"Well, I, uh," Kersh continues with his pathetic boy-like stammering. "While Ion is laid low, I will be your escort."

She graces him with one of her brightest smiles. "That's the only good news I've had all week. And you are?" she asks politely, turning to Baylor.

"Baylor, my a'deve. We're to accompany you on your trip."

Rina throws me a scathing look before turning back to him. "Thank you. Do you know how long this *trip* will take?"

Baylor shuffles nervously. "About three hours, my lady. We should arrive right before sundown."

"Unless we leave sometime today," I bluster. "We'll never arrive."

Baylor immediately snaps into action. "Of course, sir."

We slip out the gates to the sound of Crion Cyrun's howling cries of agony.

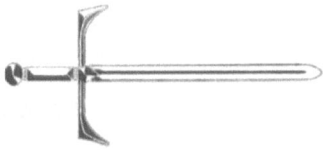

Though the weather cooperates, it's a miserable journey. Rina continues to give me the cold shoulder for unknown reasons, chatting amiably with my men, while pointedly ignoring me. Combined with the gruesome morning and the exhaustion of the past days, it feels like being swallowed by darkness when all I wanted was to bask in her light.

By the time we arrive at the cabins on the southern shores of Lake Nadore, I want her out of my sight. But the thought of sending her away to spend more time with Dion *fucking* Kersh turns my stomach worse than the memory of the rolling heads.

I dismount in front of the cabin that my grandfather had built. "Get the horses put away," I snarl as I reach up and pull Rina off her horse without any warning.

"Hey!" She grabs onto my shoulders to steady herself.

Once she's on the ground, she attempts to move away but I hold on to her. "Make sure we're not disturbed for the rest of the night."

"Of course, Deve," Baylor says, leading the horses away with Kersh.

"Would you let go of me?" Rina grouses, trying to shake me off.

Ignoring her, I dip down and yank her over my shoulder.

"Luka! Luka, put me down! Right this instant, you will put me down."

Every step I ascend to the cabin's porch sees her protests get louder. I push the door open and get hit with the musty smell of disuse. As I open the shutters on the two windows to let light and air in, she continues to rant and squirm.

"Luka! So help me, I will . . ." the rest gets muffled in the back of my travel cloak.

Tired of her screeching, I flip her back over onto her feet and she promptly starts to topple over. Batting away my attempts to keep her upright, she staggers back, awkwardly swiping at the hair in her face.

"You think this is funny?" she fumes.

My grin dims. "Actually, no. I'm so . . ." Somehow I reel in the more offensive words that come to mind. "So *displeased* with you."

"Displeased? You're displeased? With me?"

Her outrage clashes with mine, and to stop myself from ringing her small, feminine neck, I swing around to the hearth. Busy hands commit no murder.

"Don't keep me in suspense, *my deve.* Do tell. Why, exactly, are *you* displeased with *me?"* I hear her angry steps coming closer on the wooden planks of the floor.

"You will address me with respect, princess." I'm practically growling now as I chuck kindling onto the grate.

"Or what? You'll chop my head off?"

Pushing to my feet, I whirl on her. "What?!"

She doesn't heed the warning in my tone. "You heard me. Am I next on your list?"

Rage and indignation burn through me like wildfire. *What*

ridiculous bullshit is this? Her head tilts back as I step right up to her. "How dare you even suggest such a thing to me?"

An icy smile forms on her lips. "How dare I? How dare you?! You're gone for nine days, then are home for two more, and you don't have a single word for me. Not a single word! You just leave me to imagine the worst."

If her small balled up fists are anything to go by, she's livid.

"Guess what, Luka? *The worst* is pretty horrible. Especially when I'm given a front row seat to the severing of heads."

I have to unclench my jaw before I can speak. "You should know better. I would nev–"

"How would I know that?! You don't tell me *anything!"* She spins on her heel and starts pacing. "I thought you had decided what to do with me. And it had to be bad news if you wouldn't talk to me."

She looks a bit nauseated and it only serves to further fuel my disgust. "Oh, really?" I drawl. "And you thought your fate would involve a pole axe? You're so full of bullshit."

My sarcasm has her hauling in a sharp breath. "You don't understand! Without you, I have no recourse, Luka. None. With no husband and no family, I would have no protection. And if you *did* let me stay in the realm, I'd end up a serving girl like Lorna, who's on her back half the time."

That catches me off guard. *A serving girl? How on earth did she come up with that?*

"I feel so stupid," she goes on, her voice cracking. "For missing you, for loving you, for worrying about you every single hour that you were gone only to be brushed aside like a flea as soon as you returned."

"I had things to take care of!" I roar at her.

"Things that involved me directly!" Her roar matches my own. "You could have spared me a moment of your time. You didn't even check on me."

I'd watched her closely on the ride here and she barely favored her shoulder. She's fine . . . but I guess that's not what she's referring to. I'm lifting my hand to reach for her when she closes the gap between us and hits me, right in the middle of my chest. "And then," she rants on, turning to pace away again. "You can't even be bothered to mention we're going away? As if I'm less than an afterthought."

Stubborn, defiant, self-absorbed; they all fit her perfectly. "I am a man with many responsibilities. Catering to your needs does not rank among them."

My gut clenches as something that might be described as devastation slowly crawls its way across her features. "So this *is* the end?"

"Infernal woman! This is not the end of anything! It's the beginning."

Her brittle laugh fills the cabin. "Oh, really? The beginning of what exactly?"

It finally comes to me. She's not being contrary or stubborn. She actually doesn't know what I'm talking about. How have I failed so utterly to convey everything she is to me? And looking upon her now, it's obvious that I *have* failed.

CHAPTER 23

RINA

The dam finally broke. All the worry while he was away in the Wolf Realm, the ordeal with Teo, and then the build-up of dread over the last day came pouring out of me.

The initial shame and self-loathing had almost crushed me when Luka left me in our room. *Why hadn't I gone with Bron?* My miscalculation – my absolute error in judgment – had led to my complete humiliation in front of the entire realm. And worse, so much worse, it had forced the man I love to kill his own uncle. I was heartsick. I still am.

And being left alone had compounded everything. *Had I ruined my chances at a life with him? Could he forgive me? Was he done with me?* And still he didn't come. In the past, he'd included me in the discussions about the letter and the savage incursion. But not this time. This time he'd cut me out entirely and I was truly afraid of what that meant.

This morning, when he'd crept from our bed without a word was the final blow to my confidence. I was sure all was lost and a kernel of resentment had begun to grow. *Why couldn't he just tell me what was going on?* Then I'd sat through the executions with a ball of ice in my belly. Luka wouldn't even look at me until it was all over.

Then, suddenly, according to him, all was well.

All was well?

Now, here I am, standing in front of my brooding barbarian. He's *displeased* with me and I'm . . . I'm slowly being emptied of my indignation. I'd never believed he was going to use the poleaxe on me, but my anger had pushed me to provoke him. I'd wanted to hurt him the way he hurt me. Petty, I know. But that horrible feeling of having no control over my own life that I've lived with for so long was rearing its ugly head with a vengeance. I just can't live at the whims of others anymore. I just can't.

And what is he saying now? This is not the end, it's the beginning?

I laugh bitterly. "Oh, really? The beginning of what exactly?" Not at all sure I'm ready to hear the answer to that question, I go to the window and push the shutter further open. The view of the lake through the trees is lovely in the waning light. If only I could appreciate it more.

Behind me, I hear him back at the hearth, lighting the fire. With sudden melodramatic despondency, I imagine that every scrape of the flint is about to set fire to the life I had hoped to have with him, one in which I had a say . . . and I enjoyed his love and respect.

But isn't any life with him better than losing him altogeth-

er?

Of course it is, I remind myself as I idly stroke the ultra-soft pelts of my new cloak. Kata had presented it to me this morning, tracing the word deve on my palm, so I would be sure to know who it was from. As if it could be from anyone else.

Once the flames are crackling, he comes up beside me and clears his throat. "Rina, I . . . I need to tell you something." His Adam's apple bobs and I feel my chest tighten.

"Okay." My reply is barely audible.

"I know," he begins, "that I haven't given you much to believe in when it comes to us." He shifts on his feet a bit before continuing. "But I want you to know that I . . . that I lo–"

He can't quite get the word out, but my heart skips several beats anyway. *Was he going to say 'love'?*

After an awkward pause, he changes tack. "Being away from you this past fortnight, I . . . well, you said you missed me, and I missed you too."

I swallow hard, feeling my dejection quickly being replaced by hope.

"I missed you so much more than I thought possible," he goes on softly. "And not only your body, but your quick wit and your . . ." He yanks on the strings of his cloak and flings it aside, clearly uncomfortable with this speech.

"My what?" I prod. "My sarcasm?"

His lip quirks. "Well, I was going to say your sharp mind. But yes, I missed your sarcasm, too."

My mouth opens, but he puts his fingers over my lips. "Let me finish, little raven . . . please."

I give him a nod, sure that my eyes are wide and glossy

with emotion. His hand moves to cup my jaw and I lean into it. *This* is what I've needed so badly from him over the last day. Some kind of connection, some kind of reassurance.

"I spoke with Koda, Deve of the Wolves . . ."

"About me?"

"Yes. He asked me if you made me stronger, and it was then that I knew for sure." His calloused thumb strokes my cheek, grounding me in this moment. "With you at my side, Rina, everything is clear to me. I don't hesitate. I don't falter. I know what needs to be done, and I do it. With no regrets."

I smile weakly. Here is the crux of the matter. "But what of your people, Luka? I fear –"

"There's nothing to fear. The women of the realm love you. You are a high-born lady with a commoner's experiences."

"But the men –"

"Shhh." He leans down to rest his forehead to mine briefly. "The men will adjust. There was discord before you arrived, and there will be discord with you at my side."

I bite at my lip, so afraid to believe in what he's suggesting. "And you want that? Me at your side?"

"Yes," he says firmly and my heart lurches. "Together, we are stronger. Wouldn't you agree?"

"Yes," I whisper, swaying with his use of the word *together.* "So much stronger." *Is he truly telling me all I've longed to hear?* "We can protect and care for one another, and . . ." And that must be the wrong thing to say because the softness in his expression vanishes.

"Coming home to you being . . . abused." He shakes his head at the memory. "That should *never* have happened."

"I know, Luka. I'm so sorry. I made a terrible mistake. If I had –"

The hand at my jaw slides into the hair at the nape of my neck, tightening until I'm forced to stop my apology. "Woman, your safety is my responsibility. Though I won't deny it chafes that you purposefully put yourself in harm's way."

I wince in his hold. "I thought maybe if I submitted myself to –"

Contempt, or maybe rage, darkens his features. "An a'deve submits herself to no one." He gives me a jerk as if to punctuate his words. *"You* will submit yourself to no one. No one but me. Do you understand?"

The automatic need to remind him I'm my own person causes a flicker of defiance, but I try to cover it up by lowering my lashes. "Yes, okay."

My tone must not be passive enough for him, though, because I lift my gaze in time to see his nostrils flare.

"Don't do this right now," he grits out, pulling me closer. He cranks my neck back further to maintain our eye contact and it causes a flare of heat between my thighs. "You've pushed me far enough today."

"I have pushed *you?"* I retort. "You are the one who –"

"Enough of this," he rumbles, marching me over to the hearth without warning by the hand in my hair.

"Ow! Luka! What are you doing?"

His free hand undoes the tie on my fur cloak with a tug, dropping it onto the floor in front of the fire.

I paw at his arm. "Would you let go of me?"

"No. We seal this bargain between us now."

"What?"

He releases me, but only to go to work on the buckles of my vest. Before I'm even steady on my feet, he's got it off and is lifting my dress over my head.

"Luka!" I fuss, still trying to bat his hands away. "We should talk."

He takes hold of my shirt and tears the linen right down the middle, baring my breasts. The rip echoes loudly in the cabin along with my gasp of shock, both sounds landing between my thighs, causing another, more intense flare of heat.

"Was that necessary?" I ask drolly, hoping he doesn't notice the blush on my cheeks.

"No more talk." He recaptures the hair at my nape, tugging me forward. "You will give me *everything*. I will have your smiles and your conversation and your full attention. *And* I will have your body. Do you understand? All of it is mine."

I try to glower at him, but it has no effect.

"And if you ever think to ignore me in favor of others, or withhold yourself from me in any way again, you will *not* like the consequences." He leans closer with every word until we are nose to nose. "Right now, I'll have your cunt. Every inch of it."

Instead of keeping my mouth shut like I know I should, I provoke him further. "And what if I have demands of my own? Maybe I want you making me come as you beg for my forgiveness."

"Oh, I'll make you come." He snaps his teeth at me, then pulls away slightly to use his free hand to grip my neck. My eyes roll back at the sensation of being trapped, one of his hands at my nape, the other on my throat. "You'll come on my cock, on my tongue, on my fingers. On my whole fucking hand if I so desire."

I don't even try to challenge him when downward pressure sends me toward the floor. Keeping my descent slow, he gets me on my knees and then onto my front until the soft pelts of my cloak are teasing my nipples into hard points.

His fingertips briefly skim over the tender whip mark on my shoulder as if checking that I'm fit for what he has planned. I must pass his test because he straddles my hips to keep me pinned down. I twist, but all I can see is the broad expanse of his back. *He's faced away from me?* "Luka?"

Smack. His palm comes down on the outside of my thigh. Even through my buckskin leggings, it stings. "Quiet." He bends my leg up and goes to work getting my boots off, one by one. When he shuffles back and hooks his fingers into the waist of my pants, I struggle a bit, still wary. His legs clamp against my ribs, sending a dose of lust into my core as he strips the last of my clothing away.

Strong hands land on the insides of my thighs, startling me. Reflexively, I resist his attempts to open my legs and another smack comes down, this one on my bare ass. I suck in a breath.

"Settle," he orders and this time I let him spread me wide. "You will give me what I want." Fingers trail up the inside of my thigh, and suddenly, the thought of him finding out how aroused I am sends a flush of mortification all the way from my head to my toes. When my legs start to close, he pries me back open and has my sex cupped from behind before I even take my next breath.

He laughs. "Is this what you would hide from me? How wet you are?" He presses into my clit and my vision whites out. Around and around he circles, causing bolt after bolt of pleasure to careen across my senses. The strange vulnerability of my position only serves to wind me up further, and combined with his other hand's exploration of the skin of my backside, it all proves too much for me with embarrassing quickness. Humping his hand for all I'm worth, I explode into a delicious hail of fragmented light.

As if my capitulation was what he was waiting for, his weight lifts. Over my shoulder, through half-masted lids, I watch him strip himself naked, keenly ogling his length, which juts out proudly from his body. When he plants his big hands on either side of my shoulders, I'm still in a bit of a daze and vaguely wonder what he's doing. Hovering over me, he keeps his body as straight as the planks I'm lying on and slowly lowers himself until his chest grazes my shoulder blades and his cock touches my thighs, he nuzzles at my ear. "I hope you're ready for me. This won't be gentle."

Bringing his knees down on either side of my thighs, he leans over me, allowing his heavy cock to land on my ass. His lips start at the top of my spine and begin to work their way down inch by inch.

Once he's back sitting on his heels, my legs caught between his, he smacks my ass. "Present yourself."

Um, what? He smacks me again.

"Get on your fucking hands and knees and present yourself for my cock."

I groan. This man's mouth is wonderfully filthy. Two more smacks.

"Ow, Luka."

"Now."

Unsure how he wants me to move with him on top of me, I start squirming forward to free my legs. "That's it," he encourages though his legs tighten around mine. The bastard. "Let me see how much you want this." I pull myself forward on my arms, continuing to wiggle. When I slip on the cloak underneath me, I push it down until my elbows can get some purchase on the wooden floor. "Good girl," he praises as I slip further from his clutches. His thumbs slip down between my ass cheeks and pull them apart, making me yelp. He smacks me again. "Come on, show me how much you want my cock in your cunt."

"Luka!" He pries my ass cheeks apart again, this time, settling his length between them.

"Or maybe I don't need your cunt after all." He thrusts forward, sliding along my crack. "Why bother, when there's a perfectly good hole available right here?"

I buck and squirm in earnest now, worried he might actually go through with his threat. "That's it," he taunts. "Work for it."

He sits back again and continues to smack my ass and threaten me while I struggle in his hold. In the end, I'm a panting mess, somehow as desperate for him as he claims me to be. Finally he lets me work myself forward enough that I can push up onto my hands and knees. "Now there's a good girl."

"Shut up and fuck me already," I gasp.

He hums with approval as I feel him push up onto his knees, dragging his length up along the crease of my legs which are still tightly pressed together. I get no warning. As soon as he finds my entrance, he shoves into me.

I cry out, a wave of euphoria hitting me.

"That's only half," he growls.

He rocks in the tight space, shoving forward again and again until, finally, he's seated deep inside me. It's dizzying. I'm so full of him. He pauses, breathing hard as he reaches under me and sneaks a hand between my breasts to my collar bone. He hauls me up by my throat.

I scrabble at the hold, trying to get my bearings as he leans back slightly, using his strength to hold me in place, impaled on his cock. His free arm lands along my spine and his fingers grip the back of my neck, effectively completing the circle. "Fuck, yes," he grunts, pulling me back tighter on his cock.

The fullness, the domination, the divine powerlessness of being pinned on his cock . . . if it's possible to pass out from sheer bliss, I'm close.

He leans to the side, startling me back into myself. He pulls one of my legs out from between his, then the other one. With my legs on the outside now, he sinks back fully on his haunches and holds my back against his chest.

The new angle allows for him to drag against some kind of magical place inside of me. I flounder, making an incoherent mewling sound.

"Yes, I feel it too," he whispers at my ear, rubbing his free hand over my belly as if he should be able to feel himself inside of me. "Snug, isn't it?"

"Yes," I breathe. And so fucking good, especially when he opens his thighs, spreading mine with them.

"The next time you ignore me, little raven, the next time you withhold yourself, I won't just re-claim you with a rough fuck, I'll spank you. And not on your ass." He gives my clit a gentle slap and my entire body shudders.

Attempting to soothe the sting, he rubs slow circles into my clit, sliding through the wetness. I moan as the blade-thin edge I'm on begins to dissolve. "You're close again, aren't you?" he murmurs. Another gentle slap, another shudder, followed by more soothing circles. "But it's my turn, not yours." Another slap, this one harder.

With no breath in my lungs, I can't protest how he pulls out and arranges my body on my elbows and knees on my own fur cloak. When he's satisfied, he grips my hips tightly and shunts himself back into me. After a few experimental thrusts, he lunges forward as he yanks me back. Holy shit.

"You better not come," he threatens.

My laugh is cut off by the next thrust of his hips, which begins a series of long, hard, possessive strokes. I can't think it's so good, I can only feel. He groans when my impending orgasm has me fluttering around him. "If you come, I'll fuck you right through it," he says harshly, pushing a palm to the center of my back, forcing my cheek to the fur. Then I feel him lift one of his legs to plant a foot on the floor. "Do you hear me?"

"Just get on with it," I rasp, my fingers curling into the cloak near my head, trying to brace myself as he withdraws and sinks deep again. And I do mean deep. We both moan as he bottoms out.

"You're going to feel this tomorrow." He thrusts again. "As you're supposed to."

The new angle is uncomfortable yet completely divine. Every thrust presses or drags in all the right places and the flutters start up again in earnest. The slap of flesh on flesh fills my ears along with my own keening as my climax barrels down on me, promising me the sweetest of oblivions. I swear it's his cock swelling even more that sets me off. I scream.

Slowly, I come back to myself, feeling fractured and raw. I'm on my side, gulping down air. A wave of emotion rolls over me along with an icy draft.

The door shuts loudly and I startle. "They left our things on the porch," Luka says, unrolling a bundle of furs as close to the fire as possible. "I guess your screams convinced them not to knock." He turns to me when he's finished arranging them to his liking and his brows pull down. "Why do you cry?" he asks gruffly. "Did I hurt you?"

"I'm not crying," I deny, swiping at my tears as I take in the tall, naked expanse of him. He's so beautiful. Every honed muscle, every scar, every nick and scrape.

He crouches down to study me. "Come," he says. "You're cold."

Feeling so very drained, I crawl forward to our more comfortable nest. The fire is going strong now and as I lie down, it warms my front. Luka covers me, but instead of joining me, he moves about the cabin. The door opens again and I assume he brings in the rest of our things. I hear him securing the shutters and pouring some water.

Kneeling next to me, he pushes back the furs and lifts my leg to press a cool cloth to the apex of my thighs, wiping gently. It does nothing to stem my silent tears. "Can I bring you something, my little raven?" he asks, his voice as soft as the firelight. "Are you thirsty? Or hungry?"

The tears increase as I shake my head. His taking care of me is setting me further adrift on a sea of my emotions.

Slipping between the furs, he slides his arm under my head and curls himself around me, his front to my back. "Tell me why you're crying, my little Rina." His hand trails over my belly. "If I didn't hurt you, did I scare you?" His lips touch on my bruised shoulder. "Or does this hurt terribly?"

"No, nothing like that." I give his hand a squeeze, hoping it reassures him. "I think I'm crying because I love you." Hearing how silly that sounds, I laugh ruefully.

"You love me?" He doesn't trip over the word this time.

"Of course I love you. I've loved you since you sat across from me in the dark and spoke of horses." I concentrate on the dancing flames in the grate, trying not to worry about his reaction to such an admission. "I might not have known it then, but in hindsight, that's where it started. Because any man who's gentle with animals is surely worthy of my love . . . such as it is."

His chest rises and falls as if giving himself time to form a response. The delay makes my stomach churn with nerves, but I don't regret my honesty. There comes a time when it's as necessary as breathing. And for us, that time is now.

"Rina?"

"Yes?"

"I love you, too."

Closing my eyes, I let his words seep into my skin. I savor them. I haven't heard such a thing since my mother died.

"I've loved you," Luka goes on. "Since you took that knife from my hand in front of all those people. Because any woman who thirsts for revenge is surely worthy of my love . . . such as it is."

I give a watery laugh. Despite the mention of Cayson Cyrun, I'm delighted. I turn in his arms, my tears forgotten. "Really?"

He grins down at me. "Really. You would have killed him in a heartbeat if I'd let you. From then, I knew you had the fortitude to be my a'deve."

I blink at him. "So you are truly offering me a place at your side?"

He leans in and kisses me gently. "Yes, little raven, I am. If you will have me."

"Oh, Luka. Of course I'll have you. I love you so much and a home is all I've ever wanted. Thank you."

"Well, don't thank me. I am not the easiest man to . . . appease." He strokes his fingers along my neck. "I may have bruised your delicate skin."

I lift my chin, giving him better access. "Appeasing you will never be a hardship."

"That's good because the opportunities will be many in our life together."

I give another soft giggle. "May I ask a favor of you, Luka?"

He scans my face warily.

"Going forward," I tell him. "I will need you to communicate with me . . . please. I will not be a spectator in my own life."

After a moment of deliberation, he sighs. "I suppose I'm not the only one who needs appeasing."

I nod, relieved I will not have to battle him over this.

He takes my hand and pulls it to his mouth, placing a kiss on my knuckles. "Koda has advised me that I must consolidate or perish, and I see now this must be applied to us as well."

That's the second time, he's mentioned the other deve. "This Koda sounds like a wise man."

Wearing a slightly sour look, he grouses, "The only man you will admire is me."

"Is that so?" I feel a giggle surfacing at his jealousy, but manage to limit myself to the wry tone. Because I never want him to believe he doesn't have every ounce of my loyalty.

"It is so," he says arrogantly, then as if he's granting me a concession, he goes on with, "Though you can judge his wisdom for yourself tomorrow."

"Oh? What's tomorrow?"

Luka stills before his gaze darts away.

"Luka?" Dread rises up in my chest. "What's tomorrow?"

His dark eyes come back to mine, heavy with . . . something. "Tomorrow is our marriage day."

CHAPTER 24

LUKA

At first, I only register confusion from her, but that's swiftly joined by indignation. Or is it betrayal?

"Marriage day." The phrase falls from her lips like a stone sinking to the bottom of a well.

"Yes."

"And you thought to tell me this, when? In front of the priestess?"

"A priestess cannot marry a deve."

She slaps my bicep and I flinch.

"That is not the point," she hisses. "How can you not even have the decency to be chagrinned?"

"You're right. I am not . . . *chagrinned* because I have no idea what that is."

She makes to strike me again, but I get a hold of her wrist. "Uh, uh. I'm to be your husband. Violence is not appropriate."

Okay, so maybe I'm taunting her now. But with my balls freshly emptied, there's not a lot that can ruin my mood.

She yanks against my grip, saying, "Oh, but you said you loved me for my thirst for revenge."

"And your sarcasm. Don't forget that."

"Luka, this isn't funny."

I lower my forehead to hers, almost expecting her to head butt me. "I know." She tries to avert her mouth from mine, but I follow her to insist on the kiss. "I will try to do better."

Her body relaxes and I take my chance to continue kissing her. "Do you promise?" she finally pants in between brushes of our lips and tongues.

"I do promise, my sweetest one." I almost apologize but fear it will set a pattern in our marriage that I'll grow weary of quickly. Instead I decide to use my trump card. "I have something for you actually."

In the low light, she appears suspicious. "You think to buy my obedience with gifts? You know I was not all that impressed with the cloak. You didn't even bother to give it to me yourself."

That makes me pause. I didn't present her with it, did I? A mistake I won't make again. "Do not pretend you don't like the cloak," I shoot back, sitting up to reach for my vest. "I caught you petting the pelts too many times to count on the ride here."

She gives me a little harrumphing noise that makes me smile.

"But I think you'll like this one. Though it's not a gift

exactly," I say, holding it out to her. Satisfaction swells my chest at her reaction.

"My mother's ring!" She takes it, sitting up to inspect it in the light as if to confirm its authenticity. She looks to me. "Where did you find it?"

Some of the satisfaction flows away. "Why are you crying?"

"Why do you think?" She starts to fit the ring onto her finger, but pauses. "May I wear it?"

I frown. "Of course."

"I mean in the open. Where people can see it?"

My poor little raven. The Fates really haven't been kind to her. "Yes, my sweet. You can." I take hold of her hand and pull her knuckles back to my mouth for a kiss, this time it includes the ring. From there, I work my way up her arm and soon passion flares between us again.

Later, we sup on bread, cheese, and apples on our furs, sitting across from each other. I'm admiring the play of the firelight over her bare breasts when she says, "Luka?"

Languidly, I meet her eyes. "Yes?"

"I want you to know how very sorry I am about your uncle. If I had known –"

I hold up my hand to stop her. "You were not responsible for his actions, Rina."

"I know." She picks at her bread. "But he was your *uncle.*"

Sighing, I admit, "He was. And I do have some fond memories of him from my childhood, but as I got older, it became obvious how weak he was."

Her eyebrows lift with surprise, so I clarify.

"Not physically weak, but looking back, I see how he didn't stand up to my father when he should have."

My tender-hearted woman opens her mouth, but I shake my head. "Don't worry yourself. I won't be losing any sleep over his death." Though that's not quite true, neither is it false. The man chose his fate, I was only forced to deliver it.

For the first time, waking beside Rina isn't accompanied by a shadow of worry or doubt. I want to shake my head at the idea that I've finally given myself permission to enjoy her presence, but that would wake my beautiful bride to be. And she deserves all the rest she can get after the workout I put her through last night . . . memories of which start flashing through my mind.

She shifts next to me, nuzzling into my bicep. My exhausted cock shows signs of life against my thigh. I'm glad we moved our furs up to the loft bedroom above the hearth last night. Otherwise, if I could see my sexy little bride in the glow of the fire, I'd have her on her hands and knees again. As it is, the only light is the faint outline of the windows down below.

Creeping from the bed, I carefully locate the ladder and climb down. After pulling on my pants, I open the door only to start like a skittish colt at the extremely loud gasp that comes from behind me.

"Luka!"

I immediately search for a weapon.

"It snowed!"

LL Meyer

Snowed? My heart slowly dislodges itself from my throat as I turn to find her peering over the end of the bed from the loft. She's transfixed by the scene beyond the door.

"It's magnificent," she breathes.

I snort as she climbs down the ladder to stand at my side.

"I've never seen such beauty."

"You've never seen snow?" *How is that possible?*

Shaking her head, she steps forward. "Can I touch it?"

"Only if you put some clothes on. I'd prefer not to have to gouge the guards' eyes from their sockets."

She cuts me a look. "That's not funny."

"It wasn't meant to be," I retort as she goes for her dress. "You do realize that the snow is not going anywhere for *months,* right?" She doesn't answer as I admire her new curves in the daylight. It's not the snow that's magnificent, but her. After almost two months of feeding her, she's filled out in very interesting ways. Suddenly it occurs to me that we might have made a baby last night. She might already be carrying my child and a swell of awe and trepidation . . . and joy overcomes me.

Stomping into her final boot, she tries to pass right by me, but I catch her around the waist. "Aren't you forgetting something?"

She gives herself a once-over. "What?"

I haul her with me over to my pack and pull out the dagger I gave her.

"You got it back!" She beams at me as I tie its sheath around her waist.

"Yes, and this time you'll use it if you need to." I plant a kiss on her lips. "Don't go far."

354

"I won't."

I follow her out onto the porch and whistle for the guards. They materialize out of the trees and I indicate their a'deve, who's currently crouched down, inspecting the snow like it contains the answer to life after death.

I take the bucket of half-frozen water that's been left for us on the porch inside with me. Building the fire back up, I pour some water into the pot and hang it over the flames to heat. It's all very domestic and surprisingly not at all tedious.

My grandfather's cabin is the only one that's private. Any members of the deve's entourage must bunk in one of the two larger, communal cabins that sit further down the lakeshore. It's there that we find Yvette, her son Rionnon, and Kata. They made the journey this morning along with six more of my men, including Noé, to see us married.

Rina is thrilled and the atmosphere is loud and boisterous as we break our fast with eggs, bread, and bacon, and more than a few pitchers of ale. Though I lament that my mother, and Eldon and Daysa can't be here, I don't remember the last time I felt so content. Now, all that's missing is the man with the authority to perform the union: Koda, Deve of the Wolf Realm.

When one of my guards interrupts Yvette's hilarious re-telling of her and Noé's encounter with a skunk as children, it's possible that I'm a tiny bit into my cups.

"My deve, the Wolves approach from the north," he says.

355

"It's about time."

"I've never met another deve before," Yvette says, sounding oddly excited.

"I have," Noé intones, forever in a competition with his sister. "I've met them all."

Noé accompanied me to the meeting of the Deve Council in the Bear Realm last year, the one where I was informed of my impending marriage.

"What's this Wolf deve like?" Rina asks.

Noé grimaces. "He's big. Scary as fuck."

"How very unlike you, brother," Yvette mocks. "Admitting to fear."

"You'll see," he tells her as I notice Rina's concern.

Sliding my hand along her jaw, I pull her in close for a kiss. "You needn't worry. I'll keep you safe." Her resulting smile warms more than my heart and we continue our murmured teasing until the door bangs open and Koda makes his entrance.

I meet him halfway to clasp forearms. "Koda," I greet.

"Luka. Well met." He looks me over, a touch of amusement drifting across his usually severe features. "I see you've already been celebrating."

"Well, you're late. I had to occupy my time."

He shrugs. "It snowed heavily further north."

I feel Rina's little hand on the side buckle of my vest, a sure sign that she's wary. Lifting my arm, I tuck her against my side. "Rina, this is Koda, Deve of the Wolf Realm." She inclines her head deeply while he looks her up and down. "Koda, this is the princess Amarinata D'heilar."

She squeaks out a little noise of disapproval at my use of her title. "Just Rina," she says, only peeking up at him fleetingly. "Thank you for your assistance with the ceremony." The southern gesture of pressing her palms to her heart takes Koda by surprise.

"Honestly," he tells her after a moment, "Luka is the only one I'd do it for."

She finally looks him square in the face. "Yes, he's a good man."

"Luka, I see now why you're so besotted."

I *am* besotted so I laugh, not at all offended.

"Oh and by the way," Koda says, crossing his arms over his chest. "That misbegotten cur of yours has been tracking our movements for hours."

I slap him on the shoulder. "I expect nothing less."

"What does he mean?" Rina asks. "Which cur?"

"He means Venna."

Rina's expression lights up. "Venna's here?" She looks to the door.

"She must be. Why don't you go get dressed? We wed as soon as you are ready."

Once Rina has gone upstairs with Kata and Yvette, who I trust will prepare her for the ceremony, we all settle around the table and I allow myself one more tankard of ale with our esteemed guest.

"She's not what I expected," Koda tells me when we have a moment to ourselves.

"Oh?"

"She's so . . . small."

My laughter is loud and obnoxious. "Don't let her size fool you like it did me. She's made of forged steel. And once her claws come out, I would counsel nothing but caution."

He lifts his tankard in salute. "A worthy a'deve, then."

"Worthy, indeed."

I leave them after that, slipping out to get myself ready for the ceremony. Back at the cabin, as is custom, I strip my top half to the skin and slip the golden torque up my arm to my bicep. The fur cloak I gave to Rina is one of a matching set that my parents and grandparents got married in. Soothed by the idea that even if my parents' union wasn't a happy one, my grandparents' was, I pull the ultra-soft cloak over my shoulders.

At the lake, I find everyone waiting at the lookout point. They stand on either side of the path that leads down to the water, forming an aisle of sorts. With so few in attendance, the walkway is not a long one, but I don't focus on that. My bride will have a big affair in the spring when Kharon shows himself in the Mountain Lion Realm for the official ceremony.

I meet Koda at the shoreline and turn in the direction from which Rina should come. We don't have to wait for long. And when I catch sight of her, I think my jaw may actually hang open, especially with Venna prowling along beside her in the snow.

Before her, Rina carries the traditional, shallow bowl that holds the honey cake. The gauzy, draped fabric of the off-white dress she wears under her cloak fits close to the skin and I can see the curves of her breasts and her hips as she walks. Her hair has been arranged into intricate braids that are adorned with metal flowers made of gold and silver and, on top, sits the gold tiara that matches my torque. She is breathtaking.

When they come to the line of spectators, Venna breaks away to give them a wide berth. She comes to join me, while I watch everyone incline their heads as Rina passes them by.

She arrives in front of me and I barely listen to Koda's words, so enthralled am I with her; the gold of the crown against her black hair, the amber of her eyes, the fullness of her lips. In fact, Koda has to gently clear his throat when the time comes to cut the cake.

I don't miss the little twitch of Rina's lips as I jerk into action, pulling my dagger from its sheath and cutting a small, bite size portion for her. "Amarinata, take this as a symbol of my ever-lasting devotion and loyalty." Using my fingers, I place it on her tongue, lingering to enjoy the feel of her lips.

I take the bowl from her and present my dagger, handle first. She smiles mischievously, giving me a little shake of her head as she pulls her own dagger from the sheath I didn't notice was tied around her waist.

"Lukaron, please take this as a symbol of my ever-lasting devotion and loyalty." She feeds me the cake, lingering at my lips like I did at hers, making me grin.

Taking the bowl back from me, she offers the cake to Koda. "Kodagon, please bear witness to our union." He uses his dagger to cut his own piece.

His shaved head reflecting the early afternoon light, Koda lifts his arms. "Those gathered, please bear witness to the binding union of Lukaron Djothar and Amarinata D'heilar." Rina then takes the cake up one side of the aisle and down the other, allowing our witnesses to cut their own pieces.

When she returns, the plate is empty except for the excess honey. Taking it from her, I set it down in front of Venna, who eagerly licks it clean.

"I don't think you're supposed to do that," Rina teases.

I only smile as I lean down to her lips and steal a kiss from my new wife.

CHAPTER 25

RINA

Luka is right. The snow at the lakeside cabin is just the beginning. Though that initial snowfall mostly melts, by the time we arrive back at the stronghold a fortnight later, it's again snowing. And this time when it starts, it doesn't stop. Over the long, bitterly cold winter, the realm is hit by snowstorm after snowstorm and we're mostly forced to remain indoors.

Little by little, the stronghold fills up with villagers whose dwellings cannot provide adequate shelter from the frigid temperatures. Every night the Great Hall is littered with sleeping bodies and during the day it's almost impossible to find a place to be alone with one's thoughts. Being packed together is not ideal, but the people obviously have experience with it. Jobs are assigned to everyone, and there are organized games and sparring every day. It doesn't stop all scuffles from breaking out, but it keeps them to a minimum.

And me? I couldn't be happier. After spending a lifetime without much company, I love being surrounded by people. My big brute of a husband in particular. We're never far from each other. Whether my days include learning to weave or taking my turn helping in the kitchen (which I insisted on), he makes a point of seeking me out. And vice versa. I love watching him spar with the other warriors in the Great Hall.

With so much time on our hands, we also work on Luka's reading and writing skills. Turns out he has very little patience for sitting still or the delicate strokes of a quill, and once he has the basics, he avoids these sessions like a plague.

Our evenings are always spent together, drinking ale and laughing with the warriors and the farmers, and our nights . . . well, our nights are spent as close as humanly possible. By the light of the fire, we make love, talk of our childhoods, and share our hopes and dreams for the future. It's more than I ever imagined for my life. *He's* more than I ever imagined.

As much as I was fascinated by the snow at first, I'm happy to welcome the arrival of spring . . . and with it, a blessing from the Mother. I am with child. Though it is still early days, Luka is unnerved at the thought of becoming a father, and it has ignited his protective instincts like nothing else.

The idea makes me smile. I expect he won't be long in appearing over the rise to check on me as I teach some more of the village children to write their names with sticks in the dirt on the training field. The project to keep the children occupied during the long months of winter has since expanded to include those who spent the time in their own homes.

"The sun feels wonderful, does it not?" I ask Ion, whose job it still is to accompany me almost everywhere.

"It does," he replies, his hand resting on the hilt of his dagger. "It's nice to finally leave behind wearing my cloak."

I give him a flat look, which results in the corners of his mouth tilting up. "That was uncalled for, Ion." Luka insists that I still wear my cloak to keep any lurking chill away from me and the baby.

"My a'deve," a small girl cries. "Is this not right?"

I make my way over.

"My sister says I've spelled Sufan, not Susan."

Smiling at them, I nod. "Your sister is right."

"But I don't want to be Sufan!"

"Well, that is the beauty of writing. You can start over."

The poor child sniffles. "I can?"

"Absolutely." I get her to erase the letters with her shoe and we start over.

Ion sidles up beside me. "Riders on the horizon."

My head comes up. We've been expecting them for over a week now. It seems Kharon, First Deve of all the Realms, does not travel at a brisk pace.

"I'd like to move you back to the stronghold," Ion announces as we watch the caravan come closer and grow longer. I guess Kharon doesn't travel light either.

I give Ion a tight, "I think not. An a'deve should never skulk, I'm sure of it." I gesture to the gold tiara on my head that Luka has required me to wear every day for the last week for precisely this moment. He claims the First Deve may need a visual reminder that my relationship with my husband is already permanent.

Ion grits his teeth. "I'd argue the point, but I wouldn't

want to waste my breath."

"Excellent," I say brightly. "Let us continue with our work here. I'm sure the high and mighty lord will head directly for the stronghold anyway."

"You there!" Ion yells and I jump, turning to see him pointing to a boy of eight or nine. "Run to the stronghold and inform the deve, or one of his men, that there are riders on the road and that the a'deve is in danger."

The child doesn't need to be told twice. He dashes off.

Susan tugs on my cloak. "Are you in danger? Do not worry, I will stand for you like the women did in the courtyard."

My heart twists in my chest as the rest of the children echo their support.

"Oh, you're all sweethearts. I thank you. But Ion is making a mountain out of a molehill. There is no danger."

A few minutes later, as if to make a liar out of me, the head of the caravan breaks off and heads our way. I laugh, but even to my own ears, it sounds hollow. "You will not stand in front of me, Ion," I order him.

"This time you're right," he replies and I follow his gaze behind us.

I let out a huge breath of relief. Keeping Nightshade to a casual walk, my husband approaches, flanked by Eldon and Noé and followed by a few more warriors. I should have known Luka would be prepared.

As the parties draw up on either side of our little group, I notice Luka isn't wearing a shirt under his warrior's vest, which leaves the thick muscles of his arms on display . . . and the torque for all to see. And even more unusual, he's armed with more than his dagger and axe; the hilt of his broad sword is peeking over his shoulder. He radiates arrogant dominance from Nightshade's back, and I straighten my own spine, wanting us to present a united front.

After a tense silence, Luka inclines his head. "My deve."

His deve, Kharon of the Bear Realm, sits atop a beautiful white warhorse with as much authority as Luka does. But he's older than I was expecting and if he didn't have huge men all around him, I'd be hard-pressed to understand how he's remained in power.

His head has been shaved on the sides, creating a stripe of thick white hair that's been braided into a long queue. It hangs over the fur mantle on his shoulders. The etched lines around his eyes and mouth are made more noticeable by the sneer on his face, one that tells me he's loath to return the greeting of a man he considers beneath him.

I knew I wouldn't like him, but Kharon has officially gained an enemy in me as he intones, "Lukaron Djothar." He shifts his disdain to me. "I assume this is the woman D'heilar sent." If he's surprised by the crown on my head, he doesn't show it. He only lifts his hand and gestures for someone to come forward. "Is that her?" he demands of the man who brings his horse up next to his.

My stomach congeals into an icy ball that slowly capsizes in a sea of nausea.

"Well," the man says on a laugh. "She's been tarted up, but yes, that's her."

The metal-on-metal shearing sound of swords being unsheathed barely registers above the whooshing rush of blood in my ears. *Is it really him?*

"Stow your swords," booms Kharon. "All of you."

His own men hesitate, but ultimately do as they're told. Luka, however, has his sword pointed directly at Mattice Dulat, High Advisor to the King of D'heilar and the man who inflicted the burn marks on my ribs. "Insults against my wife will be answered for."

"No, they won't," Kharon says like everyone in his vicinity is a simpleton. "This man is D'heilar's representative, here to witness the nuptials. He's under my protection."

The monster who serves my cousin smirks with Kharon's pronouncement, but Luka's sword doesn't waver. One of the First Deve's guards speaks up as the tension mounts. "Shall I disarm him, my deve?"

The guard's gall knocks enough of the shock out of my system that I take a better look at him. He's bigger than the rest and scarier, with a long scar running down his cheek. But he must be mad if he thinks Luka would be intimidated by him.

A burst of laughter fills the field. "You should choose your inner circle with more care, my deve," Luka says, still chuckling as he returns his sword to its place. "Fools make for poor counsellors." Ignoring the grumbles from Kharon's party at the insult and the titters from ours, Luka calls to me. "Come, little raven. We must get our esteemed guests settled. Tomorrow will be a big day as we celebrate our union once again."

Ion bends a knee and I step up so Luka can hoist me onto the saddle in front of him by my waist. Then, as if he doesn't have a care in the world, he turns Nightshade in the direction of the stronghold, trusting his men to protect our backs.

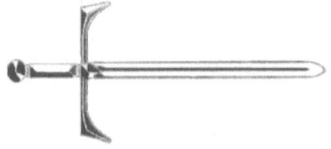

I'm not sure how I was expecting Luka to react to Mattice

Dulat's presence, but with calm composure is not it. Though he tells me not to worry, that Dulat will get what's coming to him, I'm beyond uneasy; uneasy with that man's presence in the stronghold, uneasy with his seemingly close relationship with the First Deve, and uneasy with Luka's smug confidence.

That night we enter the Great Hall for dinner to find Kharon and Dulat already seated on the dais. I almost balk at how they've seated themselves, with two empty seats between them, Luka's more elaborate chair next to Kharon and mine next to Dulat.

"Fear nothing, my love," Luka whispers as we mount the steps.

I can do this, I reassure myself even though a thin layer of sweat has broken out over my skin. *For him, I can do anything.*

We come to his chair first and I almost miss his cue to stop as he pulls it out and offers it to me. I sit and murmurs start up through the crowd. Someone yells, "Long live our a'deve," and it sets off laughter and further calls of support. I realize the entire room has taken a collective breath. It's not only me who's put off by these outsiders, an ironic twist since only a few months ago, I was the outsider.

Still on his feet, Luka grabs up his tankard of ale and raises it. "To our a'deve!"

The raucous echo of support swells and I smile back at my people, feeling a blush creep up my neck and onto my cheeks.

"How very touching," Kharon says with a healthy dose of insincerity.

Luka takes his seat beside me. "Isn't this what you wanted, Kharon? To strengthen our ties with D'heilar?"

The man's grudging agreement is lost in the noise of the platters of food being brought out from the kitchen. Luka makes no attempt to fill his plate, so I do it for him. I can't blame him for not having an ounce of appetite, especially when Dulat finally makes his presence known.

"So, Amarinata," he says in a sickly-sweet voice. "I see you've –"

Luka's fist comes down on the table like a hammer. "If you value your life, you will not address my wife."

"Really, Luka," Kharon scolds. "Is that how you treat guests?"

Luckily, we're interrupted by a mother and her young son, who wishes to present me with a posy of spring flowers. I signal my permission and the boy is lifted onto the dais. "Thank you so much, Darrion," I say, accepting them with exaggerated care. "They're lovely. Did you pick them yourself?"

"Yes, my a'deve." Though he eyes Luka and Kharon with wariness, he goes on to whisper. "I like your crown very much."

I giggle, feeling so much more at ease. This is familiar to me, this is my life now. "Thank you. Our deve gave it to me."

The boy beams at Luka, who huffs with a mix of exasperation and tolerance. "Be gone with you, then," he says not unkindly and I wink at the child.

The mother inclines her head to us as she pulls her son away, and it's then that I notice Kharon's guard, the one who dared to speak earlier, skulking off to our left. It would seem he's the official bodyguard.

Placing the flowers beside my plate, I decide I don't like the mood at our table. "Was your journey a long one, my deve?" I ask in an attempt to be a better hostess.

Kharon ignores my question in favor of spitting out his own, "What was that?" He lifts his tankard at the woman's retreating back. "They are offering her homage?" He sounds so incensed that I almost recoil. "How could you let this happen, Luka?"

I turn to find my husband with an arched brow. "Let what happen exactly? Allow a whore of D'heilar access to our people?"

My head rears back.

"Oh, ho!" Mattice Dulat crows loudly. "He knows you too well, Amarinata."

Before Luka can react, I'm on my feet and reaching around him, my supper dagger leading the way. My target scrambles back in time to avoid the blade tip that comes at him, but I soak up the fear oozing from this weasel of a man. "I distinctly heard my husband tell you not to address me," I grit out as Luka grabs my wrist to stop me from taking another swipe.

"Mmmm, that's my woman," Luka practically purrs.

"Don't you mean your whore?" I snap.

"That was for his benefit," he fires back, lifting his chin at Kharon behind me as he lets my wrist go. "It's how *he* sees you, not me. And it's clear to me now that we've both been played from the beginning. Our union was never meant to happen. Our success is their failure. Isn't that right, Kharon?" Luka glares at him as I sink down into my seat.

"I've seen and heard enough," Kharon says loudly, getting to his feet. "People of the Mountain Lion Realm."

Is he addressing our people? Without asking Luka's permission? Like most in the room, my gaze lands on Luka. He's still sprawled casually in his chair, but a muscle ticks in his jaw as Kharon goes on.

"After hearing rumors of incompetence for months and having confirmed the slaying of many of your warriors, it's become clear to me that your deve is not fit to rule."

The room erupts in shock and outrage. Profanity-laden protests and insults are launched as warriors rise from their seats, Eldon and Noé among them, looking ready to do murder.

Luka holds up a hand and slowly everyone settles down. "By all means," he mocks. "Let us hear what the First Deve of *all* the Realms has to say."

I don't think Kharon is quite as sure of himself anymore, but he doesn't outwardly falter. "The D'heilarian whore has clearly bewitched him. How else would she convince him to marry her without my presence?"

Luka laughs. *"You* sent her here."

"A mistake. Now that Teo is dead and –"

"Teo?" Luka intones. "Teo was a fool living in the past."

"Teo was a loyalist and I say this is your end, Lukaron Djothar." The room explodes once again, but over the din, Kharon shouts, "Taxon, step forward."

I fight back a niggling of panic as the big bodyguard does as he's told.

"People of the Mountain Lion, I present you with the man who will be your next deve."

Amid the utter clamor, Luka gets to his feet with chilling care, unhurried and deliberate. "What say you, Lions?" he yells in a burst of passion. "Am I headed for a downfall?"

The outpouring of support seems to rock the very walls of the hall and lifts goosebumps along my flesh.

"No, I don't think so either, my fellow Lions."

I turn to gloat at Kharon, but Luka goes on, his voice a booming echo.

"But no Northerner has ever ignored a challenge, no matter how under-handed, have they?!"

The people's intensifying roar of approval fades to the recesses of my mind as Luka's meaning hits me.

"So let this Taxon have his chance. He will not prevail!" His words are punctuated by the slamming of his dagger deep into the tabletop where it quivers in place when he lets it go.

Mother help me, but he means to fight that huge caveman?

"I suggest," Luka scorns at the man in question, "that you prepare yourself, because tomorrow I toss you directly into the Abyss."

Taxon opens his mouth, but he's drowned out by everyone banging twice on the table in unison, then letting out a collective "raaaa!" They repeat it over and over, louder and louder, until he's forced to leave the Great Hall, followed by Kharon, and the weasel, Dulat.

The experience of the chant is nothing I've ever felt before. Despite the very real possibility that Luka will die tomorrow, my heart bursts with pride and exhilaration. Now all I can do is pray that my newly-crafted life isn't over before it's barely begun.

The ale flows freely in the Great Hall after that, but Luka doesn't touch another drop. It's the only outward sign that he takes any of this seriously. He moves us from the dais to sit with Eldon, Noé, and other warriors, and they spend hours noisily re-living their battle exploits as if none of them has a care in the world.

I, however, am not as adept at hiding my feelings. I've been on the verge of screaming all night. Plus, I'm tired. When I finally mention to Luka that it's time to go upstairs to bed, I cradle my belly and he immediately takes the hint. Unfortunately, Eldon and Noé follow us upstairs to our chamber for an unplanned meeting. Because the stronghold is filled with guests, the map room has been converted into a temporary bedroom.

It's not until we're behind closed doors that I explode. "How could you agree to such a thing?!"

"I could do nothing else. Please sit down." He signals Kata, who's been waiting up for us, and she comes to place a hand on my arm. I shake her off.

"What if you die? What then?"

"Rina," Eldon cautions. "He's right. He can't ignore a challenge. Though . . ." He sets his jaw. "I've never heard of a First Deve himself presenting a challenger."

"We all knew something was coming," Luka says as he turns one of the hearth chairs and indicates that I should sit. I purse my lips, but accept.

Noé shakes his head in disgust. "We knew something was coming, yes. But not *this*. I have lost all respect for Kharon."

"Kharon is not the issue here!" I insist. "What if Luka dies?"

"Then Eldon will take care of you and our child, my love."

"But –"

"But nothing. He has sworn it to me, haven't you, cousin?"

Eldon nods gravely, and I don't know whether it makes

me feel better or worse that the situation weighs on Eldon as much as it does on me. I open my mouth to continue, but Luka stops me.

"Enough, Rina. There is only one way out of this and that is through victory. And I'm going to need your full support."

Every argument on my tongue shrivels and dies. He's right. This may be the first challenge to his leadership, but it will surely not be the last.

Kneeling down in front of me, he takes my hands in his. "You must know I have no intention of losing to that great oaf." His calloused thumb strokes along the back of my hand in a soothing motion.

"But I love you so much, Luka. I couldn't bear it if anything happened to you."

"I love you too." He reaches up to caress my cheek. "But if something does happen to me, you *will* bear it for our child's sake. I need to know that you will keep him safe."

I sniffle, hating that my emotions have been on a see-saw lately. "Of course I'll protect her. You needn't worry about that."

His lips pull into a grin. We have been calling our unborn child *him* or *her* since we discovered I was pregnant. "That's my woman." He kisses me, lingering sweetly before he gets back to his feet. "It's settled. If I should lose, Eldon will challenge and all will be well. And if things go wrong from there, you will go to Koda and the Wolves. They will give you sanctuary."

CHAPTER 26

RINA

I don't know why I'm surprised that Kharon travels with his own raised platform that can be assembled for any occasion, complete with a plush throne-like chair and lavish velvet draperies that hang on three sides to help break the wind . . . or add to the pretentiousness of it all. I'd probably be more impressed if I didn't loathe the man.

Luka had led the procession from the stronghold to the training ground, the drums thumping, as usual deep in his own thoughts, mentally preparing to fight for his life. I'd followed him, head held high and stomach quivering in my beautiful fur cloak, the crown on my head, held firmly in place by my braids. I would not dishonor him by showing even an ounce of fear or anxiety.

My husband delivers me to the platform where I'll watch this farce play out next to Kharon. At least I won't have to suffer Mattice Dulat's presence. Reportedly, he made a hasty departure last night, citing the unwelcoming atmosphere. Good riddance.

"My dear," Kharon says as I take my seat next to him.

Keeping my eyes on Luka, I offer him a simple, "Deve," in return.

The man harrumphs softly. How I wish I could join Bron, Daysa, and Yvette wherever they are in the crowd. I'm sure Ion, who wasn't allowed on the platform and now prowls at its base, feels the same way.

In the center of the clearing, Eldon announces the challenger and I rather enjoy the strident boos he receives. Kharon's little moue of disapproval is the icing on the cake until Luka is named and the crowd detonates with wild approval.

"You seem surprised by the people's love for Luka," I say blandly, watching as the combatants take up their swords and shields and start to circle each other.

"Love is not always what's best for a people."

I wince as Taxon lands a heavy blow to Luka's shield. "And I suppose you feel that your puppet is what's best?"

When he doesn't answer, I turn to find his piercing eyes sizing me up. A cheer goes up, but I can't seem to break away from his snake-like intensity. "I'm afraid, my dear, that it's time for you to go." He tilts his head to the side, indicating the drapes behind us.

Confused, I turn. My gasp is lost in the sudden deafening roar of the crowd. Through a gap in the fabric, I see Kata, a knife held to her throat by one of Kharon's guards.

"Don't make a fuss," the deve says coolly. "Just get up and go with them or he'll slit the worthless chit's throat from ear to ear."

"You're insane," I hiss. "Luka will end you for this."

"Luka has his hands full at the moment. Now, do as you're told."

I turn back, unsure. Ion is engrossed in the battle and Luka *does* have his hands full.

"Oh, look at that. She's bleeding."

Jerking around, I'm immediately on my feet at the sight of Kata's blood and jumping down off the platform through the gap. The warrior holding Kata steps back from me, keeping the knife where it is. "Take off the cloak," he orders.

"What?"

"Take it off now and give it to her." He lifts his chin at someone behind me.

She's small, like me. "Do it now or I sever her head."

"Okay, okay," I say, my trembling fingers undoing the tie at my neck and passing the woman the cloak, unable to unglue my gaze from the red rivulet trickling down into the neckline of Kata's dress.

The woman is through the gap in a flash, and the warrior drags Kata back toward another who's waiting with three horses. It doesn't take long to get Kata mounted in front of her captor and me on my own horse before we're galloping through the trees.

I can do nothing until Kata is free of that knife, so I follow them, wondering how they think this will ever work. We ride hard and the sounds of the crowd begin to fade into the background until it's a dull buzz.

Well past the last homestead of the village we catch up to a group of men on the road. More of the First Deve's men. "Please let Luka be all right," I whisper in a prayer to the

Mother. "And then let him come for us and cut every one of these bastards down."

A wagon drawn by a team of horses is stopped momentarily and Kata is handed over. Once she's chained in the bed by her ankle, I'm next, and again the wagon is moving with purpose.

"Well, well, well." My skin crawls at the sound of that voice. "Amarinata D'heilar. Are you ready to head home?"

From horseback, Dulat directs an oily smirk at me. It's exactly as I remember it. Despite all the horrible memories trying to scratch their way to the surface, I feel laughter slip past my lips. It's not tinged with hysteria or fear or anything like that. It rings with glee. "You're a dead man."

His sneer slips a little. "You always were delusional." He puts his heels to his horse and moves further up the road.

Bracing myself against the motion of the cart, I stand and cup my hands around my mouth to shout, "Whether it's my husband or one of his warriors, you're a dead man! Or me. I'm hoping it's me! Do you hear me, Mattice Dulat?! Prepare yourself for the Abyss. It's coming."

"Sit down and shut up," orders our driver as we go over a bump. Unable to keep my balance, I'm forced to do as he says, but not before I catch a glimpse of something in the trees. *Is that . . . a boy?* But it's there one moment and gone the next.

I turn my attention to Kata, sitting across from me. Her braid has partially come loose and she's paler than usual, making the blood smear on her neck stand out in sharp contrast. She's shaken, but when I reach for her hand, her grip is sure. "You okay?" She touches the cut at her neck, but nods. It's stopped bleeding mostly.

A gust of wind sends a shiver through me. It may be spring

but it's too cold to be out here without a cloak. "This is such bullshit," I mutter, checking out our situation more carefully. There's only the driver, two guards riding behind us and two in front – one of them being Dulat – but since we're shackled, there may as well be fifty men surrounding us. I inspect the chain, but there's no way out of it.

Gah! Luka is fighting for his life and I am here, chained in a cart, leaving the Mountain Lion Realm in the same way I came in. Childishly, I kick at the short chain in frustration.

"Woah!" sounds and my head snaps up. Ahead, tied to trees on either side of the road, stands a mule, blocking our way.

"What, in the name of the Father, is that?" asks Dulat, slowing to a stop.

The two guards following ride past us to join the others. "It's a mule."

"I can see that!" he snaps. "What is it doing there?"

A clatter happens in the trees off to our left, drawing everyone's gaze.

"What was that?"

More noise sounds in the distance. *Is something being thrown against the trees?*

"Damnation," one of the men says. "It's some kind of ambush."

At the same moment a small hand reaches over the lip of the wagon bed and quietly leaves first a bow and then a quiver of arrows. Oh, dear Mother. It's Rionnon. Kata and I quickly cover the weapon with our skirts.

The guards have all drawn their swords, searching the trees for the source of the noise. "Show yourselves!" one of them yells while my mind is torn between forming some kind of plan and terror for Rionnon –

"Why should we?!" echoes through the trees.

Rionnon is not alone.

"It's a child," scoffs the driver. "Go see if you can flush them out. I'll move the mule. We need to be long gone before they realize the woman is missing."

Kata gives me a discreet nod as the men on horseback move into the trees and the driver gets down from his perch and passes a lost-looking Dulat. I take hold of the bow and push up onto my knees. Kata passes me an arrow and I nock it.

I've never killed a man before and maybe if only my life was at stake, I would hesitate. But Luka and my new family mean everything to me. I won't allow this to happen. I loose the arrow and it sinks into the driver's back. He goes down with a cry and Dulat turns, shocked as I nock another one.

"Ha!" he yells, spurring his horse into the trees. I let my shot fly, but I only manage to pierce his hip. He howls like a banshee, but it doesn't stop him from fleeing.

Thwack. Kata slaps my upper arm with another arrow and gestures to our left. Having heard the cry, one of the guards is charging back our way. Grasping the proffered arrow, I clumsily nock it and shoot. It goes wide. Shit! Taking a deep breath, I accept another and this time get my bearings.

The impact at such close range knocks the man from his horse. I don't dwell on it, I simply nock the next arrow and scan the trees. I see nothing, but I can hear the boys still taunting the two remaining men, and under that, a low rumbling. Hooves. It's the thumping of hooves. "From which direction do the horses come, Kata?" I whisper desperately. "North or south?" The strain of keeping the arrow nocked has my arms trembling, but I don't dare let up. The approaching riders will either be our salvation or our demise.

I glance at the guard I shot off his horse. He's not moving. The man in the road is still twitching about, but he's in no shape to be a threat to us.

A child's scream comes from the trees and my heart freezes. I get to my feet, scanning frantically. "Rionnon!"

No answer. My sweaty grip starts to falter. I lower the bow and shake out my muscles. Kata waves to the north and I think I almost pass out from the relief. Through the forest, three men appear on horseback, two of them in the brown leather vests of the Range. The other is shirtless and as they draw nearer, the light glints off of the golden torque at his bicep. Luka.

Another scream and I tear my eyes from my husband to search again for Rionnon. There. I raise the bow once again, but there's no way I'd risk the shot, considering the scene before me. It's not Yvette's son the guard has in his grip, but one of his friends, a girl. The child is held against the man's front, his sword tip resting against her fragile chest.

"Put down the bow," the guard yells to me as Luka, Noé, and Ion rein in their horses. Luka slides from the saddle, his own sword gripped in his hand. "Back off," the man screams. "All of you!"

The girl squeals as the blade begins to pierce her skin.

"Okay, okay," I plead, slowly lowering the bow to the bed of the wagon, keeping my hands where he can see them. "Just don't hurt her."

"You too," he bellows to Luka. "Throw down the sword."

"You and I both know," Luka says, the authority in his voice echoing around us, "that the only way you come away from this alive is if you let the child go."

The guard's eyes dart every which way until finally coming back to Luka. "I only did what was ordered of me. Kharon is not a forgiving man."

"Kharon is the least of your worries right now. Let the child go and I'll –"

Luka breaks off as a spear slices straight through the man's chest with a great squelching thud right above the child's head. For a moment, nothing happens. It's as if the entire known world holds its breath until his grip on the girl falters and he topples backwards.

Shock almost bringing me to my knees, I turn and find Noé with his hands on his hips, surveying his handiwork.

"Nice shot," Luka congratulates as the children who were hiding in the trees come running. I want to go to the girl. She must need comfort after such an ordeal and I yank at my chain. "You okay, my love?" Luka asks. He's right there, looking over the edge of the cart, and the visceral feeling of déjà vu washes over me, leaving me slightly light-headed. Except this time, there's no scorn in his expression only love and concern.

A deep breath has me feeling steadier and I tug at the shackle again. "I'm fine, but there's another guard somewhere. And I only wounded Dulat. Get the key from that one." I throw my arm in the direction of the man in the middle of the road.

Luka raises a brow at me.

I huff. "Please?"

He crooks a finger at me, and I reluctantly lean down closer to him. He kisses me hard on the lips. "Don't ever get taken again, do you hear me?" he growls.

"Like I had a choice," I grumble, watching him go for the key.

When Kata and I are free, I hold the trembling girl while

Ion and Noé go off into the trees on horseback in search of the two missing men and Luka gets the story in fits and bursts from the rest of us. It seems one of Rionnon's friends, all of whom are members of Bron's little band, heard whispers this morning of a plan to take someone from the stronghold. They'd gathered their group together and followed when the men departed, only to find out I was the intended target. Half of them went back to warn Bron and the others stayed with the men.

A few minutes later, through the trees, comes muffled bellowing. I tense, but Luka puts a hand on my shoulder as, in a break in the noise, a distinctive bird call sounds. "It's Noé."

He then directs the children to find some rocks to make a small fire pit. *A fire pit?*

My brows pull down in question and he gives me a wink. "On occasion, my little raven has been known to thirst for vengeance."

His meaning dawns on me in small, incremental lurches that leave me breathless . . . and grappling with the idea of inflicting that kind of pain on someone even if it is Mattice Dulat. I'm still reeling when Noé and Ion ride up, both with men laid across their pommels. It's clear that Ion's cargo is dead when he pushes the body to the ground, revealing a gaping chest wound.

"Took it a bit too far?" Luka asks wryly.

Ion shrugs. "He wasn't willing to surrender. Unlike that one." He gestures at Dulat, who's bound and gagged, bleeding from the arrow wound I gave him. "That one surrendered right away."

Luka grabs Dulat's collar and pulls him to the ground. He lands with a thump on his arms which are tied behind his back, starting up a litany of muffled screeches.

"Shut up," Luka growls, kicking him in the ribs. "Ion, we're going to need a fire."

Ion doesn't even bat an eyelash, just dismounts and starts rummaging for what he needs in the saddle bags of the horse he's riding.

I crouch down beside Dulat and study him. He's awash in terror, and I imagine I must have worn much the same expression when he came at me with that glowing blade almost two years ago. The coward struggles against his bindings and tries to communicate something through the gag, but all I can do is stare.

"A'Deve?"

Next to me, Rionnon bends over, his hands on his knees.

"Yes?"

"What's going to happen to him?"

Returning my gaze to Dulat, I say, "I'm not sure yet." Am I really going to torture this man as he did me? Maybe I should try to scrounge together some compassion, to focus on forgiveness instead of revenge. That is the Mother's way after all. Isn't it my responsibility to model virtue over wickedness? If not for myself, then for these children?

Maybe. But I'm not going to.

Mattice Dulat showed me no compassion, and he will now reap what he sowed.

Luka calls Rionnon away from me, telling him Yvette will expect her mule – that's still tied in the middle of the road – to be back in its pen before she gets home.

"Yes, my deve," he says, laying a comforting hand on my shoulder.

I grab on to his hand, holding him there with me. "Thank you," I tell the boy. "You will make a great warrior one day."

He brightens at that and there's a notable skip to his step as he and his friends go for the mule before heading home.

I push to my feet and watch Luka place the blade of a dagger into the crackling flames of the newly-lit fire. The weight of the situation really begins to bear down on me.

Noé pulls his own dagger from its sheath and proceeds to cut away Dulat's clothing until he's left naked and moaning with dread. My stomach turns. I should be cherry-picking my targets, but all I can think about in the face of the man's pale, fleshy body is my own suffering; the searing pain, the smell of my burning skin, the sound of my piercing screams.

To escape the nausea it causes, I move to Luka's side as he returns from hoisting one of the corpses into the wagon. He picks up on my turmoil immediately, lifting one of his arms to tuck me against his side.

"You don't have to do this."

"You wouldn't think less of me?" I ask quietly.

"Not ever. I only wanted to give you the option."

I nod against his bare chest.

"You and your happiness are everything. You need only tell me your desire and it will be done."

"Thank you, Luka." After another moment of hesitation, I find my resolve. "I wish to see it through."

"Okay." He motions to Noé, who somehow knows exactly what Luka wants and wrenches Dulat up by his bound arms. The difference in their sizes is almost comical as Noé doesn't even have to strain himself to keep the smaller man upright.

Luka leans down and tests the temperature of the dagger's

handle. Deeming it acceptable, he pulls the smoking blade from the fire. "The flames are not hot enough to make it glow," Luka explains, offering it to me. I've told him of my experience with Dulat, how I feared the glow of the blade. "I'm sorry that we don't have time to do this right, but we must get back."

I take the knife from him. Even the hilt, which is made of bone, verges on too hot for my hand. Moving toward Dulat, I feel the nausea returning and I make a snap decision. One step. Two. And I drive the knife straight into his eye. It sinks in with so little resistance that the side of my hand, wrapped around the hilt, comes into contact with his face.

"Ohh!" Noé yells as I immediately let go and stumble back into Luka's arms. I dry heave a few times before I'm finally able to get a deep, calming breath into my lungs.

"Now that's how it's done," Noé laughs, letting the body fall. "Straight to the point."

Behind me, I feel Luka's chest shake and I look up. He, too, is laughing, albeit silently. "That was quite . . . deadly, wife. I thought you would make him suffer a bit first."

I exhale long and loud. "I didn't want to experience the smell or the sounds again."

"Fair enough. Let us go home."

CHAPTER 27

LUKA

I set a brisk pace on the way back.

"What do you mean you just left?" Rina asks as the stronghold comes into view. With everything going on, she'd assumed that I'd finished off my challenger before I came for her.

That is not the case.

"I could do nothing else," I claim. Though I'm not as at ease as I'd have her believe, I don't want to worry her. She's been through a trial and killed men for the first time. "When Ion exposed the woman next to Kharon as an imposter, nothing else mattered but getting you back. Without you, little raven, my life would be empty. Without you, there is no point to any of this." I gesture vaguely at the stronghold before us.

"You should have seen it," Noé says, addressing her with

a familiarity born of his new-found respect for her. "He didn't even hesitate. He just beat that great thug of a man down long enough to give himself a chance to run for a horse."

"But, Luka," she breathes. "What will happen?"

"Since I don't hear anything from the direction of the clearing, I assume that Eldon is now deve."

Or Eldon may be dead. That great 'thug' was a very skilled warrior.

At the gate, the duty guards give off a nervous energy that I don't like, and I almost insist they tell us what's happened. But I don't want to appear weak. Whatever the situation in the stronghold, I'll deal with it. My greatest priority now is Rina and the babe she carries.

The courtyard is mostly deserted, but as we ride the horses right up to the steps of the Great Hall, I can hear the drone of conversation coming from within. We dismount and enter together, hand in hand, to find the room packed. They part like a wave, giving us a clear view all the way to the dais.

Mother have mercy.

It's not Eldon who sits upon it. It's Gray.

A cold wave of anxiety starts in my throat and slithers its way down into my guts. *What the fuck?* I don't see Eldon anywhere.

Beside me, Rina murmurs a desperate, "No," and I squeeze her hand, hoping against hope that this isn't what it looks like.

I move forward, leading my wife by the hand. Head-on is the only way to face this.

Gray gets to his feet and jumps down. As we stride toward each other, I see him as the deve he should be; powerful, poised, and filled with self-assurance. I have to squash down on the rising idea that this may not go my way, especially when I notice Kharon standing at the base of the platform, wrapped in an air of patronizing triumph.

"Noé," I say in a low voice as I squeeze Rina's hand again before I let it go, trusting him to protect her while I . . . what? Do the unthinkable? Damn Kharon and his meddling to the Abyss.

In the middle of the Great Hall, Gray and I meet, separated by only a few feet. "Luka," he says simply before pulling his dagger from its sheath. Only by sheer force of will do I not flinch. We don't carry our swords in the Great Hall – ever – so I'm unarmed. My mind starts mapping out how this will go if he starts a brawl right here, right now. Though it's more likely that I'll have to challenge him formally and –

"If it came down to it," Gray starts and I dare take my attention off the dagger for a second. "I didn't want you to have to fight Eldon to re-gain the title. I'm hoping you'll accept my surrender." He flips the dagger around to present it to me hilt first.

A collective gasp goes up and echoes off the walls, including my own. A warrior never surrenders.

He goes on with, "A man must be able to think for himself in a crisis, to do the right thing when it's called for, so that's what I'm doing now. The right thing. You, Luka, are the deve we need."

Mother help us both, but he's also trusting in *me* to do the right thing in return. Everything I was ever brought up to believe is screaming at me to end his life. He's a threat now. He'll be a threat tomorrow. He'll be a threat to my leadership for the remainder of his days if I let this stand. If I let him live.

I accept the blade . . . and offer it back to him. "I accept your surrender Grayson Cyrun."

Another dramatic gasp, but this one is followed by excited chatter that quickly turns into cheers.

Unheard of emotion shines back at me from Gray as he accepts the knife and I pull him into an embrace that includes a solid pounding on the back. It takes a second, but he responds by doing the same.

The cheering suddenly takes on a horrified edge. We spring apart in time to watch Zola land flat on her back on the unforgiving stone floor not far from us.

"Mother!" Gray yells, shoving people aside as they crowd around her. Holy shit. The first thing that registers is the blade embedded in the middle of her chest. The second, the knife in her now slack hand.

Rina slams into my side. "She almost got you. She almost got you," she chants over and over. *Got me?* Noé blocks my view of Zola, putting himself between me and Gray. Eldon joins him.

"What happened?" I demand, stroking Rina's hair to reassure her I'm fine.

Over his shoulder, Noé says, "She came at you. I stopped her." Our eyes meet and I give him a nod for solving one of the longest-running problems of my reign – what to do with Zola Cyrun. He could have stopped her without killing her, but now, it is done. And I'm relieved.

Gray, however . . .

He stands and exhales heavily, his hands on his hips, his chin tipped up to the ceiling. "Damnation!" he roars with frustration. "Why couldn't you just stop?!"

He's talking to his mother.

"Why couldn't you just let it go?!"

Of course there's no answer. The woman is dead.

The chatter around us picks up again, and while some gather around Zola in shock and dismay, many begin to approach Rina and me under Eldon's and Noé's watchful eyes. "My deve, my a'deve," is repeated over and over again as heads are willingly inclined to reaffirm their loyalty.

"Are you out of your minds?!" comes from the front of the room. Apparently Kharon is offended by the turn of events. "This is not our way! This is not accep –"

"Shut up," I yell, drowning him out. "You will pack up and leave immediately. You are no longer welcome in the Mountain Lion Realm."

Pulling Rina closer and kissing her forehead, I watch a sputtering Kharon be corralled from the room by my warriors. There will be consequences for this, I'm sure, but sometimes the hard choices are the only choices.

That is leadership. Something I plan to enjoy with my wife by my side for many years.

EPILOGUE

RINA

The heat has been intense this summer, but I can't complain since I've never quite gotten used to how cold it gets during the winter here in the north.

"Papa, watch!" yells our five-year-old son, Talon, from up ahead where he's about to jump down from a fallen log at the edge of the meadow. After being cooped up in the stronghold all day to avoid the heat, he has a lot of energy to burn off this evening, something that has brought on this impromptu family walk.

Luka, not wanting to wake our six-month-old daughter, Kayla, who sleeps on his broad shoulder, waves him on, indicating he's watching as our little man has asked. Fatherhood looks so good on Luka. As any parent knows, children are not easy to deal with, and though I knew Luka would take the task seriously, I never imagined how patient and loving he would prove to be with our children. I think he wants to provide them with everything that was missing from his childhood and it melts my heart on a very regular basis.

Things have not always been easy for us though. While Talon is a hearty child, who's rarely sick, our second son, born two years later, was not. We lost him to a fever not long after he was born and with him went a very big piece of ourselves. For the longest time, I couldn't bring myself to even glance at the wall of skulls in the Great Hall. I had no idea that Luka bowed his head in prayer over our baby's remains every day until I came upon him one day by accident doing just that. A few weeks later, I began joining him. Though the grief will never completely leave me, the prayers have helped me greatly.

My pregnancy with Kayla went well, but it was stressful and I leaned on Luka more than I had a right to. Looking at him now, holding Kayla in a thin layer of muslin with such care, using his giant hand to gently pat her back, I'm in awe. He has proven himself as mentally sturdy as he is physically.

I cannot imagine my life without him.

Even when he orders me about like I'm one of his warriors, I love him. Even when he fails to communicate the most basic of information, I know he loves me. Thanks to him, the promise I made to my Mama, the one to *live* if I ever got the chance, has been fulfilled in every way possible.

"Talon has grown, has he not?" Luka asks in a rumble and I feel a grin tug at my lips. He's always so proud of his offspring. "I think he's almost ready to trade in his pony."

The boy has practically been fully-outfitted for manhood already. Glory's foal has been chosen for him and a warrior's sword was commissioned last spring. It's a good thing our son loves everything rough and tumble just like his father. They even share the same amount of interest in practicing their letters, which is none.

Before I have a chance to tease him, I spot Kata and Dion emerging from the trees not far from where Talon is now banging a stick on the log. It truly warms my heart that the sweetest woman and man in the realm found happiness together. Talon takes off like a shot to meet them as soon as he notices their presence. He loves Kata like a second mother and I wince when I envision my son barrelling into her small frame at top speed. Dion saves her though by scooping Talon up before he can make contact, setting off screams of delight as he's thrown in the air.

"Shall we go say hello?" I ask Luka innocently.

He sends me one of his famous glowers, this one saying *don't push your luck,* and I can't stop a giggle from slipping out of me. He's never quite gotten over his jealousy of Dion, the first Northerner to show me kindness.

"Well, we can wave from here and Talon can catch up. Now that she's sleeping we don't want to risk waking Kayla, anyway."

That Kayla will grow up in a different world from her grandmother's is something that I take pride in. Women come to me now when they face unwelcome attention from men and I encourage Luka to come down hard on the perpetrators. Luka's father's legacy has not disappeared overnight, but it lessens every year, and I think everyone has benefited.

Other than that, things have not changed overmuch around the stronghold. Though they've never married, Noé and Lorna, after many years of being on-again and off-again, have been given a chamber together in the stronghold. Now no man would dare ask her for anything more than a tankard of ale. Ion and Bron are still very much in love, as are Eldon and Daysa. We still go out to their home almost every week. They have another son now, much to Trudy's disappointment.

Yvette never married, but her son, Rionnon, did indeed achieve his goal to one day be as tall as his Uncle Noé and is now in training to become a warrior. To my mind, he's a little young and gangly at fourteen, but Luka claims that with the current uncertainties facing the Realms, it's never too early to start training men. While Luka has never faced a challenger from within, the eastern savages are more of a problem than ever and the Range now has men permanently stationed in the Wolf Realm under Koda's command. And worse, while Kharon has managed to hold on to power in the Bear Realm, his attempts to unseat Luka greatly rankled many of the other deves who see their realms as sovereign. Loyalties among the unified Realms were badly shaken, something that King Gaden in the south is very aware of. There have been scattered reports of men slowly amassing along D'heilar's northern border.

A soft yip carries on the warm breeze and both Luka and I turn. Venna. She stands proudly on the other side of the meadow, keeping her distance while two of her pups from this spring wrestle together in the grass. During my first summer here, she disappeared from around the stronghold. At first, Luka feared she was dead, but it turned out that she had found a pack of her own kind.

Like me, she found a home.

Now she visits occasionally to check in with Luka or, like today, to show off her pups.

"Papa," Talon says reverently from much closer than he was a minute ago. "It's a wolf."

"It is," Luka confirms, slipping a hand onto his shoulder.

"Mama." My son's tone changes to officious. "Wolves are wild animals and we mustn't bother them . . . right?"

"Wow," I tell him, trying to hide my smile. "That *is* right. How did you get so smart?"

He lights up. "My papa told me."

Luka ruffles his hair. "Come, then. Let's head over to the duck pond."

Talon's enthusiasm for the idea couldn't be more obvious as he takes off at a run while my husband follows at a much more sedate pace. Turning back to bid farewell to Venna, I'm a bit disappointed that she's already disappeared back into the forest, but I do catch sight of a crow, or maybe it's a raven, winging its way across the tree line. From there, I notice the North Star just becoming visible as dusk falls.

I smile at the sight. It always reminds me of how far I've come, how I somehow managed to endure, and ultimately thrive.

"Are you coming, my little raven?"

With a brow raised and his eyes soft with love, Luka holds out his hand to me and I take it.

ACKNOWLEDGMENTS

Wow! My tenth book and I can't thank you enough for reading it. I know barbarians are a big departure from my usual contemporary romances, but I just couldn't get Luka and Rina out of my head. In fact, the original idea came to me in the year 2000. Like I said in the dedication – yes, I dedicated my own book to myself, lol – I first considered writing a book about barbarians when I saw *Gladiator* in the movie theatre. So it's been a long time in coming.

I so hope you enjoyed the story. Please consider leaving a review! Reviews are a make or break thing for indie authors and I would be eternally grateful if you would leave a few words of support for *Under a Northern Sky*.

I want to thank those of you who helped me to bring this book to life. I'm sending lots of love to Rain, Dora, Lana, and especially Ursa for all their hard work. Also, a big shout out to Yvette Mitchell – for whom Yvette in the story was named – for her tireless support and encouragement. She's an all-round wonderful person and you can follow her @thesaucybookshelf.

There are six realms on the northern side of the River Columndra and so far I have firm plans to write two more books! *Beyond a Savage Heart* will feature Koda and is scheduled for release in 2023. After that, book 3 will showcase Kharon's downfall and is very tentatively titled *Upon a Twisted Blade*, but don't quote me on that one.

For those of you who are waiting for Desiree and Shane's duet, there's still hope. I have their story in my head, but it'll remain on the back-burner for a while yet.

I'd love to hear from you! Please feel free to contact me – or follow me – at any of the places below:

Email: lisalynn_meyer@outlook.com
Instagram: @author_ll_meyer
Facebook: Lisa Lynn Meyer
Goodreads: LL Meyer
TikTok: author_ll_meyer
Amazon Author Central: LL Meyer

All my love, Lisa.

BOOKS BY LL MEYER

The Barbarian Realms
Under a Northern Sky, #1
Beyond a Savage Heart, #2 (coming in 2023)

The Worlds Collide duets:
Not So Far Away (Scott and Ellie, #1)
The Here and Now (Scott and Ellie, #2)
Fall from Grace (Alejandro and Sophie, #3)
The Devil's Own (Alejandro and Sophie, #4)

The Penny Books
His Lucky Penny, #1
Pennies for Wishes, #2
Find a Penny, #3
Pennies from Heaven, #4

LISA LYNN MEYER

A Touch of Silence